# *Chased By Death*

Judith Copek

**Judith Copek**

**A Wings ePress, Inc.**

**Suspense Novel**

**_Wings ePress, Inc._**

Edited by: Jeanne Smith
Copy Edited by: Joan C. Powell
Executive Editor: Jeanne Smith
Cover Artist: Trisha FitzGerald-Jung



Wings ePress Books
www.wingsepress.com


ISBN-13: 978-1-61309-600-0
ISBN-10: 1-61309-600-3

Published In the United States Of America

Wings ePress Inc.
3000 N. Rock Road
Newton, KS 67114

## *What They Are Saying About Title*

What a wild ride! Unsuspecting mob wife tailed by hit men, a drug lord with dyspepsia and a submarine. Heroine Maxine leads a fast-paced chase around the US seeking bad girl sister. Great romp!

—Michal Sherring
Author of *Done For at the Danford.* An Art Museum Mystery

Great, story, well-written, a page turner for me. Wonderful descriptions of everything—food and food prep, scenery and settings, people, moods. Great, natural dialog. Intriguing movement between sub-plots and people. Kept my interest throughout. And the later action chapters—riveting. Judith is a wonderful writer, story-teller, and craftswoman.
I personally loved her insight into computer stuff, recipes and food details, and her obvious love of travel to South Florida, the great West, and our dear Southeastern Massachusetts.

—Nancy Dale, MPH
Retired from AARP

Chased to Death by Judith Copek will keep you on the edge of your seat through the entire book. It is a delicious salad of betrayal, bad choices, tension, and ruthlessness.
After divorcing her husband, whose job she has never understood, she decides to embark on a new life beginning with a search for her sister, last known address Miami. Before she leaves town, she blunders into her ex-husband's murder scene and her life will morph into a dangerous on-the-run existence, as Maxine tries to find her sister and to stay ahead of the drug cartel that wants to kill her. In the midst of all this, she finds romance.

This is a story that's hard to put down. Just when you think she has reached a position of safety, more danger appears. And Ms. Copek has masterfully engineered a twist that surprises, yet when it comes, you see it was there all along.

This is a great and entertaining read from beginning to end. The characters are true, the action follows a believable sequence, and the twists make it above the ordinary,

—Margo Lemieux MFA, M.Ed
Professor Art & Graphic Design, Lasell College
Author of Full Worm Moon and Believe in Water

Judith Copek's "Chased by Death" is an engaging and suspenseful new crime novel. The brutal murder of her accountant ex-husband and the surprising revelations of his criminal activities lead Maxine on a sometimes frightening sometimes exciting journey from New England to Florida and to the West as she tries to escape his fate. In addition to all of this, Maxine's main goal is to find her long lost sister and confront old family secrets. Along the way, she meets a man who may or may not become a romantic interest and becomes involved with his family. The complicated relationships take the characters to Colombia and Panama as well as across the United States. While the interwoven plot lines and fast action are important aspects of the book, the novel's core is Maxine, a strong compelling character who brings with a sense of humanity to the story. I enjoyed *Chased by Death* very much and highly recommend it.

—Margaret L. Dale, J.D.

*Chased by Death* by Judith Copek has everything required to guarantee a very enjoyable reading experience! There are murder, corruption, romance, infidelity and true love. The characters are people we can relate to so that we are able to empathize with their fears, disappointments and joys. Judith Copek's IT background ensures that the technological details throughout the book are accurate and intriguing. A great read!

—Debbie Weiss
Women's Book Reviews

Wow! Judith is another Sir Arthur Conan Doyle with her beautiful use of verisimilitude giving reality to the details of life, trauma, pursuit, and the cat (I love Lucy). Maxine is Sherlock. Each character has crime, pathology, and human needs which braid together for a real thriller. Death is always coming, but when? And who kills?

—Coryl LaRue Jones, PhD
Retired from NIH
Author of *Environmental Analysis of Neonatal Intensive Care* and *The Journal of Nervous and Mental Disease*

## *Dedication*

To my husband, my writers' group, and Joan,
who took me to Key West.

* * *

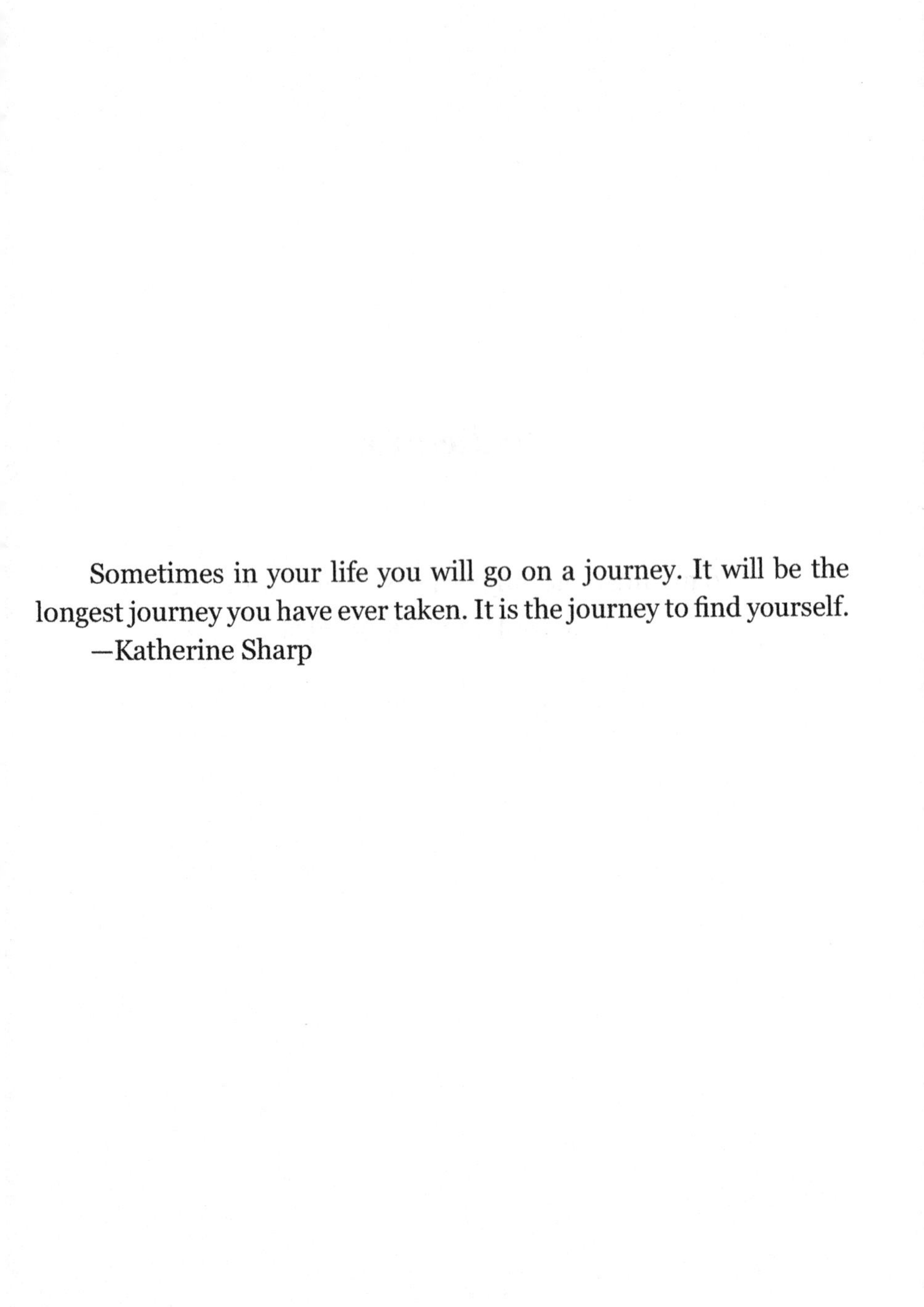

Sometimes in your life you will go on a journey. It will be the longest journey you have ever taken. It is the journey to find yourself.

—Katherine Sharp

# *One*

*Maxine*
*2008*

*Don't be a bitch.*

Maxine hadn't wanted to meet Larry here at Legal Seafood in the South Shore Plaza—their old haunt, now overrun with memories.

She spied him through the plate glass window, the ghost of husbands' past, chatting up the hostess, smiling and gesturing, flirtatious in his harmless way.

Seven years of her life.

"A most important family matter," he had explained. She had to eat, didn't she? He promised he wouldn't delay her trip. "In and out, okay?"

She pushed the door open to endure an awkward hug. Larry insisted on a table where he could see who walked through the door. The squint lines around his eyes were deeper and his face had new hollows. He had lost weight, but instead of looking fit, he seemed gaunt. Even his tan looked sallow, and his bloodshot eyes cried for

Visine. Being bronzed was part of the Summer Larry with his sports shirts, neat khakis, and Topsiders without socks. Despite the preppy clothes, Larry looked like hell.

Maxine ordered iced coffee. Larry asked for Jack Daniels. His red-streaked eyes darted around the restaurant, studying the other diners.

Turning and eyeing her, he said, "Lookin' good."

He always wanted an elegant wife on his arm, charming and all smiles. She was no longer that woman.

She had expected him to say, ditch *those clunky shoes, babe.* Now Maxine dressed to please herself. On this steamy late May evening, she wore linen shorts and a silk camp shirt. And Teva sandals.

Larry didn't comment on her practical footwear. She didn't remark on his dyed hair.

"I'm taking off after dinner," she said, hinting this wouldn't be a leisurely meal.

The harsh briny aroma of lobster drifted across their table. Lobster always tasted better than it smelled.

"Still a night owl, huh? How far you driving?" Larry's eyes swept the room again.

"Somewhere in Connecticut. South Florida by Sunday evening."

"Where you staying?" he asked.

"I'll crash at a motel until I find an apartment. It's summer. Lots of choices."

"What if I need to reach you?" His eyes bored into hers.

*Why would he need to reach me?*

"Shoot me an email."

They endured an uncomfortable silence. Maxine sipped her coffee. *Meeting Larry was a dumb idea.*

He sighed as he always did when he was resigned to something.

"When you mentioned moving to Florida, a little bird told me you were going to look for Honora. It's been a long time, Max, too long." He raked his fingers through his newly darkened hair, then swirled the ice in his bourbon. "You need to dump that old baggage."

Maxine hadn't expected Larry to guess the reason for her Florida move, her new beginning. She still clung to the idea that she could find her sister and bring her back to a normal life. More than anything, she wanted the warmth of a family being together. She and Honora cooking, shopping, even taking vacations. Her hope and her dream.

Larry drank his whiskey and peered around the dining room again as if ghouls lurked under every table.

"You okay?" she asked.

"I don't have anyone to take good care of me, but thanks for asking." His voice sounded sincere. "My family misses you, especially the kids and Corky. You're an honest-to-god member of clan Caliendo." He handed her a pale-yellow envelope. "They got together for a goodbye present and nominated me to give it to you."

Inside the envelope was a goodbye-from-all-of-us message with a Lord & Taylor gift card. She felt a pang, noting Corky's name scrawled on the card. She had missed him the most.

Besides the gift card, five crisp one-hundred-dollar bills nestled inside the envelope. Maxine glanced at Larry and raised her eyebrows.

"The gift card is from everyone. The cash is from me. I had some luck at Foxwoods last weekend."

*Gambling again.* Lapsed after all those GA meetings. The individual notes on the card made her smile. She had loved being part of Larry's family with the parties, the first communions, and the holiday get-togethers. After the divorce papers were filed, she had not kept in touch. The divorce, final today, had been her idea.

Larry seemed pleased at her reaction, with real warmth in his eyes.

"We all know what a power shopper you are."

"Oh, Lar." She held back, not wanting any strings attached. The gift card was okay., but the cash? She didn't want to be beholden to him.

"Dammit, it's a gift. okay?"

She lifted her glass in a toast. "Thanks! Tell everyone I love them."

Larry opted for baked scrod. And another Jack Daniels.

He rubbed his hand across his middle and made a sour face. "My stomach's been like a vat of sulfuric."

Maxine tried to look sympathetic while thinking that whiskey was no substitute for an antacid. After a moment, she said, "The house is in move-in condition. I hired a cleaning service."

"You didn't need to do that." He glanced at his watch.

"I'm taking just enough items to set up light housekeeping." Maxine sipped her coffee.

"You still have the Smith & Wesson?" He leaned toward her.

"Stashed in the glove box." She should have ditched the revolver, a gift from Larry when she worked nights for a while. "Do you want it?"

"God, no. A woman traveling alone is so vulnerable..." His voice trailed off. "You know, I never got around to licensing it." He glanced down at his plate. "Sorry about that."

Maxine would sell the damn gun once she got to Florida.

Florida. Her prior efforts to find her sis had failed: the web searches, the sleazy PI, the futile trips. Maxine felt antsy to get her search underway again, to talk to this new PI she wanted to hire, to take a giant step toward her goal. After the passing of so many years, Honora could be anywhere. Or dead. Whenever that possibility entered her mind, Maxine's stomach roiled and her throat felt so dry she couldn't swallow. She had to know, one way or the other. She had to.

*Think about something else.*

"When are you moving back in?" she asked.

"Tomorrow." He glanced around like a lizard searching for a rock to slither under.

Maxine had changed the locks after they separated and Larry moved out. She reached into her handbag and handed over the house keys and the garage door opener with a little card with the code for the new keypad. "Phone and utilities are still in your name."

"You make this so easy." He patted her arm in his possessive way. "You didn't notice anyone hanging around the neighborhood, did you?"

"Not a soul. Why?"

He didn't answer.

Their meals arrived. When he wasn't sneaking a peek at his phone, he was swiveling his neck to scan the room.

"You expecting someone?"

"I, uh, there's been a little business trouble, just a disagreement over some accounting practices and I, uh, pissed off somebody. Nothing to worry about."

She caught him surveying the room again. Maxine began to feel jumpy. She caught herself crossing and uncrossing her legs and picking at her cuticles. Now she, too, scrutinized the door, half-expecting John Dillinger to kick it in and spray the room with a machine gun.

The tension made her yearn for a glass of wine.

"No serious trouble, I hope," she said. Larry never confided his problems to her, not while they were married, and certainly not now.

"Only a little bump in the road," he said, not meeting her eyes. His shoulders drooped.

"Have you had a falling out with Lotto?" asked Maxine. Larry had always idolized his boss.

"No, this is an accounting problem." He smiled, but only with his lips. "Lotto is a prince."

Larry had had business difficulties before, but the new issue must be different. Maxine felt a surge of relief that Larry's troubles were no longer hers.

*I am out of here in minutes.*

They divided a slice of key lime pie for dessert, and Larry mentioned he wanted a dog.

He didn't say watchdog, but that was what he meant.

"That's funny. Yesterday I was thinking about adopting a shelter cat."

They shared a laugh.

"Tell everyone I said good-bye, and give them my love."

"Are you going to pay a last visit to our mall?" His bloodshot eyes met hers.

Maxine didn't know whether she would have a nearby Lord & Taylor store in Florida. "I need a beach bag and a new swim suit. Maybe a party dress." Dare she hope for a few parties?

"Shop till you drop, babe." His smile, no longer pained, gave a glimpse of the old Larry. "You take care now," she said. "Maybe think about early retirement."

His face turned to stone. Wrong advice.

"Bye, Larry. And thanks for the...gifts." Maxine put out her hand and he took it.

Outside, the sun hung above the horizon like a giant ornament. Maxine didn't look back.

~ * ~

The SUV's cargo area, already crammed to the gills, barely had space to squeeze in two more shopping bags. Maxine must be careful where she parked or someone would break in and steal everything.

She rolled down the window, turned on the AC, and lit a long-awaited cigarette. Three a day were her limit, a habit concealed from everyone except Larry. Maxine took her old recorder from the glove box and replayed her last messages. She had forgotten to tell Larry about the winter clothing for the Salvation Army. Maxine dialed his number from the cell phone she had resurrected when she turned in her smart phone at work. Larry's mobile number was still on speed dial. No answer. All that futzing around with his cell and now he didn't pick up. She called his apartment, and he didn't answer his landline either, so she left a message about the clothes. Maxine wondered if he had stopped by the house. It would be like him. The line at the house rang until the answering machine picked up. She felt a prickle of unease.

She gassed up and headed for I-95, thinking about her last day on the job and the farewell party. The gang in the IT department had sent her off with fun presents: a pink flamingo, sunscreen, pink clogs, an expensive beach towel, even a Carl Hiaasen book. A few miles down the road, she dialed Larry's cell again and he still didn't pick up. He had acted so hyper at the restaurant. His jumpiness, his hollow eyes.

Behind schedule, she pulled off the Interstate and tooled into Sharon where she deposited Larry's cash in the ATM. Maxine had always been a night person, and driving late energized her. The unanswered phone calls and her ex-husband's mental state—Larry must be in a dark place. She would swing by the house just to make sure everything was okay.

The split-level sat on the corner of a side street. The widow next door was in a hospice. The place across the street, in foreclosure, looked down at the heels with a weedy lawn, crud on the roof and dirty windows. Maxine hoped for livelier neighbors in Florida and thought of her new party dress, short and kind of sexy in a ladylike way.

Larry's car was in the driveway. Larry *never* left his precious Lincoln out. A narrow beam of light shown through the gap in the rec room curtains. The room contained her treadmill and step equipment, and Larry's weights and rowing machine. He wouldn't be rowing and lifting after a big dinner and all that whiskey.

Something wasn't right. She continued driving for a few blocks and made a U-turn. When she passed the house again, Maxine saw a car parked away from the light. She turned down the side street and made a U-turn, easing the Jeep behind the parked car, an old Crown Victoria with Massachusetts plates. Maxine couldn't recall neighbors with a Crown Vic. Her palms felt sweaty on the steering wheel and she wiped them on her shorts before she flipped on her recorder and noted the color, make and the license number.

Maxine drove past the house again, punching the "home" button on her cell phone. There was no extension in the rec room and anyone in the lower level would have to climb the half-flight of stairs to the main floor to reach the phone.

No one picked up, and again, the answering machine kicked in. Maxine parked next door in Mrs. Grogan's driveway. The lilacs on the hedge between the two houses were past prime, with shriveled lavender blossoms, but the rhododendrons along the garage had exploded into full bloom. Maxine crept around the hedge. Insects sang a shrill chorus, and the humid night air felt thick, almost turbid. The garage had a rear door she always kept locked.

Maxine edged along the side of the garage by the rhododendrons when she heard the garage door rumble open. She backed up between two bushes and flattened herself against the wall.

"I'm gonna put his car away. I hate fucking jobs with no lookout." Hispanic voice.

"For sure."

"For *shu-ah.*" Pure, thick, Boston accent.

Could it be the Southie Twins? Those two goons Larry used to poke fun at? South Boston and South America, he called them. Maxine remembered seeing them in Atlantic City and Las Vegas, "the Go-fers and Chauffeurs." What were those bozos doing in the house? Where the hell was Larry?

An engine started and Maxine heard the Lincoln pull into the garage. A car door slammed, and she felt the vibration of the garage door descending. She waited, and heard the front door slam and footsteps on the driveway.

Her throat squeezed so tight it hurt.

A car pulled up and she heard the thunk of another door slam. She turned her head and saw the old Crown Vic speeding toward Stoughton.

Maxine scurried next door, climbed into the Jeep, and locked the door. She backed down the widow's driveway and stared at her former house. The light was off in the rec room. She wanted to leave—head back to the Interstate and get out of there. She needed to begin her new life, not get sucked into this...whatever.

Then she pictured Larry hurt and bleeding, or locked in the trunk of his car. He wasn't a bad guy. Maxine pictured more horrors, and knew she couldn't leave. Gophers and Chauffeurs defined the words "low lifes." Why had they been inside their house?

Larry always kept a spare key in a little magnetic container under the lid of a zinc pail, near the gas grill where the barbecue tools hung. She would just nip inside and take a quick look around. She pulled back into the neighbor's driveway.

*Call the cops. No, let's think about this.*

If she called the police, she would have to report a break-in and wait until they had finished investigating. Maybe Larry had sent those guys here on an errand. He would be outraged if she brought the police into his house on a whim.

But why had the Lincoln been in the driveway?

Maxine stashed her cell phone in her pocket, grabbed a flashlight and the loaded Smith & Wesson from the glove box. Larry had given her the little revolver years ago when she had to work nights. She had taken shooting lessons. Small, less than a pound, the gun was still too big for her shorts' pocket. Bad idea to stick it into her bra. She didn't want to be encumbered by her handbag. The Smith & Wesson's nubby handle felt reassuring, but how to carry it? She found a small fabric shopping bag in the back seat and slipped the revolver into it.

Maxine adjusted the bag over her shoulder, sneaked behind lilac hedge and rounded the garage. Heart pounding, she flicked on the flashlight. The light played on the paving stones where Larry's barbecues stood: smoker, gas grill and a Weber kettle. Then it hit her. The old key wouldn't fit the new locks.

The only way to get inside was to use the garage door keypad. Maxine crept around to the front and found it with her flashlight. *2676*. Her fingers fumbled as she punched in the numbers, but the door rose with a noise like a B-52 taking off. The house was a dark hole, and Maxine didn't know if she could force herself to enter, but she scooted into the garage, hitting the door button again and cringing from the clattering sound. The automatic light stayed on for thirty seconds, and Maxine ran to the driver's side of the Lincoln and pulled the door open. The key fob was in the ignition, and Maxine used it to pop the trunk.

She had squeezed her eyes shut. Forcing them open, she peered in the big empty space with Larry's tools in a leather bag and a canvas tote with glass cleaner and paper towels. Maxine grabbed a wrench and stuck it in with the Smith & Wesson. Two weapons were better than one. The metal wrench clanked against the gun. *Bad idea.* Remembering her training about not pulling a gun unless she intended to use it, she decided to carry the wrench. With her strong arm and her coordination, the wrench would be a lethal missile. Maxine crept to the door into the house.

She turned the doorknob as the garage went dark. Taking a tremulous breath, she stepped into the laundry room, stopped, listening. Only sounds were the hum of the refrigerator and the slight drone of the air conditioner. She should flip on the lights, but what if those goons came back and saw the house lit up? Her shaking hand made the flashlight beam jerky, but the room appeared normal. She had to decide whether to ascend the half-flight of stairs to the living area, or tiptoe down to the exercise room. *Check upstairs first.*

She listened again. No sound except the AC and the fridge. Maxine crept through the kitchen, living room and dining room. Nothing out of place. No strange odors. Noticing the bags and boxes for the Salvation Army, she found a worn leather handbag with a shoulder strap. She transferred the revolver to the handbag. *Somehow safer.*

Beyond the dining room, she noticed Larry's office door open. She stood in the doorway and played the flashlight over the room. Drawers ajar, books on the floor. A shambles. What had they been looking for?

*Call the police now. First, a quick look downstairs.*

She thought about holding onto the Smith & Wesson, but she needed her right hand to grasp the flashlight. *Never pull a gun unless you are planning to shoot it.*

Maxine retraced her steps and stood on the landing to the downstairs rec room. Feeling like she was descending into hell, she swept the beam over the stairs. She tried to clutch the railing with her shaking left hand, which made her drop the wrench. Her body froze as the tool made a loud clank as it hit each wooden stair.

*Holy shit!*

At the bottom of the stairs, she picked up the wrench. Everything in the exercise room looked normal. Her nose caught a whiff of stale sweat, but someone had been here—she had seen the light through the curtains.

Still quaking, she flicked the light over the sofa, and the television, then the treadmill, and her step equipment. Her heart lifted. Nothing out of place. The beam grazed the weights, the yoga mat and finally Larry's rowing machine. Where Larry slumped. *Not moving.*

"Larry?" she tried to whisper, but her voice croaked. She edged closer. "Larry, are you all right?"

Obviously not all right. She stiffened, unable to move, unable to think. Her paralysis seemed to last forever. Somehow, she approached the rowing machine, gripping the flashlight like it was a life preserver. Larry's hands and feet had been taped to the rower.

"Larry?" Almost a shriek. "Omigod! Larry!"

She was next to him, and in the flashlight's beam, his face was bluish with little pinpricks of red all over. Then she noticed his alligator belt was wrapped around his neck. Every impulse urged her to get the hell out of there, but she steeled herself and approached the machine. She touched his face with hesitant hand. Was he still alive? So hard to loosen the belt which was godawful tight. She couldn't get it loose without tightening it more. Larry's eyes were open, and he had slumped into an awkward, unnatural posture. She whispered his name once more, but she knew he was gone. Dead.

She ran into the half-bath. Locked herself in.

# *Two*

"I w-w-want to report a murder."

Trying to hold herself together, Maxine related what she had seen. Larry, the strange car, the two men. The police dispatcher said to stay right there, that a squad car was on the way.

Maxine had the light on in the powder room, and she clutched the sink, cowering. *Larry. Oh God, poor Larry.* Then a wave of nausea hit her and she vomited into the toilet. She turned on the tap, splashed water on her face, wiped her eyes and rinsed her mouth.

The handgun in her bag. Unregistered. Maxine opened the bathroom door and tore up the stairs, flicking on light switches as she went. She raced out of the garage through the back door and rounded the lilac hedge. Her keys were still in her pocket, and she clicked the Jeep open, tossed the handbag into the back and stuffed the Smith & Wesson under the seat. Maxine ran down the sidewalk to the house. She sat hunched on the front stoop with her arms wrapped around her knees, trying to control her tremors. *Larry was dead.* She knew he had a big problem, but nothing like this. She shivered and clutched her arms closer, trying to stop shaking.

Moments later, she saw blue lights flashing on the squad car that barreled in and squealed to a stop. Maxine jumped up and waved.

~ * ~

Twenty minutes later Maxine sat in the cruiser. More police arrived, along with an ambulance and crime scene investigators. A detective appeared and she repeated what happened. This time, she mentioned the divorce, dinner, and the return of the house keys. When she said "Caliendo," Larry's surname, she thought the cop's eyes held a glimmer of recognition. She provided the address of Larry's apartment in Canton.

More cops came, some in uniform, some not. She imagined everyone clomping up and down the basement stairs. She was appalled to feel a surge of relief that the house was clean.

Trying to stay calm, she waited with her hands in her lap and her knees pressed together, with Florida drifting further away with each minute that passed. She mentioned her recorder with the license plate number, and one of the cops escorted her next door to her car and she handed him the recorder. By then, she felt numb, in survival mode, wanting only to get through this nightmare. Half an hour later, one of the detectives told her the police had apprehended two men ransacking Larry's apartment in Canton. They asked her to come to the station and give a statement.

Still later, Maxine stood in the Canton police station picking "gophers and chauffeurs"out of a lineup.

She stared at five men through the one-way glass and honed in on the one with mean eyes, noting his widow's peak and his shoulders packed with muscle and flesh. He looked boiling with energy, as if he wanted to tear the place apart. She said, "That's Spida Webb," pointing to the second man on the left.

In the second lineup, Angel Garcia, dark and dangerous, sneered, as if he were slumming and expected to be delivered to the Ritz afterward. Maxine pointed out Garcia among the five. It crossed her mind that she should have said she had never laid eyes on either of them.

Webb and Garcia had an attorney at the line-up. They must have yelped for their lawyer right away. Maxine had noticed him in the parking lot, hastily slipping his arms into a sport coat, which he wore over a white polo shirt. He had looked at her in an appraising kind of way. At least he hadn't given her the stink eye, like Webb staring through the one-way glass, as if he could *see* her.

The evening continued, hour after ugly hour, a slice of time she would always remember with despair.

"Now what?" Maxine asked the cop who had escorted her to Canton from Sharon.

"They'll be taken to the Norfolk jail for processing." He noticed her glancing at the lawyer. "These two won't get out on bail, not after what they allegedly did."

*Allegedly.*

Another cop drove her back to the Sharon police headquarters and invited her into the station, like maybe she had a choice, but he asked if she wanted water or coffee. Maxine hated being the center of attention. She remembered to give them the contact information for Larry's oldest brother. He could claim the body.

*After the autopsy.*

A ruggedly handsome man with weary blue eyes took Maxine into the chief's office. He introduced himself as George Blaisdell. The chief gestured for them to sit down but Blaisdell stood, and mentioned something about NORPAC, an anti-crime task force, and Larry's murder investigation.

"Did your husband give any indication where all the money might be?" the chief asked.

Maxine stared at him, wondering what would happen if she stood and ran out of there.

"What money?"

"Your husband was reputed to have a stash of drug money."

"Ex-husband, please."

Had whoever ransacked Larry's office been looking for drug money? Maxine examined her cuticles, first one hand, and then the other. She sighed, forcing herself to look at the cops. "I told you tonight was the first time I've seen Larry since I filed for divorce and he moved out. We met for dinner so I could give him the house keys." Maxine met the chief's eyes. She took them through the evening again, and the chief asked for her receipts: Lord & Taylor and gasoline. "To get an idea of the timeline," he said. She didn't produce the bank deposit which would require an awkward explanation, but she did tell them she and Larry had never had a joint bank account.

"I know nothing about my ex-husband's business." Maxine crossed her legs and watched the cops. The handsome one tried not to stare at her legs but failed.

Nobody spoke.

"When can I leave?"

She gave them her cell number and her Florida P.O. box address, which was all she had. They photocopied her driver's license, and the chief said her tape recorder would be kept as evidence. They took her fingerprints to eliminate them from others in the house. Someone had already driven the Jeep to the police station.

George Blaisdell gave Maxine a stern look, and said, "You are free to leave."

He glanced at the chief, who raised his eyebrows, then nodded. "It would make sense to get out of town." He rocked back on his heels. "Webb and Garcia didn't act on their own." He paused a beat. "You'll be called upon to witness in court. If the crime goes to a grand jury, you might have to testify there, too."

"When will that happen?" she asked.

He didn't know. Criminal proceedings could take a long time. In the meantime, she should stay out of sight. "Florida is a good idea. We'll be in touch."

Later Maxine might need to go through some photos to help identify people, and to try to recall any information she might have picked up earlier.

She felt a cold spasm of fear. Stay out of sight. Grand juries. Testify. Maxine stood. "Sure. No problem."

Outside, the air had a poisonous quality, as if full of toxins. She locked the door the instant she was inside her Jeep. When she pulled onto the street, she glanced behind her.

She felt a leaden fatigue beyond mere tiredness and thought about checking into a motel on Route 1, but an inner voice advised *get out of town*.

Before pulling onto the interstate, Maxine stopped at an all-night Dunkin' Donuts for two glazed donuts and a large iced coffee. She stashed the Smith & Wesson back in the glove box.

Maxine dreaded the trek from Boston, bumper to bumper in the heat and the exhaust with the aggressive semis, the blunderbuss campers, the cowboy pickups, all the crazies cutting in and out of lanes, texters tapping away, cell phone addicts yakking, a demented 1500 mile circus parade plunging down the east coast to South Florida. The sugar, the grease and the caffeine kept her going until she was past New Haven. That and two more cigarettes.

# *Three*

Lotto wanted to coax Angelika into the Rum Bar at the Shore Club near the pool. He could count on craziness at the pool—horny women in thongs, and other pleasant distractions while he sipped his favorite *Ron Zarapa Centenario.*

Angelika insisted they sit on a red sofa in the Red Room with its gauzy floating curtains and everything so blood red the back of his eyeballs glowed. Red. Red. Red.

What a sexy creature Angelika was, arranging herself on a crimson cushion, taking the first sip of her Passionata, with the strawberry garnish in her pouting scarlet lips. Pert and seductive. Lotto admired her red bra through the sheer dress. Who would have guessed a German girl could be so hot? The German girls in Colombia went to the German school and the Lutheran church and had turned up their Teutonic noses at local boys like him. Boys who weren't coffee heirs, but pharmacists' or grocers' sons.

"You wore a Pink shirt for me, Lotto," Angelika said with a bright smile. He liked her faint accent and the way her throaty voice said his name, "Lowto."

Lotto glanced down at his linen shirt. He had a closet full of Thomas Pink shirts, bought by the half-dozen at the Bal Harbor Shop on Collins Ave. He bent to kiss Angelika when his cell phone buzzed. As he glanced at his watch, Lotto felt a rush of irritation. Who would dare call him late on a Friday night at *this* number? He touched his finger to Angelika's still puckered lips and flipped his phone out of his belt. With a vague wave, he parted the filmy drapery and walked toward the beach.

He saw the "encrypted" message on the phone, and pushed his encrypt button, too. "What the fuck?" he asked.

"Problem in Boston," said Enrique's voice, gruff but pitched higher than normal. "Didn't think this could wait."

Those who worked for Lotto knew two things: Lotto detested bad news and would threaten the messenger with a painful, ugly future. Even worse was *withholding* bad news. A Colombian necktie adorned anyone stupid enough to try it twice.

An unexpected audit had tripped up Lotto's supposedly loyal accountant. What had possessed Caliendo to think he could get away with his blatant skimming of two million? Lotto had given a few simple orders, orders that anyone in his employ should be able to follow. Find out where he stashed the money. Get his computer with all that damning evidence. Kill him.

Enrique reported that the men sent to carry out Lotto's orders had killed Caliendo by accident. Before they learned anything. No money, no computer, no information. *Mierda*! And the *putas* had broken the set-in-stone rule about posting a lookout.

The litany of mistakes massed until the *Ron Zarapa* was a fiery broth in Lotto's stomach. He strode to the empty beach, an expanse of pale sand and dark water.

His men had been arrested and taken to jail. What if they *talked*?

"Have someone take care of those *idiotas*!" He stared at the surf, white foam against the black ocean. "The same for the *puta* who picked them to do the job—you know what to do. *Me entendió?*

Enrique assented. Lotto thought for a moment. "Why wasn't El Tigre doing the Boston job?

"He is in Colombia. A family crisis."

"And now the crisis is here." Far out in the water, Lotto saw the lights of a freighter shimmering on the horizon. "Caliendo's wife? Where is she?" he asked.

Enrique droned on. Their lawyer had seen the wife at the lineup. Maxine Harvey. They had a make, model, and plate number for her car, recorded days earlier. For at least a year she had lived alone at the house, but she wouldn't be there now.

"It is a crime scene," Enrique's patient voice continued. "Maybe she stays with a friend. Maybe she takes off."

"Get a tracker on the woman. *De una*. Find her or you will be digging graves in Allapattah." Lotto trusted Enrique, but liked to keep him on edge. Productive anxiety.

Lotto turned to stare seaward. The inky ocean and the salty tang of the air brought back memories of Cartagena. Miami couldn't compete with Cartagena or beautiful Cali, his hometown with its *caleqas*, those sensual women and the six-day salsa parties. Lotto wondered if he should get away, just for a weekend, to escape from here and the *putas* who made his stomach churn. His wife and sons lived in Cartagena. He missed them, especially his boys. He should visit more often, but the damned business required his total attention *Ah, God*, Lotto sighed, feeling a longing for home.

# *Four*

Maxine crashed at a motel in Connecticut. She awoke with the twisted sheets shackling her legs, and a stiff neck from the tension-filled drive. She climbed out of bed and peered through the drapes. Dense gray clouds hovered low in the sky. Maxine sat on the bed and found a Wi-Fi connection for the laptop. Her email contained only farewells from friends at work, and a message from the Florida woman whose condominium she had agreed to rent. Nothing about Larry's murder in the online edition of the Boston papers.

She had to call Larry's brother before he left the house. The police would have told him of Larry's death, but she needed to call him, too, to soften the blow, as if anything could. She felt queasiness in the pit-of-the-stomach. Could she find the right words?

Maxine dressed in shorts and sandals, scanned the room to make sure she was leaving nothing behind, grabbed her purse and her keys and left the motel. In the parking lot, she found that the Jeep had survived the night without a break-in. The slime balls that killed Larry must have followed him home from the restaurant. They might have been following him for weeks. They had most likely seen the Jeep in the driveway. *The Jeep has to go.*

Her thoughts wandering, Maxine recalled when they had first met. Larry said he was an accountant for an import-export marketing company, and mentioned complicated financial dealings. "Fiduciaries." She rarely crossed paths with his business associates, mostly men with Hispanic accents, men who didn't look like they knew a fiduciary from a Bloody Mary. "Marketing" could be anything, and Maxine soon suspected Larry's occupation was on the wrong side of the law: illegal gambling or numbers. "Don't ask, don't tell," worked for marriages, too. He had toiled long hours, traveled frequently, and worried twenty-four/seven.

The years had rolled on, and finally she understood their marriage was dead... that silence had taken the place of conversation.

What Larry's secrecy had said about his employment had poisoned their marriage. When she first voiced the "D" word, Larry hadn't acted surprised. When she told him she wanted neither money nor house, he had smiled like a man cashing a pile of chips. Which he had done last weekend. During their marriage, he had been generous, insisting she put away her entire salary and live on his. Now Maxine had a hefty bank balance, more than enough to pay a high-priced PI to find out what had become of Honora.

Sitting in the Jeep, she dialed her brother-in-law's number and swallowed hard when she heard Charlie Caliendo's gruff voice.

"Charlie, I can't tell you how sorry I am."

"We're all just devastated, Max. Forty-five years old! He was only forty-five years old," he said. She heard him choke back a sob.

Maxine told Charlie about her evening with Larry and what had happened.

"Bastards."

"There are other things...The cops think Larry had a stash of drug money. *They think.*" She heard him gasp. "And when the police caught up with those thugs, they were going through Larry's apartment in Canton." Maxine hesitated. "It might be a good idea to hire a lawyer to look out for everyone's interests. Larry's will is with his lawyer. Corky is his sole heir. I didn't know if you knew that."

Larry's youngest brother, Corky, only twenty-eight years old, had been born with cerebral palsy. He and Maxine were special buddies and his wheelchair was always parked by the bay window of the breakfast area when Maxine entertained the Caliendo clan.

Corky's brown eyes sparkled with mischief when he'd ask, "What's for dinner? How about some ziti with Grandma's special gravy? I always make a mess eating spaghetti." He'd lower his voice and ask, "Hey, know why the Italian army lost the battle? They ordered ziti instead of shells."

Maxine would laugh, and joke back. Corky was one of the few people Maxine always felt easy with. She would miss him more than anyone.

Charlie's voice interrupted her memories. "Max, are you still on the line? About the will?"

"The house is in Larry's name. Free and clear." She took a deep breath and continued, "I needed to tell someone. I'm going to be traveling, and I have to get a Florida cell phone, so the best way to contact me is through email." She cleared her throat. "I'll have a mailing address once I get settled and you can send me the obit and the card from the funeral. I'm so terribly sorry. Give everyone my condolences, will you?"

"Sure, Max. You were the best thing that ever happened to Larry."

He didn't blame her, and that helped a lot.

She checked out of the motel, bought a few groceries, stuff she could nibble in the car, snatching up a hot coffee and orange juice. Sitting in the car, Maxine went online and bought a "Spoofcard" for her cell phone so that no one she called would see her real phone number. She realized she should have kept the five hundred dollars in cash to avoid credit card charges. How deep could your paranoia go?

Having decided to sell the Jeep in Jersey, Maxine would rent a car for the drive. Before she got on the interstate, she found a Best Buy and replaced her old data recorder with one that had loads of new features. She noted her mileage and expenses on the recorder. When her inner life was in tumult, she needed something orderly in her life. Dishes done, bills paid, clothes dropped off at the cleaners. Managing the details of living gave her the illusion of control.

Today, gassed up, maps within easy reach, food and her drink handy, she would drive. Every mile moved her further from the killers and her demons—and closer to new worries that could make the problems in Boston seem piddling.

~ * ~

When she crossed into Jersey, Maxine stopped to top off the tank. While the clerk was getting her change, she called the Sharon house and punched in her password to check for messages.

"That was a dumb thing you done," said a sneering voice with a Boston accent thick as a milkshake. "You shoulda kept your big mouth shut, cunt. We got friends in the police."

The menacing tone and the profanity sent a ragged chill along her spine. Was he telling the truth? She must act as if he were.

Still at the gas pump, she unfolded the road map with sweaty palms. If she hadn't needed to conserve her cash, she would have bought a GPS too. Hell was navigating a strange metropolitan area. But she was in good old Jersey. If a state had casinos, then Maxine had visited them with Larry. Atlantic City was a two-hour drive.

She found another Wi-Fi connection, and used her laptop to locate a used car dealer specializing in creampuffs like the Jeep. Glad for the spoof phone ID, Maxine called the number. They said to bring the Jeep in. She promised to be there in the late afternoon.

In Atlantic City, she checked into the Hilton, a familiar place not far from the airport. Maxine gave a bellhop twenty dollars and he unloaded the car and schlepped everything up to the room for her. After calling the used car dealer for directions, Maxine had the Jeep washed and vacuumed. She felt a pang of regret for her big solid wheels, but this was no time to be sentimental.

At the sales lot, a mechanic checked out the Jeep and Maxine accepted the offer from the two men in the office. She signed the papers and exchanged the Jeep's title for a check. They gave her the license plates, and she put her former phone number and address on the bill of sale.

The men wouldn't hear of Maxine calling a cab and one of them drove her to the airport.

At the Thrifty counter, she rented a white Ford Freestar Mini-van and drove to a hairdresser she remembered, just off the boardwalk.

In the salon chair, gazing at her mirror image, she knew she looked like hell with dark circles and no makeup and her hair pulled back with a scrunchie. If Maxine had tried to cut her own hair, it would look like she'd been attacked with hedge clippers.

Pointing at a magazine's hairstyle photo, "Cut it short, like this," she told the young woman.

"Oh, what a shame. you have such pretty hair!" the stylist said. "Not a bit of gray."

Maxine studied her reflection in the mirror. Larry would have a conniption fit, but Larry was gone.

Forty minutes later, shorn and restyled, Maxine even looked younger, never a bad thing, if you were going to be thirty-seven next Friday.

She drove back to the Hilton where she took a long nap. At nine o'clock, she paid another bellhop to tote the boxes and suitcases down to the new rental. Maxine was climbing into the Ford when a voice shouted, "Max! Is that you?"

Her head jerked around to see a dark-haired guy getting out of the car next to hers, smiling and waving.

"Hey, Tony!" She hoped she wasn't staring at him with the horror she felt, as she stood half in and half out of her car.

"I almost didn't recognize you with short hair. Down for the weekend?"

"Yeah. For the weekend."

"Where's Larry?" He grinned at her.

Jesus. Larry. "He's...in Boston."

"You come down by yourself? Naughty, naughty." Tony's perfect smile wavered, like he was trying to figure out why Maxine would be at the Atlantic City Hilton alone.

She remembered to breathe. "A girlfriend. Ladies' weekend."

"Great. You have dinner yet?"

Larry had always bad-mouthed Tony.

"We're gonna hear a band."

"Have fun." He flashed a gleaming smile.

She watched Tony enter the hotel, and then she slammed the car door and yanked the Ford into reverse. Her hands shook like Corky's had.

At a stoplight, she opened a frappucino and chugged half the bottle. *Jesus. Tony.* Thank God he had not heard about Larry's murder. He didn't even know about the divorce.

Maxine drove back to I-95. Driving with the window down, she imagined she smelled salt-water taffy. Larry always brought a box home from Atlantic City. She liked the chocolate and the peanut butter flavors best.

Maxine couldn't stop thinking of Larry. *Sometime I'll have a good cry, but not yet.* She had to keep moving, stay off the radar, take care of herself.

~ * ~

Maxine drove into Sunday morning, arriving in Brunswick, Georgia, so tired her eyeballs ached. Groggy with fatigue, she drove over a causeway to Jekyll Island and found a motel, where they let her register before check-in time for an extra half-day's rate. She slept until four p.m. and awoke disoriented. A swim in an over-chlorinated pool and a quick breakfast made her alert again. She returned to Brunswick through the suffocating afternoon with the brackish, almost rotten smell of tidal water in her nose.

The humidity sucked her southward, toward sleaze and forty-nine dollar motels and funky bars on the beach, bars she imagined where everyone knew your name and the moles on your butt and your brand of beer. Even your sexual preferences.

She drove on, eighty miles an hour through the hot southern night, until early Monday morning when she crashed at a secluded motel in Delray Beach. The town felt deserted with most of the shops closed for the summer. In the too-cold motel room, she checked her phone messages.

George Blaisdell from NORPAC had called. The rugged, handsome one. He said Larry's murder and the arrest of Webb and Garcia had stirred up a hornets' nest. "All hell broke loose." Please get back to him as soon as she picked up this message. He left a number, which she put into her voice recorder, but it was too late to call him back. Now that the long drive was over, she felt as fragile as a thin wine glass. Even the idea of leaving the motel room and walking to her car seemed dangerous. What had Blaisdell meant by "all hell broke loose?" Hadn't all hell already broken loose on Friday night?

Looking out the window onto A1A, she opened the window and lit the second cigarette of the day, inhaling deeply, wanting to hold onto the smoke, and wanting to crawl into a safe refuge and sleep for days.

# *Five*

The slot machine exploded into flashing green, yellow and red lights and pulsing electronic music. Honora's heart thudded as she gaped at the snow-covered mountain peaks emblazoned on each of the three reels. The paytable for three coins read *5000*. A message said *Please call attendant.*

"Oh my God!" She jumped off the stool and thrust her hands in the air.

"Holy shit!" Next to her, bug-eyed, Steve stared at the gaudy display. "You hit the jackpot. Five thousand bucks! Wow and double wow!"

Honora couldn't take her eyes off the three-across good news. Behind her, people stopped and stared over her shoulder. A jackpot! And to think she had almost blown off this weekend excursion.

Under his breath Steve said, "Look, you'll be in deep shit if they find out you've been gambling here. Let me claim it. I'll give you whatever the IRS doesn't take. So you'll stay out of trouble." He laughed. "After my commission. Ha ha!"

"Don't be ridiculous." Her exultation turned sour. Wasn't it just like Steve to try to get his hands on her winnings? She didn't want him touching one dollar of her new wealth.

What five thou could buy! Designer shoes. A big-screen TV. Ethan would like that. Maybe she'd get him a Wii, too. And a mountain bike. A fun trip to San Francisco to buy shoes. Manolo Blahnik or Jimmy Choo, maybe even Chanel. And why not a handbag to go with them?

The attendant, wearing a shirt with the hotel logo, arrived and explained that she must produce a driver's license and social-security number or they would have to withhold twenty-eight percent. Prudence told her she should pay the tax and not have her information in the casino computer system, but damn it, twenty-eight percent was too much. She eyed Steve, grinning and gloating over her predicament. What a jerk. Why did she keep going out with him?

She handed the attendant her license and told him her social. Maybe no one in Reno would check out-of-state casino winners. They were so damn picky about employees gambling locally, but this was Tahoe. Did they process *everything* at corporate? Why hadn't she paid more attention?

Crap, the winnings would be spent before she had everything she needed. Ethan was really too young for a mountain bike. And when the taxes came due? Well, April was almost a year from May. She would save some out of her salary. A nasty little voice in her head said, "fat chance."

"Let's hit the grill for an early dinner," Steve said. "We can order a bottle of decent wine. I'm already licking my chops for a big boneless rib eye."

She'd like to mash his face into one of those steaks. He probably thought she'd spring for dinner, wine and the hotel room too. Well, the useless sponger had better think again.

# *Six*

Come ten a.m. Monday morning, Maxine called Samantha Mueller, the owner of the condominium she was renting, about the key. Maxine had found the rental on the Web, two bedrooms on the inland waterway in North Boca Raton.

Samantha insisted Maxine come over for breakfast, and Maxine was in the car twenty minutes later. Samantha lived a few miles south on the eleventh floor of an upscale condominium overlooking the waterway on one side and the ocean on the other. Maxine noted the amenities of a doorman and an ostentatious bouquet of fresh flowers in the lobby.

Rail-thin Samantha ushered Maxine into an airy room where abstract paintings shared the walls with prints of sea life. The casually elegant rattan furniture looked expensive.

Maxine sipped filtered coffee on the balcony while Sam puttered around with breakfast. A few summer residents, tanned to burnt umber, swam laps or lounged around the big swimming pool. Samantha popped out onto the balcony saying, “Breakfast is ready.”

They sat at a table covered by a heavy linen cloth and set with Italian pottery. Sam served eggs atop sautéed tomatoes and gave

Maxine two slices of bacon but only ate one herself. She was a redhead in her fifties with skin too long in the sun.

"Did you come to South Florida for a job?" Samantha asked, forking a bite of egg into her mouth with a freckled hand.

Maxine had already filled out a tenant information form. She said, "I need to put some distance between me and my ex-husband. I'm trying to keep a low profile, and I don't want the utility bills in my name, if that's all right."

"Oh, is he a stalker?" Samantha asked, raising a perfectly plucked auburn eyebrow.

Maxine tried to smile, but it felt forced. "I want to change the locks, if you don't mind. At my expense."

"Oh, the condo belonged to my father and I doubt if Daddy ever gave his key to anyone," Sam said with a laugh. "Although he did have a few girlfriends." She laughed again. "As long as you provide me with a key, too."

"Of course."

"And you're looking for work, I suppose?" Cool hazel eyes looked into Maxine's.

*Wants to know if I can pay the rent.*

"I have a job lined up teaching aerobics to seniors this summer," Maxine said. "In the fall I'll look for something else. Maybe find some consulting."

Sam raised her eyebrows again. "Aerobics consulting?"

"No, I'm a systems analyst." She added, "Computer," after a vague look came into Samantha's eyes.

"Oh, my god. I can barely manage Word and email." A deprecating laugh.

Maxine watched a sailboat motor by, passing a fishing boat going toward the ocean. The crews waved to each other.

"My father loved to sail," Sam said, apparently noticing Maxine's fascination with the waterway.

Maxine stood to leave. She still had to call George Blaisdell, the locksmith, and turn in her rental car.

"I'm sorry to eat and run," Maxine said with a regretful smile, "but I really want to get settled. The house keys?"

"I'll get them. The swimming pool is great and the patio is right next to the waterway. And there's a storage room." She stood and plucked a key ring off the sideboard.

"Great! I can stash my golf clubs out of sight." Maxine guessed she had passed muster.

"Oh, so you play golf?" Samantha seemed surprised.

"Just learning."

One of Larry's birthday presents had been golf clubs and a season of lessons, which Maxine had taken to please him, discovering she liked the game with its many challenges.

"I'm having some people in on Friday. Sixish. Please join us."

Taken aback, Maxine nodded and wondered how to weasel out of the invitation. Maybe a migraine. She wrote a check for two months' rent, and Sam gave her directions to the rental.

"Don't forget about Friday. Just drinks and nibbles." Samantha peered at her with an appraising look, cocking the perfect eyebrow again.

Samantha was being hospitable, and Maxine wished she could ditch the paranoia that governed her every move. She had come to Florida to find Honora, and she hadn't bargained on these complications. She felt the diffuse ache of exhaustion. Even innocent questions about her past life would be unwelcome. Lying was stressful. The mere thought of hiding was even more so.

## *Seven*

"Your bureau, Lotto. I must see your bureau."

When Angelika had tried to wheedle a visit, Lotto had said, "sorry, no."

A prestigious office on Brickell Avenue overlooking Miami with a view of the ocean was a setting Angelika would want to put her stamp of approval on.

He imagined her gliding in with a smile and a kiss. While he sat behind his curved teakwood desk, Angelika would strike one of her silly poses as she got an eyeful of his view. Angelika never stopped talking. *Lotto, let's go...Lotto, I'd love to...Lotto, why don't we... Lotto, those shoes, this dress, that bracelet...*

His little drama queen, Angelika. Too chatty, too predictable, but nice in bed.

Lotto didn't want her to see his office, not the brass plaque of *Marquesa Trading Company* or even the orchids along the wall, expensive fucking flowers that grew in any goddamn jungle. Business and other lives must not co-mingle.

Angelika got the clothes, the Boxster, dinners. Him. What the hell else did she need? She even had jewelry—gold and good Colombian emeralds. Greedy girl.

Now he had to concentrate on those goddamn Russians who would be here this afternoon with the blueprints for his submarine fleet. Half of this pounding stress would disappear when he didn't have to worry about freighters, planes and mules and every stupid thing that could go wrong when he brought product in. Did go wrong. Like the Mexicans. God, he hated the Mexican cartels with their avarice, stupidity, and their violence. Especially their excessive, mind-numbing violence. Imagine dumping human heads onto the floor of a disco! Shooting up rehab facilities. Those pricks would ruin the whole trade. Hijos de putas!

Lotto took a deep breath and thought again about the Russians. He tried to calm himself, but his heart pounded and his hands felt sweaty. He walked to the rosewood sideboard and poured a glass of mineral water from his Waterford carafe and popped a Xanax. While he waited for its calming effect, his eyes moved around the office. The Russians probably wouldn't recognize Lotto's pricey celadon jardinières, but they would realize he was a man of taste and culture, and not some mindless Miami mobster.

Yes, that decorator was a real woman, not one of those goddamn faggots, and she had sent him a bill so astronomical that for a moment he had been tempted to offer her a job with Marquesa Trading Company. But he hadn't. He ran his company with family and trusted friends. Trust was everything.

Lotto thought of the contrast between his Brickell Boulevard office and the warehouse near Little Havana where the product was kept until it could be distributed to the wholesalers. Lotto imagined leading the Russians into that dirty dump with potholes and no streetlights, with the ugly dogs patrolling the perimeter. He would point to the ancient wooden desk, the dented filing cabinet, and the big packets of cocaína wrapped in white plastic. "Here's my place of business."

It would freak them out.

Why weren't the submarine engineers themselves coming? Did they think he was some illiterate drug runner? That could be an advantage, but not in this deal.

Already there were too many fucking middlemen on this project with all of them screaming for dollars or Euros, whole suitcases of five hundred Euro notes. The Spanish called them "Bin Ladens" because they had become so scarce. The Russians might insist on Euros. Of course, by the time the subs were ready, the Euro might be in the toilet. Currencies went up and down like elevators.

It could be mutually advantageous if you accepted some of the product rather than cash. He rehearsed his ploy aloud, placing the emphasis on different words. Advantageous. Product. Cash.

He didn't think they would go for it. Of course, he would enjoy bullying the Russians, but they could be as inclined to carnage as the Mexicans. Lotto would be civil and correct, and even make nice-nice. He would patiently explain that the Medellin and the Cali cartels had been broken up in the nineties, now there were 300 mini-cartels and that his was one of them. He moved and distributed to the wholesalers. A boutique operation. Lotto didn't grow coca and his people didn't sell it on the street.

Welcome to Miami. You will, of course, allow me the pleasure of showing you some of our famous South Beach clubs?

Foreigners flipped out over the clubs with the Latin music and the sexy dancing, the gym-toned bodies glistening with sweat. They craved the women, the slim, tan, longhaired women, and the endless flow of Latin drinks.

Another round of Mojitos, por favor. He must monitor his drinking tonight. Booze didn't mix well with Xanax.

Maybe Lotto would invite Angelika along one evening. A beautiful model on a man's arm gave him a certain mystique. As long as no one talked business.

The señor del tinto who served Lotto's morning coffee entered with a pot of his favorite Colombian blend and a dish heaped with fat cubes of brown azucar.

"Just put it on the side table, and bring my demitasse," he ordered. He liked to watch the man bow before leaving.

His eyes landed on his always-empty leather "in" tray. *My little Potemkin village is going to impress the hell out of these Russkies.*

The telephone rang. It would be Enrique, calling about the mess of the month.

He punched "encryption," then answered, "*Sí*?"

He heard Enrique's voice with its quaver that told Lotto the news would be bad.

"Do you have good news, or are you *un muerto*?" His standard question.

"Ha! Ha! Lotto. We all know you are only a good news *hombre*."

Because Lotto's wife was his niece, Enrique always took liberties with their relationship.

"Shut up. Just tell me what's happened." He sipped the strong, sweet coffee.

Enrique reported Rocha was dead, but Webb had survived. His people had eliminated the idiot who had hired Webb and Rocha. Even on an encrypted line, Enrique always spoke his accented English with careful euphemisms, avoiding words for everyday business, words like *cocaine, mules, and shipment.* Lotto read between the lines. Webb, now in protective custody, would be hard to get at. The lawyer had promised that after Webb's near death experience, he wouldn't talk even if someone held a blowtorch to his *cojones.*

"*Mierda*!" Lotto shuddered, just thinking about it. "And the woman?"

"We sent out, you know, feelers, and Tony Rebechini ran into the wife in Atlantic City. She said *nada* about her husband being stone cold dead."

"No shit?"

"We had someone with native English make calls this morning. She called Mrs. Caliendo's workplace pretending to be checking a reference for a car loan. Everybody buys cars."

*Would Enrique ever get to the fucking point?*

"Our associate found a woman who knew this Maxine. Like all women, she liked to talk." Enrique chuckled.

"And?" Lotto sipped his coffee. The Xanax massaged his brain with its mellow fingers.

The shoeshine man came in lugging his paraphernalia. He noticed Lotto on the telephone, and gestured toward the door. Lotto beckoned to him and swiveled the leather chair toward the man and extended his new brown Ballys. Still on the phone, Enrique, always a paragon of thoroughness, droned on, but Lotto didn't interrupt.

"When the, ah, pretexter asked why Caliendo's wife quit her job, the woman said it was because of the divorce."

"Why didn't we know about any divorce?" He sat up a little straighter.

"Caliendo did not ever mention such a thing, but they did not live together for a long time."

The shoeshine man mixed two polishes to get the exact right shade of warm brown for Lotto's loafers.

Lotto heard papers rustling on the other end of the phone, and Enrique babbled on.

"Maxine wanted different things out of life, and didn't think they could go on as a couple. But they were still on good terms. And Caliendo's wife told this woman, 'I am doing okay.'

"And how does this bull shit get us any closer to finding her?" Lotto watched the shoeshine man apply the polish, wishing everyone who worked for him were so meticulous.

"The woman said Maxine was leaving for Florida. Maxine said she wanted 'to start a new life.' Look out the window. Caliendo's ex-wife is coming your way. Ha! Ha!"

"*Puta*!" He couldn't help himself. The shoeshine man applied polish with a rag, careful not to stain the soles.

"Ah, Lotto! You know I like to joke around." Enrique snorted with laughter. "This Maxine didn't live beyond her means. Must be the first woman not to. I doubt she'll apply for our 'benefits.' Ha! Ha!"

"Who has Caliendo's computer? You or the police?" *The crux of the matter.*

"The computer has gone missing," Enrique said. Lotto noted the quiver in his voice. "Caliendo would not have had much time to ditch it, so it could be with the wife... or one of his brothers. It could also be in Boston Harbor or a dumpster."

*Mierda*, he didn't want the computer floating around for anyone to snatch.

"I'll take care of the computer. You find the woman!"

Lotto had confided to Enrique that during the recent audit of Caliendo's books, Lotto had his hacker install secret software on the laptop.

Lotto smiled, knowing his thoroughness would have a huge payoff. He would ask his cousin Marta to report the computer stolen. Then, if anyone used the device to access the Internet, it would send a signal to the software company. They would report a stolen computer to the police. The GPS would even tell the company where the computer was located. The thief would be clueless until the police arrived. It would be returned to Marta.

Marta, Lotto's middle-aged cousin, had a mind like a man, but her maternal looks never roused anyone's suspicions.

Enrique said, "*Hasta luego,*" and ended the call.

Lotto drained the demitasse cup and watched the kneeling man rub the horsehair brush across the toes of his shoes.

*Where the hell is Caliendo's computer?*

## *Eight*

The condominium was in a development off Jeffrey Street. The cream-stucco three-story building with a red tile roof faced the Inland Waterway. Maxine parked and carried her suitcase past the swimming pool along a walk until she found the front entrance. The sun-drenched living room with a dining "L" overlooked the water, where a handful of boats lay at mooring along the pier.

The spanking clean apartment had spacious rooms and lots of light. Maxine found the patio just off the living room, separated from the water by a blooming hibiscus hedge that gave her a measure of privacy. The patio had a round glass-topped table, some lounge chairs and a black charcoal grill. She warned herself not to fall in love with the place, but she already had. It would have been so perfect if trouble hadn't intervened.

Her cell phone had two more messages from George Blaisdell and his voice sounded urgent on the last call, so she plopped down on the living room couch and dialed his number.

"Thank god, Mrs. Harvey, are you all right? Where are you?" His deep voice blustered with concern. Maxine reported she was in South Florida. No town.

"I'm glad you made it down there so quickly." He hesitated. "Listen, some bad news here."

He told her about the killing, and mayhem at the jail. "Your testimony will be more important than ever."

The hit men had taken a hit. She couldn't work up any sympathy for them.

"That's not the end of it. Saturday night, one of your husband's assumed associates was gunned down on the street in Lynn."

*Will they come after me next?* She felt dizzy, like she had spun around on a tilt-a-whirl.

She had no idea who this Roy Whaley was, maybe one of those oily faces with an unkempt mustache and a paunch straining against his belt.

Maxine wished she were in Alaska, or Switzerland. Somewhere safe. At the end of the road where no one could find her.

Blaisdell broke into her thoughts. "Ms. Harvey, did your husband have a computer?"

She had to keep repeating to herself, "ex-husband."

"He used to."

"Would you know where it is?"

She thought of Larry's home office, a dark, paneled room with the shades drawn and the heavy door always locked. Even after he was gone and the room was empty, Larry had left the door locked. She remembered him carrying a laptop case in and out of his office. Someone had ransacked the room, probably using Larry's key.

"We found a printer, a scanner, even a fax machine in his apartment, but no computer. We searched the Sharon house too. Ms. Harvey?"

"His computer was not at the house." She couldn't help them, and that was somehow a relief.

"Are you situated in a safe place?"

"I don't know. There's a phone message at the house in Sharon, a message threatening me. The man implied Larry's killers have 'friends in the police.'"

"Listen, we're monitoring the, ah, situation, and we should be able to keep tabs on whether you're in any danger. Right now, we think you are not. For what it's worth."

*For what it's worth.*

The phone call brought everything back, overwhelming her with fear, a physical sensation that ran up her arms and legs and settled into her belly as a nervous presence.

Maxine made several trips to unload bags and boxes from the Ford minivan, leaving everything scattered in the entry hall and the master bedroom. Not unpacking ran contrary to her innate tidiness, but other priorities beckoned.

In the kitchen, she found a phone directory and called a locksmith to come the next day. The smaller bedroom was unfurnished. She could move the living room desk in there and make a little office. If she stayed that long.

She got back into the Ford and headed for the West Palm Beach airport where she could drop off the rental and pick up something else, something local.

At the airport, she rented a Chevy Malibu for a week. The mess she had left in the apartment gnawed at her. She should have unpacked and left everything tidy. Back in the condo, she couldn't find a Wi-Fi connection for her laptop, and there was no cable modem or even a DSL line. An eighty-five-year-old man probably didn't give a rat's ass about computers.

No Wi-Fi was a problem. She drove around with her laptop on until she found a hot spot. Sitting in the car in the blazing sun with the laptop resting on the passenger seat, she read her email and found Larry's obit in the *Globe*. No mention of a wife, as she had asked, just of the family. Burial was on Wednesday with the wake today and tomorrow.

~ * ~

The cable guy came the next day and Maxine told Samantha to add the cost to the rent. "Oh, Daddy didn't need or want any of those things."

"The cable modem is for my livelihood," Maxine said.

A long hesitation followed. *Oh God*, she groaned. *I'll have to move if this doesn't work out.*

"About the party," Maxine said, taking a deep breath. "Can I bring something, maybe an appetizer?" She paused a beat. "I have a good shrimp toast."

"That would just be delightful," Sam said,

Maxine could tell from the gushy surprise in her voice that Sam hadn't expected her to appear, much less with food.

"I'll bring it to the party. About the cable—"

"Go ahead and order it."

Maxine breathed again. She would go to the party, smile a lot, drink a little, and leave early. *How bad could it be?*

The next item was to call the PI. She had come to South Florida to find her sister and nothing would deter her...nothing, not Larry's murder, not even by the vile threats about *"their friends in the police."*

~ * ~

The PI had an office in Pompano Beach. He agreed to meet her halfway late in the afternoon. She liked him for meeting with her so soon.

"At The Cove," he said. "Deerfield Beach."

Several months earlier, Maxine had made an online search of detective agencies in the area, and had narrowed the list down to three, and then spoken to each agency and checked references. Sheldon Finder, "Finder the Finder," in spite of the hokey name, produced first rate references—three different law firms had given him glowing reviews. Maxine had talked to him a few weeks ago and he told her to call when she got to Florida. She had told Finder this was a missing persons case. He said he loved finding people. Although his retainer seemed high, Maxine had decided to hire him.

After the call, Maxine sipped a bottle of water and let her thoughts drift to poor Larry. As the days passed and the shock wore off, she realized how good he had been, how kind and generous. She kept seeing his crooked smile, his brown eyes, and his tan face. She remembered how much he liked to wear tropical print shirts in the summer and his delight when she had given him a Tommy Bahama green shirt and khaki shorts.

She felt herself getting all weepy. She still needed a good cry. *Not yet. Maybe tonight.*

She unpacked her clothes, filling one corner of the vast walk-in bedroom closet. She unloaded the Smith & Wesson and stashed it in the nightstand drawer, making a note on her recorder to get a Florida gun license. She used her recorder to make an oral list of everything she needed to buy. Her golf clubs went into the storeroom.

In the bedroom, she dithered over the last box, heavy with records: tax filings, performance reviews, some photo albums and important papers. Nothing she needed today.

She showered in the pale green marble bathroom, put on a black and white sundress, and drove off to meet the Finder. She hoped he was half as good as his reputation.

~ * ~

The Cove nestled against the Intracoastal and had a small marina where pleasure boats tied up. Island music, ceiling fans with blades whirling lazily, hanging plants and the smell of grilling fish created a South Florida ambiance.

Sheldon Finder had said, “I’m the man wearing a tie,” and Maxine spotted him right away at a table by the water, a clean cut man with a ruddy face, wearing a blue pinfeather suit, a pale blue broadcloth shirt and a dark blue tie with multi-colored dragonflies, darting and swooping across the silk.

Maxine had always thought of private investigators as a grubby bunch needing a shave and dressed in worn, ill-fitting clothes. Sheldon Finder looked spiffy.

When he jumped up to shake hands, their eyes were level.

“Is it Mrs. or Miss Harvey?” he asked, handing her a business card.

“*Ms.* Harvey,” she said.

“You’re tall. Do you model?” he asked with an appraising smile.

Maxine returned his smile without answering. The server arrived and took Maxine’s daiquiri order, a classic daiquiri, nothing frozen or fruity. Finder asked for an imported beer, and took off his jacket. Maxine couldn't stop gawking at the dragonflies.

He asked about her trip down from Boston and she gave him conventional answers and watched the people clustered around the bar. The server brought their drinks. Maxine took a long sip, and realized she was grasping the cocktail glass like it was a lifeline. Nerves.

She removed the envelope with twenty one-hundred dollar bills from her handbag and tried to slip it to Finder. "Please understand, I'm concerned about confidentiality in this matter we're going to discuss."

"No cash. I'll take your check," he said, giving her a sharp look. "Let's discuss exactly what you want me to do before I take a retainer."

Where to begin? She picked up the daiquiri.

"Brass tacks," Finder said, his voice full of energy. "Who do you want me to find and how long have they been missing?"

Maxine cleared her throat and took a deep breath. "It's my sister," she said. "I haven't heard from her for seven years."

"That's a long time," Finder said, frowning. "No contact at all?"

"None." Maxine took a gulp of her daiquiri and realized she had guzzled almost the entire drink. Finder followed her eyes and observed the nearly empty glass.

"Where was she when you last spoke with her?" His sharp brown eyes glanced around the restaurant. Maybe he was always on the lookout for a missing person.

"She was here. In South Florida."

"And what have you done to locate her in the meantime?" Now he looked directly at her. He wasn't handsome, but pleasant-looking with short crisp hair and a blunt nose.

"I've searched on the Internet, written to her last address, called her old friends, looked in telephone directories, that sort of thing." Her face felt flushed.

"But you haven't hired anyone—"

"I hired someone a year after she went missing, but he took my money and found nothing, so I didn't do that again."

"And then?" His eyes were probing, but kind.

"My husband and I divorced. I have some money saved. It seemed like the right time to make one last effort."

"Okay, I'm going to need some facts." He pulled a navy leather notebook out of the suit jacket pocket which he had flung over the back of the chair.

Maxine took a deep breath.

"Let's start with you, Ms. Harvey. Full name, address, phone number."

Maxine gave him her P.O. box and her cell number. "I like to communicate by email whenever possible."

"I like phone calls, myself." He made eye contact again while he drank a swallow of beer. She thought he was around forty, maybe a few years older.

"I'm a private person and this is so difficult for me." She wanted to take another sip of the daiquiri, but it was gone. "I'm not in trouble with the law or anything, if that's what you're worried about." She made a half-hearted attempt to smile.

"Okay, let's talk about your sister. Her name and any names she might have used professionally or whatever."

Maxine stared at him. Could he read minds?

"My sister's name is Honora. Honora Harvey. She worked as a dancer under a different name, and maybe others that I wouldn't know. She may—" Maxine paused, looking down at her fingers clutching the cocktail glass. "She may have been a...a sex worker under still another name. My sister had a drug problem and did whatever was necessary to maintain her habit."

Finder's face didn't evince any shock. "Sex worker? Do you mean she was a hooker? A street girl?"

She gave a curt nod. He must hear these stories every day, like a doctor or a clergyman.

"I'll need her last known address." He didn't look up from his notebook.

Maxine handed him a piece of paper.

Finder stuck the paper in his notebook. "What's her date of birth?"

"April twentieth, 1979." *How had Honora become so old?*

"Did she have an occupation? Besides, ah, dancer and street girl?"

Finder bent over his notes, so matter-of-fact. He seemed to understand her sister on a level that Maxine did not.

"She was studying business, marketing, actually, when she dropped out of college."

"Where was that?"

"Ohio State."

"When did she drop out? What year?"

He looked up from his notes, sympathy written in his eyes. Maxine brushed a tear away.

"Middle of her junior year. I think it was in '99. Our parents died, and she took it hard. I tried to convince her to stay in school, but she wouldn't."

A white powerboat pulled into the marina. The crew helped a half-dozen people debark, all of whom high-tailed it to the bar, the women in shorts and flip-flops, the men in polo shirts and boat shoes. The server returned with menus and Finder ordered another round of drinks. Maxine didn't protest.

"Do you know how long your sister had her substance abuse problem?" he asked, picking up the conversation again.

"I think it started around the time our folks died. After she left school. She may have smoked a little marijuana in high school and college, but just...recreationally."

"Was she in Florida that whole time?

"No, she stayed in Ohio for a few months, then she went to California. San Francisco, then she came to Miami. We saw each other a few times, but she hated my nagging her to go back to school, get a job, all that big-sister bull shit."

Maxine remembered those awful conversations, her begging and pleading, Honora's massive resentment, her guilt, and her refusal to listen to Maxine's urging her not to throw her life away.

"Have you ever considered that your sister could be dead after all these years?"

Their eyes met. Finder folded his arms behind his head, posturing a typical male pose. He continued, "Drugs and prostitution are not...a healthy lifestyle, with AIDS, violence, crazy Johns, jealous pimps, the whole bit. There are always Jane Does that go unidentified. It's something we have to consider."

"I read the South Florida papers," Maxine said. "Over the Internet, and even from newsstands, and whenever I see any mention of finding an unidentified woman's body, I call the police in that city and describe Honora, her age, build, everything." She traced her finger around the rim of her glass. "Nothing has ever come of it." She swallowed. "I have her dental records, by the way. I sent them in several times, but the police never found a match."

Finder scribbled in the navy notebook. He looked up. "Unfortunately, Honora's story is not uncommon." He rubbed his chin. "There's not a lot to go on. You have photos?"

Maxine took three photographs out of her handbag. One of them was Honora's junior year sorority picture. It showed a young woman with shiny dark hair, bright eyes, and a lovely smile. Had she ever smiled again? With real joy? Maxine thought not.

Maxine handed Finder the first photo.

The second was a snapshot Maxine had taken of her sister at a bar in South Beach. This girl was blonde and hard looking and didn't smile. The big eyes looked haunted. Just looking at the photo made Maxine weepy.

The third photograph was an ad for a bar featuring pole-dancers. There was Honora with her eyes half-closed and a slack mouth, looking drugged-out but sexy. The contrast between the sorority photo and the dancer was like viewing two different women, one innocent, the other damaged goods.

"Enjoy the gyrations of Miss Mitzy Muldoon," the ad stated. They had a cat named Mitzy once. She passed the pictures to Finder who studied them with an expressionless face.

Maxine's gut instinct told her she could trust Finder. His references gave her confidence that he'd be reliable. For all his pessimism, she hoped he would likely take her case. Honora's case.

He looked up from the photographs. "These images tell the story of what happened to your sister," he said. "I'm so sorry." His voice was kindly, like an old friend's. He touched her hand, and before she could withdraw, he patted her hand. His gesture was one of thoughtful abstraction, not as if he were coming on to her.

She appreciated his words, *I'm so sorry.*

The server brought their drinks to the table. Maxine hadn't looked at the menu.

"Let's grab a bite. On me," Finder said. "Someone will always remember a pretty girl." He glanced at his watch. "The expense clock will start running tomorrow when I begin my inquiries. By the way, do you remember the date you last heard from Honora? And what she said?"

Maxine felt her pulse racing. Finder would take the case. He would find Honora. Her voice was so low he had to lean toward her.

"It was September twelfth, 2001," she said, and let him absorb the meaning. "Honora left a message on my answering machine. 'I met one of them. I know him. I'm scared.'"

## *Nine*

"No shit!" Finder's eyes locked onto Maxine's. "Did your sister meet a terrorist? One of the hijackers? My God!"

"I don't know." Maxine stared across the water at the apartments. "I kept calling the number that was on caller ID, and finally someone answered, but it was a pay phone in Miami. All the flights were grounded that week, so I couldn't fly to Florida. Both Honora's landline and her cell phone had been disconnected, and she had moved out of her apartment. No forwarding address. She just disappeared."

Maxine took a long sip of her daiquiri. "I was getting married in a week. The timing was awful. My fiancé agreed to postpone the wedding while I drove to Miami. He was the only person I ever told about her call.

"When I got down here, I looked everywhere. It was humiliating. Going into dark strip clubs in the middle of the day, talking to sleazeball managers while they stared at my chest and pushed drinks on me. Everyone pawing over Honora's photos. I filed a missing persons report."

Maxine stopped speaking for a moment, trying to get a grip on her emotions. "No one had seen her or heard from her." Maxine's voice was hoarse. "Honora just disappeared without a trace."

She remembered that ghastly trip, the September heat like a foretaste of hell...sometimes cell phones didn't work, everyone paranoid, the horrible images of the planes flying into the towers, people leaping from windows, the towers toppling, the endless repeated images that twisted into an impenetrable knot of horror, along with her sister's sad face and the ad promoting the dancers. The clubs smelled of stale beer, stale cigarette smoke and stale sweat. Stale tears, if they had an odor.

She found out that Honora had quit her dancing job the end of July. If she continued life as a "street girl," no one knew. Maxine wondered if her sister had some foreknowledge of September 11th, but she never approached the authorities about the phone call. Months passed with no further word and all her inquiries had turned up nothing. Larry told Maxine she would hear from Honora in time.

She never did.

Finder's eyes locked on hers. "My God," he repeated, his vocabulary regressing to those two words.

Maxine had talked herself out, and they sat in silence for a few minutes, then they ordered dinner and he told her about his life as a Florida cop for twenty years. He had a pension and a good business, work he liked. His new career was coming along and he still had valuable contacts in the police.

"I never make any promises, but I'll do my best for you," he said.

"It's been so long," she said. "I'm not holding a lot of hope." Yet hope was all she had.

At the end of the meal, Maxine wrote Finder a check, and they shook hands. In the background, Harry Belafonte sang, "Island in the Sun."

Leaving The Cove, Maxine glanced behind her, checking to see if anyone followed. Not tonight, but when?

~ * ~

Maxine's head pounded and her stomach rebelled against the meal. Rehashing the past had upset her. She drove back to Boca, eyes on her rear view mirror. She turned into Jeffrey Street, drove all the way to the end and parked in the spot that still bore Samantha's father's name in dark green block letters: *Schroeder*.

She sat in the car for a few minutes, waiting for her head to clear, and cursing herself for letting so much time lapse. Searching for Honora after all these years was chasing a wild goose. Still, Finder would do everything she couldn't: look in old records and talk to people, attack the problem in a professional way.

Maxine got out of the car and felt the steamy Florida night. She would go for a swim and burn off some of the nervous energy that made her feel like a roman candle with a match touching the fuse.

~ * ~

The shimmering water in the turquoise pool lit by underwater lights and surrounded by blue tiles, palm trees and planters with blue flowers looked like a tropical lagoon. A separate whirlpool was further back toward the fence. Light posts placed at intervals gave the area an ambient glow. Maxine kicked off her flip-flops and dropped her towel on the white chaise lounge. She wore a green tank suit made for swimming, not sunning. Ignoring the "no diving" sign, she plunged headfirst into the warm water and swam an energetic twenty laps. When she climbed the ladder and reached for her towel, she noticed a man stretched out on a deck chair at the other end of the pool. He looked in her direction. Her heart seized up, but he gave a casual wave and went back to his newspaper, which he read in the lamplight.

"That was some serious swimming," he said, eyeing her as she walked by with her beach towel slung around her hips sarong style. He had blond hair, an infectious grin and thousands of freckles.

"Thanks." Her voice was cool.

"Jeff of Jeffrey Street." His eyes crinkled when he smiled. "Don't suppose you'd join me for a drink?"

"Not tonight."

Not tonight sounded too much like "maybe tomorrow." She gave him a quick once-over, hoping he would think she had just paused to be friendly. His boxer-style swimsuit flattered his trim build. In the dim light, the tropical-patterned cotton fabric had a pleasant sheen. His hair, curly and parted in the middle, made him look young. “Did you just move in?” he asked.

“Yes, recently,” she said, without offering more information.

His muscular freckled legs stretched out in front of him. Maxine allowed herself to have second thoughts about the drink. *Stupid.*

“Maybe I’ll see you around then,” he said with a smile, returning to his paper.

She felt a little deflated. It was no big deal; he was just an affable guy. It wouldn’t kill her to be friendly, but strangers might not be who they seemed.

She returned to her apartment a roundabout way, so he wouldn’t be able to tell where she lived.

In the bedroom, she eyed the last unpacked box, sitting in the middle of the floor like a challenge. It could wait one more day until she bought a file cabinet.

For the first time since Larry died, Maxine slept without tossing and turning.

~ * ~

Next morning at the fitness club, Maxine introduced herself to the woman at the desk who showed her the workout room with its mirrored front wall and shiny wood floor. By nine a.m. sixteen women were in the room. Maxine introduced herself, slipped a CD into the player and started the warm-up. They were more spirited and less geriatric than she expected, and she was glad she had a lively tape, which started with “Fame” and segued into “Flash Dance,” and some Latin music. Teaching a new class of strangers was always a little tense. Would they like you? Were you too vigorous, too tame? Was the music all right? Oldsters didn’t dig rap. These women knew most of the moves, except for the boxing jabs and hooks, which she walked them through. The second half of the class was weight lifting and she used slower music for the weights.

“Lift. Lift. Lift.” Maxine watched them in the mirror to make sure everyone was using the weights properly. “We are strong women. Lift. Lift. Lift.”

Why did she feel weak when she could hoist ten-pound weights? Not physically weak, but the weak that fear sent through her body. Nervous jiggles up her arms and down her legs and even into her head. If she could face her worst fear, then maybe it would go away. She lost count of the shoulder lifts and made the women do fourteen instead of twelve. When the class ended, Maxine stayed for a few minutes to chat. For most of these women, the socialization was as important as the exercise. A little socialization would be nice in her life, too. The image of Jeff of Jeffrey Street in his cool swimming suit popped into her head. *Don't go there.*

~ * ~

Her cell phone, quiet for days, rang while she was unlocking the front door. It was Larry's brother Charlie.

"Max, they're saying awful things in the paper. About Larry. That he laundered money. It's so ugly. You lose your brother and everyone slanders a man who can't defend himself." His voice was bitter.

"Charlie, I'm so sorry. The police asked me about that money, too, but I didn't know anything." She waited for him to speak again, but he was silent. "How's everyone holding up?"

"Corky's taking it really hard. He and Larry were tight. Larry looked out for him."

"Larry loved Corky," she said softly. "I wish I could be with all of you. Is there anything?"

"No Max. I didn't think you would know about the money."

"Did you get a lawyer yet?" She sounded sharper than she wanted.

He didn't answer.

"Larry's lawyer can recommend someone."

"No, I can manage." She heard him sigh. "Will you come back to visit sometime?"

"Sure, Charlie."

Maxine felt like a first class shit running out on them in this time of trouble. She was never sure what Larry had told them. For starters, *don't ask her a lot of questions*. By way of explanation: *Her parents are dead, sister is off the deep end.* Sensitive subjects never broached. Maxine didn't know what was said about their not having kids, but no one ever mouthed the word, "baby."

Instead, they treated her kindly. Warm hugs and kisses of greeting and goodbye. Theirs wasn't a claustrophobically close clan, but they got together on holidays and for the occasional party. She remembered Larry's nieces' and nephews' birthdays and first communions.

She and Larry always hosted a big Fourth of July party and a day-after-Christmas dinner that featured a smoked turkey along with grilled sweet potatoes and Maxine's special cranberry crisp. Larry was a grill fanatic, with two charcoal grills: a smoker and a gas grill, all taking pride of place on the patio. Maxine was a decent cook, not elaborate, but she could follow a recipe and turn out a tasty meal. Larry was the rock star at the family feasts in his *Turn Up the Heat* apron and his mountainous platters of grilled, barbequed and smoked meats. The family appreciated that Maxine always made stuffed shells and sauce. Gravy they called it. Larry had given her his mother's sacred recipe. She wondered if she had brought it along.

The locksmith ringing the doorbell interrupted her reverie. He whistled as he installed new locks on the front door, the storage room and the patio. Maxine paid with cash.

The Verizon man was punctual. "Are you sure the router has a strong firewall?" she asked, paranoid about someone hacking into her computer. He handed her a booklet and said she could bump up the settings if she liked.

Wonderful to get an Internet connection on her laptop—tethered back to the world, her long umbilical cord to Boston, former colleagues, and the life she had left behind.

Online, she read the *Boston Globe* story Larry's brother had seen, a one-paragraph report about a task force investigating a money-laundering scheme. The article mentioned Larry's name, but Maxine didn't find the exposé she had feared. No headlines. She was confused because the cops hadn't mentioned laundered money, but rather drug money. Unless Larry had laundered drug money. That would make sense. All those trips abroad.

Sheldon Finder had sent an email letting her know he was "opening the case."

Later in the afternoon, Maxine went mall hopping and bought cushions and a tablecloth for the patio, and a one-drawer file cabinet light enough to lift in and out of the car.

Driving back to the apartment, she passed the verdant grass of a golf course. Why not take lessons at one of Boca's public courses? She let herself imagine hitting the ball and walking the greens, sweating a little in the sun. When she got home, she would unpack that vexatious last box, cook dinner, and go for a swim.

~ * ~

Puzzled, Maxine stared at the open carton lying on the bed. On top of the file folders and tax returns—it couldn't be, yet it was. She bent over the black leather case, her eyes fixed on the familiar initials.

L.J.C. Lawrence James Caliendo.

Her mind boggled at how Larry's laptop case had arrived inside her packing box. Maxine knew with dead certainty that *she* hadn't placed it there. She backed away from the bed, as if the case were a black mamba, coiled and ready to lunge.

*I know there is a rational explanation.*

She took a deep breath and grabbed the handle. Her fingers shook like an old woman's as she worked the zipper. The laptop was inside, along with a sheet of yellow-lined paper, the kind that Larry had always favored. She saw the familiar printing—he never used script.

> *In worse trouble than I let on. Used my key to get inside your Jeep and stash my laptop. Keep it until you hear from me. Don't tell anyone or give it to anyone. If my luck runs out, open the files Maxine and CANALBANK. Yours to share with Corky. Password for the laptop is corkycaL Do not, repeat, do not use the laptop on the Internet. I think the money men somehow bugged it during the audit.*
>
> *Larry xoxo*

Afraid her knees would buckle, she had to sit on the bed. Her mind was a whirlwind of disassociated thoughts. *Canalbank?* Larry's business trips had often taken him to Panama or the Grand Cayman Islands, sometimes Bermuda. Maxine went along when she could get time off. She soaked up some rays, had facials and massages and then they had dinner for two with a big red sun sinking behind some tropical body of water.

The cop's demanding voice kept surging through Maxine's head. *Ms. Harvey, did your husband have a computer?*

Then she saw two old red and blue Bank of America deposit envelopes, so thick that Larry had put a rubber band around them. She gaped at the stacks of hundred dollar bills. The envelope must hold thousands of dollars.

Maxine scurried through the apartment checking that all the blinds were shut. She found her handbag on the stool in the kitchen and fumbled for her cigarettes. Inhaling greedily, she wondered if anything in her life would ever be simple again.

*She had Larry's laptop.* With all his business data, damning or otherwise. Where had the money come from? Had Larry been murdered because of it?

What Maxine needed was a big stiff drink. And the insight to understand this situation where Larry had unwittingly placed her. She hadn't bought any liquor yet, so she got a beer out of the fridge and popped the top.

Shit, what should she do with Larry's laptop? Call the police? Call Blaisdell? Not just yet.

She knew there was a bad angel perched on her shoulder, whispering not to tell anyone anything until she knew more about Larry, urging her to keep the money. Just until she had this ugly mystery solved.

# *Ten*

Maxine could not cope with the laptop, so she avoided her bedroom after she had hidden the cash between her towels. She sautéed a chicken breast, steamed fresh broccoli and made a salad. While the chicken was cooking, she patrolled the apartment, throwing laundry into the washer, folding the newspaper, tidying up what was already orderly, always seeing the bedroom and Larry's computer on the bed and the last box, sitting there like an accusation—open but not unpacked.

She had to rid herself of the impulse telling her to race hell for leather out of there, somewhere, anywhere away from this new calamity.

She watched the network news on television while she ate and drank a second beer. "Buy vodka, rum and tequila," she told her ever-present recorder. After dinner, she checked her email and roamed the apartment, neatening places she had attacked forty minutes earlier. She stowed the dishes in the dishwater and wiped the kitchen counter and the stovetop. Again. She turned off the TV, strode into the bedroom, pulled on her swimsuit and grabbed a towel.

The sun hadn't set, and the temperature was ninety-one according to the big thermometer by the outdoor shower. Jeff of

Jeffrey Street wasn't reading his newspaper by the pool, but several other residents were sprawled on the lounges. A few people sat immersed in the whirlpool by the fence. Still ignoring the "No Diving" sign, Maxine executed a racing dive and swam twenty-five laps in the warmish water, trying to calm her mind, free styling across the pool, one lap after another, swimming like the Loch Ness monster was chasing after her.

Back in her apartment, she showered and put on white cotton pajamas and a blue terry robe. Leaving the laptop on the bed, Maxine unpacked the rest of the box and stashed all the paperwork in the file cabinet. She carried her computer books to an empty shelf in the living room. She felt for the cash envelopes, still under the towels. The apartment still looked ascetically bare, with cream walls and empty counters and tables. She unplugged *her* laptop and moved it from the coffee table to the compact walnut writing desk against the living room wall.

She glanced about the room, searching for something else to do, anything but the task she had procrastinated over for two hours. *Now*. Maxine returned to the bedroom, and brought the laptop case into the living room. The wires and cables were neatly coiled inside, and she laid everything out on the coffee table, found the right cable, and turned on the laptop. After it booted up, the system requested the password. As she keyed the letters, Maxine half-hoped the machine wouldn't respond. Then she could stash the damnable thing in the closet out of sight and mind.

Instead, "corkycal" performed its magic and flung open the gates to Windows XP.

Maxine rose from the sofa and again checked that the doors were locked, and made sure again that the blinds were completely closed. Her cell phone rang, and her heart began to tattoo like a mad drummer. She pressed the answer button.

Larry's brother Charlie again.

"Sorry to bother you again, Maxine. We're all back from the wake. There was a big turnout. Larry had a lot of friends."

*And some enemies.*

"I'm glad, Charlie."

"The reason I'm calling is that apparently Larry's computer has disappeared. The police wondered if *I* had it."

"Do you?" she asked, hoping to muddy the waters.

"Hell, no! But isn't it peculiar that the computer vanished into thin air?"

"Charlie, "she said, trying to get her voice under control. " I have a theory."

"Yeah?"

"Maybe Larry had it with him when he went back to the house, and those scumbags who killed him took it and passed it to somebody. That's what I think." Her voice sounded shaky and hollow, as if she couldn't breathe.

"You know, that makes sense. The police said it wasn't in his apartment, or in his car. I mean, where could it have gone?"

"Exactly."

"I'm sick of talking to cops," he said with a sigh.

"Me, too. A cop wants to interview me, but I'm stalling him."

"No shit. Like you'd know anything. Talk to you later."

Her lie gave her new resolve. She put the phone back on the breakfast bar and examined Larry's desktop, which wasn't too gunked up: some photo-sharing software, a slew of Microsoft Office products, Google Earth, Adobe Acrobat, iTunes, and a shortcut to My Documents. She lit a cigarette and took the little brass ashtray off the counter. Her fingers felt steady as she clicked on My Documents.

*CANALBANK* was a Word file, also password protected, but "corkycal" opened it, too. The document date was mid-May, just a couple of weeks ago.

> *Remember years ago when we opened a deposit box at that savings bank in Foxborough? I left everything you need to know. Find the lock box key in the laptop's inside pocket. If you're reading this, I'm dog meat.*
>
> *L.*
>
> *xoxo*

*Oh my God!* Larry really thought he might die. *I'm dog meat.* Maxine felt a stab of grief. She hadn't taken time to mourn the man she had been married to for seven years, the man she now wondered if she had ever really known. While her fingers probed the laptop case's pockets, Maxine remembered a Saturday in October with bright sun, brisk wind and falling maple leaves. She had forgotten about that long-ago errand in the neighboring suburb of Foxborough. They had put their wedding license and the mortgage for the house in the box.

From a pocket in the laptop case, her fingers extracted two heavy paper cases, just right for keys. She scrutinized the little red envelopes with the metal snaps. The box number was handwritten on one side and the name of the bank printed on the other.

Maxine carried the keys into the bedroom and hid them under the lamp on her nightstand, above the drawer with the handgun. More complications. Now she would need a Florida lock box to keep the damn keys safe.

Sitting on the living room sofa, Maxine opened Excel, and gaped at the number of spreadsheets. She clicked on "Mexrest." It looked like cash receipts from a restaurant. She opened a few more files, mousing around, noticing formulas and links, maybe even consolidations—the complexity was way out of her league, like examining General Motors' or Wal-Mart's books laid out in a maze of Excel. At work, she could have turned to someone in accounting. In this situation, she could turn to no one.

She realized she was grinding her teeth in anger and frustration, mad as hell at Larry for dying and leaving her in this mess. Did he think she was some kind of superwoman who could cope with anything he threw her way? Well, she couldn't. This spider's web of spreadsheets was beyond the limit of her knowledge. In despair, she put her head in her hands.

~ * ~

The June sun beat on the pool area with such intensity that Maxine imagined being in a kiln, baking slowly into Ceramic Tile Woman, hard but fragile. In a battle between the solar glare and her sunscreen, the sun would score a knockout. Except for a woman watching a little blonde girl play in the shallow end, the swimming pool stood empty at 11:00 a.m. on a Wednesday.

The girl climbed out of the water and wrapped herself in a beach towel, and then she ran back to the pool. The woman looked up from her book and ordered, "Kaylee, don't run." The girl sat down by the pool's edge with her thin legs dangling in the water.

Seizing the opportunity, Maxine tossed her wide-brimmed hat on the chaise, plunged into the empty pool and swam her twenty-five laps.

"That was good," the girl said when Maxine emerged from the tepid water.

"Thanks." Maxine smiled and the freckled face with sky blue eyes grinned back, displaying a missing front tooth.

"How did you learn to swim?" the girl asked.

"I took lessons at the 'Y.' And then I practiced. I still practice." Maxine toweled off and ran her hand through her hair, always surprised to find herself with a short haircut.

The girl's smooth brow wrinkled in thought. "I can dog paddle, but I swim under water best."

"I noticed," Maxine said. "You're pretty good." A small stretch of truth.

"My dad would teach me but he only gets home after dark, and then it's too late." She paused. "He's a golf pro."

The woman sitting in the chaise rose and walked over to them. "Don't mind Kaylee," she said.

"I like kids." Maxine smiled, remembering Larry's horde of nieces and nephews.

Kaylee jumped up, threw off the towel shouting, "Watch this!" and jumped into the water with a satisfying splash.

"I'm Julie Dunmire, Kaylee's aunt," said the woman, holding out her hand. "I take care of her on days when she can't go to the pro shop. Kaylee is visiting her father this summer."

"Maxine Harvey. Nice to meet you."

They chatted for a few minutes, watching Kaylee paddle around. Julie said that Kaylee's father was divorced and that Kaylee lived with her mom in Chicago and was spending the summer with her dad. Maxine thought blonde, freckled Kaylee looked the spitting image of Jeff of Jeffrey Street, and eventually Julie referred to "Jeff," confirming Maxine's notion. Julie took the girl in for lunch, and Maxine applied more sunscreen and picked up her notes from last night.

What she had found on Larry's computer made Maxine feel even more paranoid. There was accounting for each of twelve "cash" businesses. After she scrutinized Larry's spreadsheets, Maxine had turned back to the Word documents. Not many of those, and most of them password protected, but "corkycal" opened every file. Careless of Larry to use only one password. He should have asked her advice.

She found lists of people and even an organization chart with names and locations, but the job titles meant little. *Northeast accountant, Southeast Account. Midwest Distribution.* She opened the file named "Maxine," dated early last week.

> *Max,*
> *Enrique (you don't know him) asked me to turn over my laptop for a yearly audit. Just so you know, I've been skimming a bit over the years. I buried the skimming deep, but there's a new money man who's sharp. The skimmed money is in a special Panamanian bank, and if I don't come out of this, I want you to take charge. Half is for Corky. Keep the rest and make a nice life for yourself. About the account—3/4 of the money is in cash and the rest in bearer bonds. There's an envelope in the safety deposit box. Take good care of it.*
> *My company always looks after the wives financially. You'll get a hundred thou. If they don't call you, contact Lotto Lopez. Even if you're an ex-wife by then. I kept quiet about the divorce. You met Lotto once at the Pats game. He's an OKAY guy, a straight shooter. He'll take good care of you. See my Outlook*

*address book under Marquesa Trading Company. Don't email or call. Go see him.*

*xoxo*

*Larry*

Larry's other note had warned Maxine not to access the Internet from his computer in case it had been loaded with spyware. She wasn't sure, but the laptop could have software to enable someone to figure out where she was. It wasn't worth the risk.

At 2:30 a.m., Maxine crawled into bed with her mind boggling from her attempt to make sense of Larry's files and all this new and troubling information. She wondered about Lotto Lopez. Would he really help her? Why had those thugs killed Larry? Did they want the cash or had someone ordered him killed? Lotto? But Lotto liked Larry. Her head spun with confusion.

Tomorrow she would go over more of the spreadsheets and try to figure them out. She didn't know why, but learning what Larry had actually been up to all those years might help her.

Maxine picked up the recorder and listed: buy groceries, sign up for golf lessons. See Lotto Lopez?

Larry always used to say, "Lotto is a prince." Was he? If not, then she would be setting herself up for big trouble. Did she dare beard the lion in his den?

~ * ~

The next morning, time stood still during Maxine's aerobics class, and several times she lost the beat, confusing the women. She said, "Sorry," any number of times. Once she joked, "Is it Friday yet?" They were a forgiving bunch, and the hour finally ended.

Should she contact Lopez and decline the money that hadn't yet been offered? She could promise him not to testify. Did Lotto even know about Larry's murder? He wasn't on the computer organization chart. *Lotto is a prince.* Was Lotto even involved in all this? Maxine felt like she was walking a tightrope over a canyon.

On the way home, Maxine stopped at the UPS Store mailbox she had rented on her visit in April. She picked up a few bills forwarded from Massachusetts. It was a real boon to be able to call and ask if she had mail, to avoid extra trips to the mailbox. She would never be seen going in and out of the local post office.

Tomorrow loomed as her thirty-seventh birthday. It would also be a week since Larry had died and everything had gone to hell. She found nothing to celebrate except having survived. The difficulty was finding something pleasant, even neutral to think about. Certainly not the future. The past was not so wonderful either. She couldn't envision the path she must take. The only way she could see led into a dark wood, overrun with brambles, snaky vines, roots to trip over, and dangerous beasts.

Tonight she would take a break and leave Larry's computer alone. She might go for a swim, even watch TV. Right now, she would stop at Publix for the shrimp butter ingredients. Samantha's party was tomorrow evening. Tomorrow was also her birthday. The party seemed like a beacon away from that dark path.

# *Eleven*

The doorman buzzed Maxine in saying, “eighth floor on the left.” While she waited for the elevator, Maxine eyed the halves of shrimp and tiny sprigs of parsley garnishing the pinkish shrimp butter, with golden toast points spaced evenly around the pressed glass dish.

Leaving the elevator, she heard party-in-progress sounds with Latin music in the background and a babble of voices. The front door was ajar. Maxine took a deep breath and entered. Fresh flowers in pottery vases and a slew of votive candles lent a festive air. Red-haired Samantha, even thinner than Maxine remembered, wearing navy slacks and an unstructured white jacket, stood among a trio of women. Samantha noticed Maxine hesitating in the entry hall, and broke away from the group.

“I’m so glad you could come,” Samantha said, extending her hand. “Let me take your dish.” She removed the plastic wrap, exclaiming, “Oh, how tempting!”

Maxine wore the new cotton sundress from Lord & Taylor with red oriental poppies printed on a white background, Larry’s last gift on the last night of his life. She hated the morbid thoughts that flew into her head at inopportune times. She was the only woman in the room showing a lot of leg. The other women wore slacks or longish skirts.

Good at numbers but not at names, by the third introduction she was trying to remember whether the blonde's name was Jane or Joan or June.

Samantha, still holding Maxine's arm, steered her toward a group of men. "Have you met your neighbor, yet? Jeff Dunmire."

*Jeff of Jeffrey Street.*

"We met once at the pool." He took her hand, which he held for a moment rather than giving it a casual shake.

*A pleasant surprise.*

"An awfully brief meeting." His boyish smile showed even white teeth. Jeff looked athletic and well-scrubbed in his striped sport shirt and pale linen slacks.

"I know your daughter," Maxine said. Jeff's resemblance to Kaylee was almost eerie, from the blond hair to the freckles, and especially the engaging grin.

"Kaylee's a big fan of yours," he said. "She talks about you all the time."

"How do you know Samantha?" asked Maxine.

"She took golf lessons from me last winter, and her father was my neighbor. She was so relieved to find a reliable tenant after her father died."

Jeff brought Maxine a glass of wine, put his hand on her arm and led her to the balcony where the sun backlit the clouds in the west, producing a spectacular sunset of orange, pink and purple. They watched the boat traffic on the waterway. Occasionally a party boat passed with music and revelers.

"It's nicer here in the summer," he said with a sigh. "No snowbirds clogging the roads and the restaurants. Of course, they're my bread and butter, so I better not knock them." He produced an impressive golf swing that sent an imaginary ball arching over the waterway.

Maxine mentioned she wanted to take lessons, but it would have to be at a public course. Jeff nodded enthusiastically.

"Maybe we can strike a deal. You teach Kaylee to swim, and I'll help you with your golf game."

Jeff handed Maxine his card, and she guessed he thought she had bought into the idea. She wasn't sure how proficient a swimming teacher she would be, but she didn't demur.

Jeff introduced her to more people. Maxine sipped a second glass of wine and ate a small plate of hors d'oeuvres. With a pang, she remembered her mother had made the same spinach dip. Except for Jeff, most of the crowd was older than she was, and Maxine was glad she hadn't mentioned her birthday. Thirty-seven felt barely out of the cradle in this AARP group. The party broke up around eight, and Maxine thanked Samantha for inviting her.

"How do you like Jeff?" Samantha asked in a low voice.

"Very nice and...cute." Maxine wished she could have been more original in her assessment. But that's what Jeff was. She tried to locate him in the party exodus.

"I have to confess to a bit of matchmaking," Samantha said, smiling like a fox. "When you mentioned playing golf and taking lessons, I decided to introduce you two. I hope that's not too bold of me."

Jeff came out of the kitchen and his eyes brightened when he saw Maxine and Samantha with their heads together.

"Along with a great party, you get extra points for introducing me to my neighbor." He gave Samantha a quick hug.

"Can I take you two ladies out for a bite?" He turned toward Maxine. "Those appetizers gave me an appetite."

"I just want to clean the kitchen and chill on my balcony with the dregs of the wine," Samantha said. "Bottles and bottles of dregs." She had a throaty laugh. "I'm going back to New York day after tomorrow."

"Then it's you and me." Jeff's eyes looked hopeful.

Maxine's current situation didn't allow for relationships, but she took his arm, thanked Samantha for a lovely evening, and waltzed off into the steamy Florida night.

In the parking lot, Jeff's Subaru held a jumble of golf clubs and cleated shoes, Kaylee's car seat, snorkel gear and water bottles.

Maxine couldn't help but think of how particular Larry had been about his Lincoln, where no clutter dare deposit itself.

"You can drive my car," she said, clicking her key fob to unlock her car door, three spaces away.

"Sorry mine is such a mess. Kaylee is usually the only passenger."

Maxine said, "Today is my birthday,"...the words popped out of her mouth unbidden. She had received a few greetings from the girls at work, but nothing from Larry's family, who must be reeling from the funeral and the break-in. They weren't *her* family anymore, but it would have been nice to hear just one person's voice say, "Happy birthday!"

"Well, then." Jeff cleared his throat. "Guys know better than to ask how many candles to put on the cake, but this calls for a special celebration." He pulled onto A1A and drove south. "Do you like Northern Italian?"

Maxine and Larry had been in Tuscany once, and she remembered the food and wine and the sunlight on the countryside with the erect cyprus trees standing like sentinels. They drove into the ancient hill towns and Larry smiled while she shopped for blue Majolica plates, plates that Maxine had carefully transported to Florida.

"Northern Italian rocks," she said.

~ * ~

The sun was setting, and the filmy curtains teased diners with glimpses of the Intracoastal Waterway, now fading to dark. Maxine and Jeff were seated in the Boca Raton Resort and Club. The waiter stood by while Jeff sniffed the cork from a bottle of Tuscan wine. The golden globe lights cast a romantic glow over the room. An entire bottle of wine seemed like a rash idea after the cocktail party, but Jeff said, "I think we can manage."

Maxine liked his roguish smile.

"I splurged and got a golf membership here, mostly for networking and lesson contacts," Jeff said with a half smile. "Very improvident of me, but it's been fun, at least for a season."

She settled into the banquette. The restaurant, with its luxurious black and tan banquettes and white napery, looked like somewhere a guidebook would mark with a quiver of dollar signs. Maxine hadn't been out for a fancy dinner since she and Larry split. Dining alone had always seemed pathetic.

Jeff talked about how happy he was that Kaylee was spending the whole summer with him, and what a help his sister had been.

"I was on the pro circuit, the Nationwide Tour for a few years," he said. "It's a step below the PGA tour, and it was grueling. Kaylee was a toddler and we traveled all the time. I had a big old RV we drove to save on expenses."

Jeff sipped his wine. "It was crazy to subject a woman with a baby to all that travel, sometimes three tournaments a month. Occasionally I'd hit a hot streak and the money would be good. That kept us going."

"I can't imagine a life on the road," Maxine said. She preferred to feel grounded, with a familiar bed, and a view she recognized from the windows.

"It's brutal."

Maxine watched Jeff slather the butter on his roll.

"Every tournament has an entry fee, and along with all the travel expenses, I had to pay for a caddy. If I were cut midway through the tournament, I wouldn't collect one red cent. If you start playing erratically, it's a killer. It helps to have some income from endorsements, but I didn't." His shoulders slumped.

"Lisa took off when Kaylee was three and went back to Chicago. I stuck with the tour for another year and a half. My mom died and left me enough to buy the condominium and I started giving lessons, and then I landed the job as the club pro."

"Did that make you happy?" asked Maxine, looking past Jeff at a party of four men. She realized she looked at men now as dangerous adversaries, not as potential companions.

"It offered a regular paycheck and no travel."

Dinner arrived, a large platter arranged with rare tuna and all the tasty garnishes.

"Let's dive in," Jeff said, "but first, a birthday toast." He raised his wine goblet. "I can think of nothing better than being here with you next year on the fifth of June. Happy birthday."

"Thank you." She felt almost...happy. *Must be the wine.*

"Listen," he said, forking a bite of tuna. "Enough about me. What about you? Why did you move to the land of mangroves and alligators?"

"A divorce and a desire to start over." She paused. "And I'm hoping to find my sister whom I haven't seen in years."

She couldn't believe what had come out of her mouth. The divorce, yes. Starting over, sure. But Honora? Would she start blabbing about hijackers and pole dancing?

Jeff's eyes met hers. "Did I bring up a sore subject?"

"I haven't had anyone to talk to, so I'm sort of shocked I mentioned anything." She looked down at her plate and speared a green bean.

"The divorce or the sister?" asked Jeff.

"Oh, the divorce seems like old news. It became final on Monday."

Maxine never, ever, breathed a word about the *first* divorce, the awful one. No talk, not even thoughts. That wretched part of her life was gone. Like the weakling who walked out on her.

"Hey, we all have families and siblings and they're mostly dysfunctional. Do you want to talk about it?" asked Jeff.

Maxine stared at him and smiled. "Oh, nothing is more boring than someone else's family problems."

He looked like he was trying to read her mind. "Then let's talk about golf lessons for you and when we can schedule some swimming instruction for Kaylee."

They arranged for an early Wednesday morning golf session with Maxine and swimming for Kaylee tomorrow. Jeff suggested that if Maxine could join him and Kaylee for dinner, he would fire up the grill.

Jeff had a lot in common with Larry, who loved golf, grilling and good restaurants. Snappy dresser, too.

"Do you like to gamble?" she asked, as they cleaned up the platter, nibbling olives and forking up the last of the lettuce. Gambling had been Larry's one vice. *Except skimming.*

"Hell no. If there were forty prizes and thirty-nine people at the raffle, guess who wouldn't win anything? I'm a total bust on the slots and blackjack. It's like flushing cash down the toilet, so I don't do it. I won't even bet on a golf game. Not a single hole. I'm a total stick in the mud."

"No, you're sensible."

After dinner, they meandered around the vast hotel grounds, past stately palms and pristine fountains. The pink and white buildings gleamed in the moonlight and the mood felt dreamy, but Jeff drove her back to Samantha's and picked up his car then followed her home. They met again in the parking area, and he took Maxine's hand and said goodnight like the perfect gentleman. Why did she feel a bit out of sorts?

She dreaded returning to the endless complicated spreadsheets and the ever more dangerous knowledge of Larry's former life, returning to speculations about Honora and where and even who she might be, and worst of all, whether she should appeal to the man who might be plotting to kill her. Jeff felt like a safe port in a category five storm.

# *Twelve*

Maxine met Kaylee and Jeff at the pool on Saturday morning. Jeff smeared Kaylee with sunscreen, working with care around the green piping on her new swimsuit, a hot pink number printed with palm trees, beach umbrellas and hibiscus blossoms.

Jeff said he hadn't gone grocery shopping, which sounded like the dinner invitation had been rescinded. Although Maxine had misgivings about spending too much time with Jeff and his daughter, she still felt a twinge of disappointment. Still, she should be focused on digging into Larry's complex spreadsheets and deciding what to do about Lotto Lopez.

Maxine had conjured up a face to go with the name. She had met Lopez a couple of years earlier when some Miami bigwigs arrived in Boston for a Dolphins-Patriots game. Lopez had been one of a half-dozen of Larry's Florida associates. He had introduced her, and Lopez, not handsome, but a suave type of Latin man many women might find attractive, had regarded Maxine with his surprising blue eyes and said some flattering words, nonsense that Maxine didn't remember. Lopez had no Spanish accent, and Larry, proud of his boss, told her Lopez had a degree from the University of Miami, and even an MBA, something that would impress a junior college educated man like Larry. His posthumous advice to seek out Lopez wouldn't stop swirling around in her head.

*If they can't find you, contact Lotto Lopez. Even if you're an ex-wife by then. I kept quiet about the divorce.*

~ * ~

Maxine glanced down at the freckle-faced blonde girl, who was staring at her as if she were a goddess. While Jeff watched from the chaise longue, she beckoned Kaylee to the pool.

Maxine felt she and Jeff were communicating at a non-verbal level, that their chemistry happened with eye contact, a quick glance, a smile, beginning with that first exchange at the pool. It seemed eons since she had thought about a man in *that* way. Of course, she had thought about *the handsome one,* but not seriously. Maxine had never felt any compelling chemistry with Larry. He had wanted a wife, she had needed a husband, and their marriage had been like an outdated economic and social pact.

"Can we get in the pool now? Please?" Kaylee stared up at her with eager eyes.

"Right away."

Maxine and Kaylee climbed down the wide steps into warm aqua blue water, and Maxine took the girl's hand and guided her to a depth just over her head.

"First we're going to tread water," Maxine said. "You do what I do." Supporting Kaylee with one hand, Maxine showed her how to hold her head, and move her hands and feet in slow turtle-like circles.

"Hey, this is awesome! Watch this, Daddy, watch this!"

Jeff put down his newspaper.

Kaylee let go of Maxine's hand and stayed afloat, grinning with her gap-toothed smile.

At the pool's edge, Maxine showed Kaylee how to kick, and after a few tries she pushed off from the edge and kicked her way across the pool, face down and hands pointed in front of her. She came up for air one or twice but persisted to the goal. Maxine felt a surge of pleasure as she watched the girl.

"Look at this! Did you see that?" Every accomplishment needed Jeff's approbation.

The last thing Maxine wanted to do was to put Jeff or Kaylee in any danger. If she were honest with herself, she had to admit there had been no sign of trouble, of anyone following her or searching for her. Still, she had identified the bad guys and was responsible for their arrest.

Maxine and Kaylee took a break, and Maxine went into her apartment and called Samantha. Last night, Jeff had mentioned that Samantha still had her late father's car, which was stored in the underground garage of Samantha's condominium.

Samantha agreed Maxine could rent her father's gray Volvo until December.

~ * ~

Jeff helped with the car shuffling. Samantha had insisted Maxine take all the plants from her balcony, which would surely die from the heat and no water before she returned to New York. The yellow hibiscus would look great on Maxine's patio. For dinner, they stopped at Kaylee's favorite restaurant, Lucille's Bad to the Bone Barbecue.

"All this swimming gave me a whopping big appetite," Kaylee said.

Stuffed to drowsiness with barbecue and "sides," the three of them sat at a table littered with plastic baskets piled with chicken and rib bones, and a pile of dirty napkins. Kaylee finished the last scrap of cornbread, brushed the crumbs from her mouth and said, "This is almost like being a family, isn't it?"

"Sweetheart, it sure is," Jeff said, smiling at his daughter, but Maxine thought his smile was tinged with sadness.

"We could have a cookout at my place tomorrow," offered Maxine. "Burgers and my Tater Tots casserole. Kaylee can help me decide where to put the pink flamingo."

"Great," Jeff said. "I'll bring the wine and all the burger fixins." He gave Maxine a look that made her insides flutter.

The invitation had popped out of her mouth just like when she had mentioned her birthday. Still, she didn't need to be mooning around about a man with a kid. The next thing, Maxine would be telling Jeff details about Larry, Honora, and her past life.

# *Thirteen*

Lotto left his white Mercedes with instructions to the parking lackey that he expected to get the car back as delivered, and do not, repeat, do not touch the radio dial. The Sunday brunch crowd filled the Lincoln Road Mall. Lotto strolled two blocks under the baking June sun until he spotted Enrique waiting for him at a round table shaded by an umbrella, sitting outside like a *turista*. Miami was full of tourists, even in summer. Lotto hated their clunky white sneakers and their cheap tee shirts.

At least Enrique wasn't wearing a loud shirt and black socks, but he had eaten himself into a belly that protruded over the waistband of his Bermuda shorts like the prow of a boat. Lotto's fat colleague had news he hadn't wanted to phone in. Enrique didn't trust the cell phone encryption, which Lotto thought was stupid, but again, Enrique had survived longer than most in this business.

"*Hola*!" Enrique said, getting out of his chair.

"Jesus, why are we sitting outside like the *turistas*?"

"Better privacy. And I thought you liked the heat. But I can get us a table in the café." Enrique had drops of sweat popping out on his forehead and his white polo shirt looked damp already.

A mall security guard patrolled the street on a bike, apparently oblivious to the sun baking into his black shirt like a broiler. Summer in Miami. Why didn't they wear tan uniforms? Lotto would never understand Americans.

Hoping that sweating his brains out might be an antidote to last night's gluttony, he plopped into a chair across from Enrique. His head pounded. Not only could those Russians eat mountains, on Lotto's tab, of course, but they drank rivers. Vodka. Rum. Cognac. Just thinking of the overindulgence made Lotto's head pound.

Enrique had a tall mojito in front of him, almost a cliché, but the mint looked cooling and Lotto ordered one, too. Enrique asked what was good to eat, and Lotto said the Cuban sandwiches, but he sure as hell didn't want to eat all that ham, pork and cheese on top of last night's pig-out. He told Enrique to go ahead and order.

"Let's talk about what was so damn confidential you had to fly in. It better be news about Mrs. Caliendo and it better be good."

Enrique took a big gulp of his drink. "Like always, it's a good news-bad news situation, but we *are* making progress."

"I don't want to hear your goddamn platitudes. Can't I ever just get a report without all the idiotic commentary?" Lotto tossed down the menu.

"Our patience paid off," Enrique said, mouthing yet another stupid platitude. Lotto's scowl must have shit-canned the jargon, because Enrique said, "The good news is that your computer people got into the car rental records. The Caliendo woman rents a new car every week in West Palm Beach. She uses her Massachusetts driver's license and credit card—the address is still the house in Sharon. So we were ready to do a stakeout on the day when she was supposed to turn in the car."

Lotto's antennae prickled. Something didn't sound right.

Enrique cleared his throat and took another long gulp of the mojito. "She turned in the car four days early."

"And where were 'we' when she turned it in? Jerking off? Did she rent another one?" asked Lotto. Chasing the Caliendo woman was costing a fortune.

"That's the bad news. She turned her rental in just like always, but she didn't rent again." He paused and cleared his throat. "When she does, we're ready."

"You flew down here to tell me *that*?"

The waiter brought Enrique's sandwich and Lotto, still doing penance for last night's excess, ordered a bowl of chicken soup.

Lotto looked at the chesty girl at the next table, at the clothing store across the way, anywhere but at Enrique's goddam big greasy sandwich with the cheese oozing out of the sides.

"This *chica* is smarter than most," Enrique said, swallowing his mouthful and back on his favorite subject. "We can't get into her phone records at all. They're under lock and key. How do you think she knew to do that?"

Enrique's voice bored into his brain. "How do you think you'll like living in Kansas City or Tulsa?" he asked with a scowl.

"Ah, Lotto, this Maxine will make a mistake. They all do. She'll use her old Blockbuster card or something. And we'll be ready."

Lotto crossed his arms, leaned back in his chair and closed his eyes.

"So how did your meeting with the Russians go?" Enrique asked, lowering his voice. "Did you order the submarine kits?"

Lotto had mixed emotions about mentioning the submarines, even to someone as senior as Enrique, but his fat associate was always discreet.

"We gave them a fucking big down payment," Lotto said with a growl. "We'll have to manage the assembly. I'll need riveters and welders, trustworthy men who can keep their mouths shut. Did you see the paper this morning?"

"No, I was on the plane."

"If you had, you would have seen the news about our Colombian marines practically crashing into a mini-sub loading cargo. Not our sub, not our cargo, but what an expensive disaster that would be. Loading and unloading will have to be completed at night. All transport is risky." Lotto sighed and lit a cigarette. He seldom smoked.

"Heard we lost a mule this week. Along with some cargo," Enrique said. He finished the mojito. "Hope it was just a rumor." Enrique's anxious eyes met Lotto's.

"This week has been brutal. And now you fly here to tell me nothing." Lotto felt like a voodoo doll that everyone jabbed at will. The Russians, the DEA, everyone.

"Ah, Lotto. It's not nothing. This Maxine rents again and we find her."

"What about Caliendo's missing computer?" asked Lotto.

Enrique moved in his chair as if he were trying to find a comfortable position. "It wasn't at his house. Or in his apartment. Or the car." He shifted his anxious eyes to a point over Lotto's shoulder. "Otherwise, the cops wouldn't still be looking. Wherever the laptop is, it isn't online."

Nearby a rooster crowed. Enrique gaped with wide-eyed astonishment.

Lotto followed Enrique's eyes. A man on a bicycle whipped through the crowd with a brazen white *gallo* clutching the handlebars, wattles erect and trumpeting like it was the resurrection.

"Man, did you see that?" asked Enrique. "What kind of *loco* place is this?"

Lotto debated whether to tell Enrique that everybody around the Lincoln Road Mall knew Mr. Clucky, the rooster. He decided not to. Enrique would never shut up about it.

The waiter put a bowl of steaming soup on the table before Lotto, splattering a drop onto his Pink shirt. Lotto caught himself just before yelling *hijo de puta* at the clumsy waiter. Why couldn't one simple thing go right?

# *Fourteen*

Sunday evening after swimming lessons, Jeff flipped burgers on Maxine's black Weber grill. She cooked her kid-friendly Tater-Tot recipe, loaded with cheddar cheese. The three of them dined on the patio by the light of a hurricane lantern and tiki torches from the storeroom. Maxine felt easy, as if she were floating carefree in the blue pool. Jeff didn't talk much, but sat with arms and shoulders relaxed, smiling at her and Kaylee. He looked happy, and Maxine wondered if he was falling for her.

Kaylee chattered about the breaststroke, her new improved style of kicking, and how easy it was to tread water. With a sigh, she said, "Today was so much fun."

Humming, she left the table to go to the bathroom, and when she didn't return, Maxine got up to look for her. The bedroom light was on and Kaylee stood by the nightstand. She had a tense frown and staring eyes. Her freckles looked dark against her pale face. She gave Maxine a sidelong look and rushed out of the room. The nightstand drawer was ajar and Maxine understood what had happened. Kaylee had found the Smith & Wesson. *Shit.* Kaylee could have blown a hole in the wall. In herself. Or anyone in the vicinity.

Maxine stashed the gun on the closet shelf next to the souvenir box and hurried back to the patio. Kaylee hovered next to Jeff. She wouldn't look at Maxine.

"What's the matter, sweetheart?" Jeff asked his daughter. Kaylee didn't answer but buried her head on her dad's arm.

"Kaylee was in the bedroom and she discovered a handgun in my nightstand. I had never expected kids to be in there." She touched Kaylee's arm.

"Honey, were you frightened? I put the pistol in a safe place."

"Jesus, Maxine. What are you doing with a gun?" Jeff had his arm around Kaylee's shoulders.

"My ex-husband gave it to me. When I worked late and drove home at three a.m. I'm going to get it licensed in Florida," she added, sounding lamer than lame.

Jeff faced Kaylee. "You must never, ever snoop in people's drawers or closets." His voice was stern and Kaylee stared at the ground.

"I'm sorry," she whispered.

"Tell Maxine you're sorry."

Kaylee repeated her apology, but she didn't meet Maxine's eyes.

"Now let's make those chocolate sundaes." Jeff stood up. Kaylee gave Maxine a baleful look.

Maxine's stomach felt like she had swallowed a rock. Kaylee was traumatized and Jeff was accusing. She didn't think she could ever explain why she was hanging onto the gun. If she did, Jeff would remove himself and his daughter from her life.

They ate their sundaes in silence, and Kaylee sprayed more whipped cream from the can onto her chocolate ice cream.

"I made a ski hill."

Later, Kaylee changed her Polly Pockets doll's clothes several times. She drank more lemonade and Maxine hoped this business with the gun might be forgotten.

When Kaylee began to rub her eyes, Jeff gathered up the doll paraphernalia, said thanks for dinner and reminded Maxine of the Wednesday morning lesson.

~ * ~

Eleven-thirty Sunday night and Maxine felt like a pacing panther. She cleaned the kitchen, making sure all the dishes were brought in from the patio, tossing the tablecloth and napkins into the washer. She wandered aimlessly through the rooms, hyper-aware of Larry's laptop in the closet. She couldn't stop thinking about what might have happened had Kaylee played with the Smith & Wesson. Jeff hadn't asked if the gun was loaded. Maxine decided not to volunteer that information. What had possessed Kaylee to snoop in her nightstand drawer? Maxine remembered getting into her aunt's dressing table and dousing herself with perfume. All curious kids liked to snoop.

She sat at the breakfast bar with her elbows on the counter. In the morning, she would call Finder. She speculated about how much she would have to tell him, and wondered if Finder was a hundred percent trustworthy. PI's might work for many people. Would he mention a conflict of interest?

It was ungodly stressful not to be able to trust anyone, except for Jeff and Kaylee, who brought warm sunshine into her bleak life. Had she become a gun moll, damaged goods in Jeff's eyes? Still, he had mentioned the golf lesson again.

Maxine took a long shower, letting the water pound her back and shoulders, as if it might wash away her worries, even her bottomless fear. Drying her hair, she studied herself in the mirror, noticing that her face and neck looked tan against the white pajamas. What she needed was a strong drink. In her restless state, the living room felt confining. Even the patio seemed to hem her in. Maxine slipped a silky navy robe over her P.J.s, and poured three fingers of rum into an ice-filled plastic glass. Grabbing a cigarette, she walked toward the pool, which would be empty at this late hour. Sipping rum and inhaling nicotine, she could lie back on one of the loungers and stare at the dark sky.

As she rounded the corner and came in sight of the blue pool, she caught a whiff of tobacco smoke. Maybe some night owls were parked in the whirlpool. It looked empty, but a lone man sat on a lounge chair smoking.

Jeff.

She froze. He hadn't seen her. Jeff must be a secret smoker, too. Her first thought was to turn and scurry back inside, but she followed a deeper impulse. Jeff didn't hear her barefooted approach until she was right beside him.

"Got a light?" she asked, holding out her cigarette.

"Cripes, you startled the hell out of me!" Jeff jumped up and rummaged in the deep pockets of his cargo shorts. He was bare-chested, and again Maxine admired his muscular arms and well-defined pecs. He found his lighter and Maxine bent her head toward the hand cupped around the blue flame. This familiar gesture felt intimate and thrilling.

"So you're a secret smoker, too?"

"The golf pro is guilty as charged." He indicated the chaise longue next to him. His blond hair had frizzed in the humid night air, framing his freckled face. If he hadn't had a puzzled frown, he would have looked cherubic.

Maxine put her glass down on the tile and sat on the long chair with her legs stretched in front of her. Jeff sat too.

"I guess all three of us were pretty shaken when Kaylee found that gun," Jeff said.

"It never crossed my mind that a kid would find it." She took a sip of the potent rum.

"Kaylee's been told never to touch a weapon. At least she remembered." He paused. "She said she didn't."

"It's out of reach now."

"Odd item to bring down here with you. Unless you're spending a lot of time in Miami. Boca is about as safe as you can get." He tipped back his can, finishing the beer. "So you worked in an unsafe neighborhood in Massachusetts?"

"Not really. My husband was kind of paranoid. On my own, I would never have bought it.

"Do you know how to shoot?"

"I took lessons."

"Why don't you sell it?" He turned to look at her.

She shrugged, not knowing what to say.

He took her hand and caressed it, rubbing his fingers over the back. “Maxine, I get the feeling you’re hiding, well, maybe not hiding, but you never talk about any family, or friends, or the life you left. It’s as if you arrived here without a past. Are you...on the run or something like that?”

“Something like that.” She spoke in a whisper, and she wasn’t sure he heard her.

“Can you tell me?”

“Soon. Now I’m still trying to figure everything out.” Maxine glanced down. The robe had parted to reveal the white pajamas bottoms and her bare feet. She pulled it around her knees but it slid off again. She leaned back and took a deep drag on her cigarette. Jeff released her hand and produced an empty sardine can for an ashtray.

They didn’t speak for a few moments, and the silence felt strained. Then he took her hand again. In the distance, she could hear the engine of a boat moving up the waterway.

“Kaylee will be okay. She had a fantastic day.”

“She’s a great kid,” Maxine said, turning her head toward Jeff. Their eyes met.

“Now I’m going to confide something to you.” He stroked the back of her hand again, apparently deep in thought. “I think you and I could become close, very close, and that would make me happy, it truly would. But, and there’s a very big but...” He stopped.

“Go on,” she said, hating that word “but.”

“I’m a guy who goes along to get along. Kaylee and golf are my only passions.” His eyes searched hers. “Now you’ve come along and really hit my sweet spot.”

Maxine felt the warmth flood her chest, but before she could react, Jeff, continued, “The problem is, something weird is going on with Kaylee’s mother and I need to find out what. We had a contentious divorce because I asked for custody. Didn’t get it.” He lowered his head. “I’m taking Kaylee back to Chicago in late August, and I’ll have a hard look at the household setup and an even harder look at Lisa. If she seems unstable, I'll try for custody again. Trust me; you don't want to be involved."

He stared at the pool, and seemed to be choosing his words with care. "I almost fell over when Lisa allowed Kaylee to spend the whole summer here."

"Why do you think there's a problem?" asked Maxine. "Kaylee seems okay."

"Kaylee doesn't say much about her life at home. She and Lisa talk on the phone a couple times a week. Kaylee's voice always sounds strained, and she goes into another room to talk, almost whispers. She almost never tells her mom what we've been doing. Lisa talks and Kaylee listens and kind of shrinks into herself, you know?"

Maxine nodded, thinking of how shrunken Kaylee had looked standing by the nightstand drawer.

"I listened in on their conversation once, and Lisa asked Kaylee if I had a girlfriend. I just wonder if Lisa has ever moved on." Jeff stubbed his cigarette out in the sardine can. "She's volatile—and manipulative. Not the woman I thought I was marrying." He stared across the pool, his eyes brimming with sadness. "I know Kaylee's been late for school a lot because Lisa 'overslept.' She's also a TV addict—she never saw a reality show she didn't get involved in, and I don't think she can pass a piece of junk food without wolfing it down. I know she feeds Kaylee a bad diet. Kaylee even said, 'Mom is getting kind of fat, but she gets mad if I say anything.'"

Most kids ate junk food and were sometimes tardy. There must be something else.

Jeff turned to her. "So now you know *my* worries. Crazy ex-wife."

His half-smile seemed forced. "Feel free to tell me *your* problems," he said, meeting her eyes. "Dr. Dunmire, at your service."

Maxine realized Jeff had no idea about the kind of trouble she was in. And she couldn't tell him. She crushed the butt of her cigarette into the sardine can.

"Tomorrow I have to do something related to all this...secrecy," she said in a low voice. "Then maybe I can talk about it. Later in the week."

"Okay, later will have to do. I have some golf buddies, my rat pack, coming into town tomorrow. We're playing eighteen holes and having dinner." He paused. "On Wednesday, you and I will have to concentrate strictly on golf."

Maxine frowned, unsure what he was getting at.

He cleared his throat. "I'm due a few days' vacation. The pro shop isn't exactly bustling in the hot months...in fact, it's dead to the point of mind-numbingly boring." He cleared his throat again. "Life on the tour was boring, too, but with equal amounts of excitement. I'd quit the pro shop in a minute if it weren't for my child support payments."

Maxine nodded. Everyone was in some sort of bind.

"Kaylee wants to visit the Everglades. See some gators and crocs. Maybe you'd like to join us. This weekend? Plenty of room in the RV. We'll have fun. If the A.C. works. If you leave your gun at home." He looked at her again. "That robe is incredibly sexy."

Maxine disentangled her hand from Jeff's and stood. "I would love to see the 'Glades with you and Kaylee. The camper sounds super." She hadn't responded to the sexy robe comment. What could she say? *I want to rest my head against your bare chest.*

He was still looking at her. Any moment he would ask, "Your place or mine?" The drink had given her ideas. He already had them. Why did he drag the problem ex-wife into this? She lived in Chicago. And they were in Boca. Maxine hated mixed messages.

"I'll see you on Wednesday morning then," she said, breaking the spell.

"I'll pick you up at eight o'clock sharp. Before it gets too hot." He stood and took her hand again.

On the way back to her apartment, Maxine mused that nothing had happened, yet everything had happened. If she could enlist Finder's help. If she could make Lotto Lopez understand that she wasn't his enemy, then, just maybe, she could talk to Jeff, go camping and even...

Jeff's words came back to her. Did he really mean them? *I think you and I could become close, very close, and that would make me happy, it truly would.*

Maxine sat at her patio table and tossed back the now watery rum. She stared at the dark sky and wished she could read her future, their future, in the stars, but above her, the stars were few, dim, and inscrutable.

# *Fifteen*

Maxine popped her CD into the player on the Volvo's dash. Jimmy Buffet's voice filled the car. "Margaritaville." She wore cropped pants the same aquamarine blue as the sea and a soft white tee shirt that flattered her tan. She had stashed the Smith & Wesson, loaded and newly licensed, in the locked glove box. Next to the AAA Florida travel guide, her recorder rested on the passenger's seat with an earful of reminders. She had a new cell phone and a Florida driver's license.

Maxine tooled along Route 1 passing the mangroves lining the road. The placid Atlantic, the leaning palms, and the signs announcing the keys: Largo, Plantation, Islamorada, propelled her south. With each mile closer to Key West, Maxine's curiosity surged about this old friend of Honora's whom she was going to visit, Nicole Novak.

On Monday, Sheldon Finder had called early. Sounding brisk and confidential, Finder said he had located a woman who remembered Maxine's sister. The woman had told Finder that Honora took off years ago. *Your sister is out of that toxic environment, Ms. Harvey.* Maxine wondered if it would be harder to find Honora now. She could be anywhere. If she had left Florida, she could even be dead. Maxine felt the old knot of fear.

Finder pooh-poohed her worries. *This woman knew of someone living in Key West who was friendly with your sister. She gave me the lead. I don't have a feel for how legitimate it is, but I'm pursuing it now.*

Maxine envisioned a long chain of "friends of friends," half-naked women who slithered around their poles and slipped out of sight, never leading to Honora.

The straight-ahead road was hypnotic, crossing long spans over water, paralleling derelict railroad tracks and falling-into-the-gulf bridges, shooting south surrounded by a green sea scattered with purple patches, sea reaching to Cuba, the Bahamas, all the way to South America. As she drove the black ribbon of road, in her mind's eye Maxine saw Lotto Lopez' almost-handsome, dissolute face, mocking her attempts to clear the air around Larry's death.

Tuesday, Kaylee had another swimming lesson, supervised by Jeff's sister, Julie. Kaylee hadn't mentioned finding the gun, and Maxine hoped she hadn't told her mother. Who knew what kind of issues Kaylee had about her parents' divorce and their squabbles? Life was tough for kids these days.

Wednesday morning, buckets of rain had gushed out of a bleak sky. Maxine's golf lesson was toast, and Jeff had been busy all week entertaining his friends. She needed her wits to deal with Larry's computer, Lotto Lopez and the search for Honora. Mooning about Jeff was...well, whatever it was, she shouldn't be doing it.

Finder phoned again when she was staring at Larry's computer screen, bored and depressed. The rain still beat down relentlessly, but Finder was gleeful. G*ood news, Ms. Harvey. I've located the friend!*

Nicole Novak had danced at the same dive with Honora and they had shared an apartment for a while. Nicole didn't want to talk about Honora to Finder, but said she would be happy to see Maxine in person. Nicole owned a gift shop and had a tiny guesthouse on her property. *Key West is like a cereal box, Ms. Harvey. All the broken bits fall to the bottom.*

*Please call me Maxine.* Ms. Harvey had become tedious.

*Maxine it is. This Nicole said you were welcome to stay in the guesthouse. She only rents it during the winter tourist season.*

Maxine was relieved she could stay close to Nicole, her sole link to Honora. Yet, whenever she considered what Nicole might tell her...about September 11, about Honora, about "one of them," Maxine was gripped by a dizzy feeling that bad news would be part of the conversation. Just thinking about it made her hands moist on the steering wheel, her throat tighten.

Finder had reported that he wouldn't do anything else on Honora's case until Maxine had spoken with Nicole.

Ahead of her, the Overseas Highway unrolled with the Atlantic on her left and the Gulf on her right. She passed Long Key and Conch Key, with the sailboats tacking between the islands and sunlight dancing on the water. On this June day, it was hard to imagine hurricanes with huge waves pounding the beaches and the bridges, with bleak skies and wild winds.

Road signs beckoned diners with funky restaurant ads for "Big-Assed Roast Beef" and "Fish so fresh it should be slapped." Instead of stopping for a sleep-inducing lunch, Maxine ate a granola bar and a banana and sipped a bottle of iced tea. She rolled down the windows and smelled the briny ocean. The royal poinciana were opening big orange blossoms. She permitted herself a cigarette, taking the nicotine in long greedy inhalations.

The next road sign announced Marathon Key. Minutes later Maxine began the long drive over Seven-Mile Bridge to meet Honora's friend, Nicole Novak. Maxine had waited so many years; why did these few hours seem intolerably long?

It had been stupid to wait so many years, but Maxine had always been afraid of what she would discover, and she still felt that visceral fear. September 11$^{th}$. Honora tangled with terrorists. Honora never to be found. Honora dead. She had waited for her sister to reach out to her, like Larry said would happen, and Honora never did. Oh God, what news would this Novak woman have?

Maxine ticked off the last miles, passing white beaches. Cormorants convened on the electric wires, an unlikely welcoming committee. She popped Jimmy Buffet into the CD player again and sang along with the music. Getting blasted on tequila didn't seem such a bad idea. The wind whipped her hair, and she felt the sun burning her left arm, but she didn't care. She passed Boca Chica, and at three o'clock in the afternoon, she entered the outskirts of Key West, Florida, the Conch Republic.

~ * ~

Surrounded by a green picket fence, the Island Gift Shop was a hot pink postage stamp of a building with yellow shutters and white trim just off Duval Street. Every square inch was crammed with island souvenirs. Maxine admired a sea horse potholder and considered buying a jar of Key Lime marmalade and a pink flamingo refrigerator magnet. When she asked the young clerk for Nicole, she said Nicole had just left for a late lunch.

"You Maxine?" she asked.

Maxine nodded.

"Nicole left this for you." She took an envelope out of the cash drawer and gave it to Maxine.

Inside Maxine found directions to Nicole's place with a note.

> *I know we can have a good talk—I would love to re-connect with Honora. The screen door in back is unlocked—follow the walk. Don't let the cats out. The guesthouse is open. Make yourself at home. I lock up around nine, so meet me a little after at the Hasta Mañana Bar on Duval.*

Nine o'clock. Maxine hated waiting around.

Nicole's tin-roofed, one-story bungalow was white with a wide shady porch. The houses were packed so close together that privacy seemed an unlikely amenity. Maxine parked on the street and grabbed her carryon out of the Volvo's trunk. The fenced "yard" was red paving bricks interspersed with coconut palms, and blooming yellow hibiscus and red bougainvillea bushes—lush and tropical. Maxine opened a gate and followed the narrow brick walk along the side of the house until she reached a tall screen enclosure surrounding a smallish swimming pool, spa, and a patio area with outdoor furniture, a perfect open-air cocoon. Maxine found the half-hidden door between the bushes where two red chickens napped in the dirt. Uneasy about entering a strange place, she peered into the patio. A big tabby cat sleeping on the diving board opened one eye, stretched and continued her nap. A black cat snoozed on a pink-cushioned chair by a round table. A gray half-grown kitten ran up to the door and mewed. Maxine called out "hello!" but no one answered.

She unlatched the door and stepped onto the shady patio. The kitten trotted to an empty dish and meowed again. Maxine followed and shook a few morsels from a nearby bag of kitten chow into the bowl.

The guest quarters had a "welcome" sign by the door. The bed was heaped with a mountain of colorful pillows. A white fur teddy bear with a blue velvet baseball cap presided over the jumble. The room seemed like a gift shop, with candles, dolls, oversized goblets filled with seashells and a trove of books and magazines featuring the Keys. No luggage rack.

Big-mirrored tiles in the generous bathroom gave Maxine an image of her road-weary self with wind-blown hair and sunburned arm. The red-tiled shower beckoned her. She liked Nicole for the cats, the pillows, the teddy and for sharing her turf. Feeling a sense of relief, Maxine hoped Honora had picked a good friend in Nicole.

After a shower, Maxine returned to the patio with a Key West guidebook, and sank into one of the lounge chairs. The grey kitten, now a best friend forever, jumped into her lap and purred. A nap would help time pass.

~ * ~

Uncrowned queen of darts at the *Hasta Mañana Bar,* Maxine glanced at her watch. Ten after nine. *Where was Nicole?* Playing darts made her feel less like a single female hanging out in a bar. The tavern was a noisy scene with jukebox Zydeco and reggae tunes at top volume. Raucous drinkers hung out at the pool table and stood around the Budweiser dartboard. Maxine had already downed two margaritas and a third seemed like a bad move.

With her weight centered, she floated the obedient dart in an arc toward the target to win her third game. The gaggle of onlookers broke into rowdy applause. Tonight, the darts zeroed in on the bull's eye with uncanny precision. *Where was Nicole?* Two half-sloshed dudes, skunked by a woman, begged for a chance to get even while their girlfriends stared daggers at Maxine. They should thank their lucky stars that she refused to play for money. Maxine ate a handful of popcorn from the machine by the dartboard.

"Come on, just one more game. Our honor's at stake," the red-haired guy begged.

Someone touched her arm, and she stared into the green eyes of a petite blonde woman in a pink polo shirt.

"You just have to be Maxine," the woman said. "Your nose. Your mouth. I'd have known you anywhere." She spoke in a breathy voice. "Sorry I missed you this afternoon."

"Nicole?"

"The one and only." She gave a little rueful laugh.

Maxine extended her hand but Nicole grabbed her and gave her a hug. "I'm so glad you're here. Are you starving?"

"I sure could eat." The understatement of the day.

"I'll call the place next door for takeout. You eat meat, right?"

Maxine nodded.

Nicole pulled a cell phone out of her handbag, punched a number, and said "*dos Cubanos*, chips, and extra pickles." She paused. "Ten minutes? Gotcha!"

Nicole put the phone away and nodded at Maxine's glass. "*Cuba Libre*?"

"Coke."

"You don't drink?" she wrinkled her pert nose, evidently disappointed.

"Not after two margaritas." Maxine smiled.

"Gotcha."

Bouncy and energetic, Nicole seemed like the cheerleading type, the sort of girl who might have been able to pull Honora out of her black moods. Nicole went to the counter and talked to the bartender for several minutes. She glanced over her shoulder at Maxine once or twice. The bartender's eyes followed Nicole's with interest.

Finally, Nicole returned and they found a quieter corner.

"I sent you here because it's easy to find." Nicole kept staring at Maxine's face with what seemed to Maxine a critical gaze.

"I can absolutely see the resemblance to Honora. An older sister resemblance." She emphasized "older."

"That's me," Maxine said, feeling a bit miffed about the age put-down.

"So how do you like Key West? After a few hours down here, you'll be walking around like you're on Valium." Nicole's continued soulful stare was getting to Maxine.

"Oh, that's happened already."

She listened to Nicole's breathless chatter about the gift shop and how busy the summer had been. Nicole paused. "I'm dying for a cigarette. You smoke?"

"Occasionally."

"Will tonight be one of the occasions? I always say vices need company." She gave a breathy giggle.

"I'm always trying to quit smoking, but I never manage it." Hoping to head off any personal questions, Maxine lowered her voice. "I'm recently divorced and still feeling a little fragile."

"Oh, you should just let it all hang out," Nicole said with a dismissive gesture. Maxine took a deep breath, but Nicole dropped the subject. She sipped her beer and peered around the room, almost as if Maxine weren't there. Finally, Nicole's cell phone rang.

"Takeout's ready!" she chirped. "I could eat a horse."

"You must let me pay for dinner," insisted Maxine when they arrived at the café. Nicole agreed and took the money Maxine gave her, saying, "Just sit at one of those empty tables while I grab our order." As she had earlier at the bar, she chatted up the guy at the takeout counter, whispering and looking over her shoulder until a line formed behind her.

*Why is he looking at me with that funny smile?* Maxine felt a prick of uneasiness.

Maxine and Nicole left the takeout place and headed away from Duval Street.

"Friday's are always a bitch," Nicole said, yawning. "Long day. I'm beat." She fell silent and seemed introspective, walking with her head down as they covered the half-dozen blocks to the cottage. Maxine mentioned how much she liked the guest space, the pillows, the gray kitten, even Key West.

Nicole yawned again.

At the house, Nicole perked up and sashayed around the patio lighting the hurricane lanterns on all the side tables. Grabbing pink plates and napkins, she slapped the silverware onto the round white table without regard for seating.

"Beer, wine or...ta da! Champagne?" Nicole asked, holding up a bottle of champagne.

"A Coke or iced tea would hit the spot right now."

If her hostess said, "Gotcha!" one more time, Maxine might scream.

"Have to pick up my phone messages." Nicole disappeared into the kitchen. Maxine sat at the patio table and put the place settings in order. She watched the cats bathe, flipped through *Self* and *Allure*. She eyed the foil package with longing and opened a bag of chips. Nicole must have dozens of messages.

The night felt damp and close and the fragrance of flowers mingled with the smoke from the lanterns. Maxine told herself the bad vibes were ridiculous, but all the whispered conversations had made her uneasy. Her imagination rampaged, and she speculated that Finder was conspiring with Lotto Lopez and she had been lured down here under false pretenses.

Maxine got up and fed the cats, who milled around their empty dishes and then leaped onto the table, sniffing the foil-wrapped sandwiches. She thumbed through a Key West real estate guide. Half a mil for two bedrooms seemed crazy.

Nicole appeared with a bottle of beer, unwrapped the food and placed a still-warm sandwich on each plate. "*Bon appétit*!" she said with a tight little laugh. In contrast to her words, her face looked drained of energy.

Maxine, hungry to the point of nausea, waited for Nicole to take a bite.

"Go ahead and eat," Nicole said. "I'm just going to have a smoke first."

Maxine took a bite of her sandwich. The *Cubano*, with its pork, ham, cheese and pickle on the toasted bread, tasted wonderful.

Nicole lit a cigarette and inhaled in nervous little puffs. Maxine feared that if she waited any longer, Nicole might decide not to talk her about Honora and their long ago life.

"Tell me how you and my sister met." Maxine shooed the gray kitten off the table again and looked at Nicole. "Was it when you were dancers?"

Nicole's eyes looked vacant. Had she disappeared to do drugs? Maybe coming down here was a mistake. A phone call would have been faster and cheaper.

Nicole sighed. "I was in my second year of college and my parents got a divorce. They said they couldn't afford my schooling anymore." Nicole seemed mesmerized by the candle flickering in the lantern.

"That must have been a blow," Maxine said.

"For sure. In high school, I'd taken a lot of modern dance and even a little ballet, and I loved moving to music. *Dancing Queen*, that was me." She smiled, apparently at an old memory. "I found the ad for the club on Craig's List. For some reason, it hadn't occurred to me I would have to appear almost naked. Maybe I was naïve."

"You were young."

"I gritted my teeth and went topless. It wasn't so bad. I didn't do lap dances, and the customers couldn't touch us. Money was good. I put myself in another place, just the music and me. I tuned out the audience and being half-naked. Pretty soon it seemed normal." Her eyes found Maxine's.

"And that's where you met Honora?"

"She was already there when I started. She showed me the ropes, you know?"

Maxine nodded, but she didn't *know.*

Nicole ground out her cigarette in a scallop shell and attacked her sandwich.

"We discovered we were both marketing majors," she said between bites. "We had that in common. I mean, it seemed kind of odd, considering what we were doing. Honora said she had left college at the end of her sophomore year. I told her that was dumb. She agreed." Nicole laughed.

"So you just danced just for the money. I know my sister had other problems."

"Most of the girls had issues." Nicole's voice was casual. "Drugs, booze, men, even pimps." She hesitated. "STDs. Abortions. I got a quick street education."

The hurricane lanterns flickered as a warm breeze blew across the patio. Insects sang in the night. Bushes, trees, and the screen enclosed them, but Maxine felt exposed and kept staring at the screen door as if someone would stride in and...what?

"And were you close to Honora? Did she confide in you about her problems?" Maxine reached for the Coke that wasn't there. She felt parched.

Nicole jumped up, fetched Maxine a bottle of iced tea, and poured herself some whiskey. She had already drunk three beers by Maxine's count. "Honora and I were tight," she said in a half-whisper. A strong emotion, maybe anger or regret flickered in her eyes. She folded her arms across her midsection, and her face took on a hard-to-read expression as she sipped the whiskey. Maxine waited, but Nicole didn't resume her narrative.

"Can't you talk about it?"

"I feel like I'm betraying her." Nicole finished the whiskey and put her glass down hard.

"I'm her sister. I haven't seen her or heard from her in seven years." Maxine felt her throat tighten and feared she would burst into noisy tears.

Nicole shrugged and her eyes looked unfocused. "Oh crap, let's have dessert. I have some gelato. Then we'll chill in the whirlpool. I can always get down and dirty in the whirlpool. Nicole Confidential." She produced another breathy little laugh.

Maxine tried not to cringe. *Back off. Let her tell it in her own way*. When she wanted to pin this woman to the ground and demand, *Tell me. Every detail. I want to know everything.*

"No problem," Maxine said. Her sandwich was history. She chugalugged the tea, and pulled her smokes out of her handbag.

"Oh good. I'll join you." Nichole flicked her lighter and lit their cigarettes.

They smoked in silence. Maxine tried to think how to get the conversation back on track again. The grey kitten jumped into her lap and purred.

After dessert, Maxine carried the plates and bowls into the kitchen. Nicole's Martha Stewart tendencies didn't stretch to the culinary arts. Dishes and glasses everywhere, some clean, most dirty. Open boxes, jars, and mixing bowls on the counters. Pots and pans soaked in the sink. The clock on the pan-littered stove read 10:30. In spite of her nap, Maxine felt tired from the drive, waiting at the bar and the unrelenting stress of the last two weeks. She walked back to the patio.

"I'll have that drink you offered." She smiled at Nicole.

"Gotcha! Listen...stick a few lanterns around the whirlpool. Light a candle in your room so you can see to get back inside. No moon tonight. I'll turn off the patio lights except for the Italian ones. Creates a great mood. I'm going in to undress. Meet you at the pool. And I'll bring beach towels. Oh, the switch for the spa is on the wall." Nicole pointed to a spot near the screen door. "I'll open the champagne. We'll drink. We'll talk." She giggled.

Nicole said *undress,* not change. That must mean naked in the whirlpool. Maxine didn't care, but she didn't know Nicole, didn't even trust her, and now she was in this weird situation. *Down and dirty.* Maxine realized her unspoken response to nearly everything Nicole said was either "Oh no!" or "Oh shit!" If she weren't so desperate for information, she would jump into the Volvo and drive back to Boca.

In her room, she heard her cell phone ringing. Only three people had the new number: Finder, Blaisdell, and Jeff. Dashing to catch the phone before it stopped ringing, she hoped the caller was Jeff.

# *Sixteen*

Honora waited until June when school was out before making the drive over the Sierras to San Francisco for her fabulous shopping spree. She decided to make Ethan a part of the trip because he hated the Reno babysitter, an older woman whose only pleasure was watching daytime TV.

Honora found a kid-friendly motel with free parking out by the Seal Rocks, with a park, restaurants, and a Walgreen's nearby. They could ride the bus into downtown, which would be cheaper than a parking garage. She was trying to keep the trip economical because she had used nine hundred dollars to pay off a credit card and had paid the rent on time. She hadn't mentioned the mountain bike to Ethan. He already had the Wii, and she had promised they could pick up a couple more games.

Ethan hated sitting in back in a booster seat and had grumbled most of the way to Sacramento.

"Think about the Giants' sweatshirt and cap you're going to get," she said, glancing at him in the rearview mirror. Why did his dark eyes always look so sad?

"I wanted to see a ball game, too."

"The team isn't in town this week."

"Can we come back when they are?"

"Maybe."

"Maybe always means no." She saw his lower lip thrust out. "Why doesn't Steve ever want to play with my Wii? He says 'maybe,' too, but he never does."

"Steve hasn't been around kids much. He doesn't relate to them."

Ethan frowned. He probably didn't understand "relate." She couldn't say, "Steve doesn't like kids."

Steve acted stiff and uncomfortable around Ethan, who was desperate for someone to play catch and do "guy stuff" with. Steve wasn't that guy.

"I'm hungry."

"We'll eat at the motel. They have a nice dining room. You'll like it."

"How soon do we get there?"

Oh God, this was so tedious, but better than with Steve, of course, who would mooch off her all weekend and wouldn't be happy with a grilled cheese sandwich and lemonade.

At the motel, Ethan liked having a suite with his own space. His eyes lit up when he saw the small swimming pool and the ping-pong table in the courtyard.

Thinking Ethan would be a real pain in the ass while she shopped for shoes and clothes, Honora parked him in front of the television and dashed down to the front desk to inquire about a babysitter, someone who would take him to the park, play ping-pong and watch while he was in pool. She could shop in peace, try on a hundred shoes if she liked, and find the perfect pair. On second thought, maybe she could get a sitter for the evening, too, so she could have a decent meal and a few drinks. A late meal. In her new shoes. You never knew who you might meet.

## *Seventeen*

“I thought you were going to call when you got there, Maxine. I’ve been worried about you. Is everything all right?”

Maxine swallowed. Finder had become a worrywart. Still, it was nice to have someone looking after you. She gave him a rundown of her trip and Nicole. “We’re going to have girl talk in the whirlpool. She’s going to tell me about Honora.”

“She hasn’t yet?”

“Not in any meaningful way.” Maxine sighed.

“Let’s hope this wasn’t a wild goose chase.” Finder sounded perturbed.

“I’m not so sure.”

“Call me tomorrow. At my work number. Let me know what you find out.” He paused. “I have some information for you on Lotto Lopez. But I’m going on record that your idea might be dangerous and is at best harebrained.”

Maxine made some excuse and said goodbye. She would deal with Finder and Lopez later.

She peered out the window through the blinds. In the dim candlelight, the whirlpool looked like a blue grotto. Nicole, naked with a striped towel thrown over her shoulder, walked around the patio, turning on the whirlpool jets and watering the potted plants. She set a boom box close to the whirlpool, and climbed in. Her figure was slim but curvy. Maxine wondered if her large breasts were real.

Maxine stripped off her clothes and dawdled by folding everything neatly across the back of a chair. She found two beach towels on a narrow table and noticed the shelf above the table held, along with candles and shells, a row of self-help books, heavy with advice about relationships and self-esteem. Maxine wrapped a towel around her torso and walked across the patio. The gray kitten came scampering toward her.

"I can't believe this," Nicole said. "That cat hates water."

Maxine dropped the towel and submerged into the froth of bubbles. The kitten sat a few feet away, staring at her, wide-eyed. *Who would be so crazy as to sit in a tub of water?*

Nicole said, "Shit, I forgot the champagne," and popped out of the spa. The cat took off. Nicole had a butterfly tattoo right above her butt, where low-slung jeans would reveal it to the best advantage. Maxine settled into the water again. It was a little creepy to hear cars driving by on the street, not fifty feet from their naked paradise. Nicole returned, handed Maxine a long-stemmed plastic glass and climbed back into the pool. Her hair hung in wet tendrils about her face. Maxine noticed another complicated tattoo on Nicole's shoulder and a rose tattoo high on her left breast.

Nicole saw Maxine examining the tattoo on her shoulder. "Tarot card lovers," she said. "Just got it last year." She bent her head and looked at her arm. "Awesome, huh?"

Maxine nodded.

Latin music with a sensuous beat played at low volume while they sipped champagne, too sweet for Maxine's taste. She thought it would be nice to be in such a romantic situation with Jeff, not Nicole, when the latter asked, "So, do you have a boyfriend?" in a low, inquiring voice.

Maxine explained again that her divorce was *just* final. Then she wondered if telling a secret or two would loosen Nicole's tongue. "I did meet a guy at the place I'm living. So far we're just friends." She emphasized "friends."

"Gotcha!" Nicole pumped her for the details, and Maxine told one lie after another, because she didn't really trust Nicole. When Nicole stopped asking questions, Maxine said, "How about you? Do you have a boyfriend?"

"I thought I did," Nicole said, draining her champagne and knitting her brows. "We were getting along just fine...a few dinners a week, good sex, some fun parties, you know, and then he said he had to leave town for a few days and could I take care of his cat?" She scowled at the gray kitten who watched them from a distance. "He dropped the cat off three weeks ago, and that's the last I heard."

"Can't you call him?" Maxine asked.

"His message box is full. What a shit."

"So, I guess you have a third cat. She's awfully sweet."

"She jumps on the table. After what he pulled, I don't even like her." Nicole smiled, but not with her eyes. "You can do me a big favor. On your way out of town, drop kitty off at the shelter."

"Is it a no-kill shelter?"

"Who cares? I want to look him in the eye and say *I* didn't take her anyplace. I'll say she got out and ran away." She glowered. "If he ever comes back."

All evening Maxine had worked on liking Nicole, based on her impression of the guest room and the cats lounging around the pool. But Nicole never spoke to the cats and seemed barely aware of their presence. *Find out what Nicole knows and get the hell out of here.*

"Did Honora have a boyfriend?" Maxine asked, getting out of the pool to pour more champagne.

"Hey, thanks. That's the spirit. Move the bottle over here so we can stay put." She looked Maxine up and down. "God, you're tall and how about those muscles. How tall are you?"

"Five-nine."

"You're in great shape for your age. At least you don't need to worry so much about getting fat if you're tall. I'm only five-three, and it's a constant struggle."

Maxine lowered herself into the pool. She didn't mention that Cuban sandwiches and chips weren't exactly diet food.

"I asked if Honora had a boyfriend." Maxine tried to make eye contact, but Nicole was staring at the sky. The candles flickered and a sensuous samba played.

"Yeah, she did. The boyfriend was why she moved out of my place. Stiffing me for the rent." Another scowl.

The heady smell of a plant perfumed the patio. Maxine felt spacey. Must be the booze and the heat of the water. "I'm sorry about the rent. What was her boyfriend like?"

"Oh god. A rich Arab kid about her age, and he thought he was going to save her from herself." Nicole's voice indicated the futility of anyone saving Honora.

"How did she meet an Arab?"

Maxine wondered if Nicole could see her heart pounding in her chest. She dropped lower into the water and stared at her knees.

"He showed up at the club and bought a bottle of champagne for Honora." Nicole held her glass up in a toasting motion. She drank and fell silent.

"And one thing led to another?" Maxine felt like she was extracting wisdom teeth.

"He told her to quit her job. Sent her to rehab for a month. On his dime. I couldn't believe it. This guy hemorrhaged black-gold money. Rich Saudi parents." Nicole paused to sip her champagne. She wrinkled her nose and climbed out of the pool, returning with cigarettes, lighter and ashtray.

"Smoke?" asked Nicole.

"Sure." Maxine would have smoked a carton if that would have loosened Nicole's lips.

"Honora lived with him? He supported her?"

"And how. Expensive handbags. Jimmy Choos. She always loved designer labels. With the new boyfriend, no more champagne. She was stone cold sober, cooking lamb chops and rice for him every night." Nicole blew a perfect smoke ring.

"Do you remember his name?"

"God, no. It wasn't Osama, but something that sounded like that." Nicole flicked her fingers at the water in a dismissive gesture.

"They were happy?" She wanted Honora to have had the joy of love.

"Happy as clams until September eleventh. I didn't find out until later, but they were scared shitless he'd be arrested. You know. Florida. Arabs. Flight training. But this guy was just a kid. Terrorism wasn't his thing."

Maxine felt a tsunami of relief. Honora had not been involved with *them*. She had said, "One of them," but she must have meant someone from the Arab world, not a terrorist. Oh god, at last a glimmer of good news.

"Was he detained?" Maxine asked. So many had been thrown in jail. The guilty and the innocent.

"He disappeared when the planes started flying again. Honora said he was going home via London...that he'd send for her when things quieted down. They would get married. Except he never did." Nicole's mean little smile said, "I told you so."

"Did Honora ever hear from him?"

"No. She hinted about moving back in with me, but I'd had enough. Too much emo, you know. She hung around for a few months in their old apartment, waiting for some news. She got a job doing market research. Low-level minimum wage. I said she would make more money dancing again, but she said, 'I really don't need the money. I'm just a little bored with all this endless waiting.' I guess he left her with some money. She'd become a real drag."

"Did she stay clean?"

"Oh hell, who knows? One day she was gone. I think she went out West. She never contacted you?"

"No. I tried to find her."

"Well, there's your answer. If she had become a fine, upstanding citizen, she would have called, wouldn't she?" Nicole drained her champagne and gave Maxine a hard look. "You know, she always felt responsible for your dad killing your mom, and then your husband walking out on you."

Maxine felt her face crumple like a piece of tissue paper, while an enormous hand squeezed her chest. Honora had told Nicole all the awful things about their past that Maxine could never talk about.

"Whoops! I'm sorry. Maybe I shouldn't have mentioned that." Nicole's wide eyes opened still wider. "Insensitive of me. That's my problem. Always blurting out something no one wants to hear. It's from years of not being able to tell anyone. I was sexually abused as a child." She sniffed. "My father and my uncle. For ten years." She snuffled louder. "Damaged goods," she said, peering at Maxine. "Please forgive me." Nicole burst into noisy tears.

Was this an act? Maxine stared across the whirlpool at Nicole, whose anguished blubbering seemed real.

"That's O.K, Nicole, I...I..." Maxine's voice caught, and she couldn't finish her words because her throat had seized up into a tight knot. Her mind was a jumble of thoughts about her parents, Honora, her first husband's defection and finally, Larry. Poor Larry, gone just two weeks ago. Larry, who had not deserved such a terrible death. She saw his colorful sport shirts hanging in a row on his side of the closet. He was always so neat, so careful. So generous and kind to her. Hot tears spurted from her eyes and she didn't try to dam the loud sobs that convulsed her. The pain and the crushing sadness she felt for all her lost family washed over her in waves. Crying felt so good, as if with every sob a torturing demon left her soul.

Their spate of mutual weeping seemed to last forever. The timer kicked off, the bubbles stopped churning and still they sat in the placid blue water.

Nicole, face still buried in her hands, continued to weep. Maxine gained control of herself and moved across the whirlpool to put her arm around Nicole's wet shoulder.

"You couldn't have known," she said. "I'm sorry for you, too." Nicole howled even louder, verging on hysteria.

Anyone walking along the street would hear and come over to inquire if everything was okay. Or call the police. Maxine took a deep breath, and willed her last tears away. *Get a grip. Jesus. Get a grip.* She climbed out of the pool, wiped her eyes on the towel and wrapped it around her while she traipsed across the patio to her room. The gray kitten shot inside and ran under the bed. Maxine grabbed a box of tissues from the bathroom counter and a bottle of water. When she returned, Nicole's intermittent sobs were more subdued. Maxine set the timer for another twenty minutes. The spa rumbled to life again in a froth of warm bubbles. In the lantern light, each of Nicole's cheeks had a smudged blob of black mascara. Maxine handed Nicole a wad of tissues, lit two cigarettes and climbed into the whirlpool again.

"We're a fine pair, aren't we?" she asked.

Nicole blew her nose twice, loud honking noises, and wiped her eyes. She took one of the proffered cigarettes. "You're a doll," she said with a weak smile.

Maxine drank some water and passed the bottle to Nicole. They smoked in silence.

"Are those real?" asked Nicole, fixing her gaze on Maxine.

She thought Nicole was asking about her breasts, but before she could reply, Nicole said, "I always wanted diamond studs. What are they, half a carat?"

"I guess." Maxine's voice broke and she dammed up another round of weeping. Larry had given her the earrings on a St. Maarten's vacation. Larry. She wondered if he had bought all her presents, the clothes, the Majolica plates, even her jewelry with ill-gotten drug money or money he had skimmed. Tonight she didn't care. Every one of his gifts seemed precious. She took another drag on her cigarette. When had she last smoked so much?

"So, are your studs real diamonds?" Nicole rudely persisted.

"Yes."

"Gotcha."

Maxine heard a car pull up. The houses in Key West stood cheek by jowl, and Nicole's caterwauling might have alarmed the neighbors. Oh, god! She hoped someone hadn't called the cops. Then she heard footsteps coming round the house toward the screened area. Still holding the cigarette, Maxine tore out of the whirlpool and dived for the towel just as a male voice crooned,

"Hello girls. Can we come in and join you?"

"Shit!" Nicole looked over her shoulder in horror. "I forgot I invited them."

Clutching the towel, Maxine skittered across the patio and into her room, locking the door behind her. She doused the candle and peered through the blinds. In the dim light, two men stood by the pool. Nicole had a towel covering her. The bartender and the takeout guy—was that who it was? Hard to see in the flickering patio lights.

Maxine felt a flash of anger that Nicole had invited those guys over for a late party, probably knowing the "girls" would be lounging naked in the pool. What a come-on. Nicole, the sleazy bitch, had never been a good friend to Honora. Maxine wanted to slap Nicole silly, then knock those dudes' heads together. Instead, she flushed the wet cigarette down the toilet, dressed and sat on the bed in the dark with her head in her hands. Whenever she felt a shred of friendship or sympathy for Nicole, the woman invariably did something to queer it.

A timid knock at the door. "Maxine?"

"I'm going to bed."

"Don't you want to meet my friends? We can get the party going again."

"No, I'm tired."

"They'd love to meet you."

Maxine didn't answer. The gray kitten emerged and rubbed against her ankles, purring. She bent down and scratched it behind the ears. Outside, there was laughter and splashing and someone ramped the music up a few decibels.

~ * ~

All night she had slept on top of the bed, with the gray kitten curled next to her. The clock radio read 8:37 a.m. when Maxine opened the blinds to a dazzling sun. The pool area looked deserted, with the hurricane lanterns still standing sentry from last night. The kitten jumped off the bed and cried to go out. Maxine opened the door. The air was already warm and humid, but with a pleasant morning freshness, a combination of ocean breeze and flowers in bloom.

She could take the kitten and go. She could hang around until Nicole woke up and...then what? Rehash yesterday evening? Anything but that. The moments of sob sisterhood had passed. Now Maxine wanted to squeeze a few more drops of information out of Nicole. Had she really been serious about the animal shelter or had she just been ranting? Maxine didn't want to steal the boyfriend's cat. A clean break with Nicole, along with a complete understanding about the kitten, would be best. Maxine wondered where she could find hot coffee. Probably on Duvall Street.

After a shower in the bathroom with its red tiles and mirrors, Maxine dried her hair, dressed and glanced at the patio again. Nicole, in a pink bikini and enormous sunglasses, lay prone in a chaise lounge, a mug of coffee in her hand. Maxine stepped out onto the patio. "Good morning," she said, in the friendliest voice she could muster.

"Oh, hi! I'm totally wiped this morning. There's coffee in the kitchen. Sweet 'n Lo and creamer by the sink."

Maxine suppressed a shudder. "Gotcha," she said, hating herself for her pandering.

Clasping a pink mug of black coffee, Maxine sat in a chaise next to Nicole. "I've got to leave soon. Don't you work on Saturday?"

"Noon 'til six." Nicole sighed with her whole body.

"About the gray cat," Maxine said, looking at Nicole.

"Take her. You two have bonded. I'll get her carrier when I have the energy to get up."

"I don't want her if you think your boyfriend's coming back."

"He's not," said Nicole, examining her chipped pink nails.

"Are you sure?"

"He's pals with one of the guys who stopped by last night. His friend said he's got a job in San Diego. Can you believe it?" Nicole heaved another mournful sigh.

"Does the cat have a name?" Maxine asked, looking around. The gray kitten sat in the shade, washing her face.

"Grey Goose. Stupid name. She doesn't answer to it."

"Grey Goose is a vodka."

"It figures." Nicole stood up and went into the house. She returned a few moments later with a cat carrier.

"Take the kitten chow, too. And she has a little bed." Nicole looked at the cat as if she might change her mind.

Maxine's heart did a bungee jump in her chest. "That's so generous of you." She paused. "I forgot to ask a couple things the PI will want to know."

"Shoot!" Nicole said.

"Can you remember Honora's boyfriend's name? And what about the address where they lived?"

Nicole squinted, as if trying to remember. "He rented a condo on Normandy Isle. Bay Drive, I think. Nothing special." She picked at a cuticle. "I said his name sounded like Osama, but of course, it wasn't. Honora called him Samah. I never knew his last name."

"And what was your address when Honora lived with you?"

Nicole's eyes took on a foxy look. "Oh, what does that matter? Honora moved out."

"The PI will want to know. Just in case." In case of what, Maxine couldn't imagine.

"We were just off the Dixie Highway. southwest ninety-fifth." She sighed. "Nice big pool."

"I'll put my bag in the car and come back for the kitty," Maxine said, eager to leave before Nicole reconsidered.

When she returned, her new companion was an unhappy camper meowing in the carrier. Maxine realized she didn't know if her condo allowed pets. She had seen dogs on leashes. It must be okay.

"I hate to be a pest, but did you recall anything else about Honora that might help find her?" Maxine finished the coffee and put the mug on the table.

"I might as well spill the juice," Nicole said, with another foxy look. "I didn't see your sister, but right before she left town someone said she sure did look pregnant."

Nicole's face had a "so there!" expression. "Everyone thought maybe her Arab left her with some money, so she might have been able to get along. Child support wouldn't be an option, would it?"

Nicole's eyes glinted with the knowledge that Honora had been left high and dry. Maxine wasn't sure whether Nicole had ever liked Honora. She seemed to be feeding on all the misfortunes: the boyfriend leaving, the pregnancy. *Time to go.*

Maxine hoisted the cat carrier and Nicole carried the food and the bed. Nicole watched while Maxine stowed everything in the Volvo. She put a seatbelt around the carrier in the back seat.

Maxine gave Nicole a sedate hug. "Thanks for everything."

Nicole, grabbing Maxine in a messy embrace, said, "Next time we'll have a real party." She giggled.

"With bottles and bottles of champagne," added Maxine.

"Gotcha."

~ * ~

On the way out of town, Maxine found a beach parking lot and pulled in to call Finder. She rolled down the windows. The warm fresh air of an hour ago was an enervating heat with a humidity that frizzed her hair. Still, she felt the whisper of a breeze. Seagulls wheeled in the air and mooched bread from an old man. The water was a blue mirror, yet somehow moody, as if the quiet surface belied what lay beneath. In the distance, rotted pilings dotted the water. The kitten issued a questioning meow. *Can we get going?*

When Finder picked up the phone, Maxine gave him the information about Honora's Miami addresses. She relayed what she had learned from Nicole, including about Honora's possible pregnancy.

"If Honora was still hoping her boyfriend would send for her, she wouldn't change her name. So I'm betting you can find some leads." She could not contain a sigh. "*Out West* is so vague. I'll look up her former California address and email it to you."

As usual, Finder sounded noncommittal. "Sometimes we mine gold, but mostly we mine garbage. Listen Maxine, I know I asked you to keep in touch, but a long running case broke wide open yesterday and I've got a call coming in. Get back to me in a few minutes, can you?"

Maxine said she could. In the meantime, she drank a cup of coffee and attacked the cherry Danish with gooey frosting she'd picked up in town. The frosting oozed in the heat. Delicious and utterly bad. *Bad to the bone.* Maxine stared at the blue water, the long pier, and the beach barbecues. Then she turned around to peer through the grill of the cat carrier on the back seat. The gray kitten stared back at her with big sad eyes and voiced another plaintive meow.

Maxine had always been adept at compartmentalizing—tasks, information, emotions, and especially unpleasantness. For her Key West trip, she had put Lotto Lopez with his intriguing face and his significance in her troubled life into a sealed memory tube that she hadn't accessed while she was with Nicole. Now that Nicole, she hoped, was history, Maxine let herself think of Lopez again.

On Monday's telephone call, which seemed like eons ago, Finder had been stunned into silence when Maxine had expressed her desire to talk to Lotto Lopez. *I want to convince him that I am not a danger to him, that I won't ever testify. Larry is dead and nothing or no one can bring him back. The past is past.* Just thinking about it made her take a deep breath. *I'll only see Lotto if he is alone. He could conceivably have ordered my husband's murder.*

Maxine hadn't mentioned anything about Lotto being a prince. His MBA and his business acumen had dazzled Larry. Maxine wasn't so sanguine.

Finder's no-nonsense voice came back to her. *You never cease to amaze! You have more balls than*—He had caught himself and apologized.

She had been uneasy passing on the contact information for Lopez, hoping she wasn't opening Pandora's Box. *Lotto Lopez has the best business address in Miami. I Googled it. Can you find out if there's a time of day when Lopez is by himself?*

*You got a death wish, wanting to meet a man like that alone?* Finder wanted to know.

She had a life wish. Why couldn't he see that? *Please find out his schedule.*

Finder's response, even his casual voice, had been somehow reassuring. *Yeah. Brickell Boulevard is a fancy-schmancy Miami address. Let me see what I can do.*

On Wednesday, two days before she drove to Key West, Finder had reported back.

*I have someone scoping out this Lopez guy's office building. I did a little trolling using the name 'Lotto Lopez' and nothing turned up. 'Lopez isn't exactly a rare name in Miami. I got a hit on a Lotario Lopez. He's listed as the tenant in the Brickell Avenue building. Marquesa Trading Company. Miami is full of import-export outfits. This one seems to be legit. Couldn't find a residence, and I didn't find any 'reputation.' No police records, no lawsuit. Nada.*

Maxine had wondered aloud if Lotario was a real name.

*If my name were Lotario, I'd go by Lotto, too. Interesting he's so squeaky clean. That's in your favor. I should have a report ready when you're back from the Keys.*

She drained her coffee and watched a red kayak racing through the water. She re-dialed Finder's number.

"Sorry about the interruption," he said. "I'll give the same attention to your case when the time comes." He cleared his throat. "About Lotario, or Lotto, or whoever-the-hell-he-is Lopez. The deal is this: he's in his Brickell Boulevard office every day from nine to one. We think he walks there from a nearby residence. Plenty of luxury condos in that neighborhood. His Mercedes stays in the garage. At one p.m. sharp, he takes the elevator to the street and walks a couple blocks to a popular deli. Takes a table alone, orders a salad or a sandwich and a beer, reads the *Miami Herald*. So far, his routine hasn't varied. Then he walks back to his office and —this is the crazy thing—he disappears."

"Disappears?" asked Maxine. "What do you mean?"

The kitten meowed louder. The seagulls screamed and dive bombed as more bread hit the sand. The red kayak skimmed along parallel to the beach.

"The tail says Lopez ducks into the garage, but his car doesn't move from his parking spot. Lopez isn't in his office. He's gone. So obviously, somebody picks him up inside the garage. Busy place. Cars in and out all the time, so it would be difficult to pinpoint who he's leaving with. Tinted windows, etc. You'd need an army to follow everyone leaving the garage. Sometimes Lopez shows up at the office around six or seven, or maybe it's midnight or later. If it's early, he drives to South Beach for dinner. One night his companion was a knock-out blonde. He always disappears into the garage. Must have a chauffeur or something waiting down there—maybe even another car."

"I could approach him in the deli." A seagull flew up next to the car and waited hopefully.

"That would be the safest place," Finder said. "I insist on watching your back." He cleared his throat. "I don't have to like this. In fact, I don't like it. But if you're going to be stubborn, so am I..." His voice trailed off.

"Maybe on Thursday. I have an aerobics class, but I can drive down afterward. I'd have enough time." Maxine watched a small sailboat on a windward tack across the water, white sails taut.

"Absolutely not. We'll drive to Miami together. Listen, sorry, I have another call coming in. Get back to me first thing Monday morning, okay?"

"Come on, kitty, let's go," Maxine said. The kitten was asleep.

~ * ~

Maxine's new voice recorder was an electronic marvel, well worth leaving the old low-tech recorder with the Sharon police. A bit larger than a cell phone, the new device could be set for voice-operated recording, and she could bookmark passages. The machine even had a search function, and Maxine could download her recording to her computer if she bought some special software. She wondered what kind of crazy woman she was to enthuse about the lengthy battery life, light weight and long recording times of her new toy. A woman with no real life, a woman with a recorder for a confidante.

She spoke into the recorder, making her usual to-do lists.

"Pick up a book on Excel. Look for an advanced class." That should get her going on the spreadsheets. "Check out community colleges. Do a Google search on the name Samah. Get a list of rehab places in the Miami area. Maybe Finder can locate where Honora dried out. See if the library has any old Miami phone books. Check out those neighborhoods where Honora lived."

She yakked on, leaving reminders to herself. The non-essential stuff could be deleted when she got home. Home. She would really be in a bind if the condo didn't allow pets. Stupid to adopt a kitten, but this one was so sweet.

Maxine cruised somewhere between Boca Chica and Looe Key, crossing the bridges, savoring the turquoise sea, imagining kayaking with Jeff. She speculated about kayak rentals and wondered if Kaylee could manage in the quiet waters. She let herself picture the proposed trip to the Everglades.

And Lotto. Always Lotto.

She had planned to stop in Islamorada for lunch, but now she had the cat along. A bottle of tea, her water and a granola bar would be enough after that huge Danish. Maybe she would return to Key West as a tourist with no agenda except fun. Maybe Lotto was really a prince of a gentleman. Life was full of maybes.

# *Eighteen*

The aerobics club had a substitute for Maxine's Thursday class. By mid-morning, she and Finder were tooling along I-95 to Miami. Finder's plan was too elaborate, absolute overkill, but Finder insisted it was his way or nothing. Earlier, he had driven from Pompano Beach to pick up Maxine at the Boca Raton Resort and Club where she had spent the night in a room in the tower, feeling like a goddess readying herself for sacrifice. She had driven into the private grounds and registered under her own name. At least in mid-June, the rates weren't sky high. Finder was costing big bucks trying to locate Honora and getting Lopez off her back.

The gray kitten, now dubbed Lucy, was at Jeff's with Kaylee and her aunt. Kaylee adored the kitten and was beside herself that she would have Lucy all day. Cats were "legal" in the condominium, and Lucy had adapted easily to Maxine's living quarters.

The PI wore the blue pinfeather suit and the jazzy dragonfly tie Maxine remembered from their first meeting at The Cove.

At Finder's insistence, Maxine wore a black linen shift with a white jacket. Black heels and handbag. *Dressed to kill.*

"Wear a straw hat. One with a black ribbon would work."

"Why does it matter *what* I wear?"

"We want everyone in that deli to remember a woman in black and white wearing a hat. A woman of style. When you swap into a pink baseball cap, t-shirt and sandals...*adios* style, hello tourist." He glanced in the rearview mirror from time to time. "I've never been convinced this Lopez doesn't have muscle following him around that we haven't seen. That's why we're driving a rental car and why you're going back to the hotel afterward. The hotel management screens everyone coming in the entrance and they aren't likely to let any rough types in." Finder looked at Maxine with his shrewd eyes. "Are you nervous?"

"I'm okay. What if Lotto doesn't eat lunch at the deli today?"

"Lotto eats there *every* day. He's a creature of habit. And my operative has reported Lotto's already in his office. I've got a good feeling."

Maxine stared through the car window at the depressing Florida landscape. I-95 with its huge trucks and tourists and demented drivers and ramps and bleak bedroom suburbs of crammed together apartments and worst of all, the endless congestion and the stink of exhaust fumes made her edgy. Some of the palms still looked scraggly from the last hurricane. Miami's skyscrapers loomed up like a jaw of unevenly spaced teeth. Finder followed the green Interstate sign to *Miami Downtown*.

Finder's operative, as he always referred to him, would follow Lopez from his office to the deli and keep in touch by cell phone. The important thing for Maxine was to stay calm, speak her piece and leave.

A fat Florida grapefruit had lodged in the pit of her stomach. Her handbag felt heavy with the Smith & Wesson in the bottom. Finder didn't know about that. She recalled another harrowing day, when she had rescued a twelve-year-old girl from a rip tide. She hadn't been sure she had enough strength, with the girl grasping at her, trying to drown both of them. She had gritted her teeth and swum parallel to the beach for minutes that seemed like hours, with the girl in a cross-chest carry, too weak to struggle. Today's mission only required her to gut it out. Maxine felt a jolt of energy. She could do it.

# *Nineteen*

Today was hotter than yesterday. Lotto could feel beads of sweat popping out on his brow. He didn't want to be like those American wimps who couldn't walk a few blocks at midday without wilting.

He picked up a *Herald* and entered the deli. Only a few minutes after one and the line for tables was gone. Lotto had become used to Florida's early eating hours, but he had never learned to like them.

With a practiced eye, he scanned the still bustling room, listening to the clink of silverware and the babble of voices in English and Spanish. He smelled whiffs of the blackened grouper special. Shrieks of laughter rose from a table of thirtyish women. Why did women always assemble in groups like flocks of hens?

Lotto's favorite table in back was free, and he seated himself facing the diners, and then removed his cell phone from his belt holder and placed it on the gray tabletop. The waitress approached with a menu and a wide smile. Lotto tipped generously. He asked for a Bohemia beer, but he didn't open the menu.

In Lotto's head, business refused to take a lunch break. Sunday afternoon he would fly to Cartagena and shepherd the Russian submarine kits through customs. The kits were arriving as "farm implements." Thinking of the exorbitant bribes he would have to pay, Lotto drummed his fingers on the table. The cost of doing business.

Angelika had pouted when he mentioned he'd be away for a week. Lotto promised to take her clubbing Saturday, and handed over a wad of cash for spa treatments. For her and her friends...the cost of a high-maintenance girlfriend.

*Lotto, it's just no fun to go by myself.*

Women liked to cluck together over their pedicures.

*Lotto, I will be beautiful for you. In addition, we need extra for the tips.*

Extra for this. Extra for that. And fancy lunches with drinks, of course. There would be a trip to the spa's shop for cosmetics and whatever women bought at those overpriced robbers' dens.

When the waitress returned with his beer, Lotto ordered the BLT. Without mayo. He admired the golden, grainy color of the Bohemia before taking a hefty swallow. The beer had a bittersweet full-bodied flavor, not like the weasel piss wimpiness of so-called "lite" beers. He unfolded the *Herald* and glanced up as a stunning Amazon entered the room. He liked women who understood how sexy a little elegance could be. Something intriguing about that wide-brimmed hat shading her eyes. Maybe a model, but not one of those plucked runway chickens. Probably a catalog model, like Angelika. *A little meat on her bones. Muscle, too,* he thought, ogling the endless legs. Lotto noticed other admiring heads turning to watch the woman.

She removed her sunglasses and looked at Lotto. He felt a twinge—was it desire? No, recognition. Where had he seen her before?

The woman gave him a faint smile and made her way around the tables, striding across the room. She stopped in front of Lotto with her not quite intimate smile.

"May I join you?" A faint whiff of Chanel drifted across the table.

He half rose and gestured at the empty chair. The woman extended her hand and gave his a firm shake. *What the fuck?*

"I'm Maxine, Larry Caliendo's widow." She seated herself across from him and placed her sunglasses on the table.

*Mierda. Now* he recognized her. *Maxine.* Lotto's mind raced like Angelika's Boxster. The bodyguard was waiting across the street, or on the sidewalk, or in a parking lot, but *not in this room.* The woman, Maxine, saw him glance at his phone. She placed her hand lightly on the table.

Their eyes locked.

Lotto could not believe this. Could not believe that Caliendo's wife was sitting across from him. In his face. His people had looked *everywhere* for this Maxine. They had hacked into how-many computers; they had followed every lead. *Nada.* And she was sitting here and he could not even make a phone call. *How did she find him? What did she want*?

The waitress swooped down on the table with a smile and another menu.

"Nothing for me, thanks." Crossing her legs. Another whiff of perfume.

"Not even a glass of wine?" Lotto's voice sounded hoarse. *What did she want? She must be wearing a wire.* The white jacket would conceal a wire. Lotto felt his pulse skyrocketing. In spite of the air conditioning, he felt beads of sweat on his temples. He tugged at his collar.

"I hope it's not presumptuous of me, but I needed to talk to you. In private." The Caliendo woman's voice was low, with a throaty quality. Her eyes never left Lotto's as she picked up her sunglasses and twirled them. Her wedding ring was gone.

"You may know that Larry and I separated and had been living apart for a year."

He nodded, waiting. The woman's words were rushed. Nervous. Lotto sipped his Bohemia, which had developed a bitter taste.

"Larry died the day our divorce was final. A few months before that he told me that if anything ever happened to him, the company would take care of me."

Wired or not, Lotto had to say *something*. "How does this affect me?"

"Actually, it doesn't. I don't need anything. No money. Because of my last job and an inheritance, I'm quite well situated. Therefore, there's no need—"

"Are you sure you don't want some wine, Maxine?" He gestured toward his beer. "Or perhaps a Bohemia?" It was difficult for Lotto to think of this creature who had led him on such a fruitless hunt as "Maxine," but he forced himself to use her name.

"No, nothing, thanks." Maxine glanced at the table of women settling the bill and continued to twirl her black sunglasses. "I just wanted to let you know that I've declined to testify in the trial of... of Joe Webb. After the divorce, I wanted to start a new life, and that meant leaving everything behind. Larry. Everything."

The hen party was leaving, with a scraping of chairs and hugs and noisy farewells.

Lotto couldn't stop staring at Maxine, her face, her hat, her jacket, and her nervous hands. In another situation, he would have felt a tremendous attraction to this woman, but now she was the thorn that jabbed his side. Lotto glanced at his phone again. If he could just press one key. Maxine seemed to read his thoughts as they both looked at the black cell phone lying in front of them on the gray table. *Mierda.* She might pounce on his cell phone if he attempted to pick it up.

"Larry's youngest brother has cerebral palsy and Larry's estate went to care for him. I've severed all my ties." She emphasized "*all my ties.*"

The waitress deposited a blackened grouper sandwich at a nearby table, and the smell of cooked fish assaulted his nose.

Maxine knew who Lotto was. She even knew where to find him. *Mierda.* What else did Maxine know? What had Caliendo told her? And how did Caliendo know so much?

"I am so distressed to hear of your...husband's death, Maxine," he said. "Even with a divorce, it's never an easy thing." Lotto's voice was neutral, consoling, he hoped. He tried to gauge the effect of his words, but Maxine's face betrayed nothing.

"I want your assurance," she began, "that...that you understand that I...that—"

Maxine didn't finish her sentence. Lotto thought she couldn't.

"What assurance do you need?" he asked. Assurances, like all lies, were easy, He loosened his collar again.

"Your word as a gentleman that you or your goons won't hunt me down and kill me." Maxine glanced at her watch.

Speechless again, Lotto could only stare into her deep-set eyes, shaded by the brim of her hat.

"I'm only a businessman. Why would I wish you harm?" Lotto smiled, just for her, a warm smile, he hoped, without guile.

Maxine stood and smoothed her skirt. "I didn't expect you to admit to anything." She hesitated. They both stared at his cell phone. On maximum alert, Lotto stood, too.

"Maybe I can do you a favor," Maxine said. "You might be interested to know the local police were on to Larry. They asked me 'where the money was.' Of course, I don't know." She smiled. "Just food for thought."

As if on cue, the waitress appeared with Lotto's sandwich, insinuating herself between. Lotto and Maxine. She put the plate on the table and hovered, babbling something about the mayo. *Mierda!*

Maxine began walking through the deli. At the door, she turned and glanced back. The smell of Chanel still hovered about the table.

Lotto picked up his cell, pushed "encrypt" and another key. "The Caliendo woman is leaving the deli this moment. You know what to do!"

# *Twenty*

Threading her way through the close-together tables at the deli, Maxine took her cell phone from her jacket pocket and hit "send." Finder picked up on the first ring.

"He's calling someone. Where are you? I'm scared to death."

"Just turning the corner. I'll be there in a moment."

Maxine couldn't move, couldn't think. "Oh, here's a cab pulling up." She ran down the steps to the street. "Meet you at the airport. Delta arrivals." Her voice was a croaky whisper. She climbed into the taxi and shut the door. "Airport."

The driver pulled away from the curb. "Did you hear?" she asked Finder. She was so terrified she had trouble speaking.

His voice shouted in her ear, "Jesus! Get out of that cab. The driver might be one of Lopez's goons. It could be a trap. Don't hang up!"

Maxine leaned forward and said, "Sorry. Can you let me out again?"

He turned to look at her. The moment seemed to last forever.

"You must pay the minimum fare."

The driver's accent was Hispanic, which freaked Maxine out even more. But he pulled back out of the traffic into a bus stop. Maxine had an emergency wad of bills in her handbag, but her fingers didn't want to obey her brain and it took precious seconds to grab the five-dollar bill and pushed it at the driver.

"Sorry," she said again.

Maxine tossed her hat on the seat. The driver said, "*Que*?" as she lunged out of the taxi.

What did Finder's rental car look like? Maxine's heel caught on something and she went down on one knee. Looking along the street behind her, two cars down, a driver flashed his lights. Finder. Right by the maroon and white sign advertising the deli.

Across the street, an enormous man with a bullet-shaped shaved head stood by the open door of a taxi. Maxine had never seen anyone so huge. Their eyes met for a moment and Maxine's panic increased. He gave her a cold stare, eyes like ice cubes. This must be who Lotto had wanted to call. The hulk's eyes never left her as he began crossing the street through the traffic. Maxine's high heels thwarted her sprint toward Finder's car, but he had already opened the passenger's door and she clambered inside.

"That big man is after me!" Pointing to the hulk.

"We gotta get out of here." Finder shot around the corner and made an illegal left turn against the traffic. Horns honked and drivers flipped them the bird as Finder sped away. When she turned to look, there were no cabs behind them. Finder punched some buttons on the dash. The GPS said, "Turn left at the next intersection."

Maxine yanked her shoes off, tossed her jacket into the back seat, and jerked the hot pink t-shirt over her head.

Finder passed her the pink baseball cap. "You look like you've been tasered."

"That's how I feel, too." She put the cap on.

"Take a deep breath. Your shoes are on the back seat."

Finder's voice was calm, but he was sweating as he clutched the steering wheel. Maxine retrieved the pink sneakers and bent over to put them on, noticing that her knee oozed drops of blood. She leaned back against the headrest.

"It was a stupid thing to do. Right away, I realized how useless this was. When he couldn't stop looking at his phone. He didn't even have the decency to promise not to kill me."

"I never did like the idea. But you were so intent." Finder continually checked the rear view mirror. "I wonder if the goon got our license plate. We were pretty fast, and he wasn't expecting you to get out of the taxi and into another car." He paused. "A real ogre. I wouldn't want to be the guy who spit in his Cheerios."

The disembodied GPS voice directed, "Turn right onto South Miami Ave. Turn next right."

"I'll check in with my operative. He should be behind us."

The tense ride to the airport rental return took only fifteen minutes, enough time for a cigarette to balm her shattered nerves. There were so many cabs heading to the airport that Maxine's eyes almost burned out of her skull staring at all the taxi drivers. No giant man with a shaved head. No taxis followed them into the car rental return. Maxine had sweated the tee shirt damp, and she breathed easier when they boarded the bus to the terminal. Finder was on the phone to valet parking. The operative reported that he didn't think anyone was following them. Definitely no cabs. Maxine remembered the Smith & Wesson again and how she had forgotten it when the huge man appeared.

On the bus, Finder flipped off his phone and rubbed his temples. "Killer day," he said. "Let's grab a bite to eat at the hotel when we get back? Good sandwiches at the pool bar. And booze." He smiled at her for the first time that morning.

Maxine wasn't sure she could eat, but she could drink. "They're going to keep looking for me," she said. "That big guy's eyes were like ice and Lotto's weren't much friendlier."

"You must have scared the bejesus out of him."

"I could tell he was dumbfounded." Maxine thought about her rendezvous with Lotto. She had forgotten how good looking he was, with his tan Hispanic face and insolent eyes, blue eyes, actually, and his lean build. He had looked fantastically neat with his starched Pink shirt and patterned blue tie in the godawful heat. His emotionless eyes had bored right into her, but he had to be feeling a certain... vulnerability.

Maxine said, "I wouldn't have connected Lotto to Larry's murder if it hadn't been for the two creeps. The 'Chauffeurs and Gophers' who showed up at those so-called 'executive meetings.' They were the muscle, but I didn't realize it at the time." She added, "I've never seen that big hulk before."

Eyes on the road ahead, Finder rubbed his chin. "You mentioned receiving a note from your husband telling you where to find this Lotto if the shit hit the fan?"

That "note" had been on Larry's PC.

"Yes. Name. Address. Phone number. Maybe Lotto wasn't expecting that. Maybe Lotto didn't even know Larry had this information. Larry was a smart guy."

She sighed, thinking of Larry's PC with its damning evidence. If Lotto knew she had *that*, he would never stop looking for her. She didn't want Finder to know about the computer, either. No one must ever know about Larry's laptop.

Finder cast a quick glance Maxine's way. "I ran a credit report on Marquesa Trading Company. Seemed to be a real business. Legitimate letters of credit. My guess is that it's a business fronting for drug money. Lots of those in Miami."

At the hotel's gatehouse, the guard let them in. "A good feeling, huh?" asked Finder. "To know your back is covered?"

Maxine nodded. She wanted to spend a few minutes by herself, time to regroup. "I have to change. This t-shirt looks dorky weird over the dress. And the sneakers." Her scraped knee had stopped oozing.

Finder parked in front of the main building and tossed the keys to the valet.

"You go freshen up. I'm going to make some calls to my old contacts at the DEA. I'll meet you at the Gazebo Bar in fifteen minutes. By the Tower pool."

~ * ~

From her seventeenth floor aerie in the pink tower, Maxine gazed across the yacht club and Lake Boca, where the Intracoastal

Waterway ballooned. Highrises lined the water and the ocean beyond. She peered down on the hotel pool right under her window where sunbathers sprawled on lounge chairs with thick blue cushions the color of the water. Kids splashed and a gardener swept a walk lined with lush green foliage. Everything looked so normal, while she felt out of sync with the world.

Maxine took her laptop from under the spare blanket in the closet and placed it on the desk that overlooked the water view. She put the Smith & Wesson in a pocket in her suitcase. While the PC booted up, she yanked off her pink disguise, the baseball cap, t-shirt and the sandals. Since her move to Boca, Maxine received little email, but she couldn't wean herself from checking her inbox several times a day. She had an email from Brianna, a friend from work.

> *Hey Max,*
> *Weirdest thing this week— and it involved YOU!!! Someone trashed your old office. The Powers That B think they sneaked in with the cleaning crew. Manila folders all over and your file cabinet ransacked. Your nameplate still on yr cube. What gives? Did you make somebody MAD? Have you made the club scene yet in South Beach? Hear it really cooks. Love to bop down and party til I drop. Ha! Ha! Hope all is well—have to get back 2 the salt mines.*
>
> *Brianna*

The trashed office had to be Lotto's people searching for information that would lead to Maxine. They might have tried to steal her Outlook address book. On her last day, she had made a copy and then del2eted every address. Lotto would never rest until she was as dead as Larry. The idea of Brianna or any of her girlfriends from the office visiting her was impossible. How would she explain looking over her shoulder all the time?

Maxine didn't want to meet Finder by the pool and she wasn't even sure about seeing Jeff later. She wanted to go home, change into pajamas and thick white socks and fix a peanut butter and jelly sandwich. Squishy white bread, chunky Skippy and thick apricot jam. Washed down with milk. Whole milk.

Yesterday Jeff had made Maxine promise that she would explain her "mysterious errand" and why she was staying at the Boca Raton Club for two nights.

*I'll tell you everything after I'm back. Please don't call me before four.*

Whenever Maxine acted secretive, Jeff frowned and sulked a little with a thin mouth and clouded eyes. *Why can't you be just a little bit upfront with me?*

She and Jeff had spent some evenings together since she returned from Key West. Jeff grilled or Maxine cooked and Kaylee swam in the pool and played with Lucy. Every night at eleven the would-be lovers met by the blue pool, where they smoked cigarettes, drank rum, and held hands with the fervor of lovesick teenagers. She wanted to tell Jeff, "I can't get too involved with you right now because my focus is getting this man to buy off on the idea that I'm no danger to him." She hadn't spoken those words. Jeff would want to know the details. He would try to discourage her. She had to keep Jeff and Lotto spaced apart like beads on a necklace, with a little knot of time and distance between each one.

Maxine wanted to tell Jeff that her worst fear, besides Lotto, was "you will walk away when I tell you my story." Any sane person would. Especially a single dad. Still, she had to tell him. Maxine closed her eyes and pressed her fingers against her eyelids. If it weren't for Honora, she would leave Florida tonight.

~ * ~

With a bottle of beer in front of him, Finder was propping up the bar at the Gazebo. "I've lived in Florida for twenty years and I've never seen so damn much pink and blue," he said, looking around. "What do you want to drink?" He patted the bar stool next to him.

"I'll have a daiquiri on the rocks." Maxine stared at Finder's beer. "Lotto drank Bohemia, too."

"He has good taste. We'll give him that." Finder took a long swig of beer.

No one spoke for a while. Maxine liked Finder, and he had saved her butt. She shouldn't begrudge him the time it took for a drink and a bite to eat. What kind of gratitude was that?

"A penny for your thoughts," Finder said. Maxine had turned to look at the pool. She swiveled her bar stool back to Finder. His face had its customary ruddy flush, and she noticed the gray in his thick wiry hair.

"My thoughts are pretty morbid."

"Yeah. I can understand that." Finder opened the menu. "You're probably running on empty. How about a sandwich or something?" His voice was kind.

"Just a snack. A friend may join me for dinner."

Finder didn't ask about the "friend." Instead, he said, "We're grilling tonight. Ever eat beer can chicken?" Finder rubbed his blunt nose as he studied the menu.

"My husband used to make it." Maxine warmed at the memory of Larry and his grills and spice rubs and recipes. "You're married?"

"Twenty–five years. My wife teaches school, but she's off for the summer. We try to take it easy in the heat. How does a shrimp cocktail sound?"

"Good, actually." The shrimp would hold her until dinner. If Jeff decided to come.

"Lunch is on me, OK?" Finder put down the menu and ordered Maxine's daiquiri and two shrimp cocktails. Finder removed his jacket and stuffed his tie into the pocket. "You up for a rehash of Lottogate? We should figure out what we learned today, go over what went right, wrong and the surprises."

"I'm so grateful that you took over the—the management of this Lotto business." Maxine said, wishing the daiquiri were in front of her. "If I'd been on my own, I might be dead by now."

"So that's the first thing we learned. Lotto is dangerous. He has a giant-sized jack-in-the-box goon jumping out of taxis. No more Marquesa Trading Company executive. Lotto showed his hand, and now he's likely to be a pit bull." Finder studied the array of bottles above the bar. Maxine shivered.

"Lotto will think of getting rid of you as one-stop shopping."

"I should have known better." *Where was the damn daiquiri?*

Finder shrugged. "Lotto's a creature of habit who encountered a stranger in *his* space. He won't like that you ferreted him out. Lotto won't like that at all. He is going to wonder how you found out about his legit 'Lotario' side." Finder cleared his throat. "My guess would be that he would want you questioned before he takes more drastic actions. I wouldn't mention this because it will scare you, but you've got to understand the danger."

Maxine didn't confess that she was already scared 24/7. Her stomach was permanently balled into one huge knot, like a skein of steel wool. She looked away.

"Maxine, your bravery is equal to your fright. I understand completely. That's why I didn't try to quash your idea of confronting Lotto. 'We must travel in the direction of our fear.'"

She turned to meet his eyes.

"John Berryman. My wife's in the English Department. Sometimes she forgets herself and reads poetry to me." Finder grinned, apparently pleased to surprise her. "Who knew, huh?"

The waiter brought Maxine's daiquiri. Finder ordered a second beer.

"I'll do some computer searches to make sure you're still off the grid. I can work on tracking your sister. With her gone, are you planning on sticking around here? Might be safer to be in Austin. Or Podunk. Somewhere beyond Lotto Land. Any thoughts about that?"

Maxine took a healthy sip of the daiquiri, cold and loaded with rum.

Her thoughts were bleak and involved another long wearying trip. Away from Lotto Land.

"Don't use any credit cards, if you can help it." Finder said. "Is there someone who can pick up your mail for you?"

"Maybe."

"Now, if a grand jury convenes, you'll probably have to testify." Finder took a long swallow of beer. "Subpoenas don't offer any wiggle room. Everything will be confidential. At least that's the way it's supposed to work. You might want to consult a lawyer. Just to be on the safe side. I can recommend a couple."

"I'll think about it." Maxine would also think about cutting out *before* any "shipping up to Boston" was required. "I've been putting off the Boston cop who's been bugging me for information and talking about my testimony." Maxine's pulse raced. All this talk of testimony and grand juries was making her crazy. She had to get out of town. She had a vision of herself and Lucy, crisscrossing the country looking for a safe haven, with Lucy meowing pitifully in the cat carrier. If Maxine could get to the money in the offshore bank, she might be able to buy a false identity. And security.

"Hey," Finder said. "Your tan has just done a big fade."

"I'm pulled in too many directions."

The waiter put two lemon-garnished shrimp cocktails in front of them.

"I'll help you figure it out." Finder finished his beer.

They ate, Finder paid the bill and left Maxine, still at the bar, drinking her second daiquiri. She picked up her half-empty glass and found a lounge chair by the pool. Her watch read 3:55. The next minutes dragged by while Maxine waited for Jeff to call. She liked him more than she had admitted to herself. Not having begun a sexual relationship had somehow heightened her feelings for him. She tried to imagine herself speaking all the words she must say, tried to imagine his face with all those innocent freckles, his casual grin, his easy posture, hearing her recitation. In her mind, she saw his grin fade, his posture stiffen, and his freckles blanch.

She jumped when her phone trilled.

"How about I come over for dinner?" Jeff asked. "We can have a good chin wag and maybe you'll show me your room." His voice was breezy, maybe a little teasing. He paused for an instant before continuing. "I talked Sis into taking care of Kaylee tonight. Kaylee and Lucy. Can't separate those two. Hope that's okay."

It was better than okay.

"Hey, I've got some big news of my own. The un-surprise." Jeff's voice wavered a bit.

"We'll talk," she said.

"Yup. Let's plan the Everglades trip."

They agreed to meet at seven. The idea of telling Jeff made her stomach clench up worse than ever.

# *Twenty-one*

Over dinner, Jeff told Maxine his news. He no longer had a job.

Florida in the summer was a dead season, and as the economy tanked, fewer people played golf or took lessons, and *no one* was buying three-hundred-dollar golf shoes or pricey drivers.

"It wasn't unexpected," Jeff said. "They said I was welcome to keep giving lessons, but my pro shop hours were drastically curtailed. I said 'screw it.'" He stared through the window at the yachts in the hotel dockage. "I have set some cash aside for a rainy day." His blue eyes sparkled. "We can drive down to the Everglades. Maybe go to the Keys. Do some serious exploring. Teach Kaylee how to kayak." He paused and continued. "We can enjoy the rest of the summer." His words were almost an exultation.

Although she had expected him to, Jeff didn't press Maxine for *her* news. Maxine wondered if she still had that tasered look.

After dinner, he put his arm around her waist and they ambled through the lush grounds under a dark, moonless sky. The vegetation crept close, along with the cloying scent of the flowers. Something rustled in the leaves above them. Maxine hoped it wasn't one of those Florida fruit rats.

The darkness encouraged confidences, and when she told Jeff her story, she didn't try to put a good face on the facts, like Larry's occupation, or her finding his body and how her knowledge endangered her.

"Cripes, I see why you had to stay out of sight," Jeff said, beginning to come to grips with this new Maxine and her troubles. His voice sounded reasonable, but his face had frozen into a worried frown.

A huge moth, dark as the night and as large as a bird, winged by. Walking silently, like in a dream, they passed a reflecting pool. The moth returned, and seemed to be shadowing them.

"Black witch," Jeff said.

"What?"

"The moth. A black witch. Kaylee was afraid of bugs, so we studied them."

They continued along the sidewalk through the gardens.

"I've been doing my best to cope," continued Maxine. "I hadn't expected to meet anyone and drag them into my troubles."

Sometimes Jeff held her arm, and other times he dropped it and they walked side by side. He hadn't revealed how he felt about her crazy story. In fact, he seemed too quiet, like a man poised for flight. The thing that Maxine feared most.

They strolled indoors, passing under tall arches, and through a dim Moorish lounge. In a pristine white salon, they sat next to each other on a sofa and Maxine clutched a blue throw pillow while she told Jeff about Lotto and what, with Finder's help, she had done today.

Jeff turned his disbelieving face to her, with astonished blue eyes, and unsmiling lips.

"Jesus, Max. You must be out of your mind."

"I had to talk to him. Don't you see? I had to try." She took Jeff's hand. "So it was a colossal mistake. He might have said, 'No problem. I won't hurt you. We don't owe each other anything.'"

"Fat chance," Jeff said. He pointed to a dark bar next to the lounge. "Night cap?"

Except for the jungle animals painted above the bar, they were the only patrons. The bartender took their orders.

"Now, can you understand why I was so reluctant to tell you?" Maxine asked, trying to meet Jeff's gaze, but he had his head down, staring into his tequila.

"I'm getting a pretty good picture," he said in a low voice.

She had been afraid this would happen.

"I understand if you don't want to...to pursue our relationship." Pain pressed against her heart and her voice quivered.

Jeff finally looked into her eyes. "It's going to take me a while to process all this new...stuff. I knew you had a secret, but not a bombshell."

The bartender put their drinks in front of them. Jeff signed the tab.

She leaned into him a little and he put his arm around her, almost like he was protecting her.

"The moment I saw you, I knew..." His voice fell lower, almost to a whisper. "I just knew. What do you say we take our drinks and go to your room? Cuddle up, watch TV. I'll give you a killer back rub."

Jeff still wanted her, but would he be there for her tomorrow and in the days to come?

Maxine's cell phone rang from the depths of her handbag.

"I've got to check the call."

*Finder.*

"Thank god I reached you." He sounded breathless.

"What happened?" she asked. Jeff's eyes held question marks.

"I had a call from the Pompano Beach police. Someone broke into my office. Ransacked the files."

Maxine gulped. The grapefruit that had lodged in her stomach all day felt like a bomb. "Does this involve me?"

"I have to think so. Lotto may have your phone number, even your address."

"But no one knows it." The sick feeling had become a dead feeling. The image of a monkey leered from each of the table lamps and from the painted wall above the bar. Mocking her.

"I used my resources to find your address. The link to your landlady and her father. And I put it in my file. I'm sorry, Maxine."

"Oh my god." She felt a flash of rage. How could he have done that?

Jeff was frowning at her.

"How long ago did it happen?"

"The cops just called. I can come to your place in Boca and check that everything's all right."

"Do what you like. I'm just getting out of here. I'll call you from the road." Maxine pushed the "end" button. *Shit.*

"Someone broke into the PI's office and he thinks they may have my address. I've got to go home right away." *Larry's damned computer*. "Then I have to get out of here tonight."

"Are you crazy? To go back there? That gorilla could be waiting."

"I've got to pick up something important." Maxine remembered the keys to the lock box. She had to grab them, too.

"Nothing is that important." He stared at her with disbelief.

"You still don't know everything."

"Okay, I'll drive you."

"You don't need to get involved in this."

He didn't answer, but took her hand and they rushed out of the orange and brown bar, through the white lounge and the arches and past the potted palms. Jeff handed the parking valet a ten, saying, "We're in a hell of a hurry."

Maxine checked her handbag for her house key.

Jeff shifted from one foot to the other. "Where's that PI's office?" he asked.

"Pompano Beach."

"That's not very far away. Cripes, Pompano Beach, Deerfield Beach and then Boca."

"That's why we have to hurry."

The car jockey pulled up in Jeff's Subaru, and they jumped in.

"I don't have my Smith & Wesson," Maxine said.

"Good. You'd probably shoot yourself in the foot."

~ * ~

They had a straight shot four miles up the Federal Highway. The light at every intersection was red.

"It's not so bad," Jeff said, when she exhaled an impatient sigh. "We'll be there in less than ten minutes." He paused a beat. "Listen, I have an idea. You call nine-one-one and report prowlers at an address next door to yours." He turned to her. "Then in a minute, I'll report a strange noise around the same address. We'll have half the cops in Boca over there. If the heavies are snooping around, they'll take off with the police running all over the place. What do you think?"

"The police dispatchers all have GPS systems. They might know we're not at the address we're calling from. Hang up after a few seconds—before they can zero in on the location."

He gaped at her, but she had already punched in 9-1-1.

Her voice had an edge of hysteria as she reported "a man looking in the window on my patio," and another one "crouched in the bushes." She hung up with a little shriek.

A couple minutes later, Jeff dialed from his cell phone. "I'd like to report prowlers on Jeffrey Street." He gave an address and continued, "I heard a woman screaming. Better go check." He put the phone in his pocket.

"Listen," Jeff said. "Set your phone to vibrate. We can keep in touch if we're separated. Okay?"

She slipped out of the white jacket she had worn to lunch with Lotto. She pulled off her heels, too, because they would go click-click on the sidewalk.

"We'll park so we can do a Le Mans start out of here, not super-close to the building. I'll go in with you." He wasn't tentative now. Maxine felt so relieved to have a co-conspirator, someone who could plan, who hadn't been running for weeks.

"Larry, you don't have to do this."

His head swiveled. "Larry?"

"Oh Jeff! I'm sorry. It just slipped out."

They stopped at the red light at the intersection of the Federal Highway and Jeffrey Street and watched a squad car race past them.

Jeff said. "Good response time."

Maxine felt some of her tension drain away. Jeff turned at the light.

"We'll still follow the parking plan," he said. "And if the police come to the door, just give them the same story as before. I'll be the concerned neighbor."

They turned into the condo property. The clock on the dashboard read 9:47. Maxine didn't see any police in the first lot.

"Should we try to find the cop cars and park next to them?" she asked.

"No, we follow the original plan." Jeff cut the engine.

Maxine didn't argue. She found her house key, and tucked her cell phone into the pocket of the black dress. As they left the safety of Jeff's Subaru, the night felt heavy and damp, and the dark waterway smelled of brackish seawater. The parking area was well-lit, and strategically placed outdoor lamps splashed the landscaping with ambient light. They spotted the police cruiser in the lot behind the pool. A second cop vehicle pulled up next to it, blue lights flashing.

"Bingo!" Jeff said, giving her arm a little nudge.

Ignoring the police, they took the sidewalk along the waterway, passing the tennis courts and the pool. They found the pavement between the pool area and some shrubbery and approached the building entrance where the condos shared a common hallway. The lights were on in the corridor and everything seemed normal. As Maxine unlocked her front door, her cell phone began to vibrate. She pulled it out of her pocket. *Unknown caller.*

"Don't answer," Jeff said, and after a few moments, the vibrating ceased.

They went into the entry hall and Maxine locked the door behind them. "Don't turn on any lights." She tiptoed into the bedroom and took the flashlight out of the nightstand, glad that she had left all the windows shuttered. Maxine slipped Larry's computer off the top shelf of the closet, grabbed the wad of cash between her beach towels, and stuffed the money into the zippered case. She looked in her nightstand drawer but couldn't find the safety deposit box keys for the Foxborough bank. Her memory froze up. She looked in the computer case and the keys weren't there either. It would be a huge attention-getting hassle to have the box drilled open.

"Maxine!" Jeff called in a loud whisper from the entryway.

With a sinking heart, she looked in the nightstand one last time. Not there. Where was it? Oh god...

She grabbed the bag of kitten chow on her way out, relieved that Lucy was safe with Jeff's sister and Kaylee. They returned to the Subaru at an unhurried pace, with Maxine fuming about the missing key. No cops about, but the squad cars were still in the parking lot.

After Maxine had fastened her seat belt, Jeff said, "Stay here and keep down. I'm going to grab a couple of things out of my place. I'll be right back. Keep your phone on, and don't answer unless it's me. Use the panic button on the key fob if you don't like somebody's looks."

He was gone.

Maxine settled in to wait. As soon as she relaxed, she remembered about the lockbox keys. Not in the nightstand drawer—hidden under the nightstand lamp. How stupid to forget. All this unrelenting stress. Maxine shoved Larry's computer under Jeff's golf bag. She wished she still had the Smith & Wesson clunking around in the bottom of her handbag. *Relax, the cops are here. The area is safe.* Taking only her cell phone and house key, she hurried toward her condo. She saw only one squad car, a good sign. Apparently, no prowlers lurked in the bushes, imagined or real.

She edged into her building, down the hall and into her apartment. She felt her way into the bedroom where a little light filtered through the blinds. She found the lamp and under it the keys in two stiff little cases.

Maxine's doorbell rang. She froze. Who the hell was that?

She left the bedroom and crept down the hall into the living room where she peered through the louvered blinds into the patio. No one visible. She unlocked the sliding door and opened it just enough to ease herself outside. She hunkered down by the little fence that separated her patio from the sidewalk and the canal. She heard the doorbell again. It could be the police. Or a neighbor. Or Lotto's thugs.

She crept around the fence and flattened herself against the bushes, craning to see the sidewalk. A huge man with a shining bullet head walked toward her. He stopped and seemed to listen, and turned right, toward the building's front entrance, or maybe the pool. Maxine looked in the other direction, where the canal made a turn, and thought she saw another man standing by the waterway. He disappeared and she didn't know where he was. Maybe coming around in the opposite direction of the big man.

What if the big man was lurking on the entry walk or by the pool? He would see her. In a few swift strides, she lunged across the sidewalk in front of her patio and stepped onto the wooden dock where a powerboat was tied up. Another big step and she was on the boat. Two more and she was crouched behind the cabin. She waited a moment for her heart to stop pounding and then felt for her phone and pressed the "send" button.

Jeff's voice asked, "You scared the crap of me. Where the hell are you? I'm in the car."

"On a boat. In front of my patio. I saw the big man and someone else. I don't think I can get to the car without them seeing me."

"I can't hear you. Speak up." His voicc had an edge of panic. She repeated her words, as slow and loud as she dared.

"I'll come get you."

"No, that's too risky. I'll swim across the waterway. It's dark. They won't see me." Her heart was racing so that she could barely speak. "Pick me up by the condos across from us."

"Oh God, you can't be serious."

"Hurry up!" She pressed the "end" button. Footsteps on the walk. She heard her patio door slide open and the murmur of deep voices. The door closed and the night was quiet again.

She waited a few minutes to give Jeff a head start, to make sure the men weren't in her vicinity. Maxine stuffed the lock box keys into her bra and put the car keys into the other cup. Easing herself into the water and holding her phone above her head, she waited a moment. The water felt cool, not cold. She didn't see any boats in the channel. Maxine pushed off from the moored boat into the inky water and began a slow sidestroke using her right arm, with her left hand holding the phone out of the water. She tried to maintain a powerful but quiet scissors kick to aid her advance. The waterway at this location was probably less than two hundred feet wide, and Maxine was making good progress considering the soggy dress that wanted to drag her down like an anchor. About halfway across, she heard a motor. She turned her head in the direction of the noise and her left hand and the cell phone went into the water. The running lights on a boat chugged right at her, slow but faster than she could swim. Maxine let go of the phone and treaded water, trying to decide what to do. The boat loomed out of the darkness. She couldn't yell to attract the skipper's attention. The blub-blub-blub of the engine was getting louder, the boat closer.

She jackknifed into a dive, deep under where the boat would pass. The water was pitch black and she felt lost in it and panicky that she would swim into a manatee or some horrible thing submerged in the dark water. Then she heard the boat's motor, a distance away. She clawed her way to the surface. The boat was heading for docks on the Jeffery Street side. She treaded water again to catch her breath and to calm the panic that clutched her.

Were those car lights on the opposite bank? Could Jeff be there already? Maxine started swimming toward the lights, swimming harder than she ever had, harder than in a high school hundred-meter race, harder than she knew she could swim. Inhaling big nourishing gulps of air and trying not to think of her close call with the boat or the wet dress that impeded her progress, Maxine forced her muscles to greater exertion, doing a frantic fifty-yard dash through the murky water. When she was close to the shore, she turned her head enough to see the running lights of the motorboat on the opposite side of the canal. No one had followed her. Maxine treaded water for a moment to get her wind back, and then breast-stroked toward a dock. She had just enough upper body strength to heave herself out of the water. She slogged to where she had seen the headlight beams and she ran into Jeff who gave her a tight, squishy hug. She had never been so glad to see anyone in her life.

## *Twenty-two*

Lotto walked into the kitchen for more ice and rum. Angelika, in a lime-green top that showed plenty of cleavage, was making a big deal out of the veal cutlets, pounding the hell out of them with a mallet. The noise sounded like carpenters demolishing the room.

"I'm preparing them exactly like my grandma did, Lotto." She slipped her hand under his untucked Pink shirt and rubbed his back. "You look tired. A good dinner will pep you up."

In shorts and a silly little apron, Angelika did not look like Lotto's idea of a cook. Still, of all the models, actresses and various women who had passed through Lotto's life in the U.S., Angelika was the only one who knew her way around the kitchen.

"Lotto, I'll make baby Yukon Golds for you. I know you love potatoes. Do you want white or green asparagus? Lotto, do you have any more lemons?"

Lotto this. Lotto that.

"If there is one goddamned hair in that food, I'm going out to eat." Lotto said, taking his drink and returning to the *Miami Herald* and his white leather sofa.

Angelika flounced into the bathroom and returned with her hair in a ponytail and her nose in the air.

This miserable day had disaster written all over it. Angelika had pouted and raged when Lotto said he was leaving for Cartagena tomorrow instead of Sunday. Now there would be no Saturday night clubbing—after his *promise.* To calm the waters, Lotto had agreed that Angelika could cook for him and even spend the night, something he seldom allowed. Of course, she would try to extract a huge bribe for the missed night of clubbing with all the loud music, pulsing lights, sweaty bodies, half of them snorting blow.

A girlfriend was always trouble, but then whores were, well, whores were *putas* and not interesting. A real man didn't need *putas.*

Lotto's wife and children in Cartagena, a well-behaved wife and well-behaved children, would be crazy happy to see him tomorrow night. Their cook wore a proper uniform and stayed in the kitchen. In the meantime, to keep a little peace in his life, he had to dine *a casa* with Angelika.

Lotto slid open the door of his wrap-around balcony twelve floors above Brickell Avenue. The hot, humid air made him feel alive. He leaned against the railing, taking in the panorama of Biscayne Bay, and the dramatic sky at dusk. On Saturday, he would see the sun set in Cartagena. While Angelika fussed in the kitchen, Lotto forgot the spectacle in the west and glommed onto the topic that never left his head for five minutes: how to manage the fallout from his encounter with Maxine Harvey.

He had been sure El Tigre would nab this Maxine before she could get away, but El Tigre's car had been on the wrong side of the street, and Maxine had jumped in and out of the cab and then into the private car and escaped. *Mierda.*

At least El Tigre had noted the license plate and their hacker had been able to get into the car rental records almost immediately. Sheldon Finder, Private Investigator, had rented the car that picked up Maxine. So Maxine had hired a PI to find him. But she must have already had his name. She had called him "Lotto," not Lotario.

An hour ago, Lotto's people had entered Finder's office and found Maxine's home address. If the burglar alarm hadn't sounded, his people might have discovered even more, but Maxine's address had been what they wanted. After dark, his special team captained by El Tigre would find Maxine's place in Boca Raton. In a few hours, Lotto should have a report on the evening's success. Or failure. His eyes narrowed, thinking of failure.

Lotto had to steel himself for another hairy mess. El Tigre must find out what the hell was going on with that woman. Had she talked to anyone besides Finder? Of course, if she had blabbed to the DEA or the police, if anyone had discovered Lotto's network, then the whole problem would require massive adjustments. Before Lotto left for Cartagena at noon tomorrow.

Lotto had a plan in place to leave the U.S. quickly and anonymously, but that was the *disaster plan.* It was all he could do to keep himself from pacing up and down on the balcony like a caged panther.

The sliding door opened, and Angelika untied her apron and announced, "Dinner is on the table."

A green platter heaped with Wiener Schnitzel surrounded by boiled potatoes and a mountain of white asparagus waited. Angelika served him very properly. The veal tasted mild and tender. Lotto liked the little squeeze of lemon on the asparagus and the meat. He ate with gusto, because his appetite for lunch had disappeared when the Harvey woman had stood in front of his table. *Mierda*, the thought of it still made him crazy.

Angelika chatted during the meal, and Lotto had only to nod or look at her sometimes. Finally, he crossed his knife and fork on his plate and put down his napkin.

"Lotto, you ate like—like a truck driver. Did you like my cooking?"

Another nod. He had eaten everything in sight. What more did she want? Women always fished for a man's compliments.

"It was an excellent dinner," he said, lavish with his praise.

"Thank you. Now I have a little favor to ask—"

*Here it comes.*

"It would be so cool if I could learn the *cumbia*. Please, please teach me."

Now he had heard everything. "That's *negro musica*," he said. "For slaves and peasants."

"Lotto! I could learn a few steps. I brought a CD."

He had just agreed to this insane request when his cell rang. He stepped out onto the balcony and pressed, "Encrypt."

El Tigre reporting in. Maxine's page in the PI's files listed two addresses. The first was garbage, a UPS mailbox. The team was leaving for the second Boca address.

"Make her talk before you kill her." Lotto remembered Caliendo's botched death in Boston.

Angelika popped the disc into the CD player and shook her round little butt to the song. She bopped around in front of the sideboard where the area rugs didn't cover the rosewood floor. Lotto didn't tell her how this music recalled carefree teenage years with his friends, the best years before he arrived for college in the U.S.

"Okay, the cumbia is something like a tango, but more like a jitterbug," he said, taking Angelika's hands in his. "Bend your knees a little and watch my feet."

"You have nice legs, Lotto. I like you in shorts." Angelika's eyes caressed his knees, calves and ankles all the way down to his loafers. He felt a little surge of desire. The cumbia was desire set to music. *Negro musica.*

More rum. Music blasting away. Getting into the rhythm of the cumbia, he could recall Maxine, her deep eyes, her hat, her long legs. For a few minutes, he imagined he was dancing with her, admiring her rippling muscles, watching her inhibitions falling away. *Absurdo!*

Angelika noticed he had spaced out and yanked his arm. "Where are you?" He turned his attention back to her, seeing the sweat between her breasts, and her little frown of concentration. Angelika made a decent *cumbia* partner. He wiped his forehead with the hem of his shirt while Angelika sashayed over to the CD player.

A moment later, he heard the pulsing electronic rhythm of the lambada. Angelica called it "our song." She began swinging her hips in a suggestive movement and he joined her, their pelvises grinding together back to front, front to front—sex set to music.

~ * ~

"It's all those freaking phone calls," Angelika said in a low, emphatic voice. "How can you concentrate on anything with your damn cell ringing every ten minutes? Maybe if we got a little sleep..." She touched his hand and nestled into him. What was a king-size bed for if women never let you out of their grasp?

He grunted an assent, feeling eaten by anger and shame. This... this *failure* had never happened before. This was Maxine's doing. He recalled her scent, imagined her dead body, her dead naked body under his merciless gaze. The bedroom, cloaked in the dark of the moonless night, allowed Lotto to glimpse that face with those deep-set eyes staring into his soul. She wasn't dead, not yet. But she would be. He touched her cheek. Warm. Soft moist lips. He ran his finger along her collarbone and caressed her ear, her neck. She caught her breath.

Lotto continued his exploration of the not-quite-dead Maxine, astonished that she began to move and even moan under his caresses. She thrust the sheets away. Progress was swift and sure—like the old Lotto. He couldn't believe his good fortune that Maxine was responding to him, clutching him like a crazed nympho while he showed her who was master. It lasted until they were sated and drenched in sweat, and her still perfumed body felt relaxed and slack against him. She gave one final gasp, and whispered, "Oh Lotto, that was the best ever!"

The faintly German accented voice pulled him out of his fantasy, away from Maxine. *Mierda*. Angelika! The sex had been so real. So good. He was still enjoying the lingering sensations when his cell sounded on the nightstand.

# *Twenty-three*

Finder, in an orange and blue flowered tropical shirt, strode back and forth at the main entrance to the hotel. When Maxine climbed out of Jeff's Subaru, he said, "Oh thank God, you're back! I've been talking to Boca PD—" He did a double take. "You look half-drowned. What the hell happened?"

"I swam across the Waterway."

Finder gave her an uncomprehending look as his eyebrows zoomed toward his hairline. Maxine noticed the half-moons of perspiration on his shirt and beads of sweat on his brow.

Even in the warm, humid night, she couldn't stop shivering. If she could only ditch the wet, soppy clothes. Jeff came up behind her. She introduced him to Finder. Maxine watched them shake hands without any cordiality.

Finder turned to Maxine. "We need to talk."

"Jeff is taking me to his sister's. I can't go back to my place." The dress still dripped canal water. Maxine had sat on Kaylee's beach towels on the ride over.

"Right." Finder rubbed his fingers over his chin. Under the lights of the entrance, his five o'clock shadow gave him a saturnine appearance.

They worked out the logistics. Jeff took off in his Subaru. Finder would act as bodyguard until Maxine was safe with Jeff at Julie's house in West Boca.

A second man joined them. Finder introduced him as Hank, an off-duty cop. "Hank is our bodyguard. He'll follow us."

Hank held up a meaty hand in greeting.

Maxine gave Finder a rundown of the last hour, including seeing the enormous bald man and another creep entering her apartment.

Finder said the police had just missed apprehending the intruders. "The cops think Lotto's men had posted a lookout."

"Did you mention Lotto's name?" she asked.

"Damned right I did."

Up in her hotel room, Finder sprawled in a chair watching TV while Maxine showered and dressed. From the bathroom, she heard gunshots and sirens. A cop show. She put the pink clothes on again, with white slacks, dried her hair and scooped all the hotel toiletries into her bag.

Maxine realized her only clothes were the few garments she was folding into the small suitcase. A handful of cosmetics. One swimsuit. She had become a refugee. Her hand found the hard metal of the Smith & Wesson in the suitcase pocket, which she zipped shut. The little Maxine owned she'd left for Lotto's thugs to paw over. She wanted to scream. For the last time, she glanced out the window at the view. Bright lights and dark water. She looked at the room with its soft linens and perfect decorating. She wouldn't likely be staying anywhere this upscale for a long time.

Finder hadn't said much, but he looked like hell, with his black whiskers and bloodshot eyes. She couldn't forgive him for his snooping, and she didn't like that he was the weak link, the link connecting her to Lotto. She had to think about this some more. Tomorrow on the road.

When he realized she had finished packing, Finder stood.

"Whatever I say now won't begin to tell you how sorry I am."

"I guess this was bound to happen sooner or later." She always knew she was living in Florida on borrowed time.

"The Boca cops locked up your apartment. They'll keep an eye on the place. They didn't think anything had been taken. Did you get everything you needed? That was a damned close call."

"I grabbed some cash and cat food." Nothing could make her tell Finder about Larry's PC, or the deposit box key.

"I'll go over and clean out the fridge for you, if you like." He paused and their eyes met. "Did you get some clothes? I can send you some if you'll tell me what—"

He looked so abject, standing with his hands by his sides, staring at her with his wrinkled forehead. "Jesus, Maxine. Say *something*."

"I'm leaving for Boston tomorrow with Jeff. In his RV. With his little girl and my cat. I'll call you when I get a new phone."

"Lotto must have traced me through the rental car," Finder said. "It's the only thing that makes sense. He must have someone working at the airport. Probably bribed a counter clerk. Or he has a hacker on his payroll."

"Doesn't matter. I'm on a cash only basis." Maxine looked around the room once more to make sure she had left nothing behind. She had wadded up the black dress and stuffed it into the hotel laundry bag. It might be ruined. She chided herself for being selfish, making such a big deal out of leaving with nothing but the clothes on her back. She had plenty of money, two computers, a ride, and maybe a bonanza waiting in Panama. She had Jeff, who was putting his life on hold for her. And sweet, loving Lucy. Even the imperfect Finder.

"You have plenty of money?" Finder reached for his wallet.

"I'm good." She grabbed the laptop. He turned off the TV and picked up her suitcase.

In the elevator Maxine said, "You'll keep looking for Honora, won't you?" She had actually considered sacking Finder for snooping on her, but what good would that do? She'd have to start all over, and she had done such diligent research to find somebody competent. He had simply satisfied a PI's natural curiosity.

Finder gave a vigorous nod. "Absolutely. Honora is my priority."

She checked out and they left the hotel. Hank was standing in the entrance, shooting the breeze with the car jockey. She handed over the valet ticket.

"Hank will follow us in my car and I'll drive yours," Finder said. "We'll make sure everything looks all right around the sister's place. Then we'll get out of your hair."

"You'll take my car back to my condo?"

"The least I can do. We'll go through it and make sure there aren't any receipts, anything pointing to you."

The valet zoomed up to the entrance in Maxine's Volvo. She gave Finder Julie's address which he punched into his GPS. Maxine had to restrain herself from ordering him not to save the location. He must have been reading her mind because he said, "I'll delete the destination after we get there."

They left the safety of the hotel grounds, and Finder cleared his throat and rubbed his chin.

"About your sister Honora," he said, turning to look at Maxine. "I don't have much to go on. Is there anything else I should know, something that may help me locate her? We've got old addresses, here and on the West Coast, and maybe a kid born about six and a half years ago. Maybe a drug habit, but that could be in the past. Any more old friends? Relatives? You said she freaked when your folks died. You mentioned guilt. What was that all about?"

Maxine didn't speak while Finder turned right onto the Federal Highway. The GPS said, *Follow the road.*

She felt so alone, so desolate, as if this were her last night on earth. She leaned her head back and spoke in a toneless voice.

"I was married and living on Long Island. Honora was a college sophomore. Somehow she discovered our mother was having an affair. Honora was always a daddy's girl and she was terribly upset. So she hinted at...at the situation to our father. He always had a hair trigger temper." Maxine remembered the cycles of shouting and gesticulating and then the abject apologies. Her throat tightened. "He might have found out sooner or later, or maybe the whole thing would have blown over with no one the wiser." She paused, uncertain if she could continue.

"So what happened?" ask Finder. His voice was gentle. Maybe he had already guessed.

"My father went crazy. He followed Mom and her boyfriend to a motel. Broke into their room. Shot them both and killed himself. " Maxine thought she would hyperventilate, relating this horrible story one more time. The years had not made the telling any easier. She still recalled Honora's hysterical voice on the telephone, screaming, "Daddy is dead! Mom is dead! It's all my fault."

"Jesus. And so your sister blamed herself. For letting the cat out of the bag."

Maxine winced, but that was exactly what had happened. "She said she couldn't go back to school. Locally, of course, there were endless stories and coverage in the paper. I wanted Honora to come and stay with me for a few weeks, but she got in my mom's car and took off for California. Some old boyfriend lived there, but it didn't work out. According to the will, Honora's share of the estate was in trust for her until she turned twenty-one, which happened a year later. She went through the money like it was water."

Finder lit a cigarette and handed it to Maxine. He cracked the window.

"God, I'm sorry. That must have been rough." Finder paused. "How did *you* handle it?"

The GPS said, *Prepare to turn left onto Glades*.

"Somehow I got through the scandal and all the horrible publicity. My husband couldn't cope with it. He hung around for a year, and then he asked for a divorce. That's when it hit me. *I had lost everyone.* My entire family. By then Honora was doing drugs, sleeping around, refusing help, stonewalling me. I had a useless degree in history, and so I went back to school and learned computer programming." Maxine felt tears building up. She stared out the window so Finder couldn't see her cry.

"That really sucks. You poor kid."

Pity never helped. Actually, nothing helped. Maxine stared at the streetlights, the strip malls, the banks, the fast food places, everything looking normal. The Florida Turnpike loomed ahead. She tossed the half-smoked cigarette out the window and wiped her eyes with the back of her hand.

*Turn right in 200 feet. Prepare to turn right on Meridiana.*

"If Honora can be found, I'll do it. Promise." Finder's solemn voice reassured Maxine. She tried to imagine Honora a mother, even picture a little niece or a nephew, a dark, solemn child with big eyes, a kid about Kaylee's age.

"Julie's house is on the right." Maxine was relieved to see Jeff's Subaru in the driveway. Finder parked by the curb. Maxine moved to get out of the car, and Finder jumped out and held her door for her. Another car pulled to the curb and Finder gave Hank a thumb's up. Finder popped the trunk and handed Maxine her luggage. She grabbed the hotel laundry bag with the soggy black dress.

The neighborhood was quiet with the only sound the drone of the television in Julie's living room. The entrance courtyard was a mass of green leaves and yellow hibiscus. Foliage gone wild.

"Now you take care, "Finder said. " Is this guy reliable?" His scowling face indicated that maybe Jeff wasn't.

"Yes. I trust him. He's my neighbor."

"I'll take care of whatever needs doing. Just give me a heads up when you're coming back. Stay away for a while is my advice."

"That's the plan," Maxine said, although there was no plan.

He gave her a bear hug. Jeff came out of the house and stood by the front gate, shaded by the shrubbery. They watched as Finder pulled away.

Jeff said, "I'm glad you're here," and put his arm around her.

"What did you tell your sister?"

Jeff held the front door for her. "Pretty much the truth. I said if anyone comes looking for me, tell whoever it is I'm back on the golf tour."

"Is Julie okay with everything?"

Jeff's answer was a quiet "Yup," making Maxine wonder.

"Your computer's in Kaylee's room." He noticed the case Maxine carried. "*Another* laptop? Cyber girl!"

She knew he was trying to make a joke, but any reference to Larry's computer yanked her chain.

Julie came out of the kitchen to meet them. She gave Maxine a quick hug. Maxine was always astonished to notice the cut-from-the-same-mold resemblance among Jeff, Julie and Kaylee.

"What rotten luck!" Julie said.

"I'm sorry to arrive on your doorstep like this," Maxine murmured.

Maxine and Jeff stepped onto the red tiles of the living room floor where Kaylee's dolls and books littered the area. Lucy came scampering out and rubbed against Maxine's legs. "Hi, sweetie," Maxine said, bending down to pet the purring kitten.

"Kaylee loves that cat," Julie said. "I'm making some good strong tea."

"Pour a little rum into it," advised Jeff. He turned to Maxine. "Julie says you can sleep with Kaylee and I'll take the couch.

Maxine nodded. *Not tonight*. She wondered how awkward this must be for Jeff. She wished they were already on the road.

Julie returned with a tray holding the tea paraphernalia.

Now that she was safe and normalcy had returned, Maxine experienced a sudden fatigue so overpowering she feared she would fall asleep on the sofa, mug in hand.

Jeff must have noticed her exhaustion. "You need shuteye." he said, and led her into the bedroom where Kaylee slept. "I'll get your suitcase."

The nightlight revealed Kaylee sprawled on the sheets clutching a rabbit that was all ears and legs. Maxine sat on the bed with her head in her hands. Maybe this trip wasn't a good idea. The cat, the little girl...everything seemed fraught with complications.

Maxine heard Jeff and Julie whispering in the living room. If she had her Volvo, she would just take off and drive. Drive until she dropped, like on the way down here. Drive to Boston and find the Panama bank account number in the safety deposit box. Then what? A trip to Panama and newfound wealth? California and search for Honora? The idea of so much travel was daunting.

Jeff popped in and put her suitcase beside the bed. "We can do a quick load of wash in the morning," he said in a whisper. "Julie put your wet dress in the laundry room. Will Kaylee ever be surprised when she wakes up with you in the other bed?" He put his arms around her. "Wish it would be me. Do you need anything?"

"I'm good."

"Julie has to leave early tomorrow, so we won't be in her hair."

Maxine felt too stupefied with tiredness to answer, but not too tired to share a long kiss. If not for Julie and Kaylee, it would happen now.

"You smell like soap. Nice," he said.

"Better than canal water."

"I was crazy the whole time you were swimming." His hand brushed against her cheek. "When I saw you come out of the water, I was the happiest man in Florida." He pulled her to him again. "Tomorrow we'll be alone...kinda sorta."

~ * ~

Maxine woke to the low sound of voices. She had no idea where she was, and then she saw the nightlight and heard Kaylee's even breathing. Julie's voice, from her tone, not happy. Maxine rose and tiptoed to the door.

"I don't like the idea of Kaylee taking off on this crazy trip. You don't know anything about this woman, but it looks like trouble follows her around like, like that cat. Leave Kaylee with me for a week. I'll hire a babysitter during the day. She'll be fine. Mark my words, that cat in the camper will be nothing but trouble. I wish just once you would listen to reason."

Maxine couldn't hear Jeff's answer.

Julie's voice rose shrilly. "Why do you always latch on to these damaged women? First Lisa, and now this one."

Jeff's reply was still inaudible.

Julie's "big sister" voice. "'Running's not a plan. Running's what you do when a plan fails.'"

"Did you just make that up?" Jeff asked.

"No. It's from a movie. Remember Earl Basset?"

"Well, running is the new plan."

"I didn't know you were sleeping with anyone." Julie's voice held an accusatory note.

"We're just friends."

"That takes the cake." She paused. "You better get some sleep."

Maxine darted back to bed. She wanted out of there as fast as possible. In the morning, she would suggest what Julie said. Leave Kaylee and Lucy behind. She and Jeff could zip up to Boston. Maybe take Jeff's car instead of the big RV. Run fast.

~ * ~

The first argument came early in the morning. When she found out they were traveling to Boston instead of the Everglades, Kaylee's face turned red, and she threw her rabbit across the room and stomped her foot.

"Sweetheart, it's too hot for the 'Glades. We'll go this fall. I promise."

Then Kaylee insisted on a bath instead of a shower. "I hate showers," she screamed at Maxine, and charged out of the bathroom in her underpants. "You're not my mother. You can't make me."

Jeff took Kaylee's arm, walked her back to the bedroom, and closed the door. Aghast at this defiant side of Kaylee, Maxine sat at the round kitchen table with a mug of coffee. All kids had issues. Surely, this was a storm that would blow over. Lucy rubbed against her legs and purred.

Maxine had that hollow feeling in her chest as if someone had died. It could have been her. Not once yesterday, but twice. She felt so vulnerable. Talking about her parents with Finder brought the old pain to the surface, a hurt that never healed.

And she craved a cigarette with an unrelenting urgency. Jeff didn't smoke in front of Kaylee. How would they be able to indulge their nicotine habit? This is what it came down to. Sneaking behind a seven-year-old's back for a smoke. Disgusting.

Jeff had nixed the idea of leaving Kaylee and Lucy behind, an idea that sounded better to Maxine with each passing minute.

"Lotto could find out about Kaylee and use her to get to you," he said. "She's safer with us."

End of discussion. Then, Jeff's voice rose in exasperation when Maxine had expressed concern about taking Lucy along. "On the tour there were cats, dogs and hamsters. Someone even traveled with a rabbit. I've got a big motorhome. It's a non-issue. We'll stop at a pet store and get a leash. Lucy's young. She'll adjust."

Jeff came out of the bedroom and Maxine heard him running a bath.

"Lots of bubbles!" Kaylee shouted from the bedroom. When Kaylee was in the tub, Jeff returned to the kitchen and poured a mug of coffee. His shoulders slumped and his face lacked its usual optimistic smile.

"New problem," he said, sitting across the table from her. "Are you up for a trip to Chicago after we're done in Boston?"

"I guess so."

Jeff splashed milk into his coffee and stirred. Frowning, he seemed to be picking his words. "The reason Kaylee is such a mess this morning is that her mother called last night." He stared out the kitchen window. "Lisa told Kaylee she might have to live with her Aunt Peg this fall. Peg is Lisa's older sister. She lives way the hell in a western suburb of Chicago. Kaylee would have to change schools. Peg's two boys bully Kaylee. I can't imagine where Lisa would get such a hare-brained idea."

"Call Lisa and ask her what's going on." Maxine operated under the theory that the only dumb question was the one you didn't ask.

"She won't pick up the phone when she's sees my number."

"Call her from here."

"She sleeps late. She wouldn't be up."

Maxine wanted to say, *wake her up*, but she wanted to avoid involvement with Jeff's high-maintenance ex-wife.

Life had become a demented scavenger hunt. Find the key to the Foxborough lockbox. In the lockbox, you'll find Larry's secret account number for the offshore bank. Drive to Chicago and discover why Kaylee's mother has gone nuts. Fly to Panama and get the skimmed money. Avoid Lotto and his "helpers." *Or not.*

~ * ~

They left Julie's around ten, heading for the RV storage in Delray Beach. The morning sun promised today would be another "hot one." In the pale sky, an unhealthy looking haze erased the normal blue. The television weather predicted thunderstorms in the afternoon. Confined to the cat carrier on the back seat, Lucy emitted her mournful meow at regular intervals. Maxine hoped she didn't howl all the way to Boston. Sometimes Maxine peered into the rear view mirror, relieved that no one was following them.

"We'll leave this car sitting in the RV spot," said Jeff over the cat's wails. "The storage area is fenced and secure, so no one can get in without the code." He paused. "Should anyone try."

"Is the camper registered in your name?" asked Maxine. She wondered how long it would take Lotto to learn about Jeff and maybe even locate Julie.

"I incorporated myself when I was on the golf circuit, and the camper is still registered to *Closer to the Hole.*"

That would buy them some time.

Maxine pulled her recorder out of her handbag and said, "Buy a cat harness. Buy a gun safe. Inventory the camper supplies. Make a grocery list. Get underwear, socks, sneakers, and t-shirts. Some shorts and a hoodie."

"Why do you talk into that thing?" Kaylee asked, still prickly as a hedgehog.

"I leave reminders for myself."

"Can't you just write it down like a normal person?"

"I could, but I like to do it this way. Here, do you want to leave yourself a reminder?"

"How do you turn it on?" Kaylee looked intrigued in spite of her snide remark.

"The sound of your voice activates it." Maxine explained, handing the recorder to Kaylee.

"Awesome." She assumed a serious expression, like a news anchor, as she held the machine to her mouth. "Sound of voice, ready, actibate. Visit Plymouth Rock when we get to Boston. I want a little red lobster toy. And please God, could we go to a water park?"

Jeff and Maxine laughed and agreed this was an excellent list. They turned onto Military Trail and a few minutes later, they were at the RV storage facility. Jeff punched in a code and the gate swung open.

"Awesome," Kaylee said. She held the recorder next to the cat carrier. "Say something, Lucy."

Lucy obliged with another plaintive meow.

The lot looked like an encampment. Motorhomes of various lengths rested alongside folding camping trailers, fifth wheel trailers and towable RV's of every length and color parked in neat rows. Jeff pulled up next to a blue and white behemoth.

"My god, it's a bus!" Maxine took in the expanse of wrap-around windshield, big windows, and the long body that went on forever. She had envisioned something more primitive, a camper with at least a tentative connection to roughing it, maybe a truck camper. This looked like a huge...target, visible from miles away. *Get a grip.*

"Twenty-seven feet of comforts," Jeff said, beaming like a proud father as Maxine gaped. "1995 Monterey Cobra with all the amenities. A home away from home. What made being on the tour actually bearable."

Maxine toted Lucy inside and placed the carrier on an upholstered sofa behind the driver's seat.

Jeff said, "We can stash her litter box in the shower stall."

They dumped all the luggage on the full-sized bed in the rear, a bed Maxine was pleased to notice, had privacy if the compartment door was shut.

"We'll gas up and take on some water. See what's in the larder. Probably not much." Jeff started the engine, and said, "Whew! She's rarin' to go."

Kaylee had climbed into the big swivel chair on the passenger's side. There was a small television set where a rear-view mirror should be. The kitchen and dinette had storage and even a microwave.

Twenty minutes later they were on the road again, tooling north on I-95 to the gun store in West Palm Beach. Lucy, free again, sat on the big bed in back, staring out of the window with the same look she had had when Maxine sat in Nicole's whirlpool in Key West. *I can't believe my eyes.*

While Jeff and Kaylee waited in the hot parking lot, Maxine purchased an aluminum handgun safe, a five-foot security cable and even a padded shoulder strap for transporting the safe. She stuck the safe and accessories in a locker high above the bed. Back in the passenger seat, she booted her laptop and found a wi-fi connection. Pet store. Dollar store. Lunch.

When they had zoomed through various strip malls in West Palm Beach, Jeff eyed the receipts Maxine was stuffing into an enveloped marked *trip expenses*. "Spending money like drunken sailors in a Mexican whorehouse on New Year's Eve," he said, grinning, "but that's strictly hearsay."

Back in the driver's seat after lunch, Jeff traced his finger up the map of the Florida coast along the red line of I-95. "We can make Jacksonville by evening and still have time to buy groceries and cook dinner."

With each mile she put between her and Lotto, Maxine felt a little safer. After a thousand miles or so, maybe she could feel almost normal. She might even shower without the willies, walk into a store without glancing around, and meet strangers without paranoia. Still, a woman who was running for her life, a woman who had a Smith & Wesson and a gun safe, a woman who looked in the rear view mirror every few minutes could never be totally normal. And she was cool with that.

"Won't we need a reservation tonight?" asked Maxine.

"I have a campground guide. Try the glove box."

"There's a Starbucks up ahead. Can you stop for a minute?" Maxine put the computer on her lap and picked up the wi-fi signal. One message from Finder.

*We touched a hot button with the mention of L.L. Now the DEA is having a shit fit. Probably stewing that he got the wind up when you interrupted his lunch. Call me tonight.*

"What?" asked Jeff, who must have noticed that she hadn't breathed for the last thirty seconds.

"Complications. I'm wondering if the DEA had Lotto under surveillance and they're afraid Finder and I screwed everything up."

"Cripes, Max. Isn't that good news if Lotto's been under surveillance?"

"But the big bullet-headed man apparently wasn't."

"Matter of time."

Kaylee sat at the dinette table, engrossed in the toys from the Dollar Store. Lucy slept on the bench across from her in the new Berber faux sheepskin bed.

Kaylee's voice piped up. "I want a cookie." Pause. "Please."

Waiting in line at Starbuck's, she thought this trip with Jeff and Kaylee was like being married without the courtship, certainly without the honeymoon, but instead with a complicated married life of children and problems.

When she returned, she gave Kaylee the cookie and popped open two frappucinos.

Jeff said, "Let's talk about this new Lotto development." He glanced back at Kaylee, but she was engrossed in the cookie and dressing the dolls. "Do you want to quick buy a phone?"

"This evening is soon enough."

"We're five minutes from every chain store in the world."

"I want to get going," Maxine said, with what she hoped was finality.

"Cripes, Max, you think Lotto's going to stalk you in the Palm Beach Radio Shack?"

Maxine laughed, but she didn't back down, and Jeff pulled onto the Interstate.

"So what's your real opinion of this Finder guy?" asked Jeff, driving north in a mix of trucks, cars and buses. "I was surprised you didn't sack him after the way he snooped on you."

Maxine took a sip of her frappucino. "When I found out, I was angry. But the thing is, I spent so much time doing due diligence on every PI down here. He's the best. Why get rid of him for snooping when that's his job? I had only given him my PO box address." She put the drink in a holder on the dash. "I guess I was too coy, *too* mysterious."

"He really got on the stick for you last night."

"He did."

"You don't think your search is a lost cause?" asked Jeff.

"I have to give it my best shot. I know that's what Finder will do, too." She drained the frappucino. "My main regret is that I waited so long."

Maxine leaned back in the chair, and pressed her fingers to her temples. Her well of pain would never run dry. For years, she had blamed Honora when she needed to forgive her sister, and tell her everything was all right, tell her that their parents' deaths weren't Honora's fault.

~ * ~

In the early evening, they found a large, clean KOA campground in North Jacksonville, a peaceful spot surrounded by tall pines.

"Oh cool! A swimming pool and a playground. And kids!" Kaylee ran to the bed and began rummaging through her suitcase. "Can I go swimming? Can I?"

Jeff promised to go out with Kaylee once the hookup was complete. He took her outside while Maxine unpacked the just-purchased groceries and made a quick dinner. Maxine was having fun playing house and getting the hang of the motorhome. She liked sitting high enough to see above the traffic.

Kaylee had met a girl her age at the pool, a girl whom she had promised to see again at the playground. A red-haired girl popped her head in with Kaylee, looked around and said, "Cool!" Maxine heard more comings and goings while she was in the bathroom.

At dusk, the sky turned black in the west and thunder rumbled in the distance. The wind whipped up, and the pines swayed. The motorhome would be a snug cocoon as long as there weren't any tornados.

Then Jeff came in with a white face spotted with freckles and said he couldn't find Kaylee. She wasn't at the playground. The pool had closed. He had insisted she stay where he could see her, and he had walked around the motorhome once and talked to the family camped next to them for a moment and now Kaylee was gone.

"I'll help you look."

"No, stay here in case she comes back."

"Maybe she's with her new friend. The little redhead."

A thunderclap startled them. Jeff left again. Moments later, the rain came, driving sheets against the motorhome. Thunder boomed and lightning flashed. The pines swayed like stalks of corn in a summer wind. Maxine peered out the windows, but the rain was so intense she saw only the lights burning in the campers. She put on Jeff's windbreaker and opened the door. Warm rain blasted her face. A few hardy souls streaked through the storm from the showers or raced to round up folding chairs and picnic gear. No Jeff. No Kaylee.

Maxine went inside and checked the bathroom and bedroom again. That's when she noticed Lucy's absence. She searched the motorhome. Lucy was gone, too.

Maxine waited on the step, oblivious to the pounding rain and the thunderclaps.

Alone. Jeff was alone, sopping wet, trudging toward the camper. As he got closer, Maxine saw that his eyes were crazy with worry.

"I looked everyplace, the laundry, the johns, the little store. I called myself hoarse. Where the hell could she be?"

"Lucy is gone, too. Maybe Kaylee accidentally let her out and ran after her. I'll bet anything Kaylee is snug and dry in someone's RV."

Jeff stood in the rain, craning his neck first one way, then the other. "She's never pulled anything like this before. Maybe we should call the police."

"I'm sure somebody saw a little girl out in the storm and took her in." Maxine tried not to dwell on Julie's prophetic words about Kaylee, the cat and the camper.

"I'm going to knock on doors until I find her." Jeff brushed some rain out of his eyes. "We don't know these people. There could be low-lifes or criminals. Escaped cons. Pedophiles Anybody."

A chill went through Maxine. *Even Lotto's goons.*

Jeff had turned back into the rainy night. Maxine's stomach was a cave of writhing snakes and she shivered in the rain. Kaylee just had to be okay. Most people were kind. Most people would take a scared, wet kid in. Most people.

# *Twenty-four*

At five p.m. Friday, with heat rising from the tarmac, Lotto's flight left Miami for Houston, and not in wide-bodied comfort, but in a 737. Tonight's so-called first-class dinner would make Angelika look like an Iron Chef. Worse, he had to change planes in Houston to get to San Diego. No direct flights and these robbers were ripping him off for over two thousand dollars.

In normal times, Lotto would have hopped on a flight to Cartagena or even Bogotá, but he had switched to furtive mode. Thanks to Maxine Harvey, who had disappeared from the face of the earth after the break-in of her condo. Lotto had no idea where this infuriating cunt might be.

First there was business in San Diego—nothing he was looking forward to. Colombia and the dockyard with the submarine kits was where he wanted to be.

Lotto's black Tumi bag was in the overhead compartment, with a change of clothes and a dumb-ass one-quart plastic bag with his sample size Royal Lime and the rest of his travel-sized toiletries. He had a full tropical wardrobe waiting in Cartagena. At least he was spared the aggravation of traveling with Angelika and so many freaking cosmetics that she had to check her bags. He had a Wii and some games for his kids, along with new sneakers, sweatshirts, and the Harry Potter films. Godiva chocolates and a Ralph Lauren dress for his wife. In his briefcase, he had stashed his laptop, his cell phone, catalogs of Marquesa Trading Company products, along with today's *Miami Herald* and yesterday's *El Universal* that he had grabbed at the airport. Lotto's laptop held the resumés of the three final candidates for Larry Caliendo's job. If anyone searched his luggage, he was a family man traveling on business.

Caliendo's job, cartel accountant for the Northeast region, wasn't advertised in the *Herald* or *El Universal*. There were no trade newspapers in his business. Lotto had extended feelers throughout his underground, and the résumés he had received were reassuringly traditional. Tomorrow at the hotel, he would interview the final three candidates: a Colombian, a Cuban and a North American woman. Interview and evaluate. All had excellent recommendations. He didn't see how any of them could possibly be a plant, but the thought made his heart race.

El Tigre sat in the tourist section with the rest of the peons. To avoid scaring the bejesus out of everyone with his massive bulk and his executioner's eyes, El Tigre wore a 48 XL navy sport coat, khaki trousers and a panama hat with a madras hatband. He could pass for a gentleman if no one looked him in the eye. Lotto actually didn't like El Tigre, but his menace and special skill set were a necessary evil. No one could get answers out of anyone as speedily as El Tigre. No one could kill with such offhand elegance.

Lotto put his head back, reclined his wide leather seat and slept. The flight attendant awoke him for a tiny overdone steak with dribs and drabs of potatoes and vegetables. He almost wished he had taken along the plastic container with Angelika's leftover veal cutlets. He picked at a few bites and dozed again.

Enrique joined them at Bush Intercontinental in Houston. Lotto, Enrique and El Tigre all boarded the plane en route to San Diego, but they didn't sit together or make eye contact. Lotto drank some generic airline rum while he thought about one of the items on his San Diego agenda, a late dinner with his mother. He was paying a visit like a proper son, because she hadn't wanted to dress up and drive all the way from La Mesa to the Del Coronado hotel. He would have provided a lavish meal, but she couldn't be bothered.

Lotto saw his mother once a year, usually in San Diego, although one year they met in Palm Springs and once in San Francisco. He calculated that she must be sixty-two. Stylish, thin, and still intent on her bohemian ways, she never seemed old to him. Better looking and more energetic than these flight attendants with their pasted smiles and support stockings who looked like they should be home with their grandchildren.

Lotto's mother had landed in Cartagena in the mid-sixties, a hippy girl with long blonde hair, a backpack and a fistful of travelers' checks. Trying to cadge drugs, she had cast a spell on his father, an earnest but gullible pharmacist's son, and she had obstinately refused to marry his father. They had christened him, the baby, Lotario, of all silly names, obviously his mother's idea. At the age of two, he had renamed himself Lotto, a name that even as a toddler had suited him better. His mother stayed for three years, until the Summer of Love called her back to California, leaving a confused, blue-eyed boy who spoke childish but fluent English. Her wealthy family had arranged a trust fund for his education, not generous, but enough for Florida schools. Birthdays and Christmas, she remembered, unless she was trekking in Nepal or learning to make batiks in Bali and would not be heard from for months until a card or an exotic gift arrived. "For my precious Lotto."

For his mother, Lotto was hand-carrying a ceramic sculpture of a *chiva*, a colorful Colombian bus, with produce and chickens piled on top and peasants and animals inside and crammed onto the open rear area of the bus.

Lotto's stepmother, Maria, had raised him and two half-brothers in a middle-class, conventional household with Sunday Mass a given, respect for elders, and attention to studies. He appreciated his stepmother for her dedication to raising him to respectability and his mother for her spontaneity and passion for whatever her current interest was. He wondered what she was "into" this year.

The plane banked and he could see the blue Pacific. The jet skimmed down over the San Diego hills, so low it must clip trees and telephone poles, and then they were on the ground.

*Welcome to San Diego. The local time is six-fifty p.m. The temperature is seventy-six degrees. Our captain and crew have enjoyed serving you...*

Enrique had rented a Lincoln town car. Lotto followed him to the parking garage at a distance. El Tigre would make himself scarce until Sunday when he would drive them to Tijuana for a flight to Mexico City and on to Cartagena. So tedious, all this misdirection. Tijuana with its rival cartels and violence was a special hell these days, and Lotto wanted El Tigre's menacing bulk and canny protection. Once Lotto and Enrique were on a flight to the Mexican capital, El Tigre could return to look for Maxine. She wouldn't escape again. What was the saying? *Third time's a charm.*

# *Twenty-five*

Mitch called and wanted Honora in his office. What now? He always came out to her cubicle to discuss VIP events or marketing strategies because his office was a clutter of filing boxes, folders and stacks of paper to rival the height of Donner Pass. Even worse, he kept the temperature so low she needed a down parka to keep from freezing.

Actually, he wasn't a bad boss if you got him out of his office. Honora recalled the horrible managers of the strip clubs where she'd worked. Compared to them, Mitch was all right. But why did he want her in his office? A promotion? No, that would be an occasion for lunch.

She applied fresh lip gloss, touched up her eyeliner and pulled her red V-neck blouse down to reveal more cleavage, then put on her suit jacket. Honora always wore a suit to work—short and tight to make the best of her assets, yet professional looking. She didn't work strictly in the casino back office. Sometimes she assisted operations to make sure key events went off without a hitch. She always wanted to look good.

Mitch, with his short-sleeved shirts and wrinkled khakis, hated the people part of his job and left that to her. His forte was compiling the stats on the success or failure of each marketing event or campaign.

Honora walked by the half-dozen cubicles to Mitch's office. Imagine having a window view of the mountains blocked by the clutter of decades-old campaigns. Why did he keep them?

As usual, his door was closed. She knocked and heard his gruff, "come in."

Mitch sat in his paper-obsessed untidiness. A lock of greasy hair hung over his forehead and flopped across his eye. He looked up and didn't smile, but squared off one of the stacks of paper on his desk. The room felt like a meat locker.

"What's up?" she asked, with an uneasy feeling, like she had glimpsed a snake slithering behind a filing box.

"Yesterday I received a letter from corporate, along with a surveillance tape," he said, looking at his papers.

*Shit.* After three weeks, she thought she was home free.

Mitch looked up at her with a puzzled frown "Why in God's name didn't you just pay the taxes on the jackpot? No one would have ever known you were playing the slots in Tahoe." He waved the letter at her. "Now, I've got no choice but to dismiss you."

"I've got a kid to feed, rent to pay. You'll never find anyone as good as me to do the events." Her voice sounded like she was down on her knees, begging.

"Company policy is company policy. No exceptions."

"But—"

His eyes had an odd gleam. He cleared his throat. "My hands are tied, but there's one thing I can do to help you."

*And I'll bet there's one thing I can do to help you, too, you dirty bastard.*

He cleared his throat again. "The only thing I can do is lay you off instead of firing you. You'll be able to apply for benefits." His smile was conspiratorial. "I'll pull the wool over HR's eyes, but I'm taking a risk, so you need to do *me* a little favor."

"Sure, Mitch, whatever."

He stood and walked past her to lock the door. "And of course you'll get a good reference."

Shit. Mitch and his greasy hair. Why had she thought he was different? Men were pigs.

Honora suppressed her revulsion. Not just of Mitch, but of doing it for money again, like any street girl. What the fuck? This would take five minutes. Not such a bad deal, really. Mitch was gross, but then, life was never fair.

## *Twenty-six*

It had been forty-five minutes, but it seemed like years. Kaylee was clutching Jeff's hand, hanging her head and dragging her feet. Seeing Kaylee safe, Maxine wanted to weep with relief.

"Oh my god, I'm so glad you're back. Where was she?"

Jeff's hair was plastered to his scalp and his mouth was a narrow line. "Kaylee was out looking for Lucy and got lost in the storm."

They climbed into the camper. "I found her on the other side of the campground. A family had insisted she come in out of the thunder and lightning. Kaylee says she took Lucy out to show her to a new friend. Lucy jumped out of her arms and ran under a camper."

Maxine handed Jeff a towel and he dried Kaylee's face and rubbed his hair.

Kaylee burst into tears and said through a spate of sobbing and chattering teeth, "I'm sorry. I just wanted to show Lucy to Emily. The storm scared her and then I couldn't find her anywhere." She threw her arms around Jeff's waist and howled. "And then I got lost."

Maxine crouched by Kaylee so they were at eye level.

"I know you didn't mean for Lucy to get away," Maxine said.

Kaylee cried louder, with gasps and choking noises.

"You love Lucy. She's probably waiting out the storm in a safe, dry spot." Maxine allowed herself to imagine the gray kitten hunkered under a long RV chassis, waiting for the rain to stop. "Cats are good at taking care of themselves." Maxine put her hand on Kaylee's arm.

"But she hates water," sobbed Kaylee. "She doesn't like one drop." Her chin quivered.

"She's under someone's camper," Jeff said. "Probably next door. Let's get you out of those damp clothes."

"I'll take a quick look around." Maxine grabbed a flashlight. "Lucy knows my voice." She clamped the pink baseball cap on her head so the rain wouldn't blind her.

Outside, the lightning and drum rolls of thunder moved east as the storm swept out to sea. Soon the pelting rain had soaked Maxine to the skin. She crept around, calling softly, and bending down to shine the flashlight beam under the campers.

When had anything gone right? Not since the night Larry died. Had only three weeks passed? Last Friday she had been with Nicole. One week and she couldn't even keep a kitten from peril. Like Kaylee, she wanted to howl with frustration, grief, and anger. Instead, she returned to the motorhome and sat on the little metal doorstep with the rain coursing off the brim of the baseball cap. She had to call Finder. Might as well get it over with. Then she could go out and search for Lucy again. She stepped inside to grab her new cell phone.

A pajama-clad Kaylee, eyes bloodshot, sprawled on the dinette bench with her long-eared rabbit clutched in one hand. In the other, she curled and re-curled a strand of damp blond hair around her finger.

"That bad Lucy is still hiding," Maxine said, in as upbeat a voice as she could manage.

Jeff came out of the bathroom. "No luck, huh?"

Looking at Jeff, Maxine said, "I'm going to call Finder." She hung the dripping baseball cap on a hook by the door, and tossed her wet t-shirt into the bathroom sink.

"Sweetheart, you get in bed and I'll read you a story." Jeff tried to take Kaylee's hand, but she pulled away.

"I want to wait for Lucy."

"First a story."

Kaylee made a noise like a long, drawn-out whine. Maxine admired Jeff's patience, as he led Kaylee off to the big bed in back. Maxine had already allowed herself to think of it as *their bed.* Her patience felt like a thin crust on a rumbling volcano. She put on Jeff's sweatshirt, took the cell phone out of its bag and sat on the dinette bench. She wrote down her new cell number and dialed Finder, wondering what he would have to say.

*Finder, pick up the damn phone.*

"I was getting antsy that you weren't going to call me." Finder's voice sounded hoarse, like he had been talking too much. Maxine recalled his haggard appearance last night, the red-rimmed eyes, his unshaven face, so different from the man in suit and snazzy tie who had met her for lunch weeks ago at the Cove.

"So why is the DEA 'having a shit fit?'" Maxine asked.

"They're afraid we've compromised an investigation," Finder said.

"The DEA is investigating Lotto?" Maxine got up, found her handbag by the passenger's seat and took out her mosquito spray. She eyed the cigarettes with longing.

"By the way, we aren't having this conversation," Finder said. Gruffness personified.

It seemed to her that they *were* having this conversation.

"All my information comes from law enforcement people," Finder said. "If I told you something and anyone traced that back to me...I could lose my license. I was a cop for a donkey's age before I became a PI, and sources still talk to me."

Over Kaylee's querulous voice, Maxine heard Jeff reading aloud.

"If you can't tell me anything, then why did I have to call you?" She hated being stonewalled like this.

"It's going to sound stupid, but I've been instructed to warn you that you are not to make contact with Lotto again. Not that you would. And some cop in Massachusetts, Blaisdell, wants to talk to you."

Maxine watched a late arrival lumber down the muddy campground road, headlights on bright.

Finder continued, "My guess is he'll want to know why you didn't tell him about Lotto. Cops kinda get an attitude when witnesses omit crucial facts. You'll need to provide whatever document you have from your late husband that mentioned how to get in touch with Lotto."

Maxine's mind raced like the mechanical rabbit with the greyhounds sniffing its tail. Everything always came back to the information on Larry's computer. "It was just a note and I threw it away after I gave you the information."

Finder said, "Jesus," under his breath. "That's destroying evidence. Tell me you didn't. Was it an email maybe?"

"Just a scrap of paper with the Marquesa Trading Company address. I copied it into my electronic contact list." A half-truth.

Silence on Finder's end.

"So how did the DEA pick up on Lotto?" Maxine asked.

"Could have been an informant, but the Feds have nothing concrete to charge him with yet. They're watching him. That's all I can tell you."

Maxine peered out the window as the big camper plowed through the mud, looking for an empty site.

Finder asked, "You still there?"

"I'm here." She opened the door to look for Lucy. A light rain still fell, but the air smelled clean with a whisper of ocean tang and a few wisps of smoke from the charcoal grills. Puddles glistened under the few lights strung around the campground, showing the way to the showers and the little store. RV generators hummed, keeping the AC going in the always-muggy air. Maxine stood on the little step, waiting for a wet cat to appear.

Finder was talking again. "...the DEA will be able to link your late husband to Lotto. That should help."

Maxine stood rooted at the door. "You mean the investigations weren't connected until now?"

"No. So, in that respect, the Feds should be kissing your ass."

Still no kitten. She lit a cigarette and inhaled the smoke deep into her lungs.

Finder continued, "I told Blaisdell you'd stop by when you were up his way. He's expecting you. Give him a call."

*"You told him what?"* Finder had overstepped the boundaries. Again.

"It won't hurt you to talk to them. Locking up Lotto would increase your chances of survival, don't you think?"

"In the future, please don't tell anyone I'll call or meet with them. From now on, your job is finding my sister. Is that clear?"

"Have you been upfront with me, Maxine?" Finder asked.

"Of course." *As much as she dared.*

She flipped off the phone, and heard her cigarette sputter as she tossed it in the mud. Finder was still a loose cannon, making promises for her.

All was quiet inside the RV. Jeff must have fallen asleep, too. Maxine doused herself with bug repellant, grabbed a lantern and stepped outside again. She had to find Lucy.

Calling softly, she made the rounds of the muddy campground, again. In the morning, she'd have to go knocking on doors. Of course, she could start now, but some inhibition held her back.

A big spray of drops hit her face as the wind blew the water off the overhead leaves. While she prowled through the darkness, Maxine thought about what Finder had said. In her heart of hearts, she knew he was right. She should meet Blaisdell and turn over Larry's computer and the Panama bank account paperwork. That would be the ethical, honest act, and one that might take the heat off. *Might.*

She felt the "bad angel" perched on her shoulder stir, advising secrecy and delay before making such a game-changing commitment. And Maxine would be going back on her word to Lotto, but if Lotto had really believed her, he wouldn't have sent in his goons.

What convinced Larry that Lotto was an "an OKAY guy?"

*We all have our delusions.*

Maxine returned to the motorhome; she felt hollow inside, like a dead tree split down the middle by lightning. Sitting on the metal step, she made some calculations. With her inheritance and what she had saved, she had accumulated almost half a million, but that had been in free fall with the stock market and the economy tanking. Finding a job would be difficult. She didn't want to work in IT anymore with the deadlines, the constant stress, and the self-important people. She didn't own a house, not even a car, little more than the clothes on her back.

The X factor was whether Finder would locate Honora. If Honora had a child, who would pay for college? Not the overseas father. Probably not Honora, who might need months of detox, rehab, or even years of therapy. Those costs could be huge. Finder might plow through a big wad of cash just trying to find Honora. Maxine saw her nest egg dwindling.

It would be crazy to give up the Panama bank account until she could see what lay ahead. She could turn over the money anytime. Larry's money, paid for with his life. And Corky. In the years to come, he would need a small fortune for his care. Maxine would play a waiting game until Honora was found. *If* she were found. In the meantime, Corky had Larry's money for support.

Maxine woke with a start. She had dozed off, perched on the little metal step with her head propped against the door. Something furry purred and rubbed against her ankle. Maxine reached for the kitten. "Come here, you bad cat." Lucy, not even damp, nestled against Maxine's chest.

"I hope you learned your lesson," whispered Maxine, burying her face in the gray fur.

~ * ~

Coming into New Haven Wednesday afternoon with Jeff behind the wheel, the motorhome crawled through the endless traffic jam on I-95.

"West Haven, East Haven, New Haven. I would say No Haven should be next." Jeff was still able to joke with all three lanes mired with cars, trucks, and buses.

One of the things Maxine liked about Jeff was that he stayed calm, and that kept her calm, too.

"Wouldn't it be awesome to have a motorcycle?" Kaylee watched two Harleys find paths through the clogged mess that a bigger vehicle couldn't.

A jackknifed truck had shut down two lanes. In the ninety-degree furnace, vehicles overheated, compounding the horror show.

Kaylee, sprawled in the dinette with Lucy curled up at her side, began singing "Hot Child in the City," for the umpteenth time.

Maxine checked her watch again as she did every two minutes. The bank closed at 4:00. Jeff wanted to drive beyond Albany where they would have a straight shot to Chicago tomorrow. If they could find a campground. If they got to the bank on time.

Maxine realized that during the past few days, they had become like a traditional family, with Jeff making decisions and doing most of the driving, while Maxine planned menus and entertainment. Kaylee and Lucy stayed in kid and pet roles. Fights and arguments in the confinement of the motor home would be a special hell.

~ * ~

Late last Saturday, with the storm behind them and Lucy safe in her faux sheepskin bed, they had driven to Myrtle Beach and camped at a huge RV park on the ocean.

Sunday, Father's Day, with Kaylee at the park's kids' program, Maxine and Jeff had cemented their couplehood with two hours of privacy in the big bed with rambunctious Lucy, who lunged at any movement under the covers, locked out. Maxine confided to Jeff that with a year of no sex she wasn't sure if she remembered how, but Jeff said it was like riding a bicycle—something you never forgot. That made them both laugh. She and Jeff seemed right for each other, a little awkward at first, then passionate. Maxine felt more relaxed with the sexual tension abated, but she was glad they had waited. With Larry, Maxine had always pretended her ardor and imagined an attractive actor or rock star in the bed, but with Jeff she didn't have to.

On Monday, while they waited for an expensive new water pump in Fayetteville, North Carolina, Jeff called his sister who reported that the DEA had a tap on her phone and someone watching her house after a guy pretending to be Jeff's friend came to her door. When Julie told the "friend" that Jeff was back on the tour, the guy obviously did not connect "tour" to "golf," and Julie had called the number scribbled on Finder's business card.

Lotto's people had probably used the simple expedient of asking around the pool, talking to neighbors. Everyone had seen Maxine, Jeff and Kaylee together. Maxine prayed Lotto's people hadn't found out about Jeff's motorhome.

From the road, Jeff had finally reached Lisa, the ex-wife of wrath. When he asked if anyone had been asking about him, she barked so loudly Maxine could hear her words on Jeff's phone. "What have you got yourself involved in now? I suppose you owe money on your credit cards. Just make sure your child support isn't late. I'll be happy to tell those leeches to go to hell, but right now I'm waiting for this goddamn heat wave to break. Put Kaylee on, will you?"

Kaylee told Lisa about the water park, the beach, the big pool, and even the kids' club, but the words *Boston, Myrtle Beach* and *motorhome* didn't cross Kaylee's lips. Kids instinctively knew what not to say. Her little girl voice grew low and solemn as she said, "yes," and "okay" in response to Lisa's words. Talking to Mom must be stressful.

Yesterday Jeff taught Maxine how to drive the Cobra, but she was so cautious they only covered 400 miles. Maxine always parked in the wide-open spaces at the end of the lot when they stopped for groceries or supplies. "Walking is good for you," she reminded a grumbling Kaylee, as they trekked across the asphalt in the heat.

Maxine had received an email from Finder confirming the DEA was watching Julie's house in case Lotto's henchman showed up again. Maxine felt guilty and low about involving others in Lotto's vendetta. Julie would never forgive her, yet Jeff acted unfazed. Was he in denial or did he just roll with the blows?

Finder's email confirmed he was on Honora's trail again. California recognized his Florida PI license and he could work there if necessary. Only a sliver of good news, but it was something.

~ * ~

Pulled back into in the endless sludge of traffic on I-95, Maxine heard a report indicating the accident had been cleared and traffic through New Haven was nearly back to normal. They had less than two hours and one hundred miles to go to arrive at the Foxborough bank. Jeff drove like a demon.

At 3:45, he pulled into the CVS parking lot, and Maxine, toting a carryall, ran across the busy street to the bank. Earlier she had retrieved one of the lock box keys from a pocket in Larry's computer case, and a few minutes ago, she logged on to Larry's computer to double-check the bank information. Maxine found the bank in Larry's Outlook contacts with the note: safety deposit box, and the box number. *Larry being Larry.*

Jeff had promised Kaylee a Burt's Bees kit and the two of them were going into CVS. Inside the bank, a woman ushered Maxine downstairs to the vaults. She thumbed through the Cs in a metal box of cardholders' information and pulled out a card with Larry's signature scrawled on the bottom line. Maxine's name was at the top, but she had only signed into the box once. Larry had many signatures, the last one three days before his death, May 26th. Looking at the familiar scrawl made Maxine want to weep.

She took the key from its red case and handed it to the woman. Maxine wondered if it was illegal to get into the box with Larry dead, but she ignored her qualms. The box looked larger than she remembered, and it felt heavier than expected. She hurried into one of the small rooms off the vault.

Maxine pulled open the metal lid on the long gray box. In spite of the air conditioning, she felt sweat on her back and underarms. On top, an inventory of the contents. Larry's orderly ways again. She glanced at his list. He had itemized half a dozen manila envelopes, each crammed with five thousand dollars in one hundred dollar bills. Maxine's trembling fingers riffled through a wedding license and the paid off mortgage on Larry's house. Their house.

She found her expired passport. Larry must have stashed it there. If anyone ever quizzed her about getting into the box, she could say she had picked up her passport.

Where was her current passport? Not with her. She hadn't seen it in Florida, either. She stared at the navy cover with "United States of America" embossed with the ornate seal. Maxine flipped the passport open and glanced at her photo. God, she looked young. Fifteen years ago. She was young. Had she left her current passport at home in Sharon? Impossible to fly outside the U.S. without it. Maxine noticed the stamp from her first honeymoon. *Bermuda Immigration Admitted, October 4.* Yet her heart felt a needle-stab of anguish. She tossed the passport into the carryall. Too many memories.

At the bottom of the box, she found a fat envelope labeled "Panama." There was a single sheet of paper inside, another inventory listing the account number, a lawyer's name and contact info. Notation of paperwork for an offshore corporation. Paperwork for the sale of a house in Panama. A debit card and hundreds of C-notes, crisp and new. And some bearer bonds for $100,000 each. *Jesus.*

Maxine jammed the Panama envelope inside her carryall. She grabbed one envelope with five thousand dollars and the inventory, and stuffed everything else back into the box—all those envelopes stuffed with cash. *Leave them be.* Maxine opened the door and said, "All set" to the vault custodian who was waiting by the card file.

Did anyone else know about the safety deposit box? The bill would land with Larry's executor. Of course *she had the keys.* They would have to drill the box open. Her signature would show the date of her visit. *Worry about that later.*

Maxine felt a rush of relief as the custodian returned the box to its slot and locked it twice. She slipped the returned key back into the red case. Clasping the carryall firmly under her arm, Maxine glanced at the wall clock. Three fifty-eight. Thirteen minutes had passed. She climbed the stairs, crossed the lobby and pushed open the door, nearly colliding with a man in a hooded sweatshirt and sunglasses.

Kind of hot for a sweatshirt. The man brushed by Maxine without apology. Everyone always in a hurry.

Maxine reached the crosswalk, and waited for an impatient pickup to pass. The rush hour was in full swing, but the traffic stopped for her. She threaded her way across the CVS parking lot to the motorhome. Inside, she found Kaylee at the dinette table examining a new Burt's Bees travel kit. Jeff sat across from Kaylee.

She gasped. Jeff was reading his email on Larry's computer. In her hurry to get into the bank, she had left it on. Password enabled.

*The computer that was never, ever to go online was wide open.*

"Oh my God!"

Jeff looked up.

"What's the matter? Did you find what you were looking for?"

"Turn that off right now. We've got to get out of here."

"I'm not done with my email."

Maxine kept her voice low so that Kaylee wouldn't be alarmed. "That's not my computer. It's Larry's. It could be sending a message pinpointing our location. To the police or to Lotto. Turn it off!"

Jeff pushed the button. "Cripes, Maxine. How much skin do you have in this game?" His wary eyes searched hers.

"Plenty. We have to put some distance between this parking lot and us. You drive."

"Did you rob the bank or something?" Jeff didn't smile, but climbed into the driver's seat. Maxine walked to the back of the RV and put the laptop and the contents of the carryall into the locker with the gun safe. She counted out five hundred dollars, which she stuffed in her pocket

The street crawled with traffic; Jeff had to wait behind a line of cars exiting the parking lot. Maxine saw the guy in the sweatshirt and sunglasses carrying a white shopping bag dart toward a gray Corolla in the bank's parking lot. While she watched, the bag emitted a big puff of red smoke. The man stared with horror at the bag, and dropped it. He leaped into the Corolla, which jumped the curb and veered into the traffic, causing brakes to squeal.

In the distance, Maxine heard a siren. That man had robbed the bank.

Jeff gave her a questioning look. Even in her heightened state of paranoia, Maxine understood that the car with the siren was coming for the bank robber, not Larry's laptop, but she felt her body tense, each nerve taut like a guitar string. A second siren sounded, a few blocks away. *Oh God.*

Kaylee pulled her attention away from the little tubs and tubes of Burt's Bees and looked out the window. "I hear a lot of sirens, Daddy."

Jeff scowled.

The motorhome was next in line to exit the parking lot. A cop car with flashing blue lights pulled into the bank, and another squad car raced in from the opposite direction. Jeff's face had paled, making his freckles pop out. From nearby, Maxine heard a third siren. Jeff backed the motorhome the entire length of the parking lot and slowly jockeyed a turn around, pointing them to a second exit. Squad cars blocked the street in front of the bank. Siren wailing, another one arrived.

"Cool!" Kaylee said. "Maybe somebody robbed the bank."

Jeff shot Maxine a look.

"It was the guy in the sweatshirt," she said.

"You *saw* someone?" Jeff's voice was incredulous.

"When I left. He practically pushed me out of the way."

"Oh crud!"

"No, it's good. They're looking for the robber, not us."

Jeff pulled out of the CVS' back entrance, and the motorhome lumbered around the town square, passing the bandstand and the hardware store. They zoomed east past the big Victorian houses on the tree-lined street.

"Let's get out of here before someone remembers you."

"Right," Maxine said. Whenever she doubted Jeff's dedication to their cause, he surprised her. Another squad car, blue lights flashing, siren howling, passed by them en route to the center of Foxborough.

Kaylee had returned to her examination of the Burt's Bees kit.

"Sweetheart, check on Lucy," Jeff asked, and Kaylee got up and went into the back bedroom.

Maxine heard her say, "Hi Goosey-Lucy," and turned her head to see Kaylee sprawled on the bed next to the kitten.

"Let's hear it," Jeff said.

Maxine had promised herself never to tell Jeff about Larry's computer. Dangerous knowledge did not belong in their relationship. Except now it did. "What?"

"About the computer, for starters. Why the hell do you have it? Why didn't you turn it over to the police?"

Maxine went into a long explanation about how it might be impossible to delete all Larry's damning notes to her before she got rid of it; notes for her eyes only. A permanent irretrievable deletion. "Even if you reformat the hard drive, some information might be retrievable." Her old company had reformatted the drives four times before they got rid of old computers.

Jeff scrunched his mouth the way he always did when he didn't like what she was saying.

"We could run over it a few times and dump it into Lake Michigan." He braked hard. "Aw, crud, clueless driver!"

Trying to reason with someone navigating a gorilla motorhome through Boston's suburban rush hour traffic was a bad idea.

"We can talk later. Can you pull into that Walmart up ahead?"

Maxine ran in to buy a portable GPS, a little Tom-Tom, paying cash with the deposit box money. She also bought a flash drive to offload Larry's files with those damning notes.

Back on the road, Maxine took the Tom-Tom out of its package and began to set it up, but it was hard to concentrate on the GPS when her mind was racing from the money she had ripped off, to Larry's laptop and back to the situation at the bank.

When Larry's brother had the safety deposit box drilled open, he would discover all that cash. She saw his astonished face, mouth ajar, eyes wide, and heard his oft-used exclamation. *Jesus, Mary and Joseph.* Would he assume she had not taken any, with so many gorged envelopes still crammed inside?

Maxine felt like she had descended into a dark cellar only to find that the staircase had rotted and she had no safe way to return. She had tried not to let Jeff know how seeing Larry's laptop online had made her crazy. Larry's note had warned about his computer being "bugged," and in those first days in Florida, Maxine had researched companies that could track computers.

She discovered Lo-Jack for Laptops, which worked just like for cars. She wasn't enough of a PC guru to delve into the BIOS to determine if the tracking system had actually been installed on the laptop. She needed a knowledgeable IT friend, someone she could trust. Maxine cast her memory back to her former workplace, but no one came to mind. Finder probably knew someone, but then she would have to explain to Finder about having Larry's laptop.

The critical issue was whether Larry's bosses had been ballsy enough to report the computer stolen after it disappeared. With all that damning information. On the other hand, the police weren't likely to parse the mind-numbing Marquesa Trading Company spreadsheets down to the nitty-gritty. She absolutely could not take the chance that Larry's laptop could be traced to her. To the motorhome. To Jeff and Kaylee.

Ninety minutes later, they were rolling along the Massachusetts Turnpike. The traffic had thinned out, and Kaylee had fallen asleep with her arm around her floppy rabbit. Worcester flew by. Strips malls, shopping centers, and the usual urban sprawl, reminding Maxine of the unrelieved relentlessness of this month.

"Now we can talk," Jeff said. He glanced back where Kaylee slept, rolled down the window, lit a cigarette and passed it to Maxine. "I can't understand why you hung onto that laptop with everyone looking for it. All you had to do was drop it off a bridge. Or return it to the cops. Let them handle Lotto."

Why *had* she held onto Larry's computer as if it were the Holy Grail?

"It's the...the reason we had to stop at the bank." Earlier Maxine had told Jeff that she had to pick up some "personal stuff" from the safety deposit box. He hadn't questioned her about the details.

"The laptop?" He flipped the driver's side visor down to keep the sun out of his eyes. Maxine pulled on her pink baseball cap. "It had nothing to do with the bank. Larry left a note about an offshore account in Panama. I had to get the account number out of the lock box."

"I can't believe this." His face had flushed.

"The Panama account is for Larry's brother Corky and me. Honora, if I ever find her. I need to fly to Panama City and get the money, but there's a problem."

"There's always one more problem, isn't there?" His voice was brusque.

This was a different Jeff, neither genial nor calm.

"I don't know where my passport is. Unless I find it, I can't travel outside the U.S."

She could apply for a new passport, but suppose she was on some sort of watch list of witnesses who refused to testify or cartel accountant's ex-wives. Any connection to Larry could get her on a list. Even if she found her passport, it might be too risky.

"You're prepared to fly to some freakin' country to get money out of a bank, drug money that isn't even yours?" His arm flailed the air. "That's the most insane idea yet."

Maxine thought Jeff, who was usually so easy-going, had lost it. Coming north with him and Kaylee was a bad idea. As a dad, Jeff must be worried about Lotto's muscle catching up to them. Lotto wouldn't care about a kid. He only cared about drugs, money, and staying out of jail.

She and Jeff beat the dead horse about Larry and the laptop and Maxine's apparent death wish until Kaylee woke up. Without consulting them, Jeff stopped on the turnpike for fast food. In another week, she would develop a serious dislike of generic pizza.

*If there was another week.*

With shoulders hunched, hands gripping the wheel and with a scowl that would send wild beasts skittering, Jeff drove across the state line onto the New York Thruway, around Albany and on into the hot, summer night.

Maxine stared at the red line of highway on the GPS. She had entered Lisa's Chicago address on Leavitt Street as their destination. God, it would be a relief to get to Chicago and out of this RV where there was no privacy and less peace.

Slouched in the dinette with her dolls on the table, Kaylee watched iCarly on the small TV above the passenger seat. Maxine heard Lucy's vigorous scratching in the litter box. Lucy had been a model cat since her adventure at the campground. Sometimes she stood on her hind feet and gazed out the windows with a pensive look. *Are we there yet*?

"When are we going to stop?" Kaylee asked Jeff.

"We'll be lucky to get to the campground by nine-thirty. Around bed time."

Kaylee's face reddened. "But then it will be too late to swim and play on the swings."

"I'm sorry." He didn't sound sorry.

"But I wanted to swim, dammit. Maxine said there's a pool. And tubing on the river."

"Hey! Calm down." Jeff glanced back at his daughter. "And watch your language."

"Why don't I read you a story?" Maxine read Dr. Seuss for half an hour and placed a glass of milk and two mint-chocolate cookies on the table. She glanced at her watch. Almost nine. The campground closed at ten. She didn't want to park the motorhome at a rest stop with fifteen long-haul trucks. Maxine felt the vulnerability of their little trio, and she didn't want to sleep along the road.

Kaylee devoured her snack, hugged Maxine, and said "Goodnight, Daddy," to Jeff, still hunched behind the wheel. Clutching her floppy rabbit, she trundled off to the big bed in back. Kaylee had rubbed her eyes and yawned all day. Being on the road was tiring.

Maxine hated that she had put this sweet kid at risk. And Jeff. He had been so nice, even chivalrous and what did he get? A woman bent on self-destruction. Dragging them all down into the muck with cocaine conquistadors and stolen laptops and trips to empty out offshore bank accounts. Hardly the Partridge Family.

Maxine poured herself a Coke and sat in the passenger's seat. "Want a soda?" she asked Jeff.

"I want you to talk to me."

*Here we go again.* Whenever he said, "talk to me," Jeff wanted reasons and explanations. She had already told him far too much. Talking only made things worse.

"I'm watching the GPS for the turnoff to the campground." Maxine held the cold Coke can to her forehead.

When they finally arrived, they found the campground was strung out along a river. After Jeff paid and did the hookups, Maxine carried a plastic glass of rum and ice and her cigarettes to a picnic table. Jeff plopped down next to her, rubbing his temples.

"Brutal day," he said, exhaling. "We can sleep late tomorrow, then I want to push on to Chicago." He put his arm around her shoulders in a comradely way.

"I'm sorry about everything," Maxine said. "I'll help with the driving." *Can't get there fast enough.*

Sounds of muted music and television programs drifted out of the long row of hooked-up RVs facing the river.

Jeff cleared his throat. "Max, in my head, your situation, your decisions...are a muddle inside an enigma. I don't understand you at all. Let's start at the beginning this time? Why did you marry Larry?"

In the dark, she didn't have to meet his eyes drilling into hers. Jeff didn't intend to be cruel, but he was waterboarding her with questions. She would have to tell him. Lay her soul bare. Again.

Stalling, she took a cigarette out of her pack and sipped the rum, then passed Jeff the glass. The white noise of the river and the chirping of the crickets grounded her in this place. A half-moon had risen, casting its pale light on the water. Maxine pulled her white cotton sweater around her shoulders.

In a toneless voice, she retold the story she had confided to Finder a few days ago, and either because of the peaceful setting, or because of the repetition, the telling felt easier. In Key West, when Nicole had mentioned, "your father killed your mother," Maxine had a meltdown. When she told Finder, she had shed a few tears. Tonight, her eyes were dry.

"God, what a horrible thing, Maxine. I'm so sorry. I had no idea. You must have been devastated."

She nodded and clutched the glass of rum. The night air smelled of farmland, maybe hay or alfalfa mixed with river water. Smelled green. Maxine held a lighted match to her cigarette, inhaled and passed it to Jeff, who touched her hand in sympathy.

They were silent for a few moments. Jeff spoke again.

"So you married Larry on the rebound? Was that it?" His voice had changed from demanding to a walking-on-eggs funereal tone.

"No, I was alone for two years. I met Larry on a singles cruise." She tried to sound matter-of-fact, finding it easier to talk about Larry than her folks.

"Get serious. You?"

"I went with a girlfriend. Just on a lark. It was one of those cheap three-day affairs from Miami to the Bahamas and back."

"Affairs is right."

Maxine ignored the jibe, put her elbows on the wooden table and let the memories return. The moonlight on the river tonight reminded her of the big romantic moon that had accompanied the cruise. "I met Larry the first night out at a cocktail party. We had dinner, some drinks, danced. He was a good dancer, sharp dresser, and he seemed like a decent guy. I liked that he didn't drink to excess." She didn't like his gambling. Maxine wondered if Larry had begun skimming to pay his gambling debts. A year after they married, he had gone to Gamblers Anonymous at her urging.

"Did he tell you his occupation?" Jeff watched a man going back to an RV toting a laundry basket piled with clothes topped by bottles of detergent and bleach.

"Larry said he was an accountant. And he was."

Jeff snorted. "And did he fess up that he cooked the books for a drug lord?"

"He told me he managed the financial end of an import-export business." She didn't like Jeff dissing Larry.

'True, as far as it went." Jeff passed the cigarette back to Maxine. "So you married him?" A little smoke escaped from his mouth with each word.

"I met his family, and they were so nice to me. He gave me his mother's gravy recipe. You have to understand what that meant. How it felt to be welcome, included into their circle after two years of having...no one. No one. After two years of feeling like a pariah. I needed some friendly people in my life."

"Did you love him, then?" Jeff's words were so low they were almost drowned out by the chorus of crickets.

"Probably not. But he was so good to me. Always respectful. He liked that I had a serious job, and he insisted I keep every cent of my salary. When he introduced me to someone, he just beamed with pride. The way he said, "This is Maxine," made me feel special. After my first marriage, I was afraid of the kind of love that breaks your heart. My heart needed mending, not the big passion."

Jeff seemed to understand. Maxine had never discussed Larry or their years together. She swiped at tears that flowed unbidden from her eyes. She passed the cigarette back to Jeff, who ground it under his shoe and put the butt in his shirt pocket.

"When you walked into Samantha's party, you looked special, like that." Gazing up at the moon, he paused a beat. "So how did you find out that Larry's company imported drugs and exported cash?"

"I always wondered. His associates seemed uncouth. Except for Lotto. Larry really liked Lotto. But Larry's home office *was* creepy." *The locked room that must never be entered.* "Larry made a lot of trips out of the country. Panama. Bermuda. The Cayman Islands. He even went to Cartagena."

Once when she had mentioned all the places Larry traveled, someone had joked, "Does he launder money?" Everyone had laughed, but she remembered the growing stress that became Larry's ever-present companion, his edginess, and his constant surveillance of his surroundings.

She couldn't see Jeff's expression, but she imagined his mouth twisting in disbelief. How could anyone have been clueless for that long?

"I guessed he was involved in a racket. Numbers or gambling. Drugs had crossed my mind, but Larry just didn't seem like the kind of man who would earn his living from someone else's pain. I didn't *know* what he did until the police mentioned that drug money. And asked if I knew where it was."

"Unbelievable." That one word, spoken in a harsh tone.

Maxine swallowed, hoping the lump in her throat would recede.

"I want you to take me to an airport tomorrow." Maxine was surprised at how little emotion her voice revealed. "Cleveland will work. Lucy and I will fly back to Florida. I'll have Finder meet me, and I'll lease a car and take off again. I have my own path to take, and I can't follow yours. You and Kaylee will be safe once I'm out of your lives. It will be better this way, you'll see."

She drained the rum and stood.

"Oh God, no! Stay with me through Chicago. Please? I need you. Kaylee needs you. We went to the wall for you in Boston."

Maxine felt like a first-class shit. She stood, riveted to the ground.

"I can't face Lisa alone. You can't bail on us now!"

~ * ~

Half an hour later, Maxine, in a robe and pink clogs, returned from the campground showers. Jeff already had his towel over his arm and carried his Dopp kit.

"I didn't mean to come on like the Spanish Inquisition," he said, his eyes still clouded with worry, as they had since Maxine had come out of the Foxborough bank. "Drug money and hit men and foreign bank accounts are a lot for an average guy like me to grasp. Just give me a little time to—to digest everything, okay?"

"I don't want to put you and Kaylee in harm's way. And I need to get to the West Coast. You'll want to go home."

"What difference does half a day make? You can leave Lucy with us."

*Lucy will be all I have.*

"Let's discuss it after I've washed off the road dust." His eyes searched her face. She thought he was trying to find a weakness in her resolve. He winked. "Pour us a little more rum. Nobody has to drive."

Maxine went into the RV and checked on Kaylee and Lucy who slept in the big bed, with Lucy curled up against the pillow next to Kaylee, emitting soft purrs.

A few minutes later Jeff returned, smelling of soap and aftershave. *Old Spice*? He eyed the generous glass of rum and ice.

"Anything under that robe?"

So the wind was blowing that way. He must know by now she couldn't resist his easy smile, his boyish blond good looks.

"P.J.s."

Jeff motioned her to stand up, and then he pulled the couch into a narrow bed and sat down. He patted the area next to him. Maxine slipped off her robe, and took the glass of rum. It was pointless to fight when they had so little time left.

# *Twenty-seven*

Lotto's condominium on the Castillogrande beachfront had the best view in all Cartagena de Indias. He stood on his balcony, enjoying the play of light on the water and anticipating dinner. In the kitchen, Fernanda the maid was fixing his favorite *bandeja paisa*. His wife turned up her nose at so much meat, the fried pork rinds with the rice and beans and potatoes; a calorie bomb, she called it, and asked for a salad. He knew she would sneak a few bites before bedtime. His boys loved it, too.

"Here is your rum, Papa." Andrés, at seven the oldest, carried Lotto's glass of rum to the balcony table.

"Mama says this is for your drink." Christian, the five-year old, his brows furrowed in concentration, placed a tile coaster on the table and reached for Lotto's glass.

"No, I'll do it," Andrés said.

"Watch out!"

The glass toppled onto the white stone floor and shattered. "Go inside! Don't touch the broken glass. Tell Mommy to get Fernanda."

Andrés took off while Christian burst into tears.

"Nothing to cry about," Lotto said, bending over to pick up the largest shard. *Mierda!* He hadn't noticed the jagged piece next to it.

A thin trickle of blood oozed out of his index finger. *Oh God, no. Not this.*

Lotto groped for the chair behind him as he felt the wooziness overtake him. He mustn't faint. He must not...

He awoke with a cold towel on his forehead, held by his wife in her new Ralph Lauren dress. The boys, both bug-eyed, stared at him.

"You know your father can't look at blood," Sarita told them in a matter of fact voice. "Now go and ask Fernanda how long until dinner."

Sarita adjusted the towel and put her slim hand on his arm. "Are you all right, Lotto?"

He nodded, feeling once more the shame and humiliation of a man unable to endure the sight of blood. "I am fine. It's just so... disconcerting."

"I understand."

But she didn't. No one did. How could Lotto Lopez, cartel *jefe,* a man who had ordered many interrogations and killings, faint at the sight of a few drops of blood?

~ * ~

White sails billowing, a stately forty-foot sloop glided into the yacht basin of the Cartagena Marina Club Nautico. From next door on the tiled terrace of the Club de Pesca, Lotto and Enrique watched the crew take the sails down and prepare to tie up to the dock. Beyond the breakwater, a regatta of sailboats tacked around the buoys.

Enrique took a long sip of beer and brushed his hand across his forehead. "Tastes good in this heat."

Lotto liked to be outdoors. He spent too much time in his Brickell Avenue office and the grungy place in Little Havana where he conducted his "real" business. This week he had enjoyed his excursions to the shacks on a remote tributary of the river south of Buenaventura, walking along the planks set on the swampland where his Russian kits would be assembled into submarines. The roar of motorboats coming and going with workers and supplies was music to his ears. Lotto even liked the fetid odor of the barely flowing tropical water mixed with fumes from the resins, and the humidity that would melt a man into a sweat-drenched mass of mosquito bites. He had grown up on this hot Caribbean coast. It was home. He still reveled in temperatures that made other men wilt. His wife rolled her eyes and sighed whenever he turned the AC down and opened the balcony doors.

Lotto wondered why Enrique had called him away from his family on a late Friday afternoon. Enrique had been evasive, and in the states, Lotto would have harassed him without mercy. Today Lotto felt mellower. The without-a-hitch transfer of the sub kits from the freighter to his trucks, the uneventful trips to the assembly point on the river, and being home with his wife and sons relaxed him.

"It's been a productive week, Lotto," Enrique observed, lighting a Cuban Corona. "And I have news that will make it even better." He puffed at the cigar, then removed it from his lips and admired the shape and smell of it. Lotto had never developed a taste for cigars. Enrique glanced at his boss's bandaged finger. Lotto noted that he wisely kept any questions or comments to himself.

"What news?" asked Lotto, watching the yacht tie up, lines secured to the cleats on the dock, the motor cut, sail covers tied down. Everything ship shape. A deeply tanned blonde woman wearing skin-tight white shorts and boat shoes clambered onto the dock with two men behind her.

"The answering machine at the office here had an interesting message," Enrique said, inhaling his Corona again. "A very interesting message."

Lotto tore his eyes away from the woman and stared at Enrique. "What?"

"Caliendo's computer—"

"Has been found?" Lotto's eyes widened as he stared at Enrique. "After all this time?"

"Not exactly found but heard from. For the first time since the computer went missing, someone used it on the Internet. In Foxborough. Not too far from where Caliendo lived."

"*Mierda!*" Lotto said. "Did the software people call the police? Did they locate the computer? Where is it?"

"Give me a chance to explain." Enrique's earnest dark eyes swept across the harbor.

Lotto regarded Enrique with suspicion. The man was always backpedaling.

"It's a little complicated."

"That's because you're a computer moron."

"Ah Lotto. It's just not my thing. But yes, the police were notified when the software company got the first signal from the computer." Enrique pulled a long face and looked across the harbor, obviously avoiding Lotto's stare. Enrique hated delivering bad news.

"By the time the police arrived, the signal was gone. It had come from a parking lot, not a house or office. They said the computer was only connected to the web for a few minutes."

"*Mierda*! Always bad luck." Lotto wanted to swear at Enrique, but of course, Enrique was only the bearer of this news, which overall was good. Caliendo's computer was not at the bottom of a landfill or deep in a river. It was only a few miles from his house, suggesting a local situation.

Lotto picked up his glass of rum and sipped it. "What has it been, four weeks?"

"Why would someone use the computer now? Do you think Maxine? If she left Florida, she maybe went home. Or Caliendo's brother? We always thought he could have it. The software people said the cops took a long time to get to the parking lot."

Lotto noticed that the name of the yacht was *Perdido*. What idiot would christen a boat *Perdido*?

"Send a man to Massachusetts to investigate. Now. Chances are good someone will use the computer again. In Foxborough or in Fresno. I want the money that bastard Caliendo skimmed. I want his wife. Either the wife or the computer is the key."

Lotto felt his mellowness melting away. He gazed across the harbor, with the old fort, the sleek yachts and the blue Caribbean. What he didn't tell Enrique was that a viselike fear gripped him whenever he thought of returning to the states. He had a powerful hunch that one of his higher-ups was disloyal, plotting a takeover, or worse, planning to turn the Feds on him. The incidents with the PI's office and Maxine's apartment were badly planned and poorly executed. His people should have been more careful.

To proceed with boldness and cunning, yet cautiously. That required judgment and nerves. Lotto knew he had both, but sometimes he wanted to stay in Cartagena and enjoy the life he had created. Every January he told himself just one more year in Miami in this damnable business. Six more months to go. This time he meant it.

# *Twenty-eight*

The next morning, their trek across the heartland passed endless cornfields and baking-in-the-sun white farmhouses stark against the ocean of green. Matching the cornfields, interstate signs loomed out of the flat horizon. The GPS had a single command. *Follow the road.*

When they crossed the Chicago skyway at ten-thirty at night, Maxine marveled at the vastness of the city laid out before them. Streetlights and highways lit stretched to the horizon. Chicago loomed before them, a giant of a city.

Jeff remembered a motel with a lot big enough for the RV. They checked in and crashed, wiped out by the long drive.

In the morning, Jeff asked a pajamas-clad Kaylee, "Do you know where we are?"

Still half-asleep, she shook her head.

"Chicago."

Kaylee assumed her thoughtful expression, with a faraway look and a slight frown, an expression Maxine had never been able to read.

"Are we going to see Mom?" she asked in a small voice.

"We are. Shower and put on a nice outfit. Maxine will help you."

"No shower," Kaylee said.

While Maxine ran Kaylee's bath, she asked Jeff, "What's the plan?"

"We'll descend on Lisa around ten-thirty. She sleeps late." He watched Kaylee, still with her pensive frown, select and discard one shirt and shorts set after another.

Jeff turned to Maxine. "We'll all go in together."

"I don't need to go," Maxine said. "I can't bring anything to the party."

"Lisa will behave better if there's a stranger in the mix. On a scale of one to ten, everything is a twelve with Lisa."

"You're the expert," she said, getting the iron and ironing board out of the motel closet.

Jeff replied, "Ha!" in a dubious voice.

"Let's rent a car so we don't have to park the motorhome in the city." Maxine plugged in the iron.

"I thought you didn't want to charge anything," Jeff said.

"We give them a credit card to hold, but we pay in cash." She hadn't told Jeff she had filched one of the money-crammed envelopes in the safety-deposit box. Her bad angel had perched on her shoulder in the bank vault, whispering advice. And Maxine had listened.

~ * ~

They left Lucy in the motel room with a "do not disturb" sign on the door. Maxine, in a short white cotton skirt with a black tee shirt and black sandals, wanted to look casual but classy. In the just-rented white Chevy Malibu with everyone crisp and clean, they pulled up to Lisa's apartment building in Ravenswood, a three-story structure of limestone. Big oak trees softened the gray stone, and small but tidy lawns grew in front of the city houses, most of which had been converted to apartments, Jeff said. "Lisa lives on the top floor." Under his breath, he whispered, "Housekeeping isn't her priority."

Kaylee had been quiet, even subdued during breakfast. Maxine's feeling of dread began to build like dark thunderheads billowing up on the horizon. *Bad weather ahead.*

Jeff found parking a few doors from Lisa's building. "Let's go say good morning to Mom," he said in a tone of forced cheerfulness.

"Aren't you glad to be seeing her?" Maxine turned to face Kaylee, still buckled up in the back seat.

A tiny, uncertain "yes." Kaylee had insisted on bringing her flop-eared rabbit along. Now her fingers twisted the worn red ribbon on its neck. Kaylee looked cute in her blue top and shorts with the white trim and a little sailboat on the front of the shirt, with her just-washed blonde hair shiny in a ponytail tied in a blue ribbon. If only she would smile.

"Your mom will be happy to see you. And surprised." Maxine wondered why Jeff hadn't called to give Lisa time to tidy up. It seemed to Maxine they might be taking unfair advantage.

They left the car and walked up the sidewalk. Jeff and Kaylee shared the trait that when they became overwrought, their skin blanched and freckles popped out like a leopard's spots. Kaylee clutched her floppy rabbit. This visit had dysfunction written all over it.

Jeff used a key to enter. They climbed the polished stairs to the third floor. The paint looked fresh. Old, but stately, the building was well maintained. Not a bad place to live. Peering over the banister at the strollers and baby buggies in the hall, Kaylee lagged behind. Jeff waited for her to catch up and knocked on the door.

A female voice called, "Who is it?" Jeff replied, "Your neighbor."

*What's with Jeff?*

A blowsy young blonde in a flowered pink robe opened the door. Her pupils widened as she recognized Jeff and Kaylee. Maxine's eyes were pulled to her enormous stomach. Lisa was pregnant, very pregnant. She had definitely "moved on" after the divorce. Maxine racked her brain to recall if a fiancé or boyfriend had ever been mentioned.

Under his breath, Jeff whispered, "What the fuck?" He recovered, saying, "We were in the neighborhood and we thought we'd drop by." His joke fell flat with his attempt at a chuckle sounding coming out more like a croak.

Lisa's wide blue eyes stayed on her daughter. "Kaylee, my baby! What a surprise! Give me a big hug!"

"Gosh Mom, you're fat."

Out of the mouths of babes. It was hard to see anything except Lisa's bulging, swollen-with-child abdomen. Maxine tore her gaze from the enormous bulge to Lisa's tired but pretty face, framed with long curly blonde hair. Maxine couldn't help noticing the dark roots in need of attention, and the stains on the robe. Jeff should have called in advance.

"Oh honey, I know Mommy's fat. I have a surprise for you, but I wanted to keep it a secret for a little longer."

"This is Maxine," Jeff said, and Maxine felt a frisson of pleasure. Jeff had introduced her with the same pride as Larry had. She didn't feel any jealousy in Lisa's glance, only admiration.

Maxine held out her hand, but Lisa grabbed her in a hug, and Maxine could feel herself pressed against Lisa's hard round stomach. "Kaylee told me how you taught her to swim. That's great. I'd look like a whale in the water this summer." She had a self-deprecating laugh that made Maxine like her.

"The place is a mess. It's been so friggin' hot, and my energy just got up and went." Another laugh. Lisa hugged Kaylee again and said, "Baby!" She led the way into a living room dominated by a large television. Cold air blasted from a window air-conditioner. Magazines, candy wrappers, and bowls with a few kernels of popcorn littered the coffee table. Lisa lumbered through the room, stacking the magazines and handed Kaylee the bowls. Maxine noted she didn't have a wedding ring. No engagement ring either.

"Just rinse these out, honey," Lisa said.

With Kaylee in the kitchen, Jeff said, "Lisa, this is absolutely impossible. Why didn't you tell me you were having a baby? Are you even married?"

Lisa shot back, "None of your business." Frown lines creased her forehead as she glowered at Jeff. Her hands went to her hips, supporting her back. "You were always such a prick."

"You've got custody of my daughter, and this damn well *is* my business. What kind of example are you setting? Who the hell is the father? And what's this craziness about Kaylee moving in with her aunt? She'd have to change schools. And you goddamn well know she hates those stupid dogs."

Unseen by either parent, Kaylee came back to the living room, her face a mass of freckles against her chalky skin. Maxine wanted to whisk her out of the apartment, but she felt rooted to the spot.

Lisa collapsed into a La-Z-Boy chair, and rested her hands on her stomach. "The baby's due early August. I can't cope with a newborn and getting Kaylee off to school. Isn't that obvious?" Her blue eyes seemed cunning as she looked at Jeff.

"I'll put Kaylee in school in Boca," he said. "Until you get on your feet again."

"I have zip money, so I still need the child support."

"Sorry. I've been laid off until November when the weather is decent and the golfers come back." He glared at her. "Surely you don't expect me to pay for someone else's kid."

Lisa's voice rose to a wail. "Laid off? When did that happen? Oh my god, are you on the tour again? The big money-suck?"

"I'm *not* on the tour." Jeff folded his arms across his chest and stared at his ex-wife.

Kaylee's pale face looked from one parent to the other.

"Oh my god, I'll be on welfare, with Medicaid. How will that look? Who's going to pay for this baby?" She jabbed her stomach. "Who's going to pay?"

"The father?"

With obvious difficulty, Lisa rose to her feet, crossed the room to an end table that held an enormous black handbag, and rummaged until she pulled out a half-crushed package of cigarettes.

Maxine felt like she was watching a soap opera. "Can I take Kaylee to the park or something?" she asked.

"Jesus, Lisa. Are you nuts?" Jeff watched her light the cigarette.

"Shit...can the lectures. I just have a few smokes a day." Lisa returned to her La-Z-Boy. Jeff began again, "Your baby's father—"

"Is married." Lisa put her head in her hands. "My only luck is bad."

"I'll be glad to take Kaylee for a walk. Maybe ice cream." Again, neither of the warring duo responded to Maxine's offer. She wanted to grab Kaylee and run out of there.

"Married or not, you can make him support you."

Lisa heaved her bulky frame out of the chair again. "I have to pee." She waddled out of the room.

Jeff looked like a man standing in front of a firing squad. He noticed Kaylee cowering by the kitchen door.

"Mom is going to have a baby?" asked Kaylee in a voice full of wonder.

"Yes, she is." He paused. "You'll have a half-brother or sister."

Kaylee hung her head.

"We could give Lisa some money," Maxine said. "Sounds like she really needs it. Maybe you could help her get public assistance."

"Don't *you* get involved! Lisa's a drama-queen sponge that sucks her world dry."

Kaylee went into the kitchen and returned carrying a mug. "I got this for Mom. There's no food, just some beer."

A toilet flushed. When Lisa appeared, Kaylee said, "Mommy, I poured you some juice."

Lisa said, "Baby!"

At last Jeff asked Maxine to take Kaylee for a walk. Outside, Kaylee asked, "What's wrong with Mom and Dad?"

Maxine was on the verge of saying, "Ask them," when she realized she was talking to a child. Kids always thought they were responsible for everything bad that happened. Even Honora, Maxine thought with a pang.

"Kaylee, sweetie, they're just having a rough time. It's not your fault." She repeated with as much emphasis as she could, "It's nothing *you* did."

"Mom's gotten so weird. And I don't want to go to Aunt Peg's. Her boys are mean, and they have two big dogs. They always jump on me and scratch my arms."

Maxine took the girl's hand. "I think your dad can figure out how to fix things."

Kaylee's shoulders had a dejected droop. "Maybe," she said, in a little voice.

Maxine was wondering how Jeff would deal with Lisa, when she heard her phone ringing in her handbag.

She dived into her bag. She couldn't afford *not* to answer it.

"Hi Maxine." *Finder*. "The cops are going to kick my ass if you don't check in with your local hometown bunch. Blaisdell is batshit that you haven't called him."

Squirrels played tag around a tree trunk, distracting Kaylee.

"Something came up and we decided to get out of Massachusetts," Maxine replied.

"A Lotto problem?"

"Something weird." She sounded like Kaylee. Everything was "weird."

"Just touch base with Blaisdell."

*When she got good and ready.*

Maxine and Kaylee walked along the street while Maxine talked and Kaylee peered into the store windows.

"Everything is good on this end. Just drop a dime, will you?"

"When I get a chance." *In my own sweet time.*

"I believe I've got a lead on Honora."

Maxine felt her feet grow light. "That's fantastic!"

Kaylee had walked ahead and Maxine hurried to catch up with her.

"I should have more news in a day or two. I picked up some information on the West Coast. Then followed the trail to Nevada. Nothing certain yet. But be ready to take a trip west."

Maxine found a bench at a bus stop and sat. Kaylee marched up and down the sidewalk in front of the seat, dragging her feet and the rabbit and kicking the already scuffed toe of her shoe along the pavement.

"Can't you tell me any more?" Maxine asked Finder.

"I believe you're an aunt. Honora has a seven-year-old son. If it *is* Honora. It looks like your sister changed her name and her identity several times. She could have been worried the boy's father would return to the States and try to snatch him. We're lucky she made the usual mistakes when she decided to disappear. There's no evidence the father ever came looking. He wouldn't know about the kid."

"I can't believe you found out so much."

"Some of it was luck." Finder sounded pleased.

"No way. I'm so grateful."

"I'll be getting back to you in a day or so. When I find Honora, I want you to go there. *Don't call.* She might panic and run again.

"One more thing," Finder said. "Ask Jeff if his sister has a new boyfriend. She took off this morning with a guy in a red Ferrari. The cops have noticed that car in front of her place a couple times. He's some moneybags with a big house in Key Largo. No known connection to Lotto. Clean as a whistle—not even a parking ticket."

"She's a realtor. Maybe he's a client."

"Could be. Except she took a suitcase along."

Maxine glanced at her watch. "I'll ask Jeff," she said and hung up.

She and Kaylee had been out for half an hour. Kaylee slumped down on the bench beside her, still kicking her shoe against the sidewalk.

~ * ~

Jeff and Lisa were drinking coffee at the small kitchen table when Maxine and Kaylee returned. Like some ungainly giant, Lisa rose to pour Maxine a mug.

Kaylee said, "I'm going to play with my dolls."

Lisa slopped Maxine's coffee all over the counter and splattered her hand.

"Ouch, dammit! Kaylee, honey, please don't go into your room."

Kaylee was already gone. Lisa said, "Oh shit!" as she charged out of the kitchen.

A shrill scream came from the bedroom. Jeff jumped up and tore after Kaylee and Lisa.

*Oh God, what now?* Maxine wiped up the spilled coffee while Kaylee shrieked over Jeff's angry voice and Lisa's defiant one.

Jeff stormed into the kitchen, holding a sobbing Kaylee by the hand. Lisa was waddling behind him, waving her arms in the air. "I didn't toss anything. It's all packed up to take to Peg's. Her toys, her bed, her school clothes—they're all ready to go. The bedroom's small and I only have space for the crib and one dresser and the changing table..."

"You could have squeezed the baby stuff into *your* bedroom." Jeff put his arm around Kaylee, whose shoulders convulsed with sobs. "Mommy didn't throw away any of your toys."

"I absolutely cannot cope with this." Lisa swiped her hand across her eyes.

"Get dressed, Lisa. Maxine will drive you to the grocery store. There's no food in the house. The milk is sour."

Lisa left the room. Kaylee hiccupped and clutched her rabbit to her chest.

Maxine asked herself why *she* had to take Lisa shopping.

"I want to make some calls and get Lisa squared away," Jeff said. "She's not into cooking, so see that she buys simple stuff: bagged lettuce, canned soup, milk, bread, tuna, some cold cuts—you know."

"Got it. I'll make suggestions." *No whole chickens*, no "*ingredients.*"

Jeff turned the giant television set on to a kid's channel for Kaylee, who was still snuffling.

Lisa appeared in shorts, flip-flops and a cotton top with pink and yellow flowers. She grabbed the mammoth black handbag and rummaged until she found a hairbrush and a pink scrunchie. While Maxine waited by the door, Lisa tore through the piles of magazines and old mail in the living room.

"I've got a shopping list started someplace."

"That's all right," Maxine said. "We can manage." She waited for Lisa to make one more trip to the bedroom for lipstick.

As they went out the door, Jeff had the gall to say, "You girls have fun."

~ * ~

Lisa picked up pork chops and hamburger patties. Baby carrots. Not as clueless as Jeff had implied. They wheeled the cart into a checkout line. Lisa rummaged in her black hole handbag, and found her cell phone. She punched in a number.

"Have you got that paperwork I filled out and sent in?" Long pause. "No, I didn't get it notarized."

Maxine unloaded the shopping cart onto the conveyor.

Lisa's voice grew more agitated. "I know there was a deadline, but I've been sick and..."Another pause.

Several carts had lined up behind theirs.

"I can come in and pick it up?" Lisa's troubled eyes, intent on her conversation, hadn't registered that the clerk had rung up their groceries and was waiting for payment.

"This is probably the worst week of my whole life. Oh, hold on, I've got another call."

Maxine broke in to ask, "How do you want to pay?"

Lisa made a helpless gesture and said to whomever was on the line, "I'll call you back. No, I promise I will."

Still with the phone to her ear, she performed another scavenger hunt through the black hole. A checkbook appeared, but the last check had been used. Lisa found her wallet and swiped a card. She looked at the little screen above the keypad. "Shit! I'm overdrawn." A gasp. "No, no, sorry, I wasn't talking to you. Listen, can I call you back?"

Lisa propped the black hole on the counter, and pawed through old receipts, sunglasses, and a half-eaten bag of Goldfish. Maxine handed the clerk a hundred dollar bill. Anything to stop the people behind her harrumphing and rolling their eyes.

"You just saved my life," Lisa said.

Back at the apartment, Maxine helped Lisa unload the groceries. Jeff had opened some of the boxes in Kaylee's bedroom and was toting toys and clothes down to the car.

"Stay for lunch now there's some food," Lisa said.

Jeff said, "No, we've got to leave."

And Maxine added, "Sure, I'll help you make sandwiches."

Jeff gave Maxine a look. Maxine thought it better to end on a friendly note. If all hell didn't break loose again.

They had a decent lunch of roast turkey sandwiches, real turkey. Lisa sliced tomatoes and got out the tapioca pudding for dessert. Maxine felt relieved that Kaylee was eating with gusto.

Afterward, Jeff handed Lisa a list. "Here are some phone numbers you might need. The important thing is to get money from the father. You can have a DNA test if he refuses."

"I was trying not to rock the boat," Lisa said, staring at the list.

"Don't be a fool. He owes you." Jeff handed her a check. "Here's for July."

"Thanks." Lisa cast a miserable look down at her swollen belly.

"Kaylee can start school in Boca Raton," Jeff continued. "I'll make sure she comes to Chicago for a visit. At least by Columbus Day, okay?"

Lisa heaved a sad sigh, and turned to Kaylee whose shoulders still had that dejected droop. "Okay. Come here, baby. Give me a hug. I miss you so much."

Kaylee hugged Lisa. Maxine thought both of them looked the picture of woe, with bleak eyes and down-turned mouths.

Lisa grabbed Maxine for a hug. "Thanks for everything. I owe you!"

"Take care of yourself."

Had Honora experienced these awful moments before she had her baby, moments of despair and loneliness?

~ * ~

"I couldn't believe you said we'd stay for lunch when I wanted to get the hell out of there." Jeff spoke under his breath while Kaylee played with a doll. They were driving back to the motel.

"I feel sorry for Lisa," Maxine said. " Any idea who the father is?"

"None whatsoever. She wouldn't give me a name." His narrow eyes looked bitter. Maxine had never seen Jeff so angry.

"The reason I wanted to leave," he said, "was Lisa told me that two days ago, some guy stopped by looking for me. I'm concerned it was someone Lotto had sent."

"Whatever made you think that?" Maxine was instantly alert, turning around to look behind them. Nothing but an ordinary white panel truck.

"Lisa said he asked which tour I was on."

"Oh, my God!" With the internet and public record searches online, it was easy to find anyone. And now Lotto might have zeroed in on Lisa.

Jeff grinned to himself. "She told me she let him have it with both barrels." He did a decent imitation of his outraged ex-wife. "'Tour, as in golf? I'm not married to the man and if he's back on the tour, how the hell would I know? Listen, tour is a four-letter word and golf is a four-letter word! Ask him, not me.'

"She said he looked 'ordinary. Nobody you'd ever look at twice.'"

They pulled over while an ambulance, siren screaming, barreled through the intersection.

Maxine stared at Jeff for signs he was as antsy as she was. His eyes were on the road, his hands on the wheel. Had he recovered from this morning's drama? He said, "We don't want to hang around Chicago."

How could Lotto have traced Jeff to Lisa? There must be thousands of Dunmires in the country. Maxine closed her eyes, as if she could block out the idea that Jeff and Kaylee might not even be safe after she left them. Maxine prayed Lotto didn't know about the motorhome. Lotto could use Jeff and Kaylee to get to her. It was naïve to think he wouldn't. She stared at her hands, with the right hand grasping the left until her knuckles were white.

"The good news is that I found a guy who can look into that laptop and figure out if it has Lo-Jack software installed. If it doesn't, you can stop worrying. At least about the computer." He gave her a sideways glance. "He said to come over after dinner. He's an old friend...a college roommate I stayed in touch with."

Maxine stared at the street again and looked behind them. A red pickup. With its gritty urban look, Chicago seemed a world away from tropical Florida, yet Chicago wasn't far enough anymore. Maybe Timbuktu. *Maybe*. Maxine remembered she hadn't told Jeff about Finder's call.

After she related her news, he said, "That's great for you. Nevada, huh?"

They had stopped for a red light and he pantomimed shuffling a deck of cards. "Maybe Honora deals blackjack in Vegas."

Maxine had hated gambling since she realized what it had done to Larry. She hoped Honora had a respectable job, but she reminded herself not to judge. *A single mother doesn't always have good choices*. Look at Lisa.

"Finder said Julie has been tooling around with a guy from Key Largo. He wanted to know if you knew who that was."

"Probably a client. Julie's business was hit, but people are still buying and selling."

"He drives a red Ferrari."

"I'll give her a call and congratulate her."

# *Twenty-nine*

"What do you say we check out the Millennium Park? Kaylee can bring a swimsuit. We've got all afternoon." Jeff swiveled his head to Kaylee, who bounced up and down on the back seat.

"The fountain is awesome. You can *see* people in it. And play in the water."

"Sounds good," Maxine said, when she really wanted to get the hell out of Dodge.

After visiting the park, they returned to the motel. Kaylee and Jeff napped, but Maxine felt too hyper. Against loud protests and an outraged hiss, she strapped Lucy's harness on and took the cat for a walk in the parking lot. Lucy slunk along with her gray belly touching the ground and complained with sad little meows.

Maxine tried to imagine meeting Honora again. Hugging her, catching up on the past years, meeting her little nephew. In her mind she saw the sister she remembered, the one in Finder's photo, the wholesome girl with her life in front of her, not the pole-dancing druggie. Would Honora be happy to see her? Or would she turn her once sweet face away, still estranged and angry? Did Maxine have the courage to face whatever she found? *I must see this through.*

When she and Lucy returned to the motel room, Maxine sat at a desk copying all the files from Larry's computer to her new flash drive. Then she deleted every document in *Word* and *Excel. Take that, Lotto!* She would ask Jeff's friend to make sure no one could restore the files. Maxine removed the Windows password. She had only been at the keyboard for a few minutes.

Maybe, just maybe, she could find out if LoJack had been installed on the computer. If it had not, they could rest easy. She didn't want to put too much faith in Jeff's friend or let him know many details about Larry's computer. When had *three* people ever kept a secret?

First she did some Google searches, which confirmed that the LoJack software had been installed not at the factory, but after the computer had been purchased. What Larry had written. More Googling told her how to determine if LoJack was on the machine, but she had been a business programmer, not a systems programmer. The different was huge, like piloting a piper cub versus a 747. This was technical turf where she had never ventured. She discovered the LoJack program would likely be hidden between the disk partitions. In spite of the air-conditioned room, Maxine began to sweat. How humiliating would it be if she screwed everything up and the laptop became unusable? Finally, she found the dropdown list for the physical drives. What had people done without search engines? She couldn't imagine life without them. She clicked on the first drive, sector zero. Her fingers felt spazzy. The table indicated unused space between the last sector of partition four and the first section of partition five. And something was there! Not very big, but something. The raw disk viewer couldn't tell her what. The anonymity was what made her decide it was LoJack. Her heart raced and she clicked out of the systems area before her twitchy fingers did something bad. Still, she had done it! She had discovered LoJack. She had deleted all of Larry's files, every Word doc and every Excel sheet. Her exhaustion made her slump over the keyboard, ready to fall asleep.

Jeff and Kaylee woke up hungry. "Hey, Cyber Girl!" Jeff said, "Are you dozing at the keyboard?" Max jerked to attention.

They all fancied Mexican food. Kaylee wanted a burrito, and Maxine craved *enchiladas verdes*. "Red snapper Veracruz." Jeff licked his lips with exaggerated gusto. In Jeff's guidebook, Maxine found a Mexican restaurant en route to the Hyde Park neighborhood where Jeff's computer guru lived. She would drink a big margarita and have a Mexican beer with dinner.

After visiting Lisa, Maxine had no reason to stay with Jeff and Kaylee, except that she loved them and leaving would be a knife through her heart. The problem was that on this road trip, Maxine had fallen for Jeff. She glanced at his tan, freckled face and his blond hair, and her heart beat faster. Jeff was more than just an okay guy. *He* was the prince, not Lotto. And this might be their last day together. She felt a cloud of gloom descend.

On the way to the restaurant, she tried to make her voice ultra-casual. "You can drop Lucy and me off at O'Hare on your way out of town tomorrow. I'll find a flight where the cat can ride in the cabin." She put her sunglasses on because she didn't want him to see how those words made her feel. She and Jeff had had several arguments about her desire to take off.

Jeff countered, "Cripes, what difference can two days or three days make? Lucy will be happier if you ride back to Florida with us." He flung his hand in her direction. "For God's sake, you know I don't like these discussions in rush hour traffic."

Maybe she *should* return to Florida with Jeff and then fly or drive to Nevada when Finder was positive he had located Honora. On the other hand, what awful Lotto surprise might be waiting in Florida? She imagined ambushes, booby traps, snakes let loose and slithering around her condo. She envisioned the big bullet-headed man lounging by the pool, his bulging biceps tattooed with guns, nooses, and a graphic count of his victims. The very thought made her sweat. Could she sneak in and out of town in a day? Have Finder bring her car to meet her at the airport? Lucy could stay with Jeff and

Kaylee. Cruel to drag a cat around the country in a passenger car. Nevada was a long trek from Florida. She should fly out.

*Making this decision is making me crazy.* Before long she would be a mad woman with wild, staring eyes, her shirt on inside out, and hair sticking out like a fright wig.

~ * ~

They found the restaurant, with a green neon cactus in the window, but no parking place. They left the Malibu a couple of blocks away on a side street.

The plump waiter teased Kaylee, who seemed her old self again. Jeff rested his hand on Maxine's knee whenever the opportunity presented itself, and he pressed his thigh against hers until their legs seemed fused together. The food was tasty and the drinks strong. Maxine relaxed for the first time all day, not thinking of Lisa, Lotto or how to get to Nevada.

After dinner, the sun was still above the horizon and heat radiated from the sidewalk as they strolled back to the Malibu. *Hot Child in the City*. Here, the neighborhood shops had metal gates in front of the display windows. A drunk staggered by, and wished them a tipsy, "evening!" raising his bottle in a toast. Mouth open, Kaylee stared. In the distance, a siren sounded. They were alone on the street. Jeff took Kaylee's hand and put her between him and Maxine. They walked a little faster until they reached the car.

"Daddy, there's broken glass on the sidewalk."

Jeff stopped. "What the hell?"

Disbelief mingled with horror as Maxine gaped at the broken window on the passenger's side of the Malibu. Her heart thumped as Jeff pulled the door open. She knew they had locked it. Maxine had shoved the laptop case partly under the front seat, and left an unfolded Chicago map on the floor to cover it. Now, the map with its red and blue lines, lay on the front seat. The glove box gaped open. She peered over Jeff's shoulder as he bent down and moved his hand around under the front seat. He straightened up and turned to her. Maxine knew by his angry eyes and compressed lips that the laptop was gone.

She and Jeff stared mutely at one another. Then Jeff said, "Probably not the ideal way to get rid of that damned thing. On the other hand..." He had a quirky, lop-sided grin.

"I hid the laptop. Not even a corner was visible. How did anyone know it was there?" She stared at the bits of broken glass.

"Lotto did not follow us and steal the laptop. There's a perfectly plausible explanation, a garden-variety thief."

"Who's Lotto?" asked Kaylee.

"Somebody Maxine doesn't like very much," answered Jeff.

"Daddy, why is the window broke? Are my dolls all right?" Kaylee asked her last question in a high-pitched wail.

Jeff reached into the back seat and handed Kaylee both Polly Pockets dolls.

"I'm more worried what the car rental people are going to say," he said over his shoulder. "You don't ever want to damage a rented car. They throw the book at you."

Maxine remembered a huge hassle when Larry had a fender-bender in his rental.

While Jeff checked the back seat for the rest of Kaylee's toys, Maxine retrieved the Malibu contract from her handbag. Under her breath she said, "We don't mention the laptop to the police, because it might have already been reported stolen."

Jeff nodded. "All your doll stuff is safe and sound, sweetheart," he told Kaylee.

Maxine called 911 and reported the break-in. Jeff called his friend and cancelled their visit. They waited on the empty street by the car, nervous at standing around in this dicey neighborhood with darkness falling. Jeff made Kaylee sit in the back seat.

Maxine, still eyeing the shards of broken glass, said, "When the cops come, I'll take Kaylee a few doors down to look in the variety store window. Tell them someone stole our portable GPS."

The bad angel had a permanent spot on her shoulder, suggesting lies at every turn.

Two hours later, with a completed police report and the rented car turned in with a damage deposit, they were ready to check out of the motel. It had been such a shitty day that Maxine decided to call Blaisdell and get a chewing out, but he was on vacation for a week, a temporary reprieve.

"Now drive Lucy and me to O'Hare," Maxine said, as Jeff pulled the RV out of the motel parking lot.

"I don't want to hear these bullshit airport suggestions," he said, his mouth a thin line. "We're going to Nevada. That's final." Maxine opened her mouth to protest, but Jeff held up his hand, signaling her not to talk.

"I've been thinking. With Lotto on the loose and that PC god-knows-where..." he paused, and took a deep breath, "...and men who knock on doors asking questions, 'Dunmire' has become a dangerous last name. We aren't going back to Florida yet."

Maxine opened her mouth again and Jeff said, "Just hear me out for a change." He waited for a red light before continuing.

"I don't have a job. You don't have a job. School's out. We're up to our asses in alligators, but we have a little money and the Cobra. We can dawdle along and see the country until you hear from Finder. We can take Kaylee to some national parks, bum around, and maybe I'll play a round of golf somewhere."

Jeff's face always lit up when he mentioned golf.

It sounded good, Jeff's plan. Maxine felt a surge of optimism. She glanced back to Kaylee and Lucy asleep in the RV's bedroom. *Keep them safe.*

The further away they were from Florida, even from Chicago, the better. They could disappear into the great American West. That's what everyone did...outlaws, misfits, people on the run. Pay cash and keep moving. *Drift along with the tumbling tumbleweeds.*

"All right," Maxine said. "We'll follow the road."

Once they were out of the urban congestion, Jeff pulled over and Maxine got into the driver's seat. Jeff tried to call Julie but her answering machined kicked in at home, and he left a message on her cell phone. *Who's the dude with the red Ferrari? Are you keeping secrets from your little bro?*

Juiced on nicotine and iced coffee, Maxine drove across Illinois to Davenport, Iowa. Iowa seemed an unlikely state for Lotto Lopez to hunt them. Maybe if Lotto got his hands on Larry's computer he would back off.

## *Thirty*

Trying to ignore the noise and the smell, Lotto struck a pose, legs hip length apart, shoulders relaxed, hands in pockets, face with a slight air of puzzlement. The engine's shrill whine as the plane pulled away from the gate was like a fingernail on a blackboard. The acrid odor of jet fuel burned his nostrils.

After disembarking his flight from Cartagena, Lotto had been pulled out of the Miami customs line and escorted into the hot bowels of the airport, where his checked baggage lay open on a waist-high shelf along with his briefcase, wallet, passport and cell phone. A German Shepherd straining on a leash sniffed around Lotto and his luggage. The dog's nails clicked on the concrete floor. Lotto had not uttered a word, neither had he smiled nor frowned. *Observe but do not comment.*

The customs *puta* had unpacked his Tumi carry-on and his duffel bag. Now he conducted a meticulous exploration of the suitcase's lining. He slid open the zipper and moved his hand, patting here, feeling there, probing everywhere. What did these idiots hope to find? Did they think he would carry drugs? Apparently, they did, because this officious *naco* had just dumped Lotto's expensive

Acqua di Parma Talc onto a paper plate. The panting dog sniffed, but showed no interest in Lotto or his possessions. *Good dog.*

They inspected his briefcase next, but it held only brochures and paperwork for Marquesa Trading Company, and a few models of rickety *chivas* autobuses wrapped in bubble wrap. His mother had loved her little painted bus. Or so she said. Lotto was relieved he no longer had the job applications for northeast cartel accountant. Not that the word "cartel" was mentioned anywhere, but no one should see those names.

His phone might be a problem, but maybe these *putas* wouldn't scrutinize the device. Lotto used every power of concentration not to glance at his phone. Made in England, the Tripleton Enigma Crypto phone was mainly for military use and not available for export beyond the Common market without a special license. Customs people might know these facts, but the phone, in appearance like all others, had no distinguishing look.

The muggy space, the noise and the reek of the fuel along with the dog tugging at his leash would give anyone a nervous jolt. Twenty feet away a girl in tight pants and high heels underwent a similar inspection. She pushed her dark hair from her eyes and fingered a gold cross around her neck. Nervous as hell. Lotto wondered if she was a mule. How ironic if she were one of *his* mules. He didn't use many these days, only when necessary.

He removed his hands from his pockets and clasped them loosely behind his back. He doubted they would strip search him, but the idea made him crazy. His composure would disappear with his clothes. *Think about something else.*

Think about Caliendo's computer, now in the hands of the Chicago police, and soon to be in Lotto's possession. A little good luck at last. The chief *puta* gave him a sidelong glance. He hoped his face expressed mild interest, nothing more.

*Just don't examine the fucking phone.*

The wait felt endless, but he noticed they were repacking his suitcase, if you could call the careless stuffing of his possessions back into the bag "packing." The heavy-handed *naco* eyed the silver framed photos of Sarita and the boys, and Lotto felt a spasm of rage. A drop of sweat trickled down his rib cage. With the suitcases repacked, they flipped through his passport one more time. His wallet was getting the second degree again. Now, finally the phone. The crypto and GSM cards had the virtue of being invisible. The *naco* flicked through the menu, scanned a few contacts and put the phone down. Lotto, pulse racing, kept his gaze fixed on his duffel bag. The *puta*, intent on finding a contact of interest, hadn't noticed the "encrypt" key. Did he think Lotto would have "hit man" and "cartel headquarters" listed? Stupid.

The man returned Lotto's passport, wallet and phone. As Lotto stuffed them into various pockets, he asked, "Am I entitled to an explanation?" He made an effort to keep attitude out of his voice.

"Just a routine check." The man gave him a faux smile, which Lotto returned.

The *naco* carried his suitcases to the public area of the terminal.

"I can manage from here," Lotto said in a gruff voice.

He wondered if someone would follow him. As a man who had nothing to hide, Lotto would take a cab to his condo, drop off his luggage, and meet Enrique. They must discuss the miraculous appearance of Caliendo's computer. Lotto considered what an innocent man in his circumstances would do. He picked up his luggage and headed for the line of taxis. While he waited, he used his cell phone. He was late for his meeting. Standing at the curb in the Miami heat, he felt himself breaking out into a well-deserved sweat.

## *Thirty-one*

Maxine and Jeff crashed at a campground off Interstate 80 in Davenport. A week ago they had been in Myrtle Beach on Father's Day making love in the motorhome. This Saturday, Maxine's sense of order told her to do laundry and stock up on groceries. Jeff dialed his sister every half hour, but no one answered her home phone, and she didn't pick up her cell. His unease affected Maxine and she got jumpy, too. She imagined Lotto's thugs jumping out from behind every tree, popping around the aisle at the supermarket, looming at the door of the laundromat. Grabbing a screaming Kaylee. *Get a grip*. Julie was enjoying a wonderful weekend somewhere with her cell turned off.

"I'm not going to be worth shooting until I find out what's up with Sis." Jeff crossed his arms, not budging.

Maxine glanced at her watch. "You want to hit the road now?"

"I want to be in striking distance of an airport. Are you taking this problem with Julie seriously?"

"Maybe Finder knows something." Maxine picked up her cell phone. When Finder answered, she apologized for calling on a Saturday.

"No problemo. And no news about Honora. Maybe middle of the week. Where the hell are you?" Finder asked.

"Iowa."

"Pick me some corn."

"Jeff is worried he can't reach Julie. She's with the guy in the red Ferrari. You said Julie's phone had been tapped. Can we find out about her conversations with this guy?"

Finder chuckled. "You never ask for much, do you? Not without a court order."

"We think Lotto's people questioned Jeff's ex-wife in Chicago."

Silence while Finder digested that bit of news. "Put Jeff on the line."

Jeff shifted from one foot to the other, inspected his knuckles, and made noncommittal replies, ending with "Julie's usually pretty cautious." He returned the phone to Maxine.

"I'll find out what I can," Finder said.

Finder's staying calm helped her stay calm. Because Jeff appeared to be losing *his* calm.

Maxine dreaded the drive to Omaha, three hundred plus tedious miles into the stark western sun, with another late night arrival. Jeff had made a reservation at a campground on a lake. Kaylee played with her dolls with Lucy next to her, licking her paws.

*Follow the road.*

Jeff drove the dark band of highway through more ripening corn. They stopped at a park in Des Moines and had a picnic.

Jeff hurried them through the meal. "We need to make tracks."

He tried his sister one more time. No luck. He looked angry enough to pitch the phone out the window. "Can you believe her message box is full?"

"Maybe you filled it up."

At eleven p.m., with Kaylee still awake, they pulled into the Omaha campground. Kaylee asked about the swimming pool in a hopeful voice. Jeff said it was dark and past bedtime. Maxine felt too weary to sleep. When she closed her eyes, she saw tandem Mack trucks barreling down the interstate, past tall silos and acres of green corn. Next to her, Jeff tossed and turned. Kaylee emitted soft moans. They were on a pilgrimage into pain.

Sunday morning and Finder hadn't called. Jeff phoned Julie one more time. Nothing.

After breakfast Jeff said, "We're driving to Denver today. Monday morning, I'm getting on a plane to Florida."

"What about Kaylee?" Maxine glanced toward the dinette where Kaylee dressed dolls. "I'm going to look for Sis, and Kaylee will just be a hindrance. Plus, I don't want her within a thousand miles of Lotto." Jeff always pronounced Lotto's name like he were something that had come out of the sewer.

"What if Kaylee doesn't want to stay with me?" Maxine turned to look at the little girl with the Polly Pockets dolls in a swimsuit parade, singing, "*Here she comes, Miss America.*"

"I talked to her already. About what we'd do if I had to go back to Florida for a few days. She wants to go swimming every day. And to see "a real cowboy." He paused. "Are you okay with it? Colorado seems safe."

She was not okay with it. Jeff was deserting them on a whim about his sister. Maxine would have to drive the RV by herself, a stomach churning thought. Kaylee could be a handful. But since the mess they were in was Maxine's doing, she couldn't make waves. Go along to get along. But his leaving really sucked.

# *Thirty-two*

Lotto paced beside Enrique like a raging tiger as they made their way through Lincoln Road Mall. Still bullshit from being searched, he spat, "airlines!" rather than explain why he was late. Being detained in customs like some pathetic mule—demeaning.

Enrique peered up and down the busy sidewalk. The farmer's market had been packed up, and in the cafés, Sunday afternoon brunch was in progress with the usual chatter of voices and the clink of silverware.

"What?" Lotto did not attempt to hide his impatience.

"Looking for that *loco* rooster on the bicycle," Enrique said.

"Forget the fucking rooster," Lotto said, plopping down at a round table in the shade of a blue umbrella. He ordered a double espresso and rolled up the sleeves of his pink linen shirt. "Let's get to work!"

From his expression of concentration, Enrique seemed to be formulating a question, but apparently thought better of it. A dumb question, no doubt.

Lotto glanced at the menu. Too much vegetarian crap. The idea of eggs turned his stomach. He ordered a steak sandwich. Enrique asked for an omelet, so Lotto would have to look at eggs, even smell eggs. His stomach lurched.

He looked at Enrique. "Your report on locating Caliendo's widow?"

Enrique broke into a smile showing many white teeth. The news must be good. "Ah, Lotto, that plan to find a boyfriend for the sister was brilliant."

Lotto continued to stare at Enrique.

"A man from Key Largo. Beach house, sports car, money. Our lawyer kept his son out of jail, and now he owes us a favor. He works off his debt this weekend. More like play than work." Enrique chuckled. "He flew to Nassau with the Dunmire woman. He reserved a suite on Paradise Island. He will be attentive, even romantic." Enrique made an extravagant gesture. "Much good sex. And the Key Largo Romeo passed us the sister's cell phone number. We have made sure her message box is full. Now we wait for the worried brother to appear." Enrique met Lotto's gaze. "How did you ever think of that?"

"I saw it on television."

"Ha! Ha! How do you know it will work?"

Lotto didn't know, but he knew the police had watched the sister's house. The sister sold real estate and her new Key Largo client was no one the cops had reason to be suspicious of. No one connected to Lotto or Marquesa Trading Company. Lotto understood people—in his business, knowing whom to trust was critical. Lotto especially understood nervous people on the run. This Jeff Dunmire would be beside himself if his sister "disappeared." He would go running back to find her. And Lotto's people would follow him right back to Maxine Caliendo or Harvey or whatever she called herself.

Their orders arrived. At least the steak was medium rare. Enrique's eggs didn't look that bad. For the first time all day, Lotto smiled.

# *Thirty-three*

Honora sat in the security office of the department store, a crummy room: airless, windowless, claustrophobic. All because of a stupid Clinique lipstick, fifteen goddamn dollars. The store detective had called the police, who were probably going to give her a citation, and there was no weaseling out of this because the detective was a woman who wouldn't give a rat's ass if Honora showed cleavage or hiked her skirt up to her crotch.

For some reason, the detective didn't buy her story of having bought the lipstick here weeks ago. They had probably caught her on the security camera.

Honora eyed the woman sitting across from her with distaste. Middle-aged and spreading through the waist and butt. "Broad in the beam," her father would have called it. She felt a familiar stab of grief when she thought about him.

*Don't go there.*

The police would arrive any minute.

"May I have my handbag back?" She remembered to add, "please."

Fatty Patty returned it with a sour look. It was the new Coach bag from San Francisco, not her first choice, but she'd blown too much on the shoes.

The filched lipstick, shiny and new, gleamed like a beacon on Fatty's desk.

Honora dug through her wallet until she found the sleazy lawyer's card. She knew some legal-eagle from when she had been caught DUI, and he had gotten her off with a warning. Maybe he could do that with the shoplifting charge.

"I've never been in any trouble at all, not even a traffic ticket." *Not around here, anyway.* Honora tried to smile, but her face felt frozen.

A cop came in. He wasn't in uniform, but she could always tell a cop. Fatty Patty explained about the lipstick, and Honora pleaded affronted innocence. The cop asked for her ID and used some handheld computer to check her record. "Clean as a whistle," he said, and looked at the store detective. "Do you want to press charges? It's just a lipstick."

"Shoplifters should be taught a lesson." Her mouth was a thin line.

"If she took the class?" asked the cop.

"If she takes the class and makes restitution, I won't press charges." She narrowed her eyes at Honora, like she knew Honora thought of her as "Fatty Patty."

The cop explained the court would dismiss the charge if Honora took a class about the evils of shoplifting, why people shoplifted and how to overcome the impulse, yada yada. Nothing would appear on her record.

Good news with her being in the middle of a job hunt. She opened her eyes wide and nodded, saying "Oh, thank you so much. I won't disappoint you again," looking Fatty Patty right in the eye.

"If you've got a computer, you can take the course at home. It doesn't take long," the cop said.

"That's wonderful. Thank you, too." Now she wouldn't have to pay a lawyer.

"Just watch yourself. Don't let there be a next time." The cop gave her a stern look.

Taking the lipstick had been a stupid thing to do, and she wouldn't repeat that mistake. She wouldn't gamble at the new job. She wouldn't leave Ethan with the sitter he hated. She would try harder to stay out of trouble. A lot harder.

# *Thirty-four*

Coming across the arid Colorado plains, the massive white tents of Denver International Airport loomed out of the prairie, looking like a vast Arab encampment in some money-soaked oasis of petrodollars. With sweat oozing from her palms, Maxine drove the RV from the interstate exit toward the airport. She had driven most of yesterday, too. Like a pilot racking up hours in the air. They were still in the boondocks and traffic was light. The idea of cabs, buses and distracted drivers on cell phones converging into the departure lanes made her insides feel like a clothes dryer loaded with tennis balls.

A brown haze of smog hung over Denver, causing Kaylee to complain. "I still can't see any mountains."

Jeff had an eleven forty-five flight to Fort Lauderdale with a stopover in Dallas/Fort Worth. Monday morning and Julie still didn't answer her phones.

Leaving the big bed in back to Kaylee and Lucy, Maxine and Jeff had spent the night on the sofa bed, with long passionate kisses and frantic but quiet lovemaking under the covers. With Kaylee only a few feet away, they were always hushed, and stealth added an extra dimension to their lovemaking.

Maxine pushed romance out of her mind to give Jeff instructions about what to tell Finder, where to look for her passport, and all the last minute details.

Jeff seemed distracted, glancing from his watch to the stark landscape and back. "Once I find out what's up with Sis."

"She's probably going to be snug in her condo when you arrive," Maxine said, hoping she was right.

"I wish," Jeff said. Julie's disappearance was worrisome, no matter what Finder thought.

Maxine followed the road around to "Departures." Driving the motorhome on an elevated roadway was nerve wracking. She had decided to skip the Denver scene, and she couldn't wait to head back to the empty eastern part of the state and the little town they had passed through yesterday with the upcoming rodeo. Her mood reflected the brown haze and parched earth landscape. *Just get the hell out of here.*

Kaylee hunched her shoulders when Jeff said, "Mind Maxine and be helpful." She perked up when Jeff handed her a plastic shopping bag. "Here's a disposable camera for pictures of the rodeo. I'll be back in a few days after I've talked to Aunt Julie. I'll bring more dolls and books. Take care of Lucy. Okay?"

Kaylee nodded, but Maxine wasn't sure she had bought into the "mind Maxine and be helpful" advice. Maxine's recorder was replete with instructions and advice about the RV. *Don't back up. Easy on the brakes*. She hoped she could manage to hook up the electricity and water. This morning they had filled up with gas, checked the tires, belts and hoses, and had the tanks pumped. Ready to roll.

"I'll give you a heads up when I'm coming back."

Maxine was not overjoyed about being saddled with so many responsibilities: Kaylee, the cat and the motorhome, especially the motorhome. She pulled up to the terminal a little away from the crowd of drop-offs. The scream of a jet taking off pinned their ears back. Maxine and Kaylee got up and stood by the RV door like flight attendants.

Jeff kissed Maxine and squeezed her hand. He hugged Kaylee, and picked up his duffel bag. "You two hang in there. Just for a couple of days."

"Us *three*." Kaylee corrected him. Lucy was locked in the bedroom.

Maxine wanted to clutch Jeff and not let go. "Be careful. Watch your back."

Jeff managed a crooked smile. The breeze ruffled his blond hair, making him look young, and for the moment, almost carefree. Kaylee waved long after Jeff had merged into the crowd. Kaylee and Maxine climbed into the motorhome, and Kaylee set Lucy free. Maxine could still smell Jeff's aftershave. She felt a pang of loneliness already. While pulling away from the curb, she checked the mirror several times. Cautious and slow. *Like a giant tortoise*. And about as gainly.

Big-eyed Lucy stared out of her faux sheepskin bed on the dinette bench.

"We could stop in Hudson and eat another buffalo burger," Maxine said. "Then we can check out the town with the rodeo."

"Awesome!" Kaylee bounced in her seat as much as the seatbelt would allow. "I want another buffalo burger."

Yesterday's long trek through Nebraska and eastern Colorado had ended at a campground in Hudson, Colorado. For dinner, they discovered an old-timey restaurant with buffalo heads mounted on the walls and real western food, including buffalo.

Maxine maneuvered the RV back to I-76. A few miles outside of Hudson her cell phone rang.

Kaylee turned to her. "Why don't you answer?"

"While I'm driving?"

"Dad does." Kaylee's pale-lashed eyes were scornful.

"I haven't driven the Cobra as long as he has." Maxine glanced at Kaylee and nodded at the phone in the cup holder. "Tell me what the number is."

Kaylee read it off. *Finder*. He might have news of Julie. What if she had come home? Jeff wouldn't be in the air yet. Was there time for Maxine to stop him from boarding the plane?

She pulled onto an exit and called Finder back.

"Hey, I've found Honora!" His voice was gleeful, with a note of triumph. "She's living in Reno in an apartment on Kuenzli. With her son. She works for a casino. Doing marketing, not dealing blackjack."

Maxine stared across the distance to the brown hills and behind them, the Front Range. Looming behind, still snow-covered, the Rocky Mountains. Her throat constricted like a giant hand was squeezing her. She wanted to weep tears of joy and relief.

Finder rattled off an address and a phone number and Maxine wrote everything down with a shaking hand.

"Go see her," Finder said. "But no phone calls before you do. Hey, are you still with me?"

"Yes. Now that I know where she is, I'm just...speechless. And scared."

"That's normal," Finder said. "Where the hell are you, anyhow?"

"I'm in Colorado. We just put Jeff on a plane back to Ft. Lauderdale." Maxine lowered her voice, turned her head away from Kaylee toward the driver's window and gazed at the mountains again. "He's still crazy with worry." She cleared her throat, which felt tight.

"Julie has a rich new boyfriend." Finder laughed. "We should all have it that good."

Maxine reminded Finder that Jeff needed to get into her condo to look for her passport and pick up some clothes.

"You're leaving the country?" he asked. *Suspicious*.

"I just don't know where my passport is." The document that would get her to the bank in Panama if she dared go. "We're taking off for Reno right away."

"We? The kid is with *you*?"

"And the cat."

"No shit, Maxine. Can you drive that monstrosity across the country?"

"I have to."

Brave words. Actually, Maxine could not imagine herself driving the RV over the mountains with the high peaks. With a kid and a cat and one scared-shitless driver.

"Why don't you hunker down somewhere safe until Jeff comes back? The world is full of *crazy* people."

Thanks for reminding me.

~ * ~

*Follow the road.*

They drove across high plains toward Rawlins, Wyoming. Maxine pulled the brim of her straw cowboy hat down to keep the sun out of her eyes. Kaylee, sitting next to her, mimicked her gesture. Her pale blonde hair matched the color of the hat.

The rolling hills to her right showed a bit of green grass. In the distance, behind those hills, the Rocky Mountains rose, blocking the path to Honora. They would cross the Continental Divide tomorrow. Twice. The thought of driving the RV along precipices on narrow roads gave her the willies.

The route across Wyoming into Salt Lake City on I-80 appeared to offer less stress. Every mile driven was a mile nearer her sister. Maxine tried to keep Honora's face in her head, but sometimes she saw the blonde, slutty Honora, half-naked, slithering around a pole. She tried to push that image out of her mind and concentrate on the wholesome young woman Honora had once been.

Maxine let a big rig pass. With both hands on the wheel, she stayed in the slow lane and drove the speed limit. Tonight, they would have a cabin where she wouldn't have to worry about hookups or backing up. Earlier they had stopped at Little America outside Cheyenne and bought western hats. Kaylee had seen "real" cowboys in scuffed boots and worn jeans. For all Maxine knew, they were drugstore cowboys, but a happy Kaylee had snapped some photos with her new camera.

Kaylee also bought three red bandanas, one for each of them, but Lucy had balked at wearing hers, so the floppy eared rabbit wore it.

Maxine bought an Indian doll in a real leather dress with beaded moccasins. Kaylee held the doll and stared through the windshield at the stark landscape.

"The Wild West." She pointed at the mountains in the distance. "And we are Wild West cowgirls." She swung an imaginary lasso. "Yippee!"

"The cowgirls are going to have a serious talk," Maxine said.

Kaylee turned to look at her, then glanced down at the doll, smoothing its dark braids.

This was going to be harder than Maxine thought. Her hands gripped the steering wheel. Kaylee assumed her "thinking" frown.

"There are things that I need to do that will get us to Reno and you have to help with some of them." She turned to Kaylee, who stared at the road ahead with intense eyes.

"I wanted to go to that rodeo. Why are we going to Reno? Why didn't we wait for Dad to come back?" For the first time, Kaylee looked worried and her frown deepened. She pushed her hair off her freckled face with a thin little wrist.

Maxine slowed to let another RV pass while she pondered what to say to Kaylee.

"Sweetie, for the last seven years my only sister has been missing. I never knew where she was. Then I hired a man who helped me find her, and he was the one who called this morning. He said my sister lives in Reno. I want to see her so badly after all those years I can't wait anymore."

Kaylee's eyes looked huge and her mouth opened to form an 'O."

"My sister has a little boy about your age. You can meet him."

Kaylee still didn't speak and she hadn't asked any questions. Maxine wished she knew more about kids. Why was this conversation making her palms sweat? Or was it the traffic converging on Rawlins? Friday was July 4th, and the road ahead was mostly trucks and RVs. Everyone between Cheyenne and Salt Lake City must be going camping. Maxine took a deep breath.

"Kaylee, we have to talk about how you can help."

Kaylee hugged the doll to her chest.

"Don't worry," Maxine said softly. "It'll be easy." She kept her eyes on the road while she patted Kaylee's thin arm. "The first thing is that I'm going to smoke a cigarette every now and then. I know you probably won't like it, but that's the way it will be. I'll try to stop smoking later, once everything has settled down."

"I know you and my dad smoke sometimes. I've seen you and I can smell it." Kaylee wrinkled her nose. "I just wish *he* would stop, too."

"He will," Maxine said. "It takes time."

"My mom smokes, no matter how much I ask her to stop."

"I know."

"Now, with your dad in Florida, we're two women travelling alone," began Maxine.

"Three women. You forgot Lucy."

"Okay, three women travelling alone. Sometimes that can become a problem if a man or men we don't know try to be too friendly. Or mean." Maxine glanced at Kaylee who was straightening the Indian doll's skirt again.

"We must not let anyone know we're alone. We'll always act like your dad is just gone for a few minutes, and we're expecting him back right away."

Kaylee nodded with the wisdom of her seven years.

"We only have to pretend for a few days." Maxine continued. "We won't talk to strange men unless we have to, and we'll never tell them your dad is in Florida, okay?"

"Okay. It's like what my mom said about not talking to strangers." Kaylee looked at Maxine for affirmation.

"Yes. Your mom is right. If anyone asks if we're alone, we say your dad is with us. Being alone is our secret, okay?"

Out of the corner of her eye, Maxine saw Kaylee nod.

Maxine had to speed up to get a big semi off her bumper. This eternal vigilance behind the wheel was exhausting. How far was Rawlins?

Maxine said, "We don't need to be afraid, but we need to be careful."

"Is Dad worried about us?" asked Kaylee.

"He knows we've got good sense."

Maxine hoped she hadn't scared the bejesus out of Kaylee, but they had to be careful. Along the road there might be drifters, drunks, escaped convicts—lots of people to avoid besides Lotto's goons. *The world is full of crazy people.* Still, the further they were from Florida, the less she worried about Lotto.

"Now, the big question is, do we cook tonight or eat out?"

"Could you make some flan like I ate at the Mexican restaurant?"

"It takes a long time to chill. We'd have to eat it for breakfast."

"What's wrong with that?"

"Absolutely nothing. Flan for breakfast it is."

Maxine thought of her mother's favorite pie, an eggy custard sprinkled with nutmeg inside a flaky brown crust. It had been Honora's favorite as well. She and her dad had liked apple.

*Follow the road.*

~ * ~

Promising herself a stiff drink with dinner, Maxine gassed up the RV and found the campground, a short distance off the interstate in Rawlins. Their little log cabin contained a double bed and a tiny kitchen. The porch had a wooden swing that seated two, and a rustic picnic table sat in the gravel yard, but the gale force winds would not be conducive to eating outside. Beyond the campground, the brown Wyoming hills sloped upward.

The campsite swimming pool teemed with screaming kids letting off steam after a day of driving. Kaylee crossed the pool with a fierce face and a determined breaststroke, not speaking to anyone.

*Two more days.*

Jeff phoned from Fort Lauderdale while Maxine was helping Kaylee towel off. He was driving in a rental car en route to his sister's.

Maxine explained about Honora and her decision to head across Wyoming instead of Colorado.

"Max, are you sure you're okay driving the Cobra?" asked Jeff.

"So far, so good. Say hello to Kaylee." She handed the phone to the shivering girl.

"Dad, did you find Aunt Julie?" Kaylee listened for a moment and said, "We're going to see Maxine's sister. And she has a boy my age."

Kaylee returned the phone to Maxine. Whatever Jeff said seemed to reassure the girl.

"I want to make Reno on Wednesday," Maxine told Jeff. "We'll pick you up at the airport."

Jeff repeated he wouldn't leave Florida until he'd talked to Julie. *Where the hell was she?*

~ * ~

Maxine and Kaylee ate soup and sandwiches for dinner, and afterward, with Kaylee's "help," they made the flan using custard cups from the camper.

Afterward, they sat on the porch swing and watched the drama of the setting sun behind the mountains with crimson streaks and purple whorls and huge clouds rimmed in gold.

"What's your sister's name?" asked Kaylee.

"Honora. It's an old fashioned sort of name. Maxine is old-fashioned, too." Maxine clinked the ice cubes in her empty glass. The rum packed a wallop, a relaxing wallop.

"What's the boy's name?" asked Kaylee.

"I don't know."

Kaylee frowned.

Maxine wondered how she could get through tomorrow, the tenth anniversary of the day her father had shot her mother, her mother's lover and himself at two o'clock on a bright summer afternoon at the Kozy Kove Motel on the first of July, now a day to clench her teeth and endure. Her stomach froze into a knot of dread. In truth, she welcomed the long drive to Salt Lake City, across Utah and into Nevada, four hundred sixty-two miles of mountains, deserts and stark landscapes.

She hadn't told Kaylee that tomorrow's campground had no pool. Maybe they could explore the town and go for ice cream cones. *If it seemed safe*. On July first, even ordinary things felt fraughtwith danger.

~ * ~

Maxine's phone rang at six a.m.. Jeff called to relay the news that Julie had turned up late last night. She was tan and glowing from the long weekend in the Bahamas. He met Nick, the new boyfriend. "He seems to be an all-right guy."

"We could pick you up in Salt Lake City this evening."

Outside, she heard the rumble of a camper pulling out early and smelled bacon frying as the campground came to life.

Jeff said he hadn't been into Maxine's condo yet. Finder was bringing the key. Jeff had run into an acquaintance at the golf club and had an opportunity to make five hundred bucks giving a foursome lessons on Wednesday. He could be in Reno on Thursday. Was that soon enough?

Didn't Jeff know how Maxine yearned to see Honora?

"Five hundred dollars will pay for my flight and all the extra baggage."

What was one more day? "I'm glad Julie's all right. Thursday's fine."

Maxine heard the relief in Jeff's voice when he told her that Julie had left her phone in the boyfriend's car.

"Any sign of Lotto?" Maxine wanted to whisper the dreaded name.

"Maybe he's given up."

Maxine didn't think Lotto ever gave up. Lotto with his wary eyes...vigilant, circumspect, and cunning. Her personal nightmare.

They said goodbye, and with a jolt, Maxine remembered today was the first of July. Someday she would have to move beyond this date. Maybe today with the long drive, and their destination in sight. How bad could a day be that began with caramel flan?

# *Thirty-five*

The workers had launched a new drug sub. Lotto got daily updates of the sub's maiden voyage as it plowed the long, low trek through the Caribbean to Mexico, where the cargo would be off-loaded for the trip to the U.S. It was pure hell to deal with the Mexican cartels. Lotto had feelers out to replace the Mexicans: in Jamaica, the Bahamas, Puerto Rico, Haiti, even Cuba.

In his office, he paced in front of his desk, stopping at the wide window to peer at late-afternoon Miami and the blue water beyond. On the street below, people popped into bars for a drink before the drive home. Lotto imagined a pleasant stroll through Lincoln Road Mall, and Angelika waiting for him later, wearing a silk dress, expecting a nice dinner, one *not* cooked by her. He had made a reservation for two at Azul, an evening that would surely cost five hundred dollars with drinks and food. Lotto hoped to hell the boutique would be closed by the time they arrived. The subs and their cargo had put a dent in his discretionary cash. Of course, he and Angelica could make the scene at Mango's but too many people in his trade partied there, and Lotto always kept business and pleasure separate.

He walked back to the desk and drained his demitasse. Once the sub's cargo was out of Mexico with the endless hassles and the exorbitant bribes, Lotto would be a happy man. He had been scheming for a year to avoid everything Mexican, but those arrangements took ungodly amounts of time and money. Negotiations. Relationships. Understanding whom to trust. When he had all his ducks in a row, it would be *adios putas. Adios Mexicanos.*

Last week, El Tigre's domestic situation had become a new crisis. His Colombian wife was sick. Cancer. Lotto had advanced him some money for travel and doctors. Now El Tigre wanted to take her to Houston for treatment. Lotto had given grudging consent. The wife had family, didn't she? They could tend to her needs. He needed El Tigre back on the job. Right away.

Yesterday, Marta, a middle-aged woman in a business suit, a woman whose appearance inspired trust, made a trip to Chicago and produced a document showing that her employer was the rightful owner of Caliendo's missing laptop. Soon Lotto would have her report.

How long had they been tied in knots by the disappearance of this infernal machine? Today the hacker Lotto kept on the payroll, the one who had cracked his way into the rental car companies' records, was making a forensic examination of the recovered laptop. It took all Lotto's patience not to call and check with the guy every hour. The hacker, hunkered down in a tiny, anonymous office, insisted he needed to concentrate and interruptions were unproductive.

Lotto sipped from the demitasse, surprised it was empty. He didn't want to bring attention to this laptop business. He had already sent two men to Chicago to debrief the laptop thief. They had been instructed not to hurt him. *Don't scare the shit out of him, either.* Conduct a serious conversation, with only the understated amount of menace to get the truth.

He fetched a bottle of water from the mini-fridge. Maxine's boyfriend Jeff had arrived on schedule. Lotto's men were tailing him and if they were lucky, he would lead them to Maxine. Of course, luck was a variable, not a constant, and good planning and follow-through often produced so-called luck.

Lotto drank the water and checked his Rolex. He realized he was humming a popular salsa tune from Colombia, but before he could recall the lyrics, his cell rang.

An encrypted call from Enrique. Lotto arranged to meet him in Miami Beach at 21st Street where the beach boardwalk began. They could talk free from the worry of electronic bugs.

~ * ~

Enrique appeared, sweating after the short stroll from where he had parked. Wearing flip-flops. Lotto glanced down at his own New Balance UK Sneakers, shoes that could hike all the way to Ft. Lauderdale.

"What?" asked Enrique, noticing Lotto's look of displeasure and glancing down at his feet.

"Dumb ass shoes for a walk."

"I didn't know..." Enrique's hand made a vague gesture toward the flip-flops.

"You know now." Lotto's eyes narrowed. "This better not take half the night, because I don't have time." He tapped his watch. "Two reports. The computer and Maxine's boyfriend.

Lotto started down the boardwalk.

"Hey, wait," Enrique said, "I have to get my notes."

Lotto stopped, turned and said, "You will tear each page into pieces, very small pieces, and put one page only in each trash container we pass."

"Sure, Lotto." Enrique opened a small spiral notebook and flipped through the pages. Lotto began walking again, but slower.

The evening still oozed heat and humidity, but shadows from the palms fell across the boardwalk and a whisper of breeze came off the water. The sky was a pure blue with a brush of white clouds, and the ocean edging the pale beach was a greener blue. Lotto closed his eyes and thought of the Caribbean.

"Marta said the computer was still in the evidence room in Chicago when she arrived."

"Get to the point."

"They handed over the computer *and* the police report."

"I know about the laptop. My hacker is already working on it."

Enrique had begun to sweat and to wipe his forehead, so Lotto slowed his pace even more, resigning himself to a stroll, not a walk.

"Marta passed a copy of the police report to the questioners before she brought back the computer."

Enrique kept flipping pages. His shoes made a maddening flop-flop-flop.

His eyes met Lotto's. "The thief said he broke the car window, snatched the laptop, and carried it home. He reported the laptop was 'empty.' Just Window's Internet Explorer. Does that sound right?"

*It did not sound right at all.*

"The *ladrón* spent all night and part of the next day surfing the web and installing a game. While he was playing, the police came to his door, asked for the computer and arrested him."

Lotto permitted himself a snarky smile. "If he was online for that long, then naturally the police would have shown up."

Enrique found a handkerchief in his shorts and wiped his forehead. "The *ladrón* lived less than a mile away from where he grabbed the laptop."

"And no one reported the laptop stolen?" asked Lotto.

Enrique craned his neck to check out two young women in tank tops and skimpy shorts.

"Will you stop gawking?"

Enrique tore another page to bits and dropped them into a trash container.

"Think about it, Lotto," he said, his dark eyes serious with concentration. "If you ripped off a computer and then someone took it from you, well, would *you* report it stolen?"

"It would be fucking stupid. But not all thieves are smart." Lotto stared out to sea. "Was the thief's story to the cops the same one he told our questioners?" he asked.

"Identical. We gave the guy a couple hundred bucks and said, 'This conversation never happened.' The thief said the car was a white sedan. Illinois license plates."

Lotto stopped walking and leaned against the wooden railing.

Enrique still panted slightly. The man ate too much and was getting a shape like a manatee. His plump elbow nudged Lotto.

Next to them a woman in tight blue shorts was stretching her hamstrings. Lotto glared at Enrique, pulled his own eyes away and stared out to sea, watching a cruise ship disappear over the horizon.

"Your second report. Maxine's boyfriend."

"Good news, Lotto. Just like you said. This *hombre* Jeff arrived at his sister's house Monday night. Talked to some neighbors. That's where our followers picked him up. We have a big team in place because, well, discretion is required, and the police may still be watching the sister's house. It may not be so easy to find out which flight he's taking."

Lotto scowled. "Tell the followers to pressure the sister's boyfriend for the information. And the team will need a photo of this Jeff."

He turned onto a short boardwalk that led to the beach. Seagrape grew in the sand, and the breeze ruffled the fronds of the few palms. Enrique turned his face into the faint wind and smiled.

Lotto was concerned about the laptop's files. He couldn't understand why the laptop had no files. Had LoJack deleted *everything?* Lotto rubbed his hand over his chin and turned back to the main boardwalk.

"The first signal from the laptop came from Foxborough, only one suburb away from Caliendo's house where Maxine lived. Now Caliendo's laptop shows up in Chicago where Maxine's boyfriend's ex-wife lives."

"Yeah, Lotto, but all the way across a big town. I'd say a coincidence." He looked to Lotto for confirmation.

Lotto didn't believe in coincidences. In his mind, Maxine had always had her husband's computer.

Enrique kicked the sand out of his flip-flops. "Hey, we walked all the way to Thirty-fifth Street. Getting a good workout in today, huh, Lotto?"

"Not as good as you will get in the future. You're joining a gym."

"Ah Lotto! I hate exercise."

Lotto could order his people to put the screws on the Chicago thief or Jeff's ex-wife, but the most direct approach was to find Maxine and ask her in a way that would produce answers. Then Lotto had another thought. Maxine had hired that PI who had driven her to the deli. The PI had given Lotto's name to the cops, who practically met El Tigre at Maxine's front door. Nobody had a shred of evidence, but now they were all walking on eggs. The PI must know where Maxine was. If Lotto proceeded with caution, this could be a fruitful avenue of inquiry.

And this nonsense with El Tigre's wife had to stop. He needed El Tigre here, ready to travel, with his mind on business.

# *Thirty-six*

*Follow the road.*

They got an early start under a generous blue canopy of sky with the sun at their backs. The wide open spaces made Maxine want to take a deep breath all the way to her solar plexus, and then slowly exhale, ridding herself of all the bad stuff.

Not far from Rawlins, the first Continental Divide crossing was not a terror-filled inching along under a towering peak on a winding road, but rather endless ribbon of I-80. Maxine would not have noticed the crossing except for the large green interstate sign announcing the divide at altitude 7,000 feet. The second "divide" was also an easy crossing with the interstate four lanes wide and only a few hills spotted with low greenery. After days behind the wheel, Maxine felt more confidence in her ability to maneuver the RV and she occasionally passed a slow-moving car or truck.

Every exit had signs advertising "fireworks." Maxine nixed Kaylee's repeated pleas for firecrackers, bottle rockets, and sparklers. Undeterred, Kaylee continued to lobby, saying "if my dad doesn't like them, can't we just give them away?"

"No way."

Kaylee stuck out her lower lip. Finally, near the Utah-Wyoming border, Maxine stopped at another Little America and bought two CDs of Western songs. Kaylee perked up to the jaunty tunes and they sang rousing verses of "Sweet Betsy from Pike" and "My Darling Clementine."

Sometimes, Maxine felt as if she might make a decent mother.

~ * ~

Maxine remained in survival mode this landmark day, keeping her mind far from her parents and the awful events of ten years ago. She did allow herself to think of Larry, gone for over a month. Unlucky Larry, who had left her with his laptop and this dangerous mess. She should have turned the computer over to the police right away. The bad angel always offered perilous alternatives to the right path. Still, Lotto could have learned that the laptop had once been in her possession, so maybe nothing would have changed. He might have even had her killed before she realized her danger. Sometimes it was impossible to know how to juggle a hot potato.

The moon landscape of the Great Salt Lake desert flew by in a pale blur. In a couple of hours they would be in Wells, Nevada, with one more day of heavy-duty driving, then Reno. Once the RV was hooked up in Reno, Maxine would rent a car. When she thought of Jeff's arrival, her heart beat a little faster, imagining his happy-to-see-her smile, his arm around her shoulder. She needed his moral support to reconnect with Honora. How could she bear it after all this effort if a surly Honora slammed the door in her face?

They stopped for lemonade in mid-afternoon, and Maxine called Jeff, who told her he had a flight to Reno on Thursday. *At last*. Maxine returned a call that she had missed while driving, a mystery number. She reached a mad-as-hell George Blaisdell, whom she had contrived to forget about since Chicago. From the sound of his voice, he hadn't had a relaxing vacation.

"You were supposed to call me. I heard you've been in the Boston area without hearing one damn word. My contact in Florida said you had a close call with some goons breaking into your house. People who might know your ex-husband. You could connect some dots for us." He really sounded pissed.

"I called, and you were on vacation. Look, this isn't a good time to talk." Maxine couldn't remember exactly what she had said last time they talked. She would have to get her story straight. The bad angel fluttered her wings and smiled darkly.

"Where the hell are you?" Blaisdell asked.

"I'm in...Utah." *Or pretty close to Utah.* She stared at a landscape of barren hills.

"What the f—" he stopped himself, "are you doing there?"

"It's a long story."

"I've got all day," he said in a petulant voice.

"I'll call you this evening. Once I get settled." Anything to delay an unpleasant conversation, or more likely a browbeating. "I've been through a lot and I don't want to be yelled at." *Set some ground rules.*

"Nobody's going to yell."

Almost five o'clock and sixty miles to Wells. The dry western heat parched her skin, which drank buckets of moisturizer. The lemonade had left a sour taste in her mouth.

~ * ~

Near I-80, the Wells RV park covered a couple acres of rangeland with a few scrubby trees and half-bare brown hills footing a mountain range still pocked with areas of snow. Maxine completed the hookups of water and electricity, and found the correct plug for the electrical cord.

After dinner, Kaylee sprawled in the dinette clutching her doll and the floppy-eared rabbit, fixing her tired eyes on the miniscule TV. Maxine opened her laptop to check her email before she called Blaisdell. Nothing of interest except an email from Finder, a little strange because Finder liked the phone. She clicked on the message:

> *"Sorry to let you know like this. Something hinky came up Lotto-wise, and I have to take my wife and leave town for a while. For both our sakes, don't call me or try to make contact. Delete this email. Be cautious. These people are very bad."*

Lotto had gone after Finder. Lotto would have reason to believe Finder knew where Maxine was. Lotto's goons must have threatened Finder's wife, because only something horrific would scare Finder.

This was Maxine's doing. Meeting Lotto at the deli had been an immense blunder. Lotto still felt invulnerable.

Dutifully, Maxine deleted Finder's email, and closed the laptop. Like a leaf in an autumn gale, her whole body quaked. Finder was her crutch and her safe haven, someone she leaned on. She pictured his blunt but kind face, his bristly salt and pepper hair, his ironic smile. Now he, too, was on the run. Still, Finder was an ex-cop. He would have resources. She wondered if the "bad" cop was down in Florida. How many cops had Lotto bought?

Maxine squared her shoulders. She had to call thorn-in-her-side George Blaisdell. She sat on the retractable step of the RV, puffing on her after-dinner cigarette and clutching her cell phone while the smell of grilling steak drifted her way. On the highway, big semis rumbled as they changed gears getting on and off the nearby interchange. The warm breeze felt soothing on her dry skin. Maxine punched "send."

She and Blaisdell went through their usual song and dance. He asked her to describe what had happened in Florida. He even sounded a little bored.

"The people who killed my husband found out that I had a business relationship with Sheldon Finder, the PI."

"Yeah, I know all about that. Finder's one of the best in South Florida, I'm told. A straight arrow.

"Did you hear what happened??"

"I want to hear it from you."

The sun descended toward the dark hilltops, sinking through a sky layered with pink and blue, a baby shower sky. Maxine ground her cigarette stub into the fine dirt.

Her pulse raced and the evening came back as if it were only last night.

*The cold dark water. The relentless fear. Diving to avoid the boat. Seeing Jeff like the light at the end of the tunnel.*

She told him what she could without too many details.

"Jesus."

"I knew I couldn't stay there anymore, so my ah, neighbor that I am...friendly with...offered to get me out of Florida. I had leased my landlady's car, and we thought that might be compromised, too. The neighbor has no job right now, so we cut and ran. We've been travelling since then, hoping to stay under the radar."

"Why didn't you tell me about Lopez?" asked Blaisdell.

Always Lotto. She saw his face, his bold, arrogant eyes.

*Never tell a lie when a half-truth will do.*

"I met him once at a football game. There was nothing to tell. Larry liked him." Silence. She could almost hear him fuming.

"Why aren't you being straight with me?"

The nearby camp laundry emitted bleachy blasts of Clorox and detergent. Another truck roared onto the highway.

"I'm scared to death. After what someone did to my husband. And to the men who killed him. Everyone connected to Larry is in danger." *Everyone connected to me is in danger.* "And I still obsess about the bad cop."

"That was just a story to scare you."

"It worked."

"How is your investigation going? Did you find the drug money?" Maxine made an effort to sound interested.

"Fat chance. Where are you and your neighbor headed?"

"California, probably."

"Stay in touch. Once a week. No excuses."

~ * ~

They made Reno and pulled into a spacious RV park in town. Playing back her recorder with Jeff's instructions, and with a pair of latex gloves, Maxine hooked up the sewer hose and opened the gray water valve.

Close to a big glitzy hotel, the park had everything a road-weary traveler needed. Their fellow RVers always dispensed helpful advice about highways and good restaurants, recommendations about campgrounds and sightseeing. Borrowing the proverbial cup of sugar was acceptable, even welcome. Increasingly Maxine was taking comfort in the nearness of nomads like themselves. The RVer next to them saw Lucy peering out the window and came by and introduced himself. She wished she could ditch her paranoia and make real friends.

# *Thirty-seven*

The next day, Maxine and Kaylee drove to the Reno airport to meet Jeff's flight. Kaylee could never walk past a gift shop without taking a look inside. At the PGA Tour Shop, Maxine bought her a junior visor but resisted the girl's entreaties to purchase a Tour straw hat for Jeff.

"Your dad looks better in a baseball cap." Maxine loved the way the cap made his blond hair curl behind his ears and along the back of the cap. "Don't you want to wear your new visor?" she asked.

Maxine gave Kaylee's fine blonde hair a quick brush and adjusted the visor to fit her head.

Last night she had rented a Ford Fusion at the airport, and she and Kaylee cruised by Honora's apartment building on Kuenzli Street along the river. The complex looked well-tended, not one of the sleazy down-on-its-luck places in other neighborhoods. Maxine felt a surge of optimism. Honora lived in a decent apartment.

Now, standing at the baggage claim, she grabbed a cart, because Jeff had called earlier from Florida saying he had a suitcase for each of them and his golf bag. Maxine allowed herself to relax, even to feel congratulatory for having driven three cowgirls and the monster RV from Denver to Reno.

"Can I go to the bathroom by myself just this once?" asked Kaylee. "I want to look at my visor in the mirror."

Maxine hesitated. Kaylee was responsible, and Reno was just an overgrown small town.

"Come back right away, then." She had begun to sound like a mother. Maxine glanced at her watch. Jeff would call when he was on the ground. She kept her eyes fixed on the restroom entrance. Kaylee came out, glanced around, saw Maxine wave, and walked back toward the luggage carousels.

Kaylee stopped dead and peered at something on the floor—a piece of paper? Maxine watched her expression change to the puzzled but thoughtful frown. Kaylee picked up the paper and stared at it.

Maxine abandoned the cart and headed for Kaylee. Airport floors with shoes from god-knows-where marching across them were filthy no matter how clean they looked. Now Kaylee would have to go back to the restroom and wash her hands. A man standing nearby held out his hand and took Kaylee's paper. She didn't speak to him. Good girl. Maxine walked faster. She should not have let Kaylee go by herself. The man flashed a false-looking smile at Kaylee, who kept her head down and continued to walk toward Maxine.

Maxine waited for Kaylee to cover the last yards. *What was this about?* She scrutinized the man who had snatched the paper out of Kaylee's hand. Neatly dressed. He waited with another man. They were dark, maybe Hispanic, not unusual in the West. Both of them had lost interest in Kaylee while they studied the mysterious paper.

Kaylee shuffled up to Maxine, still with her head down. Before Maxine could ask what happened, Kaylee said, "That man has a picture of my dad."

"What?"

"He dropped a picture of Dad standing in front of Aunt Julie's house. When I picked it up, he took it away from me." Her confused eyes met Maxine's. "I remembered what you said, and I didn't talk to him."

Why did these men have a photo of Jeff? Maxine didn't like this at all; in fact her puzzlement had morphed into the jittery fear that had become an unwelcome companion.

"Let's walk toward the ladies' room. Hurry!" She added, "You handled that very well."

"What about the cart? Aren't we gonna wait for Dad?"

"We'll find another one." Maxine glanced over her shoulder, but the men showed no more interest in Kaylee. Then she saw a third man approach the other two, a huge man in a Panama hat with a Madras hatband. She couldn't tear her eyes away. It was the frightening hulk who had come after her in Miami when she left Lotto.

"Quick! Into the ladies room!" Maxine put her hand on Kaylee's shoulder.

Kaylee raced ahead, apparently noting the urgency in Maxine's voice.

Once safe inside, with a hand quaking like an aspen leaf, Maxine groped through her handbag for her cell phone. Kaylee stood beside her, still with an open mouth. Maxine had to reach Jeff before those men saw him.

"Go wash your hands. You touched the floor." Kaylee walked to a vacant sink.

Jeff didn't pick up. She dialed again. And again. Then she stuck her head out the door and saw all three of them still standing together in front of the carousel.

Her cell rang.

"Oh my god, Jeff. Are you off the plane?"

He was at the gate waiting to disembark. In a low, breathless voice, Maxine put her head close to the wall, hoping no one would overhear her conversation. She explained what Kaylee had seen. What had happened. Where they were.

"What can we do?" she asked, on the verge of panic.

"I can't show up at the baggage claim, that's for sure." Did he sound exasperated or scared like her? Oh god, just when she thought they were home free.

There was a long pause while Jeff must have been thinking. Kaylee busied herself with the water and too much soap.

"How could anyone know you'd be on this flight? Who would have told them? Kaylee said they had a photograph of you in front of your sister's place." The tile walls of the restroom seemed to close in on her. Maxine had never felt so trapped, so hopeless. She had missed Jeff so much. And now this.

Another long pause from Jeff. "I'm thinking."

Maxine asked, "Should I call nine-one-one?" She looked in the mirror and took off her western hat. Damp hair clung to the back of her neck and her whole head felt sweaty. Her eyes looked red and squinty, with that tasered look again.

"Call the airport police." Jeff spoke calmly. "And tell them you need protection."

"I'll say there's a drug deal or somebody with a gun at the baggage claim."

"Max, that's crazy. Just take care of Kaylee."

Maxine looked at the girl pirouetting in front of the mirror, adjusting her visor.

"She's all right."

"I'll get off the phone so you can call security." He hung up.

Maxine peered out the door again at the men. Tall one in plaid shirt, short one in blue shirt and big one wearing the Panama hat with a tan sport coat. *Drug runners waiting for a pickup. Armed. Dangerous.* She had long ago blocked the ID on her cell, and she had a good vantage point from the doorway. Still by the mirror, Kaylee admired herself with her visor backwards. Maxine dialed 9-1-1. She felt panicky, almost breathless.

*Drug runners waiting for a pickup at the baggage claim. Armed. Dangerous.*

The bad angel could even save your butt.

# *Thirty-eight*

Twelve floors above Brickell Boulevard, Lotto, barefoot, paced the wrap-around balcony of his apartment. The sky was black, with a small scattering of stars. He thought of the hidden cove where his subs were assembled. There, in the impenetrable jungle, the night sky blazed with millions of stars. Insects sang and bats darted through the darkness.

Lotto looked toward Biscayne Bay. *Mierda*! Why hadn't anyone heard from the sub? It should have arrived on the Mexican coast by now, at an inlet south of Tampico. *Where was the sub?*

He hoped this blackout was simply a communications failure. He left the balcony and crossed the rosewood floor to the serving cart in the dining room where he poured himself an extra-large portion of rum. He popped into the kitchen and grabbed a few ice cubes. The oven clock read 12:47. *Where was the sub?*

Another worry was that he not heard from El Tigre and his crew. They should have reported from Reno hours ago. If Lotto was ever tempted to try his own "product," it would be on a white-knuckle night like this one.

As if the sub and the Reno situation were not enough to light a fire in his belly, the hacker working on Caliendo's laptop had hemmed and hawed and said that, although rest assured, he had found the erased files, they were all password protected. The hacker would need more time to restore the data, crack the password, and report back to Lotto. More time! A computer could drive a man *loco*.

Jiggling the ice in the glass, and taking a deep quaff of the potent rum, Lotto leaned on the balustrade and stared at the dark bay, lit by the green lamps along the waterfront and the running lights of a few pleasure boats returning late from fishing, carousing, and all the things Lotto had no time to indulge in. He gulped more rum and told himself that it took patience to acquire patience, and he had never had enough patience to get any.

*Mierda*, he had left a cigarette burning indoors. He rarely smoked, but tonight he just had to. The phone, which he had left on the outdoor table, sounded while he looked for the ashtray. He found it in the kitchen and hurried back to the balcony to answer. *Encrypted. News at last*. Lotto took a deep breath, hit his encrypt button, and said "*si*?"

Enrique, the fat, nervous conduit of information.

"Bad news, Lotto, and—"

"The sub?"

"No, the sub arrived without incident, but a crazy problem in Reno."

"Where are you?"

"In a taxi a few blocks away. Can I come up?"

Lotto's apartment was his haven. Even Angelika was not allowed to visit regularly. Now Enrique wanted admission to his private space. The alternative was to agree on a meeting place and leave the apartment at 1:00 a.m. with no bodyguard.

"Let me know when you get here. I'll ring you in." Even to Lotto, his voice sounded gruff.

"I'll just give you a quick update, Lotto."

What could have gone wrong in Reno? A cut and dried operation that should lead them to Maxine. What had Enrique called it? "A crazy problem." *Problem* was bad enough. But *crazy*?

At least the sub and its cargo had made landfall. Lotto paced up and down the balcony, bracing himself for bad news.

Within minutes, he heard the buzzer and then Enrique's voice sounded on the intercom. When he heard a hesitant knock, Lotto answered the door. Enrique gaped at his surroundings like a dumb tourist. Did he think Lotto lived in some conspicuous hideosity with ornate furniture, plastic plants and rooms full of gewgaws?

"Come in." Lotto tried not to look pissed, never an easy thing for him.

"Nice place, Lotto. Very clean and white. You got a pool up on the roof? I could get used to that."

Without a shred of hospitality, Lotto pointed Enrique to the white leather sofa.

Enrique plopped down and looked around again.

"About the 'crazy' problem," Lotto said, stalking up and down the room.

Enrique settled his bulk into the smooth leather and relaxed too much for Lotto's liking. "El Tigre called. He and his two men were waiting at the airport in Reno by the baggage claim. They had a photo of this Jeff *hombre*. Out of nowhere, a shitload of cops, airport security—they all rush in and surround them."

Lotto stared at Enrique. *How could such a thing happen?*

"All three have to produce IDs. They show their tourist visas. Then they are taken away for 'questioning.' Still at the airport. More detectives and plainclothes arrive. The DEA. Homeland security. Our guys ask for a lawyer, but nobody's listening. They are separated and questioned. 'Who are you waiting for? What plane is he on? What airline? Are you waiting for a package? A piece of luggage? If you're not meeting someone, and not waiting for a package, why are you here?'"

Enrique paused for emphasis, quoting again. They asked Florenz, "'Who is the man in your photo?'"

*Cojones de dios*. Each question stoked Lotto's rage. He bolted his rum. He had paid for those *putas* to fly to Reno and follow the boyfriend to Maxine and instead they get themselves in trouble.

Enrique, parked on Lotto's white leather sofa like a big toad, continued. "Our *hombres* hadn't prepared a story. Luis said a kid dropped the photo. He had no idea who it was. They were going to return it if they saw her again. Florenz said the three of them had met to do a little gaming at the airport. Before they hit the big casinos. El Tigre said *nada*."

"And then?" Lotto circled the room. In all this chaos, Jeff would have met Maxine, collected his bags, and they would be god knows where by now. Probably gone. Fuming, Lotto paced up and down in front of the big windows, not bothering to hide his exasperation.

"They were arrested?"

Enrique watched Lotto pace. "No. No. Not arrested. Detained. Merely detained. They were released three hours ago," he said. "After long questioning. El Tigre had a knife, but the other two had nothing. They found out that for the next hour, everyone coming off a plane had to show an ID and present a claim ticket to get their bags. The drug-sniffing dogs only found a little cannabis in a woman's suitcase. Our *hombres* were released. The police looked for the man in the photo, but he didn't appear."

Lotto paused to stare through the plate glass window to the dark ocean. The bad news rolled in like the breakers on the beach. *Cojones de dios!* Lotto's people were supposed to remain anonymous, away from scrutiny. But the most dire event, worse even than Maxine having eluded him again, was not knowing what lay behind this near-disaster.

# *Thirty-nine*

The garden apartment complex where Honora lived wasn't as upscale as Maxine had first thought. The flags at the entryway, the recently mowed grass and well-tended shrubbery gave a good first impression, but up close the buildings looked like barracks, and each unit had a room air conditioner placed below an upstairs window.

Maxine parked the rented Ford in a guest space and sat for a moment to collect her wits. She noticed a playground on the other side of the lawn and heard the squeals of kids having fun. The sight reminded her of the many times long ago when she had pushed Honora's swing.

*Higher, Massine. Swing higher.* Honora's baby name for her. *Massine.* Seven years apart. Maxine had taken care of Honora from the beginning, more mother than sister. Honora was Daddy's favorite, and he was always on Maxine's case for wanting to be with her friends instead of babysitting. *Your little sister is a responsibility you must not neglect.*

Today had been hot with that stark western sizzle that made your skin feel like baked adobe bricks, but now the light was softer and the dust had settled. In a couple of hours, the high desert would be cool. Residents had returned home for the evening and smells of teriyaki drifted her way from someone's grill. Larry's teriyaki chicken, so moist and tender with the right amount of sesame oil and garlic. Today was Friday and Larry had been gone five weeks. She thought of him less as time went by.

Maxine hoped never to have another experience like yesterday at the airport. Her chest still had that weird hollow feeling and a couple times she had started shaking for no reason. After the cops appeared in the baggage area and led those three men away, she and Kaylee left the restroom and found Jeff by the slots, trying to phone her again. Maxine told him to take Kaylee and get the car. She would pick up the bags. They exchanged her parking stub for his luggage claim checks.

A few minutes later, when Maxine returned to the baggage area, Jeff's flight number was posted and soon the carousel lumbered to life. The first bags appeared, and so did a man clutching a sheet of paper like Kaylee had described. Jeff's photo. The man didn't look at the bags, but he scrutinized the group clustered around the arriving luggage.

Maxine found *her* suitcase and recognized Jeff's golf clubs carrier, with the big "JD" on the black Callaway bag, but she had to call him again to ask what his suitcase looked like. A black wheeled duffel bag. He wanted to know what make the car was. Kaylee didn't remember. *They were like the three stooges*. It would have been funny if Maxine hadn't been so anxious. She found Jeff's bag, paid for another cart and wheeled the unwieldy collection of luggage away.

Everyone had to show claim checks and even pass the muster of a dog on a leash. The dog had shown no interest in Maxine's bags, but went crazy, straining at his harness in front of a green suitcase. Sniffing for drugs? Maxine had hustled her cart out of the terminal.

~ * ~

Sitting in the parking lot of Honora's building in the rental car, recalling those tense moments made Maxine crave a cigarette. Should she have rehearsed a speech for Honora? Her mind went blank. What would she say? This was going to be harder than she had imagined.

Maxine wiped her palms on her skirt and glanced in the rearview mirror. Her haircut looked shaggy, and she had raccoon eyes from wearing sunglasses in the harsh Western sun. Her eyes stared back at her, bloodshot and weary, as if they had witnessed too much bad stuff. Maxine gave her hair a quick brushing and grabbed *The Dangerous Book for Boys*, colorfully wrapped, a present for her nephew.

She missed Sheldon Finder, needed him. What had happened to Finder?

Maxine took a few more moments to compose herself. *Stay calm. Don't cry. Be loving.*

*Now.*

She inhaled deeply, exhaled through her mouth, and left the car. Number thirty-two was easy to find, on the ground floor. She stood, shoulders back, with all the resolution she could muster, staring at a tan door, the same color as the Nevada desert. Maxine pressed the bell, heard its ring and the approaching steps. Was Honora peering through the peephole? What if she didn't answer? Blood pounded in Maxine's ears.

# *Forty*

Who was ringing the bell at dinnertime? Honora left the frozen broccoli steaming on the stove, the onion on the chopping block, and wary as always, approached the front door. A quick glance through the peephole. Too vain to wear her glasses, she had to squint. Her eyes watered from the onion fumes. A neighbor? No, probably a saleswoman. Hadn't she seen the "no soliciting" signs? Likely some religious wingnut. Honora would get rid of her fast. She opened the door a crack.

Before she could open her mouth, the woman spoke. "Honora, it's me, Maxine." The voice sounded quivery and breathless.

Holy shit. She felt pure panic from her unsteady knees to her galloping heart. Her hands began to shake. She squinted again, and opened the door inches wider.

It *was* Maxine, turning up like a bad penny, older but still slim, with short hair and that "worried about you" big-sister look on her face.

For an infinitesimal moment, Honora felt a glimmer of gladness, but then her old survival instincts kicked in. She was tempted to close the door. No good had ever come from reconnecting with her past.

"What are *you* doing here?" She couldn't keep the words from crossing her lips. She began twisting the dishtowel in her hands, and tried to stop. *Don't show any nerves.*

Maxine said, "I'm your sister."

But before she could say more, Honora said, "I wanted to be left alone."

After the name change, and her careful avoidance of links to the past, how the hell had Maxine tracked her down?

Maxine said, "Honora, I've missed you so much. I just had to find you."

Honora couldn't stop staring, and she knew she wasn't providing the hoped for reception. Her nails dug into her palms, and her heart still hammered. For a moment she couldn't find her voice. "I...I have a new life now. I've buried the past."

She stared at Maxine, whose eyes looked so full of hope and sadness.

Maxine said, "Oh, sis—"

Honora interrupted again. "I've dumped it all behind me. Our parents. My problems." Her voice faltered. Why didn't she just slam the door? Instead, she continued, "*Everything.*" She pronounced "everything" with a grim finality. Her chin wavered. "My son knows nothing of any...family." She twisted the dishtowel again.

"But I've gone through hell to get here."

Maxine was always the family lover, wanting a crowded dinner table, women gossiping in the kitchen, birthday parties, and all that sentimental twaddle. She had an urge to brush Maxine off like a buzzing gnat. Instead, she stood stiff and prickly while Maxine wrapped strong arms around her. Jesus, what was she doing with all those muscles? Did she lift weights?

Ethan popped up next to Honora, his dark eyes staring at their visitor. "Ethan, go back to your cartoons." He hesitated, still curious. They had few visitors.

In the background, Honora heard a candy commercial. Wary, Ethan gave Maxine another questioning glance and disappeared.

Maxine looked pitiful, like she was going to weep. "Please. Just talk to me."

Honora nodded toward the sound of the television. "Ethan doesn't know anything about you."

Maxine held out her hand. "We don't have to revive the past. We can start from right now. I would love to meet my nephew."

*Get this over with.* "Sure, Max," Honora said. "No problem." She dabbed at her eyes with the towel and opened the door.

"I brought something for your little boy." Maxine stepped into the living room and held out the present.

Honora stared at the cowboy wrapping paper. *The fancy bookstore.*

Carrying the gift, Maxine followed her across the room. Honora felt a little surge of pride in the pale tan carpet with the modern beige sofa, the tile coffee table and two dark leather chairs, in one of which Ethan sprawled, his eyes on a flat screen television.

She led Maxine through a sliding door onto a cement patio. "I have to turn off the stove," she said, darting into the kitchen.

When she returned, she gave her sister a hard look. Although she needed a haircut, Maxine hadn't let herself go. She had a nice summer tan, and her figure still looked good. Those long, curvy legs. Honora felt the old ripple of envy. Maxine got the legs and she got the boobs, but any fool knew good legs lasted longer. She knew she looked older, even a bit shopworn. Honora peered at her sister's left hand. No glint from a wedding ring. Maxine had never been good at keeping a man. Her yellow shirt and white slacks weren't expensive, probably from Kohl's or the Gap. Maybe Target. Apparently no money there. Pity.

"You look wonderful!" Maxine said, as if she had expected to find the drug-addled girl of years back. Honora stood straight as Maxine scrutinized her hair, her face, and her clothes.

Honora wiped her hand across her eyes. "I had so much guilt, so much grief. No one will ever know. I decided a clean break would be best for all of us." She really laid it on, as she twisted the dishtowel into a figure eight.

A few tears wouldn't hurt, and Honora could summon them at will.

Maxine looked relieved, like she thought everything would be all right. Maxine was always a fool.

Honora gestured toward the striped patio chairs. She would be civil, catch up on Maxine's life and find out what Maxine wanted. Before she told her to get lost.

# *Forty-one*

The day after Maxine connected with Honora, she, Jeff, and Kaylee visited the aquatic driving range in the lake near their RV park. Jeff had promised Kaylee miniature golf, bumper cars, and a trip to the video arcade, but first he wanted to hit balls. The "range" was a big shallow lake with six floating island "greens." The objective was to hit the ball onto the green, not into the water. Trickier than it looked.

"Driving off the tee gets rid of all my tension," he said, eyes focused on the little islands. Kaylee stared at the hills in the distance. Maxine shot a ball into the lake.

Unable to concentrate on her golf, Maxine kept obsessing about her meeting with Honora the night before. She had hoped to include Honora and Ethan in their holiday plans, but Honora had squashed that idea.

After many consultations with her calendar, she had agreed to meet Maxine for lunch on Tuesday. "Just for an hour. I have a job, you know," spoken in a snotty voice. Maxine hoped she could warm to this standoffish Honora, with her truculent face and her cold attitude. Honora had even forgotten Maxine's divorce and remarriage to Larry, her memory paths apparently clouded by drugs. Maxine wanted the sister she remembered from childhood, not this stranger who stonewalled her. *Massine.*

She had a plan that needed Honora's participation, a plan that would ease all their troubles. If she could trust Honora. If Jeff wouldn't freak out.

"When can I meet the boy my age? When can I see Ethan? If he's almost my cousin, I think we should at least have a play date." Kaylee's voice had been querulous as she pestered Maxine.

"Maybe next week." Maxine didn't want to make promises that might be broken.

She stared at the brown hills with the cloudless blue sky overhead, thinking of the 4th of July tomorrow and recalling Larry's go-for-broke barbeques—big festive gatherings with all the patriotically colored paraphernalia—tablecloths, flowers, candles, red, white and blue lanterns for the kids. Larry had always donned his special chef's apron embellished with flag and fireworks, while Maxine's plainer apron advised: *Life is uncertain. Eat dessert first.* The nieces and nephews loved that. Corky in his wheelchair grinned and teased everyone, especially her.

*Ancient history.*

The sun shone. They had outwitted Lotto's goons. So why did this summer day feel like an ordeal?

An impatient Kaylee kicked her toe against the ground and wanted to get to the bumper cars. "This is so dumb and all the balls just go into the water. How much longer, Dad? Dad?"

Jeff executed drive after beautiful drive, mostly straight into the shallow lake. With his grip, his swing, and his legs positioned just so, shoulders lined up with the hole, he looked like the envy of every weekend duffer. Soon the golf balls began to bounce and carom off the floating islands. Finally, he whacked a ball that remained on the green, for a coveted hole-in-one.

A young woman rushed up to take a photo. Jeff held up his hand, smiled and said, "sorry, no pictures."

The girl looked crestfallen. "Don't you want a chance to win a trip to Hawaii?"

"We're in the witness protection program," Jeff said, still smiling.

"What's that?" asked Kaylee.

"A joke, sweetheart."

Maxine didn't know whether to laugh or cry. His "joke" felt like a knife slicing near the bone, too close to the truth.

Last night Kaylee's insistence that Jeff's photo had been taken in front of Aunt Julie's ("you could see the hummingbird feeder and everything") had prompted a call to Julie, but their problem didn't interest her. She said, "Kaylee has a big imagination."

What did interest her was that her new boyfriend had stopped returning calls and texts. When Maxine dared to suggest that maybe the missing boyfriend had actually taken the photo, Jeff objected.

"Finder vouched for him."

"He didn't 'vouch' for him. He doesn't even know him. He said the boyfriend was rich and had no police record."

Julie had issued a withering reference to Maxine as "that woman who is always in trouble," and planned a drive to Key Largo to her boyfriend's house. She called back later to report the house was empty. *Why was love so often terrible?*

With no particular evidence, Maxine suspected Lotto's sticky hand in all of this, and she wanted Finder's input, but Finder had vanished, too.

The one bit of good news was that Jeff had lucked into a job giving lessons at a "first rate golf club" in Lake Tahoe, an easy commute from Reno. The job was through Labor Day. Tomorrow they planned to drive to Tahoe and inspect the club. Maxine would try to find an apartment in Reno, one with two bedrooms and where Lucy would be welcome. The thought of so much privacy made her almost giddy.

Maybe Honora only needed a *little* time.

Jeff grabbed her elbow, pulling Maxine out of her thoughts. "The mini golf course is waiting."

~ * ~

The last stop, the Fun Quest Video Arcade, reeked of popcorn, too-sweet candy and sweaty kids. Already tired from the miniature golf and the bumper cars, Kaylee dragged the toes of her sneakers and wore a fearsome scowl. Her hair had straggled out of her ponytail and lay against her neck in lank tangles. In spite of the sunscreen, her nose and cheeks looked red.

Kaylee met Maxine's suggestion that they come back to the arcade tomorrow with a spate of hysterical tears. Maxine was tempted to join in. When Jeff, sunburned between his freckles, joked, "I am going to set my hair on fire," Kaylee cried louder. Maxine felt utterly exhausted, like her ankles were encased in fifty-pound weights.

Jeff said Kaylee needed down time, hell, they all needed down time, and the three of them piled into the rental car and found a Mexican restaurant. After dinner, they headed to the campground. When they arrived at the RV park, Jeff pulled the rental car up next to the motorhome. They were just in time to watch the sun set behind the Sierras. While Kaylee dawdled getting out of her car seat, their next-door neighbor, Stan, came over and spoke under his breath to Jeff. Now what? Jeff looked surprised and the men talked in low tones. The neighbor pointed at their RV a couple of times. Finally, Jeff, eyes troubled, thanked Stan and admonished Kaylee to "hurry it up."

Maxine felt twinges of anxiety skittering through her chest.

Inside the camper, Jeff barked at Kaylee to get into her pajamas, no arguments. She stomped off to the bedroom. Lucy raced out and dug furiously in her litter box.

"What was that all about?" Maxine asked, nodding toward Stan's RV.

"Two dudes came nosing around our camper. Stan said they were eyeing the Florida license plates and the 'Closest to the Hole' logo. Stan came over to find out what they wanted. They asked if Jeff Dunmire the golfer owned this camper and if his girlfriend Maxine was with him." Jeff rubbed his finger along his nose. "They said they were friends of ours, but had 'lost' our phone number."

"Oh, shit." Maxine's head felt like it would explode.

Jeff plopped down at the dinette table. "Stan asked them who he should say had stopped by."

"'Don't bother, no problem, we'll catch up with them later.'"

Jeff looked like he hadn't slept for days.

"Did Stan describe them?" Her heart raced like she'd done an hour of high impact aerobics.

He said, "'Nobody you would remember. Faint Spanish accents. Very polite.'"

Maxine's eyes met Jeff's, and a wordless communication passed between them. *They would have to run again.*

Jeff squinted. "How the hell do we find another camping spot on this weekend? They'll be at capacity." He rubbed his hand over the back of his neck. Maxine felt a spell of the shakes coming on.

"We should drive to the coast," Jeff said, watching her. "I'll shitcan the job."

"I want to stay close to Honora. The West Coast is not an option, at least not now for me."

"She can't even be bothered to see you! Or to bring her kid over here. Your priorities are skewed seven ways from Sunday, Maxine."

She put her head in her hands.

"You want to stay *here*? You're crazy." Jeff had never sounded this stressed.

"I could ask Honora," Maxine said. "She might know of a less public campground."

"Did you tell her about our...problems?"

"I could make up a story. Say it's too noisy in this park."

"Make up your story fast, because we're going to get our butts out of here."

~ * ~

Maxine was taken aback when Honora stated, "Even after all these years, I knew something was wrong from your voice." Maxine watched Honora run fingers with chewed nails through her dark bangs.

The only sound was the hum of the air conditioner. "I remembered that tone of yours, and realized that even Miss Perfect might have landed in some kind of trouble. Genteel trouble was my first guess. In a hundred years, I wouldn't have guessed you would be involved in cartels and stolen computers with a drug lord's muscle tailing you across the country."

Maxine forced a wry laugh. "I find it hard to believe myself."

She was sitting in Honora's living room drinking a Coke while they chatted and smoked. .Jeff and Kaylee were likely to be asleep in the motorhome by now. It was parked in Honora's apartment complex, in a special lot for RVs and hidden by the shrubbery that lined the swimming pool.

Maxine's call to Honora asking about camping spots had elicited the last thing Maxine had anticipated, an invitation. She drove the rental car and Jeff followed in the motorhome. Everyone was introduced. Ethan showed Kaylee his new Wii, and later, Jeff gave Ethan a tour of the motorhome, which he declared to be "awesome." Kaylee introduced Ethan to the gray kitten, with everything friendly and civilized and for Maxine, just a bit unreal.

Honora curled her legs on the beige sofa and sipped her cola. Maxine had told her, as briefly as possible, about Larry's last night, and the men who were interested in Jeff and her and the RV. She hadn't mentioned the safety deposit box in Foxborough or the Panamanian account.

"You should write a book," Honora said. "*We* should write a book. *The Harvey Sisters and All the Trouble They Got Into*. I like this better: *The Harvey Sisters and How They Fucked Up*." She laughed.

"Maybe when I get out of this mess," Maxine said.

"I had dealings with drug people in Florida," said Honora with a shudder. "They aren't a forgiving bunch."

"What I need is a place to hide out for the rest of the summer," Maxine said. "Jeff could rent an efficiency apartment close to the golf club in Tahoe. Visit on his off days. Kaylee and I need to be invisible. Jeff was well known on the tour, and the club may want to publicize his giving lessons." Maxine picked at a cuticle.

"You always did that," Honora said.

"Did what?"

"Fiddle with your fingernails. You know, all of a sudden, I just remember everything. It's crazy."

"I never forgot you," Maxine said in a soft voice.

"You should have." Honora stared at Maxine with big, questioning eyes. "Can you forgive me? Can you forget what I did?"

"I forgave you long ago," Maxine said, feeling a lump lodge in her throat. "How could you, how could anyone have known what would happen? Mom and Dad had been on a collision course for years. But none of us expected...expected...*that*." She couldn't say the words "expected our dad to kill Mom and her boyfriend and himself." Maxine started on her cuticle again and stopped. "It was ten years ago on Friday. I remembered when I was driving across Utah."

"Ten years. Jesus." Honora stood up. "How about a real drink? I've got some primo tequila."

The kitchen opened into the living room via a breakfast bar. While Honora bustled around, opening cupboard doors and the refrigerator, Maxine stared at a print of a coyote walking through a desert landscape. The red rocks, clay-colored earth and white clouds were dabbed in an abstract style, but the animal showed legs, ears, snout and a bushy tail. The artist understood muted desert colors.

Honora returned from the kitchen with a bottle of Monte Alban Mezca on a red tray with tall shot glasses, slices of lime on a plate and a shallow dish. She placed the tray on the coffee table and motioned Maxine to sit on the sofa with her.

"We'll do it right." She picked up the bottle.

The dish was a cute little saltcellar. Maxine felt a little frisson of pleasure that Honora would have such a sweet old item.

Honora poured them each a shot of tequila, passed Maxine the salt, and gave her a lime wedge. Maxine waited until Honora was ready, too, and then they moistened their thumbs, and dipped them into the salt, licked it off and tossed back the tequila. Honora squirted a few drops of lime into her mouth and Maxine bit into her lime. The tequila had an earthy, peppery taste.

"They call the lime juice a 'chaser'," Honora said. "It's supposed to balance the taste of tequila."

She leaned back into the sofa cushions. Her long-lashed eyes had a faraway look. “In those three years before Ethan was born, I went through my whole inheritance. What a freakin’ waste of money. Remember, you wouldn’t let me have it until I was twenty-one?”

Maxine nodded, recalling her suspicions that Honora would race through the money in no time. Almost two hundred thousand. Spent on clothes, drugs and who knew what?

“You spent it all?”

Honora laughed. “I thought I had. I used to take my friends to Nassau, even to Puerto Rico for the weekend. Or we’d check into a fancy Miami hotel and order drinks at the pool, snort coke all weekend, shop in the boutiques. I had shoes you wouldn’t believe. Then I met Ahmed.”

Honora frowned, still with those faraway eyes. “He made me see what a fool I was, wasting my body with booze and drugs. Sleeping around. How I didn’t get AIDS, I’ll never know.”

Maxine suppressed a shudder. “I met Nicole and she told me a little of what happened.”

Honora’s frown deepened until two tiny vertical lines appeared between her eyes.

“Nicole is a bitch. Anyway, after Ahmed left and I realized I was pregnant and maybe he wasn’t coming back, I stayed sober enough to go over my finances, and I discovered two CDs you had opened for me. I had forgotten about them.”

“That was lucky.” Maxine lit a cigarette. Her hands trembled.

“I used the money for maternity care, and to go back and finish my last year and a half of school. In California. Those CDs saved my life.”

“I would have helped you,” Maxine said.

“I was scared that Ahmed might find out about Ethan and kidnap him.” Honora cast a nervous glance toward the bedroom hallway. “That happens, you know.”

“That’s why you changed your name?”

“Twice.” Honora picked up the tequila bottle and raised her eyebrows. “One more?”

"Why not?" Maxine hoped she would be able to find the motorhome.

"The second time I went through the Chicago phone book. Wozniak. There were pages of them, a good Polish name."

"Do you have a boyfriend?" asked Maxine. Men would find Honora attractive, with her curvy figure, her wide set gray eyes and full lips.

"I see Steve, but it's not serious." She laughed. "Ethan doesn't like him. It used to be that my boyfriends had to pass Dad's muster, and now it's my kid's."

Honora poured the shots and passed the salt and the lime wedges. They repeated the tequila ceremony. Maxine felt the kick of the second shot more than the first. She took a deep breath and looked at her sister. Could she trust Honora? She had to.

"I told you that my husband was killed because he skimmed some of the money."

"How did he ever think he'd get away with that?" Honora looked scornful, like everyone knew skimming a drug lord's profits was the height of folly. Which it had been.

"He put the money in a Panama bank. Established some complicated offshore corporation. I've got the paperwork. Even a debit card."

Honora's eyes widened again. "No shit! You've got access to the skimmed money! No wonder they're chasing you all over hell and back."

"Larry left a note asking me to divide it up between me and his brothers. I've always been afraid someone would be hanging around that bank in Panama with my photo, just waiting for me to try to access that account." Maxine realized she was sweating. Maybe from the booze, but more likely this conversation. "I always thought if I could get my hands on the money, there would be enough for Ethan's college, and even a private school. He's a great kid."

Honora smiled with a mother's undisguised pride. "He's the joy of my life."

She pantomimed having another shot, but Maxine shook her head.

"Can anyone pick up the money?" Honora appeared relaxed as she leaned against the cushions, but her strong voice betrayed her interest.

"You need the account number and a password. That's what I read on the web."

"Maxine, no one would be looking for *me*. We don't even look alike. Maybe I could fly there and bring back the money. I'm about due for a beach vacation."

She had taken the bait. But could Honora be trusted? And what would Jeff say?

# *Forty-two*

Lotto had finished his blackened grouper sandwich at the deli and was strolling back to his office. Miami at noon in July was like a foretaste of hell, but Lotto thrived in the heat. As he walked through the muggy air, his mind was engaged in the problem concerning his supposedly trusted computer ace. What a stupid-ass name Bacchus was. It made the hacker sound like a wino. Bacchus had made unauthorized copies of Caliendo's restored files.

If he thought for a moment that Bacchus was selling his data, or giving it to the Feds, or just holding onto it, then that *hijo de puta* would have to be eliminated. He should never have trusted anyone named Bacchus. Lotto's twenty-year-old cousin Armando was training to replace the hacker, but the cousin wasn't ready. Maybe in six months.

Lotto arrived at his Brickell Boulevard building and entered the marble lobby, shocking in its coolness. In his office, the white porcelain coffee pot with matching demitasse cups, spoons and a white bowl of dark sugar cubes stood on the rosewood sideboard. In a few minutes Marta Sumner would arrive. In a few minutes he would have some answers.

Marta had picked up Caliendo's laptop at the police station in Chicago and passed it to the hacker. She had given Bacchus his marching orders and reported to Lotto via a phone call. Lotto did not like the idea at all of Bacchus copying files. What kind of shit was that? He wanted a face-to-face meeting with Marta.

Actually, Lotto had considered asking Marta to take over Caliendo's job as accountant for the Northeast. A plump middle-aged woman was as invisible as a ghost. Mind like a Cray computer. She could go anywhere unnoticed, unobtrusive, a nonentity. People who laundered money needed to wrap themselves in a cloak of invisibility—not flamingos but seagulls. Marta was a herring gull, with unobtrusive black, white, and gray feathers. Reception called to announce her visit.

Lotto and Marta hugged with the casualness of old friends.

"You're looking well," Lotto said, eyeing her gray silk suit and white shirt with a wide crisp collar. The drab bird wore black and gray heels with a slight platform. A woman's legs were always the last to go. Marta's still looked strong and sleek.

She settled herself into one of the chairs facing Lotto's desk with her slim briefcase beside her and took a cup of the offered coffee. Lotto noticed the lines between her brows had started to look like the pause button on the remote. Their business aged a person prematurely.

"What the fuck is going on with Bacchus?" Lotto asked.

Marta stirred her coffee with a silver demitasse spoon. She told Lotto that the hacker, all wounded feelings and outrage, admitted he had copied the files and had also put a copy out on the web. Encrypted, of course, and in a safe storage area. She imitated Bacchus' voice with its flat Midwestern accent. "*'Just using best practices, for God's sake. Make two backups, and always keep one of them off site. Jesus, everyone knows to do that. Wasn't I paid to do things right?'*"

"Like many computer geeks, he's an odd duck, but I don't believe him to be disloyal or malicious. If two backups are standard, Bacchus makes two backups. Don't concern yourself with this."

Lotto wanted to believe Marta, but his instinct was not to trust any *puta* who called himself Bacchus.

"The data recovery?" he asked, tenting his fingers and meeting Marta's intelligent eyes.

"He got everything off Caliendo's hard drive. His forensic skills are the best, but it's apparently not a quick process."

Marta hesitated and tugged at the white cuff of her shirt. Lotto wondered about the wedding band she wore, because he knew she was a widow. *Perhaps a married woman inspired more trust.*

She continued, "Bacchus made a comparison of the restored files we copied during Caliendo's audit with the restored files currently on the laptop. Besides one week of business, he found some notes to a 'Max.' Maxine is Caliendo's wife, right?" Marta eyed Lotto as if she knew he was obsessed with Maxine. How did Marta always know so goddamned much?

"Yeah. Maxine Harvey, as she calls herself," he said coolly. "What did the notes say? Did you bring copies?"

*Cojones de dios.* What had Caliendo put on the laptop for his wife to read? Had Maxine found the notes? Of course, she had found them And interrupted his fucking lunch.

"Yes, I brought copies," Marta said, her voice pleasant but emotionless. "You won't like it, Lotto." She snapped open her briefcase and Lotto prepared himself for a new and aggravating turn of events. Marta handed him two sheets of white paper.

Lotto skimmed the first. The Foxborough bank and the laptop! Caliendo's note confirmed Lotto's long-held suspicions. He glanced at Marta.

"He got the dog meat part right," she said, her face deadpan.

Lotto speed-read the second, longer note. A Panamanian bank held the skimmed money. No surprise there. And Caliendo had given Maxine the address of Marquesa Trading Company. "An okay guy?" What rot. Lotto didn't think Maxine had the money yet. She had been in Chicago and then in Reno, not Panama. She couldn't move that fast.

"You'll need to send someone to Panama," Marta spoke again. "Too bad he didn't mention which bank."

Lotto continued to stare at the longer note. " I can find out if he used one of our banks. Or lawyers." If he handled this right, he could catch Maxine *and* get his money back. One way or the other. Whether she had been to Panama or not.

"Did Bacchus read the notes?" he asked, glancing up at Marta.

"Once Bacchus recovered the information and compared the files, I took over," she said. "My impression is that his only interest is in technology, not data. I also have the second back-up."

Lotto needed ten Martas. So efficient, so intelligent, so loyal.

"*Bueno*. Any news of El Tigre's domestic situation?" he asked. Marta had a magic ear for gossip.

"His wife is getting treatment in Houston. The whole *familia* is there in a hotel." She gave a half-shrug.

"That private detective is still MIA?" Lotto's people had put the fear of god into *Señor* Finder.

"Very much so." Marta closed her briefcase and stood, smoothing her gray skirt.

The news was overwhelmingly good. Why then did Lotto have this uneasy feeling, a palpable gnawing at his vitals, almost like dread?

## *Forty-three*

"You'll be safe here," Honora had said.

*Safe? What was safe?*

Maxine thought of the black widows in the crawl space. The coyotes lurking in the hills outside of town. The meth addicts giving new meaning to the phrase, trailer trash. *What was safe?*

Honora had contrived this hideout for Maxine and Kaylee, and Maxine wavered between being grateful and appalled.

They had been hidden away in this tiny town one hundred miles from Reno, in a vast desert, a land of stark sun and blowing dust, a harsh alkali moonscape of cracked earth and sagebrush and the occasional scrawny cow.

Their rented home, which belonged to an absentee landlord, was an ancient singlewide mobile home, clean and furnished in a spare but funky style, with décor from sixties and seventies craft shows and early American style furniture. Somehow, in mid-desert, water was plentiful and the little garden was lush with roses, hollyhock and herbs, even cherry tomatoes. Lucy romped in the yard, hid in the tool shed, and sunned herself on a rock by the stockade fence. The fence, with a gate they could padlock, made them safe. The RV was hidden behind the house and further screened by the fruit trees. Maxine wondered if she would still be exiled here when the apples, plums and peaches ripened.

Jeff gave golf lessons near Lake Tahoe and lived in a tiny efficiency. He drove back here on Sunday night and left again at dawn on Wednesday morning.

They promised each other this was only for ten weeks.

Their town had a post office, three taverns and no store. Jeff kept the rental car, and Maxine bought an old maroon pickup with four doors and a backseat for Kaylee.

The freight train rumbled through town in the middle of the night, setting up a vibration in the mobile home. In the hour before dawn, someone walked along the street playing a flute or maybe a slide whistle. In the half-light, Maxine heard the coyotes howling on the mesa. Their baying froze her blood.

Kaylee longed for a real swimming pool, and when Jeff was home, they drove to one of the hot springs and floated in the warm water. Home? Would this end-of-the-world place ever be home? Would Kaylee go to school here, the only school within miles and miles? She had found an eight-year-old girl in town. The two of them lolled on the low branches of the apple tree, splashed and danced in a wading pool, and made doll clothes from scraps Maxine unearthed in an old trunk.

She glanced at her watch. Four p.m. For dinner, she would grill apples, corn and pork chops. She poured a slug of rum, added ice and grabbed her paperback novel. The best part of the day was sitting on the dust-encrusted old white sofa on the tiny deck, a dignifying term for the porch, which also had a rickety counter with a propane burner and an ancient Franklin stove, the kind one's great-grandmother had cooked on if she was poor. Maxine sipped the rum, waiting for the cool evening breeze to blow in. Out here in the middle of nowhere, a delicious quiet reigned...no airplanes, no cars, or trucks, just a tiny flock of turtledoves and the wind.

Ethan would stay with her and Kaylee next week while Honora traveled to Panama. Honora had wanted to take Ethan along, but

Maxine had vetoed the idea. She couldn't get it out of her head that Honora would disappear forever with the money, the money that offered buoyancy in this ocean of uncertainty.

~ * ~

A few days before, Maxine had left Kaylee with her new friend Petra and had driven the old pickup into Reno. She met Honora and they visited the biggest, glitziest casino. After lunch, holding her breath, Maxine used the Panamanian bank debit card at one of the ATMs to withdraw five hundred dollars. Then Honora withdrew another five hundred. In no time, they had enough money for Honora's business-class plane ticket, a four-star hotel room, incidentals and even a shopping trip in appreciation of Honora's efforts.

During lunch, Honora had said, "Maybe we should just stand at the ATM for a few hours and take it all." She looked like the cat that had scarfed down the canary...feet, feathers and all.

"That would be thousands of withdrawals, and we would run the ATM out of cash. These casinos have hidden cameras all over. We don't want to attract attention." Honora should know that. Maxine hated always to sound like the know-it-all big sister.

Driving back from Reno across the wide desert, Maxine studied the rear-view mirror, looking for a car that might be following her, but the road remained a lonesome path across the emptiness.

~ * ~

When Jeff arrived late Sunday evening with a trunk full of groceries, his kiss had been as passionate as if their separation were months, not days. Then, instead of helping put the groceries away, he plopped down on the sofa and fell asleep.

"It's a long drive from Tahoe after working all day and stopping to shop," Maxine explained, noticing Kaylee's lip jutting out. "Your dad is tired."

"I wanted to ask if I could go fishing with Petra. They invited me to the reservoir and her dad has a boat."

"*Your* dad will want to know more details, like if you kids will wear life jackets."

Yesterday, Maxine had taken the girls to visit a pottery shop in the wilderness fifteen miles from town, and supervised their purchase of clay animals. Petra had pointed out the rutted dirt road that led to the reservoir.

The pottery, the reservoir, the hot springs...every destination felt so isolated. When Jeff was gone, Maxine wanted to sleep with the loaded Smith & Wesson under the mattress, but she dare not with the kids around. Instead, she stashed it in a Ziploc bag inside a three-pound coffee can on the top shelf of the pantry, right outside the bedroom door, the mobile home being such a miniscule, compact place. She worried because there was no one nearby to call for help. The sheriff patrolled a county as big as some New England states.

Maxine put a half-gallon of milk in the fridge and a carton of Parmalat on the shelf. In Reno she had rented a phone for Honora to take to Panama. For herself, she bought an iridium satellite phone, not knowing how long she might need a device that worked in the vast reaches of this desert. To her relief and amazement, the town had reliable wifi, and she and Honora could email.

Maxine and Jeff's love life had improved by virtue of having a real bedroom with Kaylee at the opposite end of the house.

Sweet Lucy curled up and purred on Kaylee's bed every night. Kaylee's mom had been on the phone a few times. Her baby's father had coughed up some money and promised to pay her hospital bill. An upbeat Lisa seemed content to have Kaylee with them and hadn't questioned why they were living at the end of the road.

~ * ~

Jeff gave permission for Kaylee to go trout fishing with Petra's family the next day. While Kaylee was at the reservoir with her friend, Maxine and Jeff visited "their" hot spring again. Hot springs were beautiful hidden oases in this desert. First, they found the dirt road, just tracks really, heading across the *playa*, what the locals called the flat alkali desert. Maxine's eyes could gaze for miles in every direction, while behind them, the pickup had kicked up a big cloud of dust. She always expected to pass cow skeletons and old rusted wagon wheels, but the playa had an eerie emptiness, beyond any lingering remnants of civilization. When they arrived at the hot spring in early evening, they found a crowd, mostly naked, and mostly young.

"Last one into the pond is a rotten egg," Jeff said, pulling his shirt over his head.

Their sleepy little town had filled up with people working on the infrastructure of the big festival that took place over Labor Day. After a hot day on the *playa*, a dip in the warm water was bliss.

How could Maxine tell friend from foe amid so many strangers? For starters, Lotto's people would wear clothes, and they wouldn't be laid back. No slide whistles for Lotto's goons.

She and Jeff joined the group lolling in the spring. Their renting the "Wofford place" made them welcome residents. After years in the East, Maxine liked Western laid back friendliness. The camaraderie, warm water, the greenery lining the springs, relaxed Maxine to her very core.

A private plane landed on the flat playa, and the two occupants joined the crowd in the spring. What a crazy place this was.

As she soaked in the warm water, Maxine pondered Honora's upcoming trip. How risky was it to waltz into the U.S. with a suitcase stuffed with money? Customs required forms for any amount over ten thousand. Would Honora need a legitimate reason for bringing in all that cash? Maxine should tell her to think of a logical reason. Larry, whose bean-counting mind anticipated everything, had left paperwork in the deposit box indicating he had sold an expensive house in Panama, paperwork now hidden in the RV. If anyone asked, Maxine could prove her right to the money. She hadn't told Honora about the deed. Let Honora worry a little. Maxine planned to pay taxes on the windfall. She felt no qualms about raiding the account Larry had paid for with his life, his last legacy.

White contrails crisscrossed the sky, sky that dwarfed the distant brown hills and the dry lakebeds. Cows were brown specs in the distance. Only the vault of heaven, merciless and blue, felt real. Sometimes at night, military jets thundered overhead, faking dogfights over the desert against the enormity of the Milky Way.

She had become used to the coyotes howling, and now they sounded lonesome, not threatening. A person could get used to anything.

Maxine caught the herbal scent of wild sage that grew by the hot spring, pungent but pleasant. She turned her sunburned face to Jeff, who whispered, "if we leave now, we can get home before Kaylee does and have time for..." His voice trailed off. They grabbed their clothes and left.

"You seemed so tired yesterday. It must have been a brutal week." Maxine turned to Jeff as she maneuvered the pickup across the dry alkali ruts to the gravel road.

"Yeah, there's something I should have told you earlier."

Maxine glanced at Jeff again, noticing his blue eyes had clouded and his lips compressed. *Told me what?*

"When I stopped at your sister's to pick up that bicycle helmet she promised Kaylee..." He didn't continue, but stared ahead at the dust of an approaching vehicle.

"Yeah, the bike helmet. It fits fine."

"Honora hit on me."

The most absurd thing, an impossibility, but her heart still pounded. "You must have got it wrong. What did she do?" Her voice sounded angry, a little shrewish.

"She...er, backed into me, and then she put her hand on me."

"Where?" *This has to be a misunderstanding.*

He moved his hand across his crotch.

Why would Honora make a play for Jeff? Maxine had confided to her sister how strong her and Jeff's feelings were for each other.

"She wouldn't do that." Maxine said, and bile rose into her throat.

"I knew you wouldn't believe me. And I am *not mistaken.*"

"Then what happened?"

"I said I had to leave."

"And?"

"She said, 'pity.' I grabbed the helmet and left."

Maxine repressed her urge to cry, but a single tear trickled down her cheek. "I don't think I know my sister at all anymore."

"Ten years is a long time, Max. She isn't the sweet coed you remember."

She felt a spasm of disgust. "Did she ask you not to tell me?"

"She gave me a come-hither smile, and said, 'maybe some other time.'"

Her sister hitting on her boyfriend. The same sister who was flying to Panama tomorrow to withdraw money from the bank. Maxine would have Ethan, but a woman you couldn't trust around your boyfriend sure as hell couldn't be trusted with your money.

~ * ~

As he had for the past weeks, Jeff left Wednesday at first light. Maxine made French toast and sausage for Kaylee and Ethan, and boiled some potatoes for salad. Honora's treachery stayed in her mind, but Honora was in Panama.

Before Honora returned, Maxine had to decide if Ethan needed a loving aunt more than Maxine needed a backstabbing sister.

She wiped the surface of the round oak table that dominated the kitchen. A counter divided the kitchen from the living room. The three of them watched television on the ugly plaid couch, with their feet resting on the maple coffee table, and Lucy curled up on the Windsor chair cushion. The remaining furnishings were a dented bookcase and a cheap maple desk that overlooked the deck. Sometimes Maxine cooked their entire meal outdoors in a heavy cast iron skillet over the propane burner. To break the chill of evenings on the high desert, they lit the Franklin stove perched at the edge of the deck.

From time to time, a truck rumbling through town on the way to Idaho pierced the stillness. Overhead the sky remained a deep desert blue while the sun beat on the brown grass and the heat rose up with a dry smell of baked earth. Maxine had shown the kids how to make hollyhock dolls. She hummed as she picked pink roses and a handful of fresh mint for tea. The kids had the garden hose running and were making mud pies in sand castle molds. Lucy napped on the outdoor sofa.

Maxine returned to the kitchen and began making PBJ sandwiches for lunch. Ethan liked grape jelly on white bread and Kaylee preferred apricot jam on whole wheat. Maxine loved the high childish voices outside, the mud pies and the drowsy kitten, emblems of a lazy summer day.

Lost in her thoughts, she didn't hear the children stop chattering. Sensing something amiss, she turned around. Kaylee and Ethan stood at the screen door in front of an enormous man in a Panama hat with a Madras band. The man held Lucy in the crook of his arm, stroking her head.

Kaylee's small, tremulous voice said, "There's a man here to see you, Maxine. I told him Dad was home."

The man's brows were slashes across his dark forward, and his calculating black eyes bored into hers. Maxine gave a small useless scream. Fear seized her, from her wobbly legs to her dry mouth, as she darted across the room to the door.

"Please don't hurt the children." Her hand fluttered wildly, like a captured bird, as she pushed the door open.

"Please don't hurt the children."

Burly arms and a slab-like hand deposited Lucy on the floor. The man's shoulders bulged in his black Guayabera shirt.

"I hurt no child." His eyes were emotionless black holes that sucked everything into them.

Ethan's pupils were enormous and Kaylee's lips had formed a wide "O."

The man placed a huge hand on each of the children's backs and propelled them across the living room into Kaylee's small bedroom. Lucy scampered across the floor and darted under the bed.

"You remain here and play. *Sí*?" He shut the door, and then opened it again. His voice was firm. "No noise, *por favor*, quiet like mice." He closed the door.

He turned and looked at Maxine. "You sit!"

Still in a frenzy of fear, Maxine, obeying like a well-trained dog, sat on the sofa. Her heart raced like it would burst out of her chest.

The big man pulled up the Windsor chair and faced her. "I am El Tigre," he said. He removed his hat, revealing a shaved head.

*El Tigre. The Tiger. Jesus.*

His ears, fleshy and set close to his head, had points, like a malevolent elf. Pitiless black eyes stared into hers.

"Now, I must have your husband's Panama bank account number. His secret account." He smiled with a false geniality. "Please to provide. Now." He spoke in heavily accented English, but slow and understandable.

Maxine stared at him like the mouse looks at a snake. Honora had the account number and the debit card, all the paperwork with the lawyer and the corporation name. Everything except the bearer bonds and the bill of sale for a Panamanian house. She said, "I have to use the bathroom," and pointed beyond the kitchen with a shaky hand.

He shrugged, got out of the chair, checked the bathroom, and made her walk in front of him. As she pulled the door shut, he said, "No tricks. I have the children."

The *cheeldren.*

Maxine clutched the sink, wondering what she should do. *Keep Kaylee and Ethan safe.*

El Tigre had said, "I hurt no child," but Maxine didn't believe him.

She stared at her pale, wild-eyed face in the bathroom mirror.

*You got through your parents' deaths, you survived two marriages, and you found Honora. You saved that girl from the rip tide. Now, deal with this man.*

She ran the water in the sink to hide the sound of her peeing, then she flushed, and at the sink again, splashed water on her face.

*He hasn't actually threatened you. Talk to him.*

She opened the door. He stood before the kitchen sink, pouring himself a glass of water. Beads of sweat had popped out on his shaved head.

"Would you rather have some iced tea or a soda?" she asked, trying to project a normal voice, but she heard her half-hysterical quaver, and still couldn't control her fluttering hands.

He shook his head and motioned her to the table.

"I should feed the children their lunches," she said, indicating the food on the counter. He gave a curt nod.

Maxine put the sandwiches, some chips, and two sodas on a tray. She could feel El Tigre's eyes on her as she crossed the living room on weak legs with the soda cans vibrating against the tray. She opened the door to Kaylee's tiny room.

"Here's lunch." She tried to speak normally, but her voice sounded like she was delivering their last meal on earth. "Please just eat and be quiet until our guest leaves." They sat next to each other on the bed, knowing something was wrong.

"Who is that man?" asked Kaylee.

Maxine couldn't think of a plausible explanation. She shut the door without answering.

El Tigre waited at the kitchen table, his back ramrod straight, his massive hands on either side of his water glass. He hadn't shown a weapon, but his hands looked like they could split the oak table with one quick chop.

She sat across from him and their eyes locked.

"My sister is in Panama City to withdraw the money. She has the lawyer's name, the account number and the debit card," Maxine explained, "but I can telephone her."

"Now! The bank name and the account number." His eyes bored into hers. "I have killed already two men."

## *Forty-four*

Lotto and Enrique sat in the heat and the mess of the shabby office. The "cover" for product storage and distribution was a used parts warehouse, no better than a junkyard. The Little Havana structure squatted in the worst area of an ugly part of town, with rutted streets, broken lights, sullen neighbors who didn't ask questions, and mean dogs patrolling the perimeter. Lotto went there as seldom as possible, but the first sub shipment had arrived, needing to be weighed, tested for quality, and parceled out to the distributors. All done. Soon he would have his money back many times over. The last of the white shrink-wrapped bundles was en route to the middlemen.

They couldn't celebrate, because a new problem had surfaced. Enrique reported that he "had lost contact with El Tigre."

Lotto glared at the wheezing window air conditioner that couldn't keep up with the heat. A thick layer of oily dust blanketed the desktop in front of him and the smell of engine oil and auto parts irritated his nose. Enrique had seated himself in a creaky wooden office chair. Lotto wondered if it would splinter under Enrique's bulk.

"Are you sure," he asked, "this issue with El Tigre is not simply cell phone trouble? He's shuttling between mountains and deserts.

Coverage may be spotty. Maybe he lost his damned phone. *Mierda*, anything could have happened."

Enrique made a tentative movement to lean back in the ramshackle chair, which gave a loud squeak. He sat erect again.

"El Tigre has orders to stay in touch, Lotto. And he did not pass on the names of who is on the 'Maxine' job, also an order." Enrique's dark eyes glanced from Lotto to the grimy window made of one-way glass. "We've heard *nada* for three entire days." His fingers gripped the chair's wooden arms.

Lotto rose and grabbed two beers from the small fridge, noticing the dark smudges of fingerprints around the door handle. This pigsty of an office was getting to him.

"Maybe he's taking a few days off to visit his wife," Lotto said. "It wouldn't be the first time he ducked down there." He remembered the money for medical expenses he had given El Tigre. And this was the thanks he got. Still, people behaved predictably. There had to be a reasonable explanation. Enrique simply couldn't come up with it.

"I already made inquiries in Houston." Enrique wiped the lip of the bottle with his handkerchief and took a hearty gulp. "El Tigre is not there. His sister is not there. The whole *familia* is gone."

"Maybe his wife died," said Lotto.

"We would have heard."

Lotto tipped his head back and drank. "Marta argues that we spend too much money and effort on Maxine, an insignificant woman who promised not to testify against us. But Maxine knows exactly where Caliendo's skimmings are."

"Did you ever calculate how much he got?" asked Enrique. "A few hundred thousand may not be worth the trouble."

Lotto slammed his bottle down on the dusty desk. "*Cojones de dios,* it's over two million."

"Then worth the trouble." Enrique stood and walked around the office. He stopped in front of a calendar from a spark plug company and studied the month of July. "Three days," he said and turned toward Lotto. "What do you want me to do?"

El Tigre's loyalty was solid. Still...Lotto examined the label on the beer bottle. *Carta Blanca.* Everything reminded him of those greedy Mexican *putas.* "Where did you last hear from El Tigre and what did he say?"

"Reno. He said the leads had dried up, but they were going to stick around a few more days looking for that RV."

"And he didn't say who 'they' were?" Lotto finished his beer and frowned at the circle the sweating bottle made in the dusty desktop.

"No, but it was not the same men who were with him at the airport. They left Reno as soon as they were released."

Lotto stared at the ceiling. More *mugre.* Jesus, was that dried blood? He must control his nausea. "Who can we send to Panama to watch our bank?"

"Caliendo wouldn't have used our bank, Lotto. He would pick another one." Enrique returned to the chair. "You could send Marta down there, but she can't watch thirty banks."

"Maybe he used our lawyer," Lotto said. "Ask him if Caliendo opened an S.A. corporation."

Enrique made a note.

Lotto said, "I suppose it would be pointless for you to go to Reno." He still felt this woozy lightheadedness and tried not to look at the ceiling.

Enrique nodded. "Sí. Pointless. El Tigre is a pro."

The man never had an original idea in his life.

Lotto pressed his fingers to his temples. "The stink is giving me a headache. *Vamos.*"

All the way back to Brickell Boulevard, one thought occupied Lotto's mind. *Where is El Tigre?*

# *Forty-five*

They had to survive this day. And maybe the next with escape not an option. Maxine's brain whirled inside her skull, panicky, without any idea except to watch and obey.

El Tigre confiscated Maxine's computer, the pickup keys, and the kitchen knives. With the children still in Kaylee's room and Maxine confined to the john, he searched the house. Through the thin walls of the mobile home, she heard him rummaging in the bedroom, and thought she heard him lifting the mattress. She hoped he hadn't found the Smith & Wesson in the coffee can or the cash, over three thousand dollars, and the Panama bank's bearer bonds hidden in the motor home. El Tigre had pocketed her Sky Sat phone, but Maxine had no idea where he had stashed everything else.

After he released Maxine from the bathroom, the children were allowed out of Kaylee's room. El Tigre turned on the television and found a cartoon channel.

"You to call me Uncle Tio," he said, patting Ethan on the head. "This one is dark," he said, "like a little Colombiano."

*Leetle Colombiano*. Uncle Tio meant "uncle uncle."

Ethan, eyes flashing with indignation, said, "I am not little."

When El Tigre spoke, all is his i's turned to e's. *Leetle, cheeldren, and seester.*

His low chuckle scared Maxine more than his scowling. She wondered whether he liked the children or if he was only pretending to. Kaylee watched him with her usual perturbed frown that signaled, *I am thinking about this.*

"Can we watch iCarly?" asked Kaylee.

"As you like."

Kaylee and Ethan shared a package of Goldfish and sprawled on the sofa in front of the television.

He turned to address the kids, giving them a fierce-eyed glare. "You stay."

"We go out," he pointed to the deck. Like a giant malevolent toad, he squatted on the sofa, his shaved head gleaming in the stark sunlight of the torpid July afternoon. "Now we call your sister," he said, as his dark olive eyes bored into her. "She maybe has the money by now."

His cruel eyes and his big meaty arms and his demands tied her intestines in knots.

He swung her key chain around on his index finger.

Maxine waited.

"You speak Spanish?"

"No." She understood a few words, the words everyone knew.

El Tigre took her Sky Sat phone out of his pants pocket.

"Has this a speaker?"

"It's a satellite phone, and you have to stand in the yard where there's open sky."

"*Sí.* Then we go to the grass."

They left the deck and he followed her to the clothesline. Through the open window, she heard the television. Maxine noticed the front gate was still locked. Had El Tigre vaulted over the chain link fence blocking the driveway? How naive of her to have felt safe.

He punched a number and spoke rapid fire Spanish. He said, "New York" several times. Standing in the baking yard made the sweat pop out all over his shaved head covered with a hint of dark shadow.

Maxine tried to concentrate, but her thoughts wheeled around and doubled back, always wondering how could she protect the kids.

El Tigre made another call that involved clipped sentences and gesticulations with his mallet of a hand.

Maxine felt the fear shooting up her arms again. Wishing to be invisible, she slumped into a lawn chair.

He fiddled with her phone, punching buttons and scowling. "This telephone is now on the speaker. Don't try any shit," he said thrusting the phone at her. "Call your sister. She must get all of the money. In dollars."

The kids were peeking at them from the living room window.

El Tigre turned, smiled, and wagged his finger at them. They giggled and disappeared.

*Dear God. Did they think it was a game?*

Maxine keyed Honora's number, but before she could hit "send," an iron hand seized the phone and El Tigre examined what she had entered.

"No tricks. No nine-one-one." *No treeks.*

He made her want to jump out of her skin. He handed her the phone. Honora could be in the bank or at the lawyer's or shopping. She could be anywhere. The call went to voice mail.

"She doesn't answer; I have to leave a message."

He nodded, pacing up and down beside the clothesline.

"Honora, we have a bad situation here that involves Ethan. Please call right away."

El Tigre grabbed the phone again. "Good," he said. "Good message."

Maxine hated herself for trying to please him.

# *Forty-six*

The shit had hit the fan.

At 4:30 a.m., Lotto's deep cover contact at the DEA called. In a whispered voice, the contact said Lotto was under surveillance, had been for weeks. The search of Lotto's luggage at Miami airport had not been random. The contact said the DEA suspected Marquesa Trading Company of being a front for cocaine distribution and money laundering. Lotto would be arrested within the week, sooner if he showed signs of attempting to flee.

*"Todo sucede por primera vez." Everything happens for the first time.*

Lotto buttoned his favorite Thomas Pink shirt, so old and soft that every laundering might be its last. Wishing his calfskin briefcase were bigger, he slipped his laptop inside and filled the remainder with cash, U.S. twenties and hundreds, with the rest in five hundred Euro notes. The large purple bills printed with a modernist building always reminded Lotto of his Cartagena apartment with its sleek architecture. Did the DEA know about his place in Cartagena? He envisioned an endless succession of expensive bribes.

He had always known this would happen, the odds forever in favor of discovery, and now not even six months left on his own timetable. For a few minutes, he let himself mourn for the submarines he had worked for with such diligence, the respect shown his position, his life in Miami, this apartment, his office, even pretty, passionate Angelika whom he would never see again. Never. Always. Two opposite words, like the faces on a coin. Heads. Tails. Never. Always. *Mierda.*

With a brisk finality, he snapped the briefcase shut and locked it. Wearing his usual business clothes, he left his apartment at the regular time, picked up his onion bagel from the deli and walked to his office.

Fighting the stupid urge to take one last look at the Shohin bonsai, the Waterford carafe, the Venetian paperweights, even the thin white demitasse cups, Lotto unlocked his briefcase and transferred the contents to his gym bag. From his office safe, he took his maroon Venezuelan passport, only two years old with the new biometric ID. The name on the document was Carlos Léon. He grabbed three credit cards and a driver's license, all in the name of Léon.

The money Lotto had paid for those false documents had seemed preposterous, but now it looked like good planning. Along with some paperwork, he fed his American and Colombian passports into his high-security government approved shredder. The coffee man appeared with his usual pot and the brown *azucar*. Lotto told him to leave the tray on the sideboard and gave him a liberal tip.

He sat at his desk and made an encrypted phone call, the one he had hoped never to make. "Get the boat ready," he said. "I have to leave today. Around noon. Which pier? The middle one? Good."

Lotto walked into his office john and cut his hair off as best he could. *Mierda*, he looked like he had hacked at it with a dull machete. His own mother wouldn't know him. He jammed a Marlins baseball cap on his head to cover the mess, and stuffed all the clipped hair into a bag and cleaned the floor so anyone who came in to snoop wouldn't know he had cut his hair. He knew the DEA *putas* would go over his office. They would figure it out soon enough.

Wearing the black cap embossed with a turquoise Marlin, Lotto passed the shoeshine man on his way out, and handed him a twenty.

"Not today," he said. The man's face brightened. "*Muchas gracias, señor* Lopez."

*Dotting the i's and crossing the t's.* He tried not to think about how they would auction his apartment and his pristine white Mercedes. Everything. The thought of some drudge from West Palm Beach wearing his Thomas Pink shirts filled him with revulsion.

Toting the exercise bag, Lotto got his Mercedes out of the garage, and drove to his gym, like he did three or four times a week. One last drive in his sublime car. He would miss the gym with its executive locker room, buff women, and swank facilities. He would miss this life.

He stopped on the way to the locker room to buy a larger bag with the club logo, red with black trim.

"Have a good one," the clerk said. Lotto stifled a snarl. Today would not be a "good one."

In the shower, using his favorite *Colonia* shaving cream, a razor, and a non-fog suction mirror, he shaved his head. It took a long time and he had to keep running his hand over his scalp and examining the back of his head in the mirror. The shaving cream smelled of citrus. Stroking the razor behind his left ear was awkward.

*Mierda.* In the mirror he saw a thin stream of red trickling down the back of his bald scalp. The stream became a river. The tile walls began to buckle, and Lotto felt the familiar dizziness. His heart stopped beating, and he grabbed for the shower wall to brace himself. The water running down the drained turned pink. *Not now. Por favor, Dios, not now.* With what strength remained, Lotto pushed against the tiles with his arms, braced his legs, tensed his torso, and remained rigid, counting to ten, then to twenty. It seemed an eternity before the giddiness passed. He turned off the hot water, rinsed his head under the chilly stream which revived him further. It was a mere nick. He hoped the cold water would staunch any remaining ooze of blood. He couldn't leave with bits of toilet paper stuck to his scalp.

His astonishment that he had actually fought off the fainting spell was as great as his relief. But his bald head shone like a white beacon. *Mierda.* He needed some of that self-tanner Angelika always had. He looked around the dressing room but didn't see any. He slapped after-shave all over his head which made the cut sting like a Man O' War's tentacles.

When he examined his face in the mirror, the image of the gaunt man with the pale, bald head took him aback, a thin El Tigre, but not so fierce. More...philosophical. In his mind he saw his wife's startled eyes. *Hair grows back.*

Sarita was a rock. He wanted to tell her he had fought off the fainting.

Lotto found a flesh colored bandage in his shaving kit. He put on his blue warm-up suit, remembering to stick the Marlins cap in the pocket. He swapped his black gym bag for the new one, stuffing the wads of cash in the bottom. Even with his laptop, there was room for his Pink shirt, a toothbrush and a razor. Thinking of his destination, he jammed his expensive toiletries and a hand towel into the bag.

He asked the front desk to get him a cab. He considered texting Enrique and Marta in Spanish, recommending the novella, *Cronaca di una Morte Annunciata,* code for "get out of the country."

If either Enrique or Marta had betrayed him, they would know he was under surveillance. If they knew that *he* knew, the noose would tighten.

He put on his sunglasses. The Yellow Cab pulled up in front of the gym, and Lotto jumped in.

## *Forty-seven*

Until then, he hadn't hurt them, hadn't threatened them. Obeying orders hardly seemed like a plan, but she had no other. At two in the afternoon, El Tigre found the rum bottle under the kitchen sink and insisted Maxine drink with him. A drunk killer would be far more dangerous and unpredictable. He was holding out the glass of rum and Maxine took it. God knows, she needed a drink.

The kids were still engrossed in a television program and Maxine and El Tigre sat on the tiny deck outside the living room. He was in the blue metal chair and she was back on the tattered sofa. Dark half-moons of sweat stained El Tigre's black Guayabera shirt. The hot, dry wind blew a dusty swirl down the street. No cars, no people, they were alone.

"You are like a *frijol saltando,*" he said, with a gold-toothed smile.

"What's that?"

"A small bean that jumps. Now you relax. So you can tell to sister instructions. *Sí*?"

"Okay." *Always agree if possible.*

"Tell to your sister to get the money. Today! *Me entendió*?"

Maxine nodded.

They discussed the logics of Honora meeting El Tigre's "friend" who was en route to Panama from Colombia. Arranged during one of his many phone calls. Maxine suppressed a shudder, imagining some cartel thug, a man bloodthirsty and ruthless, El Tigre on steroids.

Meanwhile, El Tigre stared at the stockade fence, adorned with funky art and faux animal hides. He looked at the children's wading pool and gazed toward the shed and the hollyhocks. A strange emotion crossed his face. Sadness? He put his head in his hands and sat, shoulders hunched. When he looked up, his eyes were bloodshot. Had he been crying?

The situation had gone out of kilter. "Maybe there's another way," Maxine said, shaken by the sight of El Tigre in such an emotional state.

"My wife has the cancer." A spasm of pain crossed his face. "A bad kind." He seemed on the verge of weeping. "She has the treatment in Houston, but the doctors say they can do *nada mas*. There is one hospital in New York that has a miracle drug. It can help my wife."

He stared off into space and a tear rolled down his face. "I have the insurance only in Colombia. The treatment costs much. The air ambulance also. I need the money for the New York apartment for the *familia* for six months, the school for the children. A new passport." He made a broad sweep with his thick hand. "The money to go to another country. *Mucho mucho dinero*."

Maxine said, "I'm so sorry," and El Tigre simply said, "*Gracias*."

Was he implying that he had gone off on his own? That he was not here as an agent of Lotto?

Before Maxine could think about this new situation, El Tigre stood and began to pace up and down the small deck, only three steps each way before he reached the end. He stopped mid-stride in front of her.

"I must help my wife."

His eyes, perhaps seeing an unendurable future, stared wildly. Maxine smelled his boozy breath.

"I tolerate no delays" He waved his arms.

He stood in front of Maxine, brandishing his fist, and then he grabbed her by the shoulders, yanked her to her feet and began to shake her.

"No delays!" he growled.

"Stop! You're hurting me!"

He didn't stop and she didn't know if he would have ever stopped until her head flew off her body except that on the counter next to the propane burner, her phone began to chirp and in the living room, Kaylee began to howl.

El Tigre dropped his arms and turned toward the phone. He didn't seem to realize that he had nearly shaken her teeth out. Maxine massaged her neck. *Jesus.*

"No tricks. My associate is to charter a private jet to fly here with the money. There will be a pilot and my associate. You will say this to your sister." He picked up the phone and punched "talk."

"No," El Tigre said, his voice gruff. "I am El Tigre. Here is Maxine. You do as she say." He handed the phone to Maxine with a glare that left nothing in doubt. She must convince Honora to do his bidding. Maybe Honora would have enough common sense to contact the embassy or even call the Panama police. After all, her son's life was at stake. Or maybe that would be the worst thing she could do. They rolled the dice with the smallest action.

# *Forty-eight*

*El Tigre? Who the fuck?* Honora felt her pulse pound, then a surge of anxiety.

"Jeez, Maxine. Who was that? Is Ethan all right? Let me talk to him." Honora had a premonition that Maxine had managed to get them into a mega-mess. She sat on the bed in the hotel room and traced her fingers along the ivory coverlet. *It had been too good to be true.*

"One of Lotto's people." Maxine sounded scared. "We have to do what he wants."

Honora heard a gruff voice say, "No more Lotto."

She began to tremble all over. *Omigod, Ethan! Nothing must happen to my baby.* "Let me talk to Ethan. Right now!" She didn't have to take this shit.

Maxine said, "She wants to talk to her son."

Honora glanced out of her window, always surprised at the sight of tall sleek buildings in this steamy tropical city. Maxine had found her a classy hotel, small, boutiquey and only a few blocks from the bank. She had invited Steve along, and they had been having a ball. Wining. Dining. Partying. Steve had gone for a fitting of his custom-made suit. They had hit the Panama bank's ATM a bunch of times. Honora eyed her shopping bags piled on the chaise longue, the chair, the leather trunk at the foot of the bed—Christmas in July, as least until a few minutes ago. Why did everything always turn to shit?

"Say she is permitted to talk to the son only later." The man had a mean accented voice. Honora imagined hefty arms folded across a broad chest.

"In a minute, Honora." Maxine's voice quavered. The guy must really be creepy.

"Listen to me," Maxine said. "We are in trouble. You have to do what El Tigre says."

"Get the entire million out of the bank. Do you understand? The whole million. You didn't withdraw it yet, did you?"

Her sister's words ricocheted around Honora's brain. No way was she getting on a plane, chartered or otherwise, with any goons. She would pretend to go along with the idea, until she figured a way out of this stupidity.

*The entire million*. That meant Maxine wanted her to get just half the money out. She had to hand it to Maxine. Even with a gun to her head, she still could play the angles.

"Honora?"

"Listen, I don't have the money yet. And I'm, I'm here with my boyfriend."

Honora drummed her fingers on the nightstand, imagining what her sister was thinking, a *trip like this and she takes her boyfriend*?

"Tell him something has come up and he has to fly home without you. Get rid of him. Now! Jesus, the kids are in danger. Don't you understand?"

Maxine sounded pissed.

"What should I say? That some asshole wants to take our money?"

She heard this El Tigre bellow, "The speaker phone! No tricks!"

Maxine, sounding like she wanted to scream, said in a rush. "Tell your boyfriend you met someone else and are going off with him." There was a pause and a shout on the other end. "El Tigre wants me to use the speaker."

Honora heard Maxine's voice echoing.

"Honestly, Maxine, I don't understand how you got us into this nightmare. I insist on talking to Ethan." Honora lit a cigarette and inhaled deeply. She had almost quit smoking before Maxine showed up.

She heard Maxine ask, "Can my sister talk to Ethan for a moment?"

"He went into the house to get him," Maxine said. "He really likes Ethan."

"*Habla con su madre*," the gruff voice said, but kindly.

Ethan said, "Hello?"

"Honey, are you all right?" Honora stood and paced around the room, moved a shopping bag and sat on the orange longue. Ethan's voice had sounded so small.

"Uncle Tio lets us watch all the TV we want."

"Are you sure you're all right, Ethie? Not hungry, or hurt or anything?"

"I'm fine."

"Be a good boy for me and mind Maxine. I'll be home soon. I love you." Ethan hated it when she became emotional, but she couldn't help it.

She stood and went to the window and stared at the traffic in the street below and at all the freaking banks.

"Sure. Bye."

*What did kids know?*

"He's fine," Maxine said to Honora. "Listen. Go to the bank at four-thirty today. Make sure you get the money in hundreds or it will be too heavy. No twenties."

Honora realized there was no ashtray in the room. Smoking was forbidden. How stupid was that? She ran into the bathroom before the long ash dropped and flicked it into the toilet.

Meanwhile, Maxine told her the rest of the so-called plan. El Tigre's associate would meet her there at the hotel. He would count the money and take possession. He wouldn't hurt her. She would get a later call with more details.

Maxine was a conduit of bad news, like a pipe spewing filth.

"El Tigre wants you to call when you have the money, and before the plane leaves."

"Plane?" Honora said with a shriek. She couldn't suppress a sob. "Oh my God. Where are they taking me?"

"Everything is going to be all right," Maxine said. A sentiment that Honora didn't believe for an instant.

"Just remember the kids are hostage." Maxine ended the call.

*Like I can think of anything else.*

~ * ~

Steve came back from his outing whistling, and dumped more shopping bags on the chaise. She turned from the window to face him.

"Shit, why'd you smoke in here?" he asked. "They'll sock us for a cleaning fee." He stopped. "What?" His swagger was gone and his eyebrows knitted as he returned her stare.

"There's a glitch. You've got to go home. I'll explain later." She walked into the bathroom and dropped the cigarette into the toilet.

"What happened?" He stood arms akimbo, slack-jawed, gaping at her.

"I'll explain later. Now pack and leave." If he put up an argument, she would throw the goddamn lamp at him. She went to her handbag and grabbed a wad of cash. "Use this to pay for any ticket change charges. Get an upgrade."

"Can't you tell—?"

"No, I need to do something alone."

"I can move to another hotel." She watched his eyes travel over the swank drapes, the flowers, the oil painting, and fix on the luxurious bed.

"Steve, I said to go."

"Okay, shit! I'm outtahere. Don't expect to see me any time soon in Reno."

She watched him pack, always thinking about himself. Good riddance. When the last item was in his suitcase, he said, "Do you think you could pick up my suit?"

"No."

"Thanks a lot!" He slammed the door behind him.

Once El Tigre's "associate" had the money, he wouldn't need Honora anymore. He would have no compunction about killing her. Maxine had got her into this hideous mess. But how to get out?

Honora had a hollow echoing in her stomach. A stab of nausea and a drumming heart.

She hadn't felt this desperate for years.

# *Forty-nine*

The cab pulled up to the Dinner Key Marina in Coconut Grove, and Lotto jumped out into the muggy Miami midday. He tipped the driver, but not generously, because he didn't want to be remembered. Dinner Key was the biggest marina in Miami, with hundreds of slips and a harbor full of pleasure boats with tall masts and flying bridges piercing the pale sky.

Toting his new black and red gym bag and feeling anonymous in the marina, Lotto strode along the gray wooden planks to the long middle dock where the boat was tied up. There was one unforeseen problem. Mere minutes in the sun and already his bald head felt fried. Lotto stuck the Marlins cap on his head. *Mierda,* he hoped the captain had some sunscreen aboard.

Up ahead, he recognized *El Capitan,* the thirty-five-foot motor cruiser flying a Panamanian flag, one of many boats flying red, white and blue flags with the big blue and white stars. Caliendo had registered the vessel in Panama with the owner a fake corporation. Caliendo had been good at details like that. Too good.

Lotto expected a sleek vessel, something along the lines of a go-fast boat. Neither sleek nor new, this boat looked like a trawler.

The Colombian captain's name was Alberto and he wore a tan cap and had a short white beard and a barrel chest. Lotto thought he looked like Hemingway. The captain recognized Lotto, went to the stern, and offered a hand in boarding. The white-hulled boat was shipshape, but not luxurious. Still, the fiberglass surfaces looked newly scrubbed.

They spoke Spanish. "I am now Carlos Léon," Lotto said.

"Very good, Señor Léon. I took on water and fuel," the captain said. "There's gazpacho and sandwiches in the galley. Plenty of *cerveza*. Some good Jamaican rum. And a *tres leche*s cake."

Lotto's stomach contracted with hunger. He had not eaten the bagel.

"We're embarking for Key West and then to Havana tomorrow morning," Alberto said. "The conventional route." He paused, and looked at Lotto, probably wondering at his new baldness. "Should we get underway now, Señor Léon?"

"*Si. Immediatamente.*"

"A storm is forecast for tomorrow." Alberto showed white teeth. "'A tropical disturbance,' not a hurricane. Not even a depression. Still, one must remain vigilant."

Lotto wanted to leave ASAP. If he had eluded anyone tailing him to the gym, they would start looking for him soon. His apartment. His office. Then the airport. Lotto itched to get out of the U.S., but he recognized the wisdom of heading for the Keys first. It made the crossing to Havana much shorter. They could hole up for a few days if necessary.

"What type of vessel is this?" Lotto asked. "And how fast does it go?"

"The *El Capitan* is a working boat, built along the lines of a trawler." The captain regarded his ship with pride. "She's been to Bermuda, to Cuba, the Cayman Islands, even Panama."

"How fast?" Lotto asked again.

"Twenty-three to twenty-five knots max," the skipper said. "Four-hundred-gallon fuel tanks. You want to go to South America? I take you." He smiled again, a little roguishly.

Lotto helped the captain get the cruiser off the cleats and away from the dock, and then he went below. The cloudless sky and lack of wind would give them a good run to Key West. No weather problems today.

After lunch and a glass of rum, Lotto took a long nap in the modest stateroom. He dreamed he swam through a river of blood and he awakened swimming in sweat. Marta and Enrique were standing on the bank of the river, but they offered no help.

~ * ~

The *El Capitan* approached Key West at dusk, and motored straight to the town fuel dock in the downtown harbor called The Bight. Still reeling from his bloody nightmare, Lotto was in no mood to go gaga over the sunset.

*Lotto, we must drive to Key West. I've heard wonderful descriptions of the route, and the sunset— the lovely ceremony. I want to walk up Duval Street on your arm. We can eat conch chowder and key lime pie and make love in a quaint inn with chickens crowing in the morning.*

He had never taken Angelika to Key West. Lotto felt only scorn for the crowd of tourists on a sunset booze cruise or rubbing elbows at Mallory Square. Yet, he would miss Angelika and her boundless enthusiasm for sharing every new experience with him.

Alberto rented a slip at the end of a pier and left to get supplies for the next day. Lotto gave him five hundred dollars and a list of things he needed: t-shirts, shorts, flip-flops, underwear, a sport shirt and a decent pair of khakis. Maybe a hooded sweatshirt. Sunscreen, *mucho bloqueador*. Self-tanner. Two bottles of key lime juice for Sarita. And a duffel bag. "If I need small gifts in Cuba, what should I bring?" asked Lotto.

Alberto didn't blink. "Ah, Señor León, batteries, chocolate, mosquito repellant, aspirin. Anything from the drugstore."

Lotto handed the captain another hundred dollars. "And sturdy bags to carry the gifts."

While he watched the captain walking toward town, Lotto thought about calling Enrique and Marta, but something held him back. He no longer trusted anyone. Of course he had to trust the captain, at least until they got to Cuba. Lotto would get out of Cuba as quickly as possible. He had never been on the run. It was a detestable experience.

# *Fifty*

The kids played "Go Fish" on the living room rug. *El Tigre* had given her a small kitchen knife. Maxine grabbed the boiled potatoes along with some bacon, an onion, tomatoes, and a clamshell of baby spinach. Using the heavy cast iron skillet as a tray, she returned to the deck. El Tigre sat on the dusty couch with the phone glommed to his pointy ear, waving his arm and repeating the words *avion ambulancia*. She went back into the house for a pepper and noticed her recorder on the desk next to the window. The one thing El Tigre hadn't confiscated. His back was turned. She flipped it on. *For all the good it would do.*

Outdoors, El Tigre made more calls in Spanish, but Maxine only picked out words, not meanings. On the deck, she lit the propane burner and began to sauté the bacon, chopping and adding the onion. El Tigre said the name, "Lotto."

None of this would have happened if Maxine hadn't deluded herself into thinking she could convince Lotto she wouldn't testify. Honora wasn't the only one to screw up. Another mistake had been to go back into the house the night Larry died. She could have saved herself a world of grief if she had kept driving. Still, Larry would have done the same thing for her. *No good deed goes unpunished.*

El Tigre let out a tremendous burst of words. He spoke louder and faster with more forceful gestures. Whenever he was upset, Maxine felt his anxiety leeching into her. She forced herself to turn her head away from the skillet and look at him. His face had reddened and his eyes bulged. She had a fleeting hope he would keel over with apoplexy. Instead, he roared into the phone and ended the call. The kids stopped talking. Total silence. Dust hung in the still air.

Maxine turned away and began chopping the peppers. The knife slipped in her sweaty palm and a drop of blood contrasted with the green of the pepper. Behind her, she heard El Tigre rise from the couch. She felt him stand next to her at the propane burner. Hoping she wasn't going to lose it and start screaming or bawling, she gestured toward the contents of the skillet scenting the air with onion, bacon and pepper smells. "Is this all right?" Her voice sounded squeaky high, like she had been breathing nitrous oxide.

"You will call your sister again."

"Did something happen?"

"A change of plan. Call! Use speakerphone. No tricks!"

"What change of plan?" She glanced at her watch. "My sister will be at the bank."

"Call!" He pressed "speaker" and handed her the phone.

Maxine's pulse pounded so loud in her ears she didn't think she could hear Honora's voice. The answering machine message kicked in.

"Leave a message. Say *emergencia.*"

~ * ~

The next hour was endless. El Tigre sat on the sofa and consumed two plates of fried potatoes and vegetables. He muttered "*bueno,*" in his gruff voice. Maxine brought out two Cokes and handed one to El Tigre, and then she sat on the blue metal chair. She welcomed the sugar jolt of the soda, because she suddenly felt an overwhelming fatigue, almost as if she would fall asleep in the chair. Maxine screwed her courage up to ask, "What happened?" She pointed to the phone on the couch next to El Tigre.

"Change of plans." His voice betrayed his irritation.

"What change?"

*Order. Counter order. Disorder.* Her old navy-trained boss's mantra. Maxine felt the smallest ray of hope. Disorder could bring opportunity. Or something worse.

"They fly now to a private airport near Cartagena. There is much risk to bring the money here." He stared over her shoulder at the shed.

"Cartagena?" Jesus, Colombia.

"What about my sister?" Maxine looked him square in the eye. "And how will *you* get the money then?"

"She is released when the money is secure in Colombia." His gaze traveled to the shed again.

Maxine's stomach knotted, and the familiar jangling sensation raced up and down her arms. Honora was doomed, and Maxine's mind raced round and round, unable to think of a way out of this horrible mess.

She looked at El Tigre. "How will she get home?"

"On a plane." He stood and gave her his empty plate. His eyes narrowed. "Too many questions."

On the highway, a siren sounded, closer and closer, then raced through town and out past the dump and on the road to—Idaho? Or off into the desert. A few minutes later, a second siren and then a third tore along the highway. El Tigre's black eyes evinced pinpricks of interest.

He went indoors and Maxine heard his jubilant voice demanding, "Go Feesh!"

She tried to think what time it was in Panama, but her mind had shut down. Was it an hour earlier than Pacific time, or the same? She couldn't remember. A few minutes later, a helicopter flew overhead.

In spite of the intrusion of the sirens and the chopper, the town slept in a somnolent late-afternoon haze. On the little porch, the air was hot and dry and Maxine lit a second cigarette from the butt of the first.

They wouldn't let her sister walk away. She knew too much.

# *Fifty-one*

Lotto awakened to the slapping of the halyards on a nearby mast. He stared at the low ceiling. Where the hell was he? In a bunk on the boat. Business gone. Possessions gone. Sweating about his very survival. He remembered yesterday morning's life-changing phone call and the knowledge that his whole world had plummeted deep into the DEA's abyss.

The wind had come up, heralding the predicted storm. Through the porthole, he saw the first blush of dawn streaking the Key West sky. The strong smell of coffee from the galley mixed with the tang of the salt air. Only ninety miles between him and freedom, although few Floridians thought of Cuba as "freedom."

Lotto cut the tags off the new tan cargo shorts, a green t-shirt, and the flip-flops. Everything fit, and somehow these common clothes that anyone might wear felt right. While he brushed his teeth, he scrutinized his newly shaved scalp, dark and, thank-god, not orange from two liberal applications of self-tanner, a definite improvement over yesterday, but he still pulled on the black Marlins cap.

In the galley, the captain, ashtray at his elbow, a chart in front of him, listened to a weather forecast in Spanish. He glanced up at Lotto. "Good morning, Señor Léon." He turned off the radio. "The weather will become much worse. We can hunker down or make a run for it."

"What does the forecast say?" Lotto took the pot from the stove and poured coffee into a maroon mug, adding lump sugar and plenty of hot milk. He turned back to the captain.

"Twenty knot winds, maybe more," Alberto said. "The currents are strong. Rain. Nasty gusts. It will be wet." He removed his tan cap and ran his hand through his gray hair. "And rough. Take some Dramamine. The crossing is like a carnival ride where *los pequeños* get sick." He shrugged his big shoulders. "The front, she should pass by early afternoon." The way he stared at Lotto, he seemed to be sizing him up. *Are you* hombre *enough to brave the Florida Straits in a squall?*

"Fine. We go. We're less likely to run into the Coast Guard in bad weather, aren't we?" Lotto had first-rate false papers, but he had learned long ago that a man in his trade could never be too paranoid. There were no careless *narcotrafficantes.*

"This is a Panamanian boat. It doesn't run drugs. The Coasties have never given me any shit." He folded the map and turned off the radio.

Lotto took a sip of the coffee. Strong, the way he liked it. "Are there any stash areas for my gym bag?"

The captain gave Lotto a dour look. "I said no drugs! The Cubans do not tolerate drugs."

"Just cash." Why did everyone assume *he* carried drugs? Furthermore, he owned this goddamn boat and could load it to the gunwales with drugs if he wanted.

"One of the kitchen cabinets has a false bottom." Smoke streamed out of Alberto's mouth as he spoke. He fingered the small gold cross on his chest.

"When do we leave?" asked Lotto.

"Soon. There is good Cuban bread and ham *pastelitos* for breakfast." He opened a locker next to the sink. Lotto saw cans of mandarin oranges, black beans, tomatillos, and *dulce de leche.*

"You must remove the food to access the sliding panel in the bottom. Do it now while we're tied up. We'll eat. Then *vamos.*" He offered a thin smile. "You'll be walking along the *Malecón* in a few hours."

Twenty minutes later, the captain washed the dishes and stowed everything in the galley. *Battening down the hatches.* Lotto transferred his cash to the hidden compartment in the food locker. He gulped down two Dramamine tablets with the dregs of his coffee.

They put on foul weather gear and went topside. The light on the harbor was a smoldering golden haze. A small sun peeked over the horizon, painting a yellow glow in the eastern sky. The weird light gave the water an oily sheen, very creepy looking.

The harbor began to wake up. Lotto heard the staticky voice of another marine radio. A few intrepid boats left for the day, and sailors with towels slung over their shoulders headed along the dock to the showers. The smells of toast and bacon drifted over the marina. Seagulls squawked overhead, cruising for an easy meal. Lotto hated seagulls. With their beady avaricious eyes and opportunistic ways, they reminded him of all the people he had done business with. Those days were over. He thought about setting up a West African operation to take his *fine white fabric* into Europe, but the idea of starting again did not appeal to him. God knows, dealing with African bribes and hassles would be worse than in Mexico. At least the *putas* he dealt with there spoke a common language.

Lotto helped cast off from the dock and the captain threaded the *El Capitan* out of the Bight and to the first buoy marking the channel. Once the vessel cleared the harbor, the wind picked up and the waves grew bigger, more unruly. Lotto saw the eastern horizon and the thick strata of clouds, layers of gold, then pale brown, and dark brown and black.

*It's not an omen, but simple physics, the refraction of light.*

Overhead, the sky was a confusion of gray clouds, some pale and smooth, others more threatening. *Only ninety miles.*

An hour later, rain lashed the water and the wind lashed them in gusts. The waves had to be ten feet high. The captain said they were crossing the Florida Current, the beginning of the Gulf Stream. The boat bucked the current in the effort to slice through the enormous waves. Lotto was glad that the ship was a trawler type with a serious hull and not some fast planing boat that would be tossed around like a piece of driftwood. Alberto kept the speed up enough to surge through the waves, riding some on the crest, plowing through others in an ungodly spray of seawater. The Gulf seemed as confused as the clouds.

"*Hijueputa*!" shouted Alberto and pointed to the roof of the cabin. Lotto looked up with widening eyes. He had never heard the captain say "motherfucker" before. Over the wind and the waves and the engine, he heard a rhythmic whomp-whomp-whomp sound. *Mierda*. Through the rain-spattered plastic, he saw a Coast Guard helicopter hovering over *El Capitan*. His blood froze. What did *they* want?

# *Fifty-two*

As expected, Honora became half-hysterical when Maxine told her about the change of plans.

"What will happen to me? What will I do?" She couldn't stifle a sob.

"*Onay aneplay.*" *No plane!*

Maxine spoke rapidly in Pig Latin, the "secret" language of Honora's childhood. They had been *Axinemay* and *Onorahay*, to seven-year-old Honora's giggling delight.

El Tigre's head swiveled, and he glared with a threatening evil eye. "No tricks!"

"You will do what they tell you. Did you understand my words?" Maxine asked.

"Esyay," whispered Honora. "Yes."

"You and 'the friend' go out for a drink or something," Maxine advised Honora. "Relax a little."

The call ended.

El Tigre knit his satanic eyebrows. "My brother is a simple coca farmer. He hates cities and city people."

Maxine didn't dare think about El Tigre's rage if Honora escaped. On a busy Panama street, or in a bar, Honora would have a better chance of making her getaway. El Tigre might kill me, but not the children. Please, not the children. Kaylee would still have her father. And Ethan? If Honora made it back, Ethan would have his mother. It's just too bad for the rube brother.

Maxine fixed fish sticks, carrots and hot biscuits for the kids, with El Tigre chortling, "go feesh!" They had dinner around the big oak table. Kaylee seemed watchful, attentive to any strange currents in the room. Maxine picked at her meal, but Ethan gobbled down everything, and El Tigre cleaned out the rest. Ethan seemed happy to have a male around. He must miss having a father. El Tigre and the kids watched cartoons while Maxine cleaned the kitchen.

Jeff called as he did every day. When the phone rang Maxine jumped up, thinking the call was from Honora. El Tigre examined the caller ID and passed the phone to Maxine, mouthing "no tricks!" She recognized Jeff's number.

"Hi!" she said, trying to sound like today was any other day.

"What's going on?" he asked.

"We're just watching TV." She imagined Jeff's freckled face, his easy smile, unaware of this catastrophe.

El Tigre got off the couch and hovered a few feet away, making Maxine crazy.

With all the time in the world, Jeff chatted about doing this morning's drive in record time, the golf lessons, even how nice the club management was. He didn't notice her monosyllabic replies.

"You sound tired," Jeff said.

"I'm half-dead. Must be the weather."

"What news from Honora?"

"She should be on her way home, soon." *If only*. "She's getting the money." Maxine picked at her cuticle.

"Hey, am I on a speaker phone?" Jeff asked.

"The kids think it's cool," she said.

"Next time, let me know." He sounded miffed. Maxine said goodbye. Thank God he didn't ask to speak to Kaylee.

The children took baths, ate cookies and ice cream and watched more TV. If Maxine ever had to listen to another idiotic cartoon, she would become catatonic.

# *Fifty-three*

"*Los locos! Idiotas!* Alberto picked up the handset of the ship's radio and dialed a frequency.

"Hallo, this is the ship *El Capitan*."

A spasm of anxiety grabbed Lotto. Why would the Coast Guard fly in this miserable weather, harassing innocent sailors? Alberto's tan face looked calm, but the waves were worse now, and Lotto wanted the captain to concentrate on the goddamn navigation. They almost took a hit broadside. Lotto felt like he was riding in his son Christian's bathtub toy boat, except now the devil laughed and splashed and created havoc in the water. Fear dwelt in the back of his mind like a bear in a cave. More danger. More betrayals. He would never set eyes on Cuba. Never arrive in Caracas. Never see his sons again.

"Panama," Alberto said into the handset. A pause. "Havana."

The captain listened intently while gripping the wheel. "No." The faintest smile. "*Gracias*." He hung up the radio as the biggest wave yet slammed across the bow.

Lotto braced himself for the wall of water. After the wave had passed, he looked up through the driving rain as the helicopter veered off to the west.

"What the fuck?" The noise of the water crashing around the boat was so loud they had to shout.

"They could not see our flag," hollered Alberto. "Maybe we have lost it. They also wanted to know if we had seen any bales of 'square grouper.'"

Lotto gaped at the captain. "You are making a joke."

"No," said the captain. "A drug ship dumped a cargo of *bota*."

In spite of his lurching stomach and his paralyzing fear, Lotto laughed at the irony of the situation. He had never dealt in weed, but the humor appealed to him.

"What else did they say?" he yelled over the noise of the waves.

Alberto looked at Lotto again, exhibiting his faintly amused smile. His gold tooth flashed. "They wished us a 'good trip'."

~ * ~

The winds grew wilder and the waves more rambunctious. Alberto put on a life vest and asked Lotto to do likewise. At the mercy of the seas, he felt sloshed and churned—whipped around like a hapless sock in his wife's washing machine. Alberto muttered something about deploying the drogue chute.

"Would you be capable of taking the wheel and keeping us on course?" the captain asked Lotto, who answered with a blank stare. *Him* navigating through these seas? The man must have lost his mind. Lotto gave a faint shake of his head. He felt capable only of fear, mixed with dread and despair, his entire body locked into survival mode.

Leaving land in the storm had been stupid. He could have remained out of sight below decks in Key West until the weather cleared. He could have saved himself. Now those ninety miles seemed a wild and treacherous ocean away in this boat Lotto expected would be broached at any moment by a monster wave that would send them to kingdom come.

~ * ~

In increments so small he hadn't noticed, the fierceness of the gusts abated, and the maelstrom of waves grew calmer. Lotto asked himself if survival were possible, and now the answer was *maybe,* not the no of half an hour ago. The constant turbulence of cutting through the angry sea lessened. To the south, where Cuba lay, was that a glimpse of blue sky? He whispered an involuntary prayer.

A few minutes later, Lotto and Alberto leaned back in their seats, daring to relax for a moment. As the sea became less frenzied, the captain poured each of them a shot of rum.

"That was some bad shit," he said. "You are a decent sailor." He hoisted his plastic tumbler.

Lotto felt like a drowning man who had been washed up on a beach. He was uncertain as to whether he could even walk. "Thanks," he said and raised his glass to Alberto. The rum sloshed around the glass, which felt heavy in his hand.

Alberto lit a cigarette. "Really bad shit."

An hour later, the buildings of Havana beckoned from the gray skies. Alberto called the harbormaster at Hemingway Marina to let him know of their impending appearance.

"This is *El Capitan* arriving from Key West. We are registered in Panama and have one Colombian and one Venezuelan aboard. No pets."

"Getting foreigners through customs, the Cubans are as nitpicky as the gringos." The captain gestured toward the city. "Kilometers of red tape. It can take three hours or so. We can't leave the vessel until we are cleared. I hope you are not in a hurry."

Hurry was no longer an issue. Lotto was happy to be alive.

"No pornography," said the captain. "And no guns."

"No problem."

Lotto helped Alberto spot the big red and white buoy that was the entrance to the channel. Navigating to the marina in the still heavy seas was tricky, but Alberto didn't seem to mind. He had electronic charts and depth finders, every nautical toy. Courage and seamanship counted more than gadgets, but the salsa music in the wheelhouse made Lotto's insides stop quivering.

At the marina, a trio of *guarda* in crisp white shirts and pressed navy pants came aboard. Lotto smiled at the attractive woman member of the group, and let Alberto do the talking. In midsummer, the basin was loaded with sailing yachts from Canada, the Bahamas and even the British Virgin Islands.

Two hours later, the rain had stopped and they cleared customs with a few gifts bestowed for the *guarda* being so quick and efficient. Lotto's money remained undiscovered. He changed into dry clothes, and he and Alberto left the *El Capitan* tied up at the dock. Lotto's legs felt wobbly, unused to the steadiness of being on land. *Terra firma.*

The marina was a small city. They exchanged money, and Alberto led the way to *La Cova Pizza Nova* where they shared a pizza. Lotto, not exactly worried, but still uneasy about the cash he had left aboard the boat, casually mentioned he might be willing to sign the *El Capitan* over to Alberto for *dinero suelto,* mere pocket change, as he had no more use for the vessel. Alberto nodded with a pleased gleam in his eye and flashed a gold tooth.

Lotto called for a taxi to drive him into town. While he waited by the bus stop for the cab, he called Enrique, encrypting the call out of habit.

"Get out of the country," he said. "The DEA is onto us."

"Where are you, Lotto?" asked Enrique's worried voice.

"Havana." Lotto eyed an ancient bus that pulled up. A handful of yachtsmen and marina employees boarded.

"I am leaving for Bogotá in a few hours," Enrique said.

The bus took off in a cloud of smelly exhaust.

On an impulse, he lit the cigar he had just purchased. Normally he disliked cigars, but this one wasn't bad. He called Sarita and said he was coming home, with a stopover in Caracas. He pictured her happy smile, her soft face and sleek dark hair.

"Lotto, what wonderful news."

Would she still think so when he told her Marquesa Trading Company was no more? Would she want him hanging around all day? Thank God, Sarita was a judge's daughter and any unpleasant talk of extradition would be swiftly squashed. He tried to think of his new life as a man of leisure, sipping coffee all morning, playing soccer with his boys, meeting cronies for a drink at the yacht club. He would no longer be a stranger to his sons, make sure they didn't repeat his mistakes.

The future. It seemed unreal, like the little bit of blue sky he had glimpsed when the sea stopped rampaging.

A strange yellow and green open conveyance with hard plastic orange seats and a blue checkerboard on the front next to the painted word "Taxi" arrived. Round as a bumblebee, with one large headlight, like a cyclops, a friendly yellow cyclops.

Lotto climbed in. "*Habana. El Malecón.*"

"Ah *señor*, bad weather today." The driver turned to him. "The waves are crashing over the sea wall."

He motioned to the driver to get going. The open-air ride felt exhilarating. Lotto realized that he had seldom been irritated since getting the bad news, the worst of all possible news yesterday morning. Sometimes opportunity arrives disguised as bad news. The fear of drowning had left him feeling cleansed, almost... reborn.

The cab dropped him along *El Malecón*. Hands clasped behind his back, pitched forward into the wind, Lotto walked along the mostly deserted seawall, watching out for the breaking waves. The esplanade smelled of briny ocean, and the wind and the spray felt invigorating, not threatening. Across the street the crumbling white colonial buildings gleamed in the sun.

Lotto remembered walking the entire five miles of *El Malecón* with his mother, a feat he still recalled with pride. In 1977, after Carter lifted the embargo, they had visited Havana over a school vacation. He had been ten years old, with eyes for everything. They tapped their feet to *Son* and mambo, gobbled black beans and Cuban sandwiches, and rode around the old squares in a horse-drawn carriage. Lotto remembered the horse's hooves clopping on the cobblestones as they rounded the Parque Central in *vieja Habana*. His best memory was of an exciting baseball game. Even to his young eyes, the players looked many levels above the teams in Colombia, and he had followed Cuban baseball for a while.

Lotto wondered if his mother would visit him in Colombia. Of course, they could also meet in Mexico. Maybe Buenos Aires. It would depend on the evidence against him and any extradition treaties.

On the street, the exotic intermixture of old automobiles passed by, most of them in need of a muffler, vintage American cars of every make; some so ancient he didn't recognize them. A tan swept-wing Dodge, then a blue Buick Century clattered along the roadway. The vintage cars, the water crashing against *El Malecón,* and even the old white city seemed to have a beating heart. Lotto, too, felt alive, still mortal, after this morning's white-knuckle passage, but lustily alive.

## *Fifty-four*

"Anybody home?"

Kaylee looked up expectantly, recognizing Petra's mother's voice. Her eyes shifted to Maxine, and then to El Tigre.

Maxine glanced out the window into the summer darkness. El Tigre jumped from the sofa and flipped the yard lights on. Petra's mom stood at the end of the short driveway, leaning on the padlocked gate.

He muttered, "Say you have no time to talk. Remember, I have the kids." His arm shot out and stopped Kaylee from running outside.

"Time for you to go to bed," he said. "First chocolate, then brush teeth."

Maxine went out and walked toward the gate like a zombie. The cool breeze grazed her hot cheeks. Her heart raced and she couldn't think of a single thing to say. She couldn't even recall Petra's mother's name.

"Did you hear the news?" the woman asked.

"What happened?"

"A fisherman found two dead men out by the reservoir. Both had been shot. Didn't you hear all the sirens? The helicopter?"

"I thought...a car accident."

Petra's mother bent her head close to Maxine and lowered her voice. "Shot at close range. Like an *execution*. Keep your doors locked." She rattled the gate and smiled. "This seems pretty secure. Hey, do you want me to take the kids tomorrow? They can work in the community garden for a while. Do them good."

"Maybe," Maxine said. "Kaylee has a rash I'm watching."

"I'll come by around ten, okay?"

Maxine gave a weak nod, and turned back toward the house. She stumbled on the step leading up to the deck. She couldn't stop thinking of El Tigre's words. *For this I have killed two men*. Now, two dead men had turned up a few miles away. El Tigre had killed them and he would kill her, too if she stood in his way.

Maxine didn't mention the "news" to El Tigre. Instead, she said that a neighbor wanted to take the kids gardening tomorrow.

He gave a noncommittal shrug.

# *Fifty-five*

Getting the money out of the account had been a cinch. Honora had talked to the lawyer yesterday, who told her what to do. She wore a pink suit with a white camisole, everything glammed up with an Hermès scarf in pink, gray and gold, and gray pumps—too high to be business-like, but what the hell? The outfit had cost a small fortune, which she had paid for with the Panama bank debit card. What a joy and a wonder the card was, even more fun than spending her inheritance, because that had been her druggy self, and this time around she was sober enough to relish every dollar spent.

She had taken a new suitcase for the money, a cheap lime green affair with wheels. With this mega-load of cash, it was so tempting to drop out of sight. If it weren't for Ethan and that horrible man who had practically kidnapped him, she would have. *Adios, everyone.*

A taxi deposited her back at the hotel, and Honora changed into slacks, v-neck silk sweater and low heeled sandals, everything black for a getaway in the dark. She finished packing, lovingly folding the pink suit, the best outfit she had bought since Ethan was born. She took five hundred dollars out of the suitcase, slipping the bills out of random bundles. Who the hell would know?

Honora had called Maxine to report she had the money, and gotten the bad news about an unscheduled trip to Colombia. *Over my dead body.* They would toss her out of the plane or give her to the FARC rebels. Something horrible. She would plan her escape. Nothing came to mind. Honora tried to think how Julia in *Destiny and Desire*, her favorite *telenovela* would get out of the jam. Something dramatic, unexpected, a big surprise like floating away in a hot air balloon. Julia had endless resources.

Honora did have a stash of money. With a stomach careening with butterflies, she scanned a magazine, flipping pages and looking at the ads, not reading but thinking hard how to outwit this Jorge.

He was late. If he were too late, he wouldn't go anywhere but the airport. Where was he? She was dying for a cigarette and she had just used the toilet for the umpteenth time when the front desk called to say "*Senor* Botero" was in the lobby. Honora felt a pall of dread settle over her. She would do what she had to. She could mesmerize just about any male between fourteen and eighty into dancing to her tune. If that didn't work, there was Plan B.

"Send him up."

She gave herself a liberal spraying of her duty-free perfume, Armani *Code Pour Femme*, and tugged at her black sweater to display more cleavage. There was a knock at the door. Honora opened it with a big smile. "You must be Jorge," she said in a teasing, breathy voice.

One look and her optimism plummeted and a queasy feeling invaded her stomach. Jorge Botero, burly as a boxer, must be fifty if he was a day. Honora pressed herself against the door as he entered, reeking of cheap tobacco. Under pointy eyebrows his flinty eyes swept the room, suspicious as hell. As she followed him in, she looked with distaste at his longish sideburns that morphed into a short black beard, and his bald head fringed with black hair growing past his collar. Cheap yellowish knit shirt, black pants, white sneakers, a real fashion statement. He carried a white plastic bag.

She pointed to the loud green suitcase on the chest at the foot of the bed. "One million dollars. My kid's education."

From his sour expression, she knew he didn't give a rat's ass about anyone's education.

His grim mouth, accentuated by the pencil thin beard and mustache, looked cruel. In broken English, he rasped, "I want to see the money," or that's what she understood. Without so much as a *por favor*.

*En Español*, Honora explained that she spoke Spanish, not fluent, really, but she'd taken some classes and after living in Miami, Southern California, and Reno, well, it was good enough for everyday conversation. She gushed that she absolutely loved the *telenovelas* on the Spanish stations and watched them all the time.

While she spoke, he stared at her with no expression. His deep-set eyes looked like they never crinkled into a smile. Honora knew she was babbling and swallowed hard. She fixed her gaze on his gold medallion, gold watch and gold ring, all shiny and sparkling, totally out of synch with his clothes. Some money there.

Jorge ordered her to open the suitcase, pointing and acting like it was freaking booby-trapped. They stared at the stacks of money. Just astonishing, the sight of a million dollars. Except now it wouldn't be hers to share.

Jorge pawed around the suitcase, removed some of the packets and examined them. *Making random counts*. He grimaced as he made some scribbles on the little notepad by the room phone. He didn't complain about any shortages, although her heart was lodged in her throat. As she watched him rifle through the bills, the idea of a quick seduction of this implacable man who never stopped glowering seemed a poor bet.

When he finished counting, he put everything back, none too neatly, then he reached into his plastic bag and took out a brass padlock. He zipped the suitcase shut and slipped the lock through the holes on the zipper pull. Next he took a luggage tag out of the plastic bag, and affixed it to the suitcase.

"Call my brother and tell him I have the money." My brother. *Mi hermano*. The look in his eyes really creeped her out. He and El Tigre must be part of some horrific crime cartel.

She made the phone call, and Jorge spoke to El Tigre, and when he ended the call, he kept her phone, slipping it into his pants pocket. *Bastard.*

Somehow, she must finagle him out of the hotel room, and then out of the building. She checked her watch. Just before seven. When the bars and restaurants opened.

Honora told Jorge she needed to use the bathroom and skittered in and shut the door behind her. The bathroom, among other amenities, had a telephone. Honora ran the water in the sink while she called the front desk to send a bellhop up right away. She flushed the toilet, washed her hands, and came back into the room.

"We should have a drink," Honora said, batting her eyelashes. "To celebrate." No reaction. Maybe he didn't understand her Spanish.

She stood by the window and looked at the tall buildings. Shit, this was awful. She sidled toward the door so she could fling it open when the bellhop arrived. Almost before she got into position, there was a knock, and she opened the door. Jorge stared daggers.

She gestured to her luggage by the door. "I'm leaving my bags with the doorman," she said, in English to the bellhop. "And have him get me a cab."

When the bellhop picked up the green suitcase, she thought Jorge would lose it. "That stays with me," he said, and yanked it out of the startled man's hand.

She took her handbag and followed the luggage out of the room with Jorge right on her heels. They rode down in the elevator with him holding the lime green suitcase in his vise grip...Honora wondered if he would handcuff it to his wrist.

She bestowed outrageous tips on the bellhop and the doorman. When she stepped outside, Jorge stuck to her like a shadow, close on her heels, clutching the suitcase. The heat emanating from the sidewalk still shimmered, and the humidity would wilt your hair in a minute.

Dusk was falling. On the bustling street in front of the hotel, Jorge stood too close, while a cacophony of horns honked, buses rumbled, motor scooters sped by. Down the street, a band played salsa. The smell of exhaust nauseated her. Where were the aromas of the juice vendor and the hotdog cart when you needed them?

Jorge didn't say jackshit, just stared at her with sullen eyes, which narrowed as the doorman opened the door of a cab that pulled up. Jorge stepped back and grunted, "no!" while Honora produced her most seductive smile.

"I know a cool place in the San Felipe neighborhood," she said. "*Casco Viejo.* A jazz bar with good food. It's a fast ride from the hotel."

Seeing his creased brow, she said, "We'll stop by the hotel again on our way to the airport. We have two whole hours to kill." *You stupid prick.*

Jorge stood rooted in place, like a statue. With a quizzical expression, the doorman looked from Jorge to Honora and back again. Ignoring Jorge's reluctance, she jumped into the back seat of the taxi. Jorge, still glowering, lumbered in beside her, insisting, "We are going to the airport."

God, he had uttered an entire sentence.

She wrinkled her nose. "Of course, we're going to the airport. But we've got loads of time and I don't like icky airport food." She had begun to sweat, but she put her hand lightly on his thigh, just exerting the smallest pressure. His leg felt like a log and he pulled the suitcase across his lap. Speaking English, she gave the cabbie the name of the restaurant where she and Steven had eaten last night.

Traffic congestion made the ride anything but fast, and Honora kept up a pace of chatter, asking Jorge questions he steadfastly declined to answer as they drove along the Avenida Balboa. He held the suitcase across his knees. Desperation drove her to more inane chatter until the cab let them out in front of the arched doorway of the restaurant.

Looking around, Honora realized that maybe she hadn't picked the best area, with derelict and demolished buildings placeholders between the nice restaurants and bars. Kind of creepy if one was alone with the confusion of curving streets and the nearness of the slums.

Jorge's eyes seemed to bulge and he looked about ready to explode, yet he maintained his eerie silence. Was he a peasant from the jungle, a coca farmer or maybe somewhat *challenged*? He seemed totally out of his element, whatever his element was. On the other hand, who would send a dimwit to ride herd on a million dollars?

She avoided the busy patio and headed inside for the air-conditioning. "We can eat in the bar," she said. "Quicker that way."

The walls were used brick, covered with abstract paintings in reds, deep greens and blacks. Latin jazz played in the background. The waiter carried a plate of sizzling shrimp to the party next to them. She and Jorge sat knee to knee at a tiny table, and Honora ordered a tropical punch with tequila, orange liquor and strawberries. No ice. Jorge asked for a beer, but only at her prodding. She whipped out her wallet and put the money on the table.

"So do you live in Colombia? What's it like? I hear it's beautiful. What city do you live in? Or are you a country boy?"

He muttered, "Buenaventura," and shut up again. He kept his eye on the suitcase, under the table by his ankles.

"Oh, what a pretty name. Is it on the coast? I really love Caribbean climates."

She pretended to slurp down the tropical punch, but poured some of it under the table, and she called the waiter over and said the party sitting there before them had spilled something. Jorge, nursing his glass of *Balboa*, and looking like his boxers were crawling with fire ants, didn't respond, even in monosyllables. Honora ordered another drink.

"Jorge, I guess you are the strong silent type, very macho, I'm sure. I like that in a man." She patted his leg again, and could feel him tense. The couple at the next table smirked. After the drink arrived, Honora acted a little tipsy, talking loud and making extravagant hand gestures.

She pushed her dark hair away from her face, took a big sip of booze and slopped the drink over the table and down her top.

"*Mierda!* My brand-new silk sweater." She dabbed at it with her napkin. "I'll be right back." She took her handbag and the cocktail glass and lurched toward the ladies' room.

The entrance to the kitchen was around the corner. Hell and damnation, the ladies' room was locked.

Honora, still rubbing her sweater, wanted to chew her nails to the quick waiting for the occupant to leave.

Maxine had told her to escape. That meant Maxine must have some insight into the situation with the kids and El Tigre. If Maxine was wrong...When the door opened, she almost knocked the woman down to get into the john where she locked the door and put her drink on the counter. She pulled the plastic bag of hand sanitizer, alcohol rubs, and mouthwash out of her handbag. Matches from the bar. Oh God, she was dying of nerves, and her hands shook so badly she could barely light the matches. She doused the paper towels with the mouthwash and the sanitizer and lit the alcohol rub. Everything flamed up like the 4th of July. Once she got the paper towels on fire, she lit the contents of her cocktail glass, and then the wastebasket. She kept feeding and fanning the flames until the smoke alarm went off, emitting a shrill sound they must be able to hear on Mars.

Holding her breath, she waited a few more seconds, worried Jorge would grab her at the door. She peered out into the corridor. Kitchen noise and the scream of the smoke alarms. Patrons scrambling down the staircase from the second-floor restaurant. No sign of Jorge, but she spied a corner of a lime green suitcase on the floor just beyond the kitchen door. Crap.

Honora dodged back down the hall and flattened herself against the wall. She rummaged in her big handbag until she found the one-quart toiletries see-through bag for going through security. Inside she had four tubes of lipstick bundled together with a rubber band. She plucked the tube in the middle. Her safety net. She dug for her glasses, because she had to see to point the nozzle away from her. In the corridor, the suitcase hadn't moved.

She surprised Jorge lurking around the corner by the kitchen door, green bag at his feet. She gave him a big wide smile and aimed a blast of pepper spray at his eyes. He bellowed and rubbed his face while she turned into the kitchen. He grabbed her as she scooted by, and she lost her glasses and dropped the spray. She had to stomp on his arch before he would release his grip on her arm.

Like a crazy woman, she tore through the confusion in the kitchen yelling "*Fuego*! *Fuego!*"

Between waiters and cooks scrambling to leave, she dodged into the courtyard, and edged her way past barrels of garbage, out a gate and onto the maze of streets. Darkness had descended, and Honora had a horror of wandering into the slums. Checking behind her, she walked close to a foursome until they entered a restaurant. Finally, she got to Plaza Bolivar, but she didn't see a cab, so she hurried a few blocks further, trying to stay with people, especially Anglos. Something smelled musty and rotten. She looked over her shoulder again for Jorge, but his scary bulk wasn't visible in the murky darkness. No sign of a lime green suitcase. In a crumbling white building the long, sad tones of a trumpet sounded above the street. Hustling along the sidewalk, fearful of the shadows but needing them for cover, Honora arrived breathless and frazzled at the Plaza de la Independencia. She and Steve had caught a cab there last night in front of the big pink building. Honora had planned to return to the hotel and grab her suitcases, but now she just wanted to get out of there. She could arrange for them to be air freighted. When you had access to shitloads of money, life was so easy. Not her life, of course, and sure as hell not today.

Breathless and with a racing heart, she jumped into a taxi. "Tocumen Airport," she said, panting. "I'm late for my flight." Her one thought was to get out of Panama. Tonight.

## *Fifty-six*

A few minutes before nine, the phone rang again. El Tigre looked at the number and answered, "*Sí*? Jorge?" Almost like he knew Honora wouldn't be on the phone. He said, "*bueno,*" his voice low and intense. Maxine kept her gaze fixed on him. His eyes passed over her face and strayed to the window. It was almost dark. The conversation was short. El Tigre punched the "end" button.

"What about my sister?" Maxine felt a hard lump forming in her throat.

"We did not speak of her."

That could mean anything. Had Honora escaped?

~ * ~

Maxine and Kaylee slept in the "master" bedroom, and Ethan stayed in Kaylee's room on the far side of the living room. Lucy slunk under Maxine's bed. Maxine heard her licking herself. She had fled when El Tigre called, "*amiga dulce, ven, gatita, ven*!" Animals knew. Kaylee shifted in her sleep and clutched her floppy rabbit. Maxine wore a warm-up suit to bed.

*For this I have already killed two men.*

She saw the dirt road going uphill to the reservoir, the green reeds by the boat ramp. She remembered the pungent smell of wild sage. The sound of water running through the canyon. The vistas of blue sky and brown hills. The placid surface of the lake.

Her body tensed with fear. *Like an execution.* El Tigre was capable of anything. Maxine tried to pray, but she kept drifting into sleep.

She woke and heard paper rustling and her laptop booting. What was El Tigre doing on her computer? She tried to recall if there was any mention of two million rather than one million dollars in her files, but her mind was so frazzled she couldn't remember what was saved on the flash drive and what was on her hard drive. Her email account had a password. She floated in and out of sleep. El Tigre had turned off the living room lights. She heard faint snores. It would be impossible to awaken the children and sneak out past El Tigre, then climb the padlocked fence. He had her keys. Even if they got out of the yard by some miracle, then what? Walk along the highway? Try to wake up a neighbor? All the dogs would bark. He would come after them. *I have killed two men.*

Overhead the jets roared as pilots practiced dogfights over the desert.

# *Fifty-seven*

Since that world-changing phone call, Lotto had been acting from instincts so pure, so automatic, they must be self-preservation. At José Martí airport, he upgraded to first class on the Copa flight from Havana to Panama City. He didn't like the airlines that flew directly to Caracas from Havana. Cubana had the world's worst safety record. You could not pay Lotto to fly Cubana. Besides, in Panama he could transfer money, even ask his banker and lawyer if Caliendo had opened private accounts.

After a long wait in line, he bit his tongue lest the old Lotto say something rude to the Copa reservations clerk, words not in tune with his new mellower self.

His carried-on gym bag crammed with dollars and Euros hadn't raised eyebrows going through security, nor had his Venezuelan passport. His one Cuban purchase, not that there had been much to buy, was a white Panama hat with a black band. The hat covered his shaved head on which a field of short stubble had sprouted. He wore the silk Tommy Bahama shirt and the tan Dockers Alberto had purchased in Key West. His blue suede athletic shoes looked right. The new Lotto, dressed like Everyman, but with flair.

Who the fuck was he kidding? Sitting in the plane waiting for take-off, Lotto had a moment of sheer terror. The space around him in the cabin felt strange, not confining, but weirdly off, like he had ventured into another universe. Heart pounding, he eyed his fellow passengers, clueless about the disturbed air, the sense of his space irrevocably wrong.

*Just a small panic attack.*

The flight attendant in her navy-blue dress stopped to get his drink order and he asked for a glass of water and rum on ice. He had purchased *Death in the Andes*, a novel set in Peru. He flipped through the pages as the plane pulled away from the gate and taxied toward his new life. *Mierda*! He should have picked something lighter to begin his new life, his *nueva vida*.

As the jet lifted off, Lotto bid a silent adios to the red Cuban soil, to Miami, to his occupation, so tense and dangerous, yet so profitable. There were no old *narcotraficantes*. Most his age rotted in jail or in their graves.

A leopard *could* change his spots. He might teach business in Cartagena; after all, he had an MBA. Or maybe dabble in consulting, not in the trade, but in logistics, international business. He could resurrect Marquesa Trading Company, under another name, of course, legitimate, this time, not a front. Maybe he would do something extreme, like—learn to cook. Wouldn't Sarita and the maid be astonished if he waltzed into the dining room holding a platter of Wiener Schnitzel?

Lotto sipped his rum as the plane crossed Cuba and began the flight over the blue Caribbean. The panic attack? Just a blip on the radar.

In the aisle seat across the way, a pretty woman smiled at him. Lotto returned her smile. He would miss Angelika, but the world was rife with pretty women.

# *Fifty-eight*

Maxine sat up straight in bed when the telephone chimed in the middle of the night. Her heart raced again as the adrenaline flooded her body. She strained to hear. First, El Tigre's expectant, "*Sí*?" Then, "*Bueno. Alambre el dinero.*"

Something about the money. El Tigre went into the bathroom and the toilet flushed. She heard water running in the sink. Maxine tried to recall if El Tigre had arrived with a duffel bag or a valise. She thought not. She hadn't seen his car, either. Maybe his gun was still in it. Or at the bottom of the reservoir.

"*Buenos días*!" He stood in the bedroom door. With the hallway light behind him, he looked more like a giant ape than a human. Kaylee stirred. Under the bed, Lucy growled.

"What?" asked Maxine. "Did the plane land? What about my sister?" Her voice quavered on the word "sister."

"We did not speak of her. You and the kids to put on clothes. *Rapido*!"

"Where are we going?" If he took them to the reservoir, she thought she would die of terror before he could kill them. "They are just young children," she said. "They haven't done anything to you." Pause. "They like you."

He turned and left.

Maxine woke Kaylee and told her to get dressed. It was still dark, and the desert air held a chill that penetrated one's bones. She put on a windbreaker over red her warm-up suit.

"Wear a sweatshirt." She patted Kaylee's shoulder, but Kaylee pulled away.

Stupid to be concerned with staying warm when they were all doing to die. With Kaylee grumbling that this was the dumbest idea ever, Maxine walked into the kitchen. El Tigre stood by the sink filling a water bottle. She went into Ethan's room, and found him sitting up in bed. His dark hair stuck up in all directions.

"When is my mom coming back?" His querulous voice ending in a high-pitched wail.

"Your mother will be home soon," Maxine said. "Maybe tomorrow." She smoothed his hair and gave him a hug. "Get dressed."

The important thing was to keep calm and not let the children panic. Maxine heard El Tigre in the bathroom with water running, and she grabbed the three-pound coffee can from the pantry shelf and took it to her bedroom, where she extracted the Smith & Wesson and stashed it in the inside pocket of her windbreaker.

When the kids were dressed, she gave them granola bars. El Tigre grabbed the orange box and crammed it into a canvas carryall. Maxine noticed cookies, water and a collapsible umbrella sticking out of the carryall. Why did he need an umbrella? Then he insisted they wear hats. Maxine handed Ethan a Red Sox cap. She and Kaylee wore their straw cowgirl hats. Both kids, complaining in unison that they were still tired, flopped down on the sofa.

"Day of big adventure," El Tigre said. "Like a camping trip."

Maxine thought Kaylee looked scared. She ducked her head and scurried back to the bedroom for her floppy rabbit. Maxine had been terrified all day, but the words "camping trip," made her stomach churn, spurting acid and bile. She ran into the bathroom.

A few minutes later El Tigre banged on the door. "*Vamos! Rapido*!"

Maxine opened the door. El Tigre dangled the pickup keys from his fat finger.

"*Vamos*!"

"Please don't hurt the children."

This time, he made no promises.

# *Fifty-nine*

Lotto had napped on the plane to Panama and in the afternoon he took care of his banking and legal business. Neither lawyer nor banker knew of any Caliendo matters. With a good dinner in his belly, he sat in the Tocumen airport departure lounge of Copa Airlines, reading *La Prensa* and waiting for his flight to Caracas.

A dark-haired woman with round cheeks and big eyes stared distractedly at the gate information. Lotto cast an admiring glance at the curve of breast in the slinky black top and the firm round *nalga* straining the tight slacks, hoping against hope that she might be his seatmate. The woman frowned at the long line of passengers queued up at the counter, looked at her boarding pass and back at the gate information. She sighed and plopped down next to him.

"Are you flying to Caracas tonight?" he asked, aiming for a neutral conversational voice.

"No. Miami. Do you speak English?"

"Yes, of course." In his most measured tones. Her accent revealed her American roots.

"Talking Spanish for days has given me a brain cramp."

She checked her watch and examined her boarding pass again. Everything she wore looked new and expensive.

After a few moments he said, "You seem distracted."

"Today was one for the books. If you'd followed my footsteps, you'd be distracted, too." She sighed again. "And now I seem to be at the wrong gate."

"May I?" he asked, and reached for her boarding pass. *H. Wozniak*. She didn't look Polish. On a 12:30 a.m. Copa flight to Miami.

He said, "Your flight doesn't leave for hours. This probably *is* the right gate. I can check for you."

"Would you?"

For the first time, a smile lit her face, and Lotto felt a jab of desire. What a woman! So shapely, so needy, so lost.

He used his laptop to call up her flight information. "This is the right gate. You just have a long wait." He hesitated. "My flight doesn't leave for an hour. Perhaps we could have a drink or a bite to eat."

For the first time she examined him, and Lotto thought she liked what she saw, even the Panama hat, because she chirped, "Lovely!"

"I am Carlos León of Caracas," he said, extending a hand.

"Honora Wozniak of Reno, Nevada."

"Ah, Reno!"

She looked at him with an odd expression he couldn't read.

Lotto knew from experience that the airport restaurant didn't have the best food and the lines were often long, but his twenty-dollar bill worked wonders, and he ordered a Balboa beer, and Honora ordered a *seco* on ice, which surprised him because it was a local drink. He kept the gym bag with all his cash and his laptop between his feet.

Honora practically chugged the *seco,* betraying her nerves with her manicured hands always shifting her hair out of her gray eyes, worrying her fingernails, arranging her bracelets, and rubbing her rings, a perpetual motion machine. Lotto ordered *carne en palito* for Honora and slipped the waiter a twenty to bring the food fast.

"So tell me about your horrendous day," he said with a smile.

And over a second *seco,* to his astonishment, she did.

*Cojones de dios!* He had snared Maxine's sister, blabbing about El Tigre and Maxine herself and Reno, loading Lotto's ears with her mind-boggling story.

He gazed into her troubled eyes, murmuring, "I'm so sorry," or "that must have been awful for you," or "how frightening," and she unloaded another confidence. This Honora's anxiety whirled in a vortex of worry and fear. Every other sentence she took a deep breath and said, "I really shouldn't be telling you this but what the hell, you're from Caracas, so far from this God-damned mess." Another sip of *seco* and another confession: the worthless boyfriend, the bank account, and even the money taken by El Tigre's brother Jorge.

Jorge and El Tigre. Those filthy *hijos de puta*.

Now Lotto knew whom to thank for blabbing to the DEA. And after all the things he had done for El Tigre.

"I'm sick of Reno, sick of the U.S., and I'm getting my son and leaving. Maybe I'll even come back for the rest of the goddamn money. It doesn't belong to Maxine. It's drug money her husband skimmed. Drug money! Why should the government get it? My sister can rot in her little desert town, assuming she survives that bastard El Tigre, and if anyone touches one hair of my son's head I'll send them all to kingdom come."

*You got that right. He skimmed it from me.*

The whole story delivered to him with histrionics, even verve. Honora waved the bamboo skewer from her *carne en palito* around, making the waiter dodge.

Her eyes met his. "I'm crazy with worry about Ethan. Do you have children, Carlos?" She pronounced his name with a slight hesitation.

He mentioned his two boys and she smiled. When her eyes lit up, she was a true beauty.

"Our sons are almost the same age." She gave a wistful sigh.

Lotto put his hand on hers. "Everything will work out for the best. And if you need a place to stay, there are lots of wonderful apartments in Caracas. Even a British school. It's a lively cosmopolitan city."

He would make occasional trips and if this woman took up residence, and things worked out, then he would make regular trips. She would have that *puta* Caliendo's money in her warm little palm. Soon to be in his.

Lotto, feeling almost giddy, put cash down on the table, picked up his gym bag and laptop and took Honora's arm. His flight would be boarding.

Honora dabbed at her eyes, but he saw no tears. "It's so wonderful to find someone I can confide in. I've been so alone, so scared..."

He handed her a card, the ink barely dry, with an email address and a P.O. box in Caracas. "Email me if you decide to visit my beautiful city," he said, and gave her arm a light pressure.

As they headed toward the gate, she said, "This started out to be such a shitty day, having to give all the money to that stupid farmer, or whatever he is. And you've been such a prince to listen to my rambling."

"Email me." He took her soft hand, pressed it to his lips, and gave her his "you are very special" smile.

She grabbed him and gave him a big hug with her breasts pressed firmly against his chest.

It was a foregone conclusion that they would meet again.

## *Sixty*

They left town in Maxine's old maroon pickup. She was driving with El Tigre next to her, solid as an oak, and the children, awake and vigilant, in the back seat. She had a cigarette going and the driver's side window cracked. Yesterday she stopped rationing her cigarettes. What difference did it make when you were going to die?

When the road divided, El Tigre motioned Maxine to drive east toward where the pavement ended, not north to Idaho and the reservoir. He wouldn't return to the scene of the crime. *For this I have already killed two men.*

"The whole sky is a rainbow," Kaylee said.

"No, it's not. There's no place for the pot of gold." Ethan sounded sure of himself.

"But it has rainbow colors," Kaylee said, still adamant.

In the east, the sun crept toward the horizon. A fiery band of crimson limned the edge of the earth. Above the red, strata of orange, gold, and an eerie pale green merged into a darker turquoise. The vault of the sky remained blue-black. In the rear view mirror, Maxine saw a slice of moon hanging over the black mountain behind them.

While she drove, El Tigre studied a Bureau of Land Management topological map. Surrounded by the alkali dessert, Maxine plunged ahead for twelve miles until the pavement ended. Her stomach clenched as it had so often in the last eighteen hours.

"You must turn right. Soon. Slow down. Very slow. *Aqui mismo.* Turn."

*For this I have already killed two men.*

Faint tracks meandered into the desert, but not toward the hot spring. El Tigre would take her and the children into the vastness and shoot them. Like he had the others. Or slit their throats. The bile rose again, protesting against death. Maxine's fingers clutched the wheel.

When they left, she had noticed a white Ford minivan parked in the street in front of their house. *El Tigre's transportation.*

She took a deep drag from the cigarette. The nicotine found the sweet spot where the panic lived and calmed it. For a few moments.

"How did you find us?" she asked, astonished that her voice sounded almost conversational but with the husky timbre betraying her fright.

He turned toward her and she could make out his victorious smile. He raised his eyebrows and flashed white teeth. "Lotto's idea. *Muy simple.* Install a tracking device on Jeff's car. We find Jeff first. On the internet at the Tahoe golf club." He rubbed his hands together. "We learn that Jeff comes on Sunday and returns to club early Wednesday. Yesterday, I drive here and climb the fence."

They had been crazy to think it would be safe here in the desert with today's electronics able to track one's every move. Maxine hadn't been on Facebook since she left Massachusetts. She had only used Twitter once or twice in Connecticut. She had paid cash, ignored friends' emails. She hadn't even rented a freaking movie. And still they found her.

"Drive faster. The earth is hard. You can drive much faster."

She floored the accelerator and behind them, a great rooster tail of alkali dust swirled.

"It was Lotto's idea?" she asked. Had he said the GPS tracking device was Lotto's idea?

El Tigre smiled with a self-satisfied air and hooked his thumb toward his burly chest.

"I do not work for Lotto now. I work for me, El Tigre. Lotto is in deep shit. *Mas rapido,"* he said, leaning forward and staring ahead. "*Mas rapido.*"

Her heart beat *mas rapido* as the pickup raced down the playa, and even in the cool morning air, her palms felt sticky on the steering wheel. They drove further into the trackless waste. Could she bring herself to shoot El Tigre in cold blood, just like her father had killed her mother, her lover and himself? Maxine's throat felt dry as the dust. She had trouble concentrating on her driving because her mind still raced trying to think of another way out when there was no way out.

"Stop!" El Tigre folded the map in a messy rectangle. "Children get out. You also. Be quick! Leave keys."

Maxine braked the pickup and climbed out, surprised by her ability to stand on her wobbling legs. Kaylee jumped out.

"Why did we stop here? Where are we?" She clutched the floppy rabbit.

Ethan scrabbled across the seat and got out, too. He looked around at the vast empty space and rubbed his eyes. His baseball cap was on backwards. Both kids looked up at Maxine, waiting for an explanation.

El Tigre opened his door and climbed out. He walked around the pickup and stood stock still, looking at them. Maxine thought of grabbing the Smith & Wesson.

"Sit!' he said. They sat in the dust. He reached inside the back seat. For the children's sake, Maxine tried to control her trembling. She fumbled at her inside pocket for the gun, but she couldn't pull the zipper, so useless were her shaking hands. El Tigre would murder them while she was trying to work the zipper.

*This is it.* She put an arm around each child, trying to shelter them. She couldn't bear to look at her executioner.

"*Adios.*"

Instead of a shot ringing out, Maxine heard a thunk in the soft dirt. The bag with the granola bars, the water and the umbrella lay in front of them.

"Do nothing stupid. *Nada.* I have your sister."

He heaved his bulk into the pickup, ground the gears and made a U-turn toward the highway, picking up speed. When they turned to look, all they could see was a tornado of tan particles and the rising sun as the pale dust engulfed them.

Maxine felt the relief flood her body. She wanted to weep and hug the kids, and tell them how much she loved them, but there was no time. She had to lead them out of the desert.

~ * ~

The sun rose. Maxine calculated El Tigre had driven them four miles into nothingness. They had been hiking for a few minutes, following the pickup's tracks, three tiny specks in the vastness of the playa. Normally, Maxine could walk the distance in an hour, and run it in less, but the kids were straggling, and it might take two hours of walking if everything went well. She hoped that someone would stop for them along the road back to town. A few ranches were scattered along its length, and rock hounds in four-wheel drive vehicles explored off-road for old mines and agate beds.

To the north and west, the hills had turned purple and pink, stunning in their beauty. Kaylee, unimpressed with the panorama of big sky, continued to gripe. "How far is it now? I'm so tired. If I sit down, will a scorpion sting me?" Her uncombed hair straggled out of her Western hat.

"We have to keep walking. We're miles from the highway."

"That's so far." Kaylee kicked the toes of her shoes into the gray dust, dropped her floppy rabbit, and burst into tears. She bawled louder when Maxine held the rabbit by the ears and slapped it against her thigh. Dust flew. Ethan laughed. Maxine returned the rabbit to Kaylee, who cradled it against her chest. Minutes later, Ethan had his meltdown. A water bottle spilled, making little craters in the dust and bringing more tears.

After what had happened, some acting out was to be expected, but Maxine had to get them to the road before the July temperatures soared into the nineties. Overhead, a small plane circled around, too high to notice them. The thought of El Tigre changing his mind about leaving them alive bubbled to the surface of Maxine's brain. He could send someone back to kill them, someone who had no scruples about hurting children.

They trudged on. A whirring vibration broke the silence, almost like a train, but overhead. Maxine craned her neck toward the sky. A helicopter, passing over them and flying toward the main road. They waved and called out as if the pilot could hear. Maxine wondered if she should write "HELP" across the dirt in giant letters. She slipped out of her windbreaker to make her red warm up suit visible.

The chopper coursed onward. Too high to spot anyone. Still, why was it flying around in this nowhere land? Maybe they were looking for the reservoir shooter. She wondered if El Tigre had reached the highway yet. She kept watching the sky.

"Did they see us?" asked Kaylee, her small voice breathless.

"They're too high. And they wouldn't be looking for us."

"I'll bet they saw us. I waved my hat," Ethan said.

A glimmer of hope buoyed her spirits. Then a shadow of doubt. Could El Tigre have somehow called in the helicopter? He had her Sky-Sat phone. They were sitting ducks with nowhere to hide.

The helicopter circled and returned, flying directly overhead, sounding like a monotone drummer, thump, thump, thump. Maxine made out the word "Washoe." The sheriff? They waved like crazy, but the chopper didn't swoop down. Instead, it continued to fly in El Tigre's direction.

Up ahead, Maxine noticed a cloud of dust coming toward them. El Tigre, returning? He would be freaked out by the helicopter and he would want to grab them before the chopper landed. Shields. Hostages.

Maxine peered around. No trees, not even a tumbleweed. If she got the children away from the tracks and lying down, maybe he would drive by. She unzipped the pocket and felt the nubby handle of the Smith & Wesson. This time she must screw up her courage. She tried to visualize the scene. The pickup, the dust, El Tigre climbing out, tramping toward them. His ferocious face, his incredible bulk, his horrific intention. She would hold the gun. Aim at his body, right at the heart. Shoot to kill.

*Leave us alone.*

Already she felt such fright, from her weakening ankles to her dizzy head. How could she do this impossible thing? Sometimes she carried bugs out of the house on a broom rather than kill them.

She could never shoot anyone. *But she had to.*

In the distance, the helicopter looked like a big bumblebee. She heard the faint whump, whump, whump of the whirring blades. The chopper was flying back toward them. Much lower, now. They waved and shouted as it passed over. Surely, at this altitude, the pilot had seen them. The approaching dust cloud grew bigger.

"We have to leave the tire tracks. Let's run over there and lie down." Maxine pointed toward the east. Not to a discernable hiding place, but away from the tracks.

"No! I don't want a scorpion to sting me!" Kaylee's voice rose to a note of hysteria.

"The man is coming back. We have to hide."

"But I won't lie down in that dirt." Tears streamed down Kaylee's dusty cheeks.

Ethan stared at the arriving dust. He clutched her hand tighter. She had to protect the kids.

Maxine herded them a hundred yards away. "Hurry, hurry. Lie flat. Right here." She pushed a bawling Kaylee down.

El Tigre pulled up in an immense billow of choking dust. Leaving the road hadn't fooled him a bit. He stopped yards away. The chopper made another pass, ever lower.

Maxine sprang to her feet. "Kaylee, Ethan, stay behind me."

They obeyed, in single file like Indians. Maxine took the Smith & Wesson from her pocket and gripped the revolver, right arm straight and stiff, support arm in place, as she had been taught. *Legs apart, find your balance. Grip the trigger. Line up the target.*

The dust hadn't settled when El Tigre lunged from the pickup. A knife gleamed in his hand. He stopped and glared at her when he spied the Smith & Wesson.

"Do not be stupid." His eyes narrowed and he glanced behind him toward the noisy, hovering helicopter, which kicked up a choking cloud of dust.

"If you come any closer, I'll shoot." Her voice high but determined.

Surely, he would turn and leave.

Blades clattering, the chopper started to touch down behind El Tigre's pickup. He clutched the knife and took a menacing step toward them.

"Get in the truck," he ordered.

Dust swirled into her eyes, which teared up. Inside her mouth, a weird metallic taste, like her fillings were melting.

Maxine's arms shook as she tried to steady her aim. "Stop. Or I'll shoot."

Didn't he understand she meant to kill him?

"Put the gun away." Brandishing the knife, he began to march toward them through the mantle of dust. "Drop the gun or I kill you and take the children."

He kept coming. He came at them in slow motion. With all her strength, Maxine squeezed the trigger. He didn't stop, but kept coming. Kaylee screamed, a shrill, high-pitched little girl scream. It seemed like she had been there for hours, with El Tigre advancing toward them. Maxine shot again, and again. The noise reverberated over the desert.

Time stopped.

El Tigre's face contracted into a mystified frown as he lurched backwards. His hand touched his chest with a tentative motion. Jesus, if she had only nicked him, he would be after them like a wild boar.

Maxine stood her ground, both hands on the Smith & Wesson, waiting. El Tigre dropped the knife and crumpled into the pale dust. Kaylee was sobbing.

A man ran around the pickup and yelled, "Are you all right, ma'am?"

~ * ~

The next hours were a blur of sheriff's deputies from three counties, all of them with questions. Somehow, she was a hero for dispatching the reservoir killer. She had explained how El Tigre had appeared and menaced them, had even used Ethan to threaten her sister vacationing in Panama. Could they help find Honora? Maxine didn't know what she would do if her sister simply disappeared again. *What would she do?*

The cops found the Sky Sat phone in the pickup and noted all the numbers El Tigre had called. They took the phone as evidence. Maxine mentioned the tape recorder on the living room windowsill, which might have picked up his conversations.

*She had killed El Tigre.* Maxine felt spacey, like she viewed life from the wrong end of binoculars. They were actors in a play. Nothing felt real.

~ * ~

Hours later, back at the house, her computer was still on from when El Tigre had used it in the middle of the night. The crime lab people took fingerprints and DNA samples. Once again, the tape recorder also became "evidence." This time she wouldn't replace it, but would treat herself to a Blackberry or an iPhone. Someone fed the kids lunch. Finally, they let Maxine use her computer. The deputy told her El Tigre had been looking at airline schedules out of Reno, and they might need the computer for evidence, but she could check her email.

Weary to the bone, Maxine sat at the maple desk overlooking the sunny yard and signed on to her email.

A message from Jeff: *You sounded odd tonight. Please confirm you're okay. I'll call in the morning.*

She hit "reply" to Jeff's email but she didn't know where to begin, and her fingers were still full of tremors. Lucy ventured out from under the bed and crunched down her kitten chow. Ethan and

Kaylee had collapsed in a comatose sleep in front of the television. What they had gone through!

Among the email messages, Maxine saw one from Honora. With her fingers disobeying her brain, she finally clicked on the email.

*I'm at an internet café at the Panama City airport. Waiting for my flight to Miami, the only one to the U.S. tonight. No luggage except my handbag, and I jump out of my skin when anyone so much as looks at me. Jorge has my cell phone. I'd be afraid to call anyway, because the asshole might pick up. I'm worried crazy for Ethan, but I don't want to go to the police. I am praying everything is all right with you and the kids. H.*

Sent at ten o'clock last night.

Tears cascaded from Maxine's eyes, and she ran into the bathroom and cried. She leaned against the sink, overwhelmed by body-shaking sobs. She wept for her long dead parents, for poor murdered Larry, with relief that Honora and the children were safe. She wept because she had taken a life. Drained of emotion, she washed her face and dabbed at her red puffy eyes.

A few minutes later, one of the cops reported that Honora had returned to the U.S. She had landed in Miami early that morning and was probably on her way home.

A car pulled up outside. Through the living room window, Maxine saw Jeff looking askance at the three police cars parked in the street. She ran outside and threw her arms around him. "I was sure I would never see you again."

"Cripes, what's going on around here?"

He held her trembling hands and looked into her eyes while she told him.

"Oh, my God! Oh, my God!" He seemed stuck on those three syllables. Then they hugged again. They kissed. She wanted to stay in the safety of his arms forever.

Inside, Kaylee woke, ran to Jeff and threw her arms around him. "Daddy, there was a big man here, and he scared me, and Maxine shot him. We got to ride in a police car."

Ethan awakened too, and Maxine told him his mother was on her way home. Jeff topped off the wading pool, and Kaylee and Ethan took some boats and ducks and climbed in. While they sat in the water, talking softly, Maxine told Jeff the whole story, rationally this time, beginning with El Tigre standing at the screen door with the kids and ending with Honora's email.

"Cripes, Max. Is it really over?" They hugged each other again, and then Jeff's cell phone rang. Honora, calling from the Denver airport, upset that she couldn't reach Maxine. Her plane was scheduled to arrive in Reno in a couple hours.

"We'll come to meet you," Jeff said. Maxine had never liked him more than at that moment.

# *Sixty-one*

Honora found Maxine, Jeff, and the kids waiting for her at the Reno airport baggage claim, but Honora only had eyes for Ethan. She clasped him to her like they had been apart for years, not days. His thin little body seemed bigger and he looked older. Her baby put his arms around her waist and squeezed her like he never wanted to let go. When she said, "You're the best and bravest boy in the whole world," he ducked his head, embarrassed, but he put on the Dolphins cap she had bought in Miami.

Maxine cried and insisted on hugging the bejesus out of her. Honora felt bruised from so much embracing. She tried to return the hugs with a little enthusiasm, and she guessed she owed Maxine for taking care of Ethan, but wasn't it her sister's stupidity that had got them into this mess anyhow? It was a wonder Honora hadn't been tossed out of a plane or some other hideous thing. She kept her distance from Jeff.

"I'm so happy to be back I could kiss the ground," she said, adding, "I'm starving."

"Me, too," Maxine said.

If Maxine started the hugging business again, Honora would freak out.

At Honora's apartment, Jeff volunteered to entertain the kids while she and Maxine grabbed a bite somewhere.

Ethan asked Jeff, "Can we play catch?" and Jeff agreed. Jeff was really good for Ethan.

Honora already had second thoughts about blabbing her story to the good-looking stranger in the airport. She would definitely not travel to Venezuela. That Chavez was a weirdo and they didn't even like Americans down there. She was thinking Bahamas or Cayman Islands.

As she and Maxine drove off, Jeff was tossing the ball first to Ethan, still wearing the Dolphins cap, then to Kaylee.

"You're lucky Jeff is so good with kids," she said, craning her neck for a last look.

"Maybe *you* can find a family man," Maxine said.

*Was that snide or what?*

"Maybe I can."

"But not Jeff," Maxine said, turning, and looking her right in the eye.

"Max, I'm sorry about that." Honora tried to look contrite with sad eyes and a hangdog expression. "It won't happen again."

Maxine said nothing, and moments later, asked, "Shall we go to Mel's Diner?"

Thank God she had dropped the subject of Jeff.

"Perfect," Honora said. "Sane, safe and ordinary."

"We need ordinary," Maxine said.

They settled into a black Naugahyde booth and ordered wine. Maxine's wine sloshed around in her glass like she had palsy. Barely under control. It wasn't every day you drilled a big goon with a Smith & Wesson. Honora would never have guessed Maxine had it in her. You can't ever tell about people, even family. Especially family.

On the jukebox, Grace Slick sang, "Don't You Want Somebody To Love?" Honora thought of the hot man she had met at the airport, Carlos León, whose eyes made her melt, those magnetic bedroom eyes, but Caracas was no longer on her itinerary. She had tossed his business card into the trash.

In the booth next to them, a well-built middle-aged Latino man in a black shirt and a cowboy hat sat thigh-to-thigh with a hard-looking blonde, who looked like someone who ordered straight gin for breakfast.

Honora asked for a Reuben and Maxine ordered a French dip. Maxine had always liked French dips. While they waited, Maxine told an endless story about how El Tigre showed up demanding the money from the Panama account. Honora was only interested whenever Maxine mentioned Ethan. In between times, she allowed herself to daydream about the rest of the money in Panama and what it could buy.

"I was so scared for you," Maxine said.

Honora suppressed a yawn. "I am so beyond sleep-deprived." She tried to sound apologetic. Maxine's eyes softened with sympathy.

The blonde had ordered hot cocoa. She took a sip and smiled through her whipped cream mustache. The man said something under his breath and she grabbed his crotch.

Honora dreaded ending up like the blonde, getting long in the tooth and having to fawn over older men. She attempted to pick up the thread of the conversation. "*You* were scared. Max, I was petrified. El Tigre's brother looked like Assassins R' Us, the creepiest guy you can imagine." She shuddered, remembering, and gulped her wine. "I just knew they would hand me over to those rebels."

She let Maxine take her hand. Maxine was overdoing the touchy-feely. *I guess she really loves me.*

The waitress brought their meals, and Maxine ordered two more wines. She seemed calmer.

"I can't wait to hear how you got out of Jorge's clutches," Maxine said.

While Honora described her clever moves, Maxine's eyes grew wider, and her mouth opened. Honora continued her story, watching emotion flicker across Maxine's face: fear, amazement, and disbelief.

"I'm so proud of you, sis," Maxine said.

Honora shrugged.

The waitress delivered steak, eggs, biscuits and gravy to the next table.

"So you never saw Jorge again?" asked Maxine.

Honora rubbed her arms. "Once he had the money, I was just a girl to get rid of. They were probably worried I 'd scream 'thief' and go to the police if they let me go." She grinned at Maxine. "Which is exactly what I would have done if I hadn't been so freaked out. I was relieved to arrive at the airport in one piece. And lucky to find a flight out last night."

Maxine leaned toward her. She was practically whispering. "I don't think Jorge ever told El Tigre you were gone. He called twice, and El Tigre always acted like everything was going according to plan, but whenever I asked about you he said, 'she wasn't mentioned.' I think Jorge was afraid to tell El Tigre that you outsmarted him."

Honora noticed that her sister had stopped shaking, but she looked awful, with dark circles under her eyes and one twitching eyelid. The proverbial basket case.

While Maxine paid the bill at the counter, Honora said, "Hey, Max, let's bop next door into the casino and draw some cash out of the account." Honora flashed the Panamanian bank debit card.

Maxine hesitated and furrowed her eyebrows. *Hell! Had Honora been too quick to head for the money?* Maxine still showed no enthusiasm, but she said, "Okay."

"I'm just wiped out from this god-awful experience." Honora spoke in a rush. "I want to take Ethan and go away for a week or so. Somewhere in California. The Russian River or maybe Bodega Bay. I'll need a little cash, okay?"

Honora thought Maxine nodded with less reluctance this time.

Maxine said, "Panama was sure as hell no vacation." Then Maxine held out her hand for the debit card.

So Maxine didn't trust her one hundred percent. She would have to be super careful, or lose access to her share of the money.

# *Sixty-two*

Finder's arrival in Reno had been a surprise. He had taken his wife to Portugal because both of them had been threatened. Probably Lotto's people, but no proof. "Now that things have sorted themselves out, I'm on the grid again."

He wanted to see "some Western sights," so with a picnic lunch packed, Maxine picked him up at his hotel. His first words were, "I wanted to apologize in person for leaving you in the lurch like I did."

While she told him what had happened since they talked last, his observant eyes noted the old fifties motels along the streets of Reno, the bare hills north of town and finally, the mustang adoption center housing hundreds of captured wild horses.

The hot wind whipped through the open pickup window as Maxine drove further north. Finder had let out his low whistle when she told him about Larry's laptop, the two million in the Panama account and Honora's adventures with El Tigre's brother.

"I had the feeling you were holding back on me," Finder said, running his hand through his shot-with-gray dark hair. "So, it was the skimmed money?" He raised his dark brows.

Maxine nodded.

"My sources report Lotto has flown the coop," he said, leaning back. "One jump ahead of the DEA. He drove to his health club, strolled inside, and disappeared .Undoubtedly out of the country by now. You're out of harm's way."

"El Tigre said Lotto was in 'deep shit'," Maxine said, "but I didn't know what he meant."

"He meant deep shit." Finder laughed. "A hundred bucks says Lotto will land on his feet."

~ * ~

By the turquoise waters of Pyramid Lake, Maxine and Finder sat at a shaded picnic table eating the turkey sandwiches and sharing a bag of chips. Alone in the wilderness, they watched a flock of pelicans fly in like dive-bombers and swoop low along the shallow shore.

Maxine realized how much she had relied on Finder. She started a long thank-you, but he knitted his dark brows and said, "I've always thought I failed you."

"The failure was mine."

They sat in silence, listening to the hot wind that evaporated their sweat.

"Are you and Honora getting along in a sisterly way? I had a hunch this meet-up wasn't going to work out." He watched her as he exhaled a cloud of smoke, caught by the wind.

Maxine helped herself to a cigarette. Tobacco made the hard questions easier. She stared at the pyramid jutting out of the water. Eons of geologic history. Native American history, mostly sad. Their particular history, also mostly sad.

"I don't think Honora was happy to be found. She still seems... distant." Maxine felt a pain under her heart whenever she thought of her sister.

"How does she get so much time off to go to Panama and then take off for the Russian River?" asked Finder, raising an eyebrow.

"She says vacation and comp time."

Finder crossed his arms. "The fact that she never wanted to reconnect should tell you something."

"I know." Almost a whisper.

Maxine had received a few emails from Honora, including one with a photo of Ethan standing in the surf. She had emailed they were staying a couple extra days because Ethan was still having nightmares.

"She was so freaked out by what happened in Panama and poor little Ethan had kind of bonded with El Tigre, so he's got his issues too." Maxine had always made excuses for her sister. Now she was making them for Ethan.

*Massine.*

"You coming back to Florida now that the coast is clear?" he asked.

"We're staying here until Labor Day when Jeff's golf lessons are done. Going home via Chicago so Kaylee can meet the new baby boy. Her half-brother. He should have arrived by then. We need to be in Florida when Kaylee starts school." Saving the best news for last, Maxine said, "Jeff and I are getting married."

"No kidding. My very best wishes. By any chance in a Reno wedding chapel?"

"How did you know? Want to stick around? You can be best man. We're a few people short of a proper wedding party."

"Will I finally get to meet Honora?" he asked with an impudent grin. "And kiss the bride?"

~ * ~

On the way back to Reno, Maxine let Finder drive. Wearing Jeff's old baseball cap, with his blunt nose in profile and his strong hands grasping the steering wheel, he no longer looked like an Easterner. The sunlight and the vast spaces and the brown hills gave everyone a Western aura.

Finder's doubts about Honora made Maxine decide to phone her sister. Honora had said, "Please don't call me. I just want to chill, and take care of my boy." Maxine had respected her need for down time, but she still felt uneasy—to call it a premonition would have been too strong. Still...

*The number you have called is no longer in service.*

Jesus, no! "Her cell phone's been disconnected."

Finder's brown eyes offered sympathy but no surprise.

Maxine's dry throat had a strangled feeling, as if she couldn't catch her breath. She clasped her hands to quell their shaking and willed her stomach to relax, running the gamut of now-familiar sensations.

Maxine directed Finder to Honora's apartment. He parked and she tore up the walk and rang the bell. No answer. She leaned on the neighbor's bell. An old woman came to the door, holding it open a crack.

Maxine peered in at the wrinkled face. "I'm looking for my sister, Honora Wozniak. She and her little boy live next door and she's overdue from a vacation."

"Miss, she's gone." The woman pointed an arthritic finger toward the street. "Moving van pulled up a few days ago, and took everything, lock, stock and barrel."

Maxine returned to the pickup and sat staring out of the window at nothing. All the time, the effort, even the money, and now this. *Honora was gone. Without a goodbye. Just sneaked away.*

Head down, she picked at her cuticle, trying to stem her tears. Finder patted her shoulder with awkward tenderness.

"When we've done all we can humanly do, it's time to pick up and move on."

She nodded, still fighting tears.

"My advice," Finder said. "is for you to secure that money in Panama. Your sister has the account number and the password?"

"But I've got the debit card." Maxine, her cuticle now shredded, looked up and met his eyes. Second to her love for Ethan, Honora loved money. They drove to Mel's Diner, parked, and entered the adjoining casino.

At the first cash machine, she slipped the ATM card into the slot, and keyed the password. She punched in a balance inquiry, which showed eighty-seven dollars. She stared at Finder. "I can't believe she returned to Panama and grabbed the rest of the cash." She swallowed hard. "Five-hundred thousand. Oh, God!" She buried her face in her hands.

Finder, standing next to her, gave a low whistle. "Son of a bitch."

Feeling like a zombie, Maxine tucked the card back into her handbag. Her throat felt so tight she couldn't speak.

"Ill-gotten gains seldom bring happiness," Finder said.

Maxine felt a weight too heavy to bear pushing her down into a hopeless despair, almost like when her parents died, because the sisterly bond she had so wanted had been trampled and spat upon. Maxine remembered Honora's hard, unwelcoming face across the doorway when she first made contact. Her sister's eyes had been... implacable. *What are* you *doing here?* Maxine should have turned and walked away, but she would have always wondered if things could be different. Now she knew.

Maxine turned to Finder. "There's still five hundred thousand in bearer bonds. I have them."

All of a sudden, Maxine itched like crazy. She clawed at her rashy arms. Hives!

Still scratching, she said, "Can you fly down and get the rest? It's not for me, it's for Larry's brother Corky."

His eyes looked hard. "It'll be nothing but trouble."

"He has cerebral palsy and needs lifelong care. Larry asked me to do this."

Finder's eyes softened. "In my book, that's a pretty good reason."

Still itching, she turned to Finder. "I just wanted to have a family. That's all I ever wanted."

"You have a family. You have Jeff and Kaylee. Keep in touch with your ex's tribe. You said they loved you. Family doesn't have to mean blood ties."

Still feeling like all hope was gone, she nodded. Finder touched her arm. "Who else knew about the money?"

"Jeff. Lotto, but he's gone. El Tigre, but he's dead. You. Me. Honora." *And she's gone.*

"Blaisdell?"

"No. They didn't know it was in Panama." *Scratch. Scratch.*

"So it's our little secret. I can fly to LA this evening and down to Panama City tomorrow. I'll need paperwork and the bearer bonds."

"There's a bill of sale for a house to explain the money."

"Your Larry thought of everything."

Finder drove them to his hotel. "You have a drink while I'm checking out and then you can drive me to your place and get the documents." He paused a beat and asked, with a foxy smile, "How do you know I won't abscond with the funds?"

"Because I'm going to pay you twenty-thousand dollars for doing this."

He squeezed her shoulder. "Every trip should be so remunerative."

At the hotel's entrance, she paused before *The Spirit of Nevada*, a life-size bronze sculpture of wild mustangs at full gallop in their hot-blooded charge across a desert landscape. A colt raced with the herd, nostrils flaring.

"I hate to think of those poor bastards in that corral," Finder said.

Maxine said, "They're all up for adoption. They don't round them up to shoot them."

Inside the casino, the chords of Billy Joel's "Piano Man" melded in weird harmony with the cacophony of the slots.

She ordered wine at the bar. The red bumps on her arm itched less. Finder was at her elbow a few minutes later.

"I packed fast so I can grab a beer."

The waiter delivered a bottle of Heineken. Finder drank and said, "It's over, Maxine. You fought the good fight, and now you're going to have a good life."

She turned her head and their eyes met.

"I'm not going to obsess about Honora. She had a bad angel on her shoulder. We both did." She swallowed hard. "Mine flew away."

"Good riddance to the bad angel." Finder lifted his bottle and drank again.

"Life will be easier," he said, "if you can get Corky's bank account number so I can make a direct transfer. Easier tax-wise and so forth. And I won't have to worry about schlepping all the cash back here, or running into El Tigre's evil brother."

Maxine picked up her phone.

"I'm calling Corky." It would be so good to talk to him again.

# *Sixty-three*

Honora had opened a new account with her less-than-expected funds. One million would have been better. Maxine, that dirty dealer, had really screwed her over. Imagine not saying a word about those bearer bonds and Honora standing in the Panama bank looking dumber than dirt. At least she'd recovered her suitcase from the earlier hotel, getting her stylish new clothes back. Where to live had become a problem. The Cayman Islands were out. Likewise, the Bahamas. Forget Bermuda. Too many visa hassles. Belize was way out and she refused to even think about Panama, where she'd had the worst days of her life. It wasn't easy for a woman with only five hundred thousand dollars and a seven-year-old kid and so-so references to find a place to call home.

From her generic hotel room in Panama City, Honora perused her address book, mostly men who had "befriended" her at one time or another. She wasn't too hopeful, but she called Jack Cope anyway, asking if he knew of any casino jobs in other countries, preferably faraway English-speaking countries.

Jack called it a "crazy coincidence."

"Some associates are opening a casino in New Zealand and I have a list of jobs, one of which is perfect for you. Events planner."

He paused. "Salary is good, but not wonderful. Auckland is a cool city, a great place for your boy. He's in school by now, right?"

Honora and Ethan left Panama the next day for Las Vegas and a job interview. She looked like a million bucks in her new designer clothes and the interview went well. They checked her recent reference and made an offer. In three days, she and Ethan would leave for Hawaii, and wait there until her visa came through. She would try not to screw up this time.

Ethan kept talking about saying goodbye to Maxine and Kaylee, and she'd squashed that, telling him they were back in Florida.

Ethan would be fine once they got settled. Good schools. Lots of social services. A clean slate.

## *Sixty-four*

Leaving Jeff and Kaylee in Reno, Maxine took a plane to Boston by way of Denver to visit Larry's family and explain about the money. The explanation involved all sorts of sins and shenanigans, both hers and Larry's. Reviewing the long, mostly sad story, she hoped she would be up to all the questions and confessions.

On the phone, Larry's brother had been cordial, even elated when she announced her visit. *Maxine, we'll be glad to see you! Corky is popping wheelies in his chair from excitement.*

In Milton, the cab driver pulled up to the gracious white ranch house that handled Corky's special needs with a minimum of fuss. The familiar sight of Corky, his brown eyes sparkling, waiting in his wheelchair on the sidewalk, brought tears to her eyes. Why had she ever assumed divorcing Larry meant parting with his loving family?

Maxine jumped out of the cab, ran to Corky and gave him a hug. At thirty-two, Corky was closer in age to Maxine than to his three older brothers. He stuttered, "M-m-m-m-Max," causing tears to spill down her cheeks. Frank and his wife Michelle came out of the house and hugged her too. The Caliendo welcome made up for the one she had never received from Honora.

Dark, petite Michelle led her through the kitchen to admire the new lap pool in the backyard. "Corky used some of the money he got from selling Larry's house. It's been so good for him to be able to swim at home this summer."

Red clay pots of basil and geraniums grew along the edge of the pool.

"Great tomatoes," Maxine said, admiring Frank's side garden.

"We're eating them tonight," Michelle said. "Now it's wine time, and I know you have so much to tell us." She squeezed Maxine's hand.

They gathered in the living room with its beige couch, salmon drapes and brown wing chairs. A painting of a Cape Cod fishing shack hung over the mantel. Family photos crowded the top of a side table. Maxine recognized Larry, grinning as though he didn't have a worry in the world.

Sitting in the wing chair, Frank held a glass of whiskey. Maxine and Michelle sipped pinot grigio in generous goblets, and ginger ale with a straw for Corky.

"Start from the beginning," Frank said. "Don't whitewash anything. We're all grownups. We can take it." He clasped his hands over a generous belly.

Maxine began with her last dinner with Larry at Legal Seafood.

Fifteen minutes later, Frank said, "He got in way over his head."

Maxine knew from Corky's anguished eyes and his hands clutching the ginger ale can that he was losing his composure. She was glad when Felix, his black and white tomcat, jumped into his lap. He stroked Felix with a shaky hand.

"I feel awful I misled you about Larry's laptop. You can't imagine the shock when I found it in the last box I unpacked." With pauses and hesitations, she told more of the story in an edited version. Frank gave a huff of disgust. "Larry never understood how vicious these people are. Skimming a drug lord's profits? That's just crazy."

Maxine mentioned Jeff, "my friendly neighbor with his little girl," and how he had helped her escape from South Florida. She stopped her story to dig the lockbox key out of her handbag. "We should clean out the box tomorrow morning."

Frank whistled when she related how much cash Larry had stashed away in the Foxborough bank.

Corky said, straight-faced, "M-m-maybe we should have built a bigger pool with cabanas, and even a cabana girl."

Over insalata caprese, with Frank's tomatoes, Maxine told them something of the cross-country trek in the motorhome. Her voice quivered when she spoke about Honora and her trip to Panama and how that all turned out. No one spoke or even moved as she described El Tigre's taking her and the two kids into the desert.

When Michelle served the stuffed shells sauced with the Caliendo gravy recipe, they stopped talking and dug in.

After dessert, the family returned to the living room and Maxine told them about Finder, his errand in Panama and the five hundred thousand dollars in bearer bonds designated for Corky. The only sound in the room was the hum of the air conditioner.

"Larry wanted you to have it all, Corky. I brought along a deed of sale for a house in Panama that will explain where the money came from. It's yours, if you want."

"That," Corky said, "will pay for a skid load of drugs, therapy and doctors." He paused. "Care in my old age."

Frank poured grappa and Michelle brought Corky another ginger ale.

"In the meantime, Jeff and I have become a couple." Maxine picked at her cuticles.

"You need someone in your life," Michelle said. "He sounds right for you. I hope we'll meet him sometime."

"Me too," Maxine said.

"Hey, Max," Corky said. "Want to go for a swim?"

Maxine always packed a swimsuit. The pool had lights for night swimming. She and Corky paddled around. "Corky, you'd love to swim in the hot springs in the desert where we lived. The water always washed some of the bad stuff away. Like your pool does. I know you'd feel really great in that warm water."

"We could build a hot tub by my new pool." Corky mused.

"Or indoors for year-round use," Maxine said.

"I can't ever thank you enough, Max. You risked everything for me. Can I meet Jeff and Kaylee sometime?"

"Sure. As soon as golf season is over. We're all going to start therapy," said Maxine. "I have to accept what happened in the desert. Plus the shenanigans with the money and the laptop. Kaylee has nightmares about El Tigre, and she misses her cousin. Jeff feels guilty because he led El Tigre to us. Not intentionally, of course. When we get back to Florida, we'll find someone to talk to."

"G-g-good idea," Corky said.

They floated and dog-paddled. Maxine told Corky about giving Kaylee swimming lessons.

"You're a good person, Maxine," he said, but his voice was sad. "I miss Larry every day." After a few minutes, Corky perked up and told Maxine about his yoga class and how much he liked volunteering at the animal shelter. "I've got my family, good friends like you, and a decent life. What everyone wants."

~ * ~

The next morning, Maxine called Finder in Panama and gave him Corky's bank account number, then Frank drove her to Foxborough to empty the safety-deposit box.

They gawked at the bulging envelopes and Frank said, "Jesus, Mary, and Joseph!"

"I took an envelope along when I got into the box a few weeks ago. We had to live on cash only with those goons after us. I want to return what we spent."

"Are you crazy? After what you went through? And what you're doing for Corky? I don't want to hear another word, not one word about it."

"If you ever change your mind..."

"I damn well won't," he said with a scowl.

"We had a crazy time when we came through town earlier. "The guy in the hoodie who pushed me out of the way was a bank robber. And then I found Jeff reading his email on Larry's laptop, the one bugged with LoJack for Laptops. We tore out of there so fast you would have thought we were the bank robbers."

A shared laugh broke the ice about the cash-stuffed envelopes.

Back at the house, Frank showed his wife and son the envelopes. "Better get these to *our* lock box right away."

Michelle said, "Oh, my God!"

Corky looked skyward and said, "Thank you, Larry."

When the cab arrived to take Maxine to Logan, they all wiped a few tears, and she promised to visit and to bring Jeff and Kaylee. "A real New England Thanksgiving would be perfect."

"M-m-m-maybe I can cadge a few golf lessons," Corky said.

"Jeff would love that," Maxine said, and everyone laughed.

# *Sixty-five*

Jeff and Kaylee met Maxine at the Reno airport. Maxine hadn't checked a bag. The baggage claim area held such grim memories. Kaylee wore the hat Maxine bought at the gift shop before all hell broke loose. Better not to remind her.

"Finder's flying back from Panama to LA tonight," Jeff said. "He'll be Reno-bound first thing in the morning. How does tomorrow afternoon sound for a bang-up wedding chapel shindig complete with a best man and a junior bridesmaid?"

"Can I get a pretty dress?" Kaylee asked.

Jeff smiled at his daughter. "Something to match your freckles?"

"Dad! No way."

"I want Maxine to wear what she wore to Samantha's party, her birthday dress. I carried it from Florida, hoping for a good occasion."

"The one with red poppies. My favorite," Maxine said, impressed that Jeff remembered.

"So the wedding will be like a party?" Kaylee asked, with her thoughtful look, like she imagined the wedding, the feast, and her new life.

"Sweetheart, best party ever." Jeff put Kaylee's hand between his and Maxine's.

~ * ~

The next day, Jeff left to pick up Finder. "I still get jitters whenever I set foot in the Reno airport," said Jeff with a shiver. "Then us guys are going shopping. We'll pick you up around one and head out for the chapel. Be ready."

Maxine took Kaylee to the mall to look for a dress. Kaylee took the dress shopping seriously, and squinted at herself in the mirror with each change of clothes. At last, she fell in love with a girly pink dress with ruffles and rickrack. "It's perfect! Oh, it's all so perfect."

Maxine kept explaining that this was not a big fancy wedding, but a five-minute ceremony with a justice of the peace. It didn't matter what Maxine said, because the words junior bridesmaid and the pink dress had created a picture of fabulousness in Kaylee's mind.

Finder and Jeff returned to the apartment wearing Western duds. "Now we are drugstore cowboys," Finder said with a straight face.

"Wow, Dad! You and Mister Finder fit right in. It's going to be so perfect."

~ * ~

The small chapel, designed for thirty or more, had modest wood pews and white painted walls with a muted gray-green carpet. The altar was flanked by silk flowers. Maxine said, "No fake flowers," and Finder grabbed the waterless vases and carried the stiff bouquets to the back of the chapel.

Finder returned and said, "Wait a minute. Did you two want to write your own vows?" The ensuing discussion brought Maxine to confess that anything produced in the few minutes before the ceremony would be hopeless, and besides, traditional was best. Moments later, Finder and Jeff stood by the JP, and Maxine, carrying a bouquet of yellow roses, and holding Kaylee's hand, paced down the aisle. Kaylee's eyes looked big as eggs.

After searching two pockets while Maxine held her breath, Finder produced the gold band, and vows were exchanged. Maxine wondered if Kaylee was holding her breath the whole time.

Ebullient and sipping champagne, Maxine and Jeff posed for some photos and then Finder and Kaylee joined them for pictures of the wedding party. With everyone clowning around, and toasting with the plastic glasses, Maxine wondered if the results wouldn't look like a "crazy drunken weekend with a little girl in a pink dress."

Back at their new Reno apartment, Jeff had invited some neighbors for burgers and hot dogs on the grill. Maxine had made her famous baked beans. Everyone seemed to be truly happy for them, with hugs and back slapping. Maxine couldn't stop smiling. She finally understood the meaning of the words "a heart made glad."

Cowboy Jeff came up beside her and slipped his arm through hers. "Happy?"

"Ecstatic," she said."

## *Meet Judith Copek*

An information systems nerd for twenty-plus years, Judith segued into writing from technology and sometimes she is still inspired to write about software's scary aspects.

When Judith takes a vacation, it may spin off into a novel. *World of Mirrors* was born when Judith and her husband visited the Baltic island of Rügen shortly after the reunification of East and West Germany. Many road trips as a child, adult trips to Florida and Northern Nevada, as well as interest in the drug trade inspired her latest novel, *Chased by Death.*

Judith is a member of Sisters in Crime, Mystery Writers of America, and the Short Mystery Fiction Society. Poems, short stories, and memoir as well as two earlier novels, *The Shadow Warriors, and Festival Madness* are part of her published writing.

## *Other Works From The Pen Of*
## *Judith Copek*

***World of Mirrors*** - A high-tech consultant agrees to retrieve state-of-the art software in East Germany with a colleague and ex-lover who keeps her in the dark. As she navigates a landscape of sociopaths and unrehabilitated Stasi, Zara realizes she's in the wrong place at the wrong time with the wrong man and no exit strategy.

## *Letter to Our Readers*

### *Enjoy this book?*

### *You can make a difference*

As an independent publisher, Wings ePress, Inc. does not have the financial clout of the large New York Publishers. We can't afford large magazine spreads or subway posters to tell people about our quality books.

But, we do have something much more effective and powerful than ads. We have a large base of loyal readers.

Honest Reviews help bring the attention of new readers to our books.

If you enjoyed this book, we would appreciate it if you would spend a few minutes posting a review on the site where you purchased this book or on the Wings ePress, Inc. webpages at: https://wingsepress.com/

## Visit Our Website

*For The Full Inventory*

*Of Quality Books:*

*Wings ePress.Inc*
*https://wingsepress.com/*

*Quality trade paperbacks and downloads*

*in multiple formats,*

*in genres ranging from light romantic comedy*

*to general fiction and horror.*

*Wings has something for every reader's taste.*

*Visit the website, then bookmark it.*

***We add new titles each month!***

Wings ePress Inc.

3000 N. Rock Road

Newton, KS 67114

Made in the USA
Middletown, DE
21 April 2023